Brad Parks is the only author to have won the Shamus, Nero, and Lefty Awards, three of American crime writing's most prestigious honours. A former journalist with the *Washington Post* and the *Newark Star-Ledger*, Parks lives in Virginia with his wife and two children. *Say Nothing* is his UK debut.

www.bradparksbooks.com
@brad_parks

Further praise for *Say Nothing*:

'Grabs your heart in the first chapter, and doesn't let go until the last line.' Joseph Finder

'Parks perfectly nails the dynamics of a family under the gun and has conjured a plot that leaps straight from today's headlines. This novel's a winner!' Jeffrey Deaver

'Tremendously satisfying, packed with engaging characters and surprising plot twists and a furious build of tension until its gut-wrenching pay-off.' Chris Pavone

'A twisting, suspenseful ride that adds a new and original twist to the legal thriller: a judge, cornered.' William Landay

'A masterful suspense thriller . . . *Say Nothing* expertly ratchets up the tension and character depth with every chapter, building to a shocking and deeply emotional finale. Fans of Harlan Coben will be enthralled.' Glen Erik Hamilton

'John Grisham would be proud of the plotting in this legal thriller.' *Sunday Times* 'Summer Reading'

'With the fascinating backdrop of the US judicial system, this outstanding race-against-time, psychological thriller is as much a tale of family dynamics as of criminal behaviour . . . This twisted tale is written with such power and intelligence that you have no option other than to read it under your desk at work.' *Daily Mail*

'*Say Nothing* is a powerful, tense UK debut – the sort of book that grabs you and refuses to let go.' *Dead Good*

'*Say Nothing* opens with an intriguing premise . . . Grips the reader from the start and doesn't let up.' *Crime Pieces*

'A cross between domestic noir and the legal thriller schools . . . Will appeal to fans of Harlan Coben and John Grisham.' *Shots*

'A tense, compelling thriller . . . Grips the reader just as strongly as a Lee Child or Jeffrey Deaver story . . . Parks' characterisation is first-rate, especially in portraying the conflicting sides of Judge Sampson's personal life, law man vs family man, and the havoc that the strain of the children's kidnapping wreaks in his and his wife Alison's minds . . . *Say Nothing* shows what happens when orderly lives are twisted out of shape by crime, when the veneer of civility is stripped off . . . A remarkable and original thriller.' *Thriller Books Journal*

'The tension in *Say Nothing* is palpable . . . Perfectly plotted to maximum effect . . . Riveting storytelling.' *Liz Loves Books*

'When I get asked what book I would recommend, *Say Nothing* is now my first answer. I have just spent the last two days pouring over this thriller, devouring every word and I cannot say too many good things about it . . . An epic five stars . . . Brilliant, brilliant storytelling.' *Grab This Book*

'Thrilling . . . Reminded me a little of *The Firm*, and other early works by John Grisham, in the sheer sense of urgency pulsing through the pages . . . Fantastic – absolutely heart-in-your-mouth stuff.' *Crime Worm*

'Faultless . . . A moral dilemma of what a parent would do to protect their child, and how far they are willing to go . . . Brilliant.' *crimesquad.com*

'A superior and enjoyable thriller with an appealingly light touch.' *Sunday Express*

'An intense, intelligent and gripping legal thriller . . . An exceptional story.' *Random Things Through My Letterbox*

'Gripping, dramatic . . . A great read.' *Trip Fiction*

'An engaging and pacy thriller.' *Never Imitate*

'Parks does a fantastic job conveying every parent's worst fear while also showcasing the marital conflict and mistrust that erupts in the midst of a crisis. The complications and twists build to an unexpected climax that is both perfect and gut-wrenching . . . Fans of Harlan Coben and Lisa Gardner will love this thriller.' *Library Journal*

'The nerve-shredding never lets up for a minute as Parks picks you up by the scruff of the neck, shakes you vigorously, and repeats over and over again to a climax so harrowing that you'll be shaking with gratitude that it's finally over.' *Kirkus*

Say Nothing

BRAD PARKS

FABER & FABER

First published in 2018
by Faber & Faber Ltd
Bloomsbury House
74–77 Great Russell Street
London WC1B 3DA

This paperback edition first published in 2018

Typeset by Faber & Faber Ltd
Printed and bound by CPI Group (UK) Ltd, Croydon CR0 4YY

A CIP record for this book
is available from the British Library

ISBN 978-0-571-33269-4

2 4 6 8 10 9 7 5 3 1

I'm married to an amazing woman who, many years ago, told me to chase my dream. Then she made it possible in all the days since.

This one—especially this one—is for her.

Their first move against us was so small, such an infinitesimal blip against the blaring background noise of life, I didn't register it as anything significant.

It came in the form of a text from my wife, Alison, and it arrived on my phone at 3:28 one Wednesday afternoon:

Hey sorry forgot to tell you kids have dr appt this pm.
Picking them up soon.

If I had any reaction to this unexpected disruption, it was only mild disappointment. Wednesday was Swim With Dad, a weekly ritual revered enough in our family to deserve capitalization. The twins and I had been partaking in it regularly for the past three years or so. While it had started as a predictable disaster—more the avoidance of drowning than actual swimming—it had since evolved into something far more pleasurable. Now age six, Sam and Emma had become ardent water rats.

For the forty-five minutes we usually lasted, until one of them got that chatter in the teeth that told me they were done, all we did was enjoy one another. We splashed around. We raced from one end of the pool to the other. We played water games of our own invention, like the much-beloved

Baby Hippo. There's something about having genuine fun with your kids that's good for the soul in a way nothing else is, even if you're forever stuck in the role of Momma Hippo.

I looked forward to it in the same way I cherished all the weekly rites that had come to define our family's little universe. Friday, for example, was Board Game–apalooza. Sunday was Pancake Day. Monday was Hats and Dancing, which involved, well, dancing. With hats on.

And maybe none of this sounds terribly sexy. Certainly, you wouldn't want to slap it across a *Cosmo* cover—HOW TO GIVE YOUR MAN THE BEST PANCAKE DAY OF HIS LIFE! But I have come to believe a good routine is the bedrock of a happy family, and therefore a happy marriage, and therefore a happy life.

So I was miffed, that Wednesday afternoon, when the enjoyment of our little routine was taken away from me. One of the benefits of being a judge is having a certain amount of say-so over my own schedule. My staff knows that, no matter what crisis of justice may be visiting us on a Wednesday afternoon, the Honorable Scott A. Sampson will be leaving his chambers at four o'clock to pick up his kids from after-school care so he can take them to the YMCA pool.

I thought about going anyway and swimming some laps. Doughy forty-four-year-old white men with sedentary jobs ought not pass up opportunities for exercise. But the more I thought about it, being there without Sam and Emma felt wrong. I went home instead.

For the past four years, we've lived in an old farmhouse

alongside the York River we call "the farm," because we're creative that way. It's in a rural part of the Virginia tidewater known as the Middle Peninsula, in an unincorporated section of Gloucester County, about three hours south of D.C. and many steps off the beaten path.

How we ended up there is a story that starts in Washington, where I was the go-to policy guy for an influential US senator. It continues with an incident—might as well refer to it as The Incident, also capitalized—that landed me in a hospital bed, which tends to encourage the rethinking of one's priorities. It ends with my appointment as a federal judge, sitting in Norfolk, in the Eastern District of Virginia.

It was not, necessarily, what I had envisioned for myself when I first picked up *Congressional Quarterly* as a sixth grader. Nor was it your conventional put-out-to-political-pasture assignment. From a workload standpoint, federal judges tend to be like ducks: There's more going on under the surface than anyone quite realizes.

But it was certainly better than where The Incident might have ended for me, which was the morgue.

So I would have told you, all things considered, I had it pretty damn good, with my two healthy kids, my loving wife, my challenging-but-rewarding job, my happy routine.

Or at least that's what I would have said until 5:52 P.M. that Wednesday.

That's when Alison arrived home.

Alone.

*

3

I had been in the kitchen, cutting fruit for the twins' next-day lunches.

Alison was emitting her usual coming-home sounds: opening the door, putting down her bag, shuffling through the mail. Every day, from nine to five thirty, she works with children who have intellectual disabilities that are so severe, their local school systems lacked the ability to accommodate their needs. It is, from my perspective, grueling work that would absolutely wipe me out. Yet she almost always comes home in a good mood. Alison is a veritable force of nurture.

We've been together since our sophomore year of college. I fell in love with her because she was beautiful and yet also found it endearing that I could name all 435 members of Congress, along with the states they represented and their party affiliations. If you're a guy like me and you find a woman like that? You hang on to her for all you're worth.

"Hey, love," I called out.

"Hey, hon," she answered.

What I didn't hear, I immediately realized, were the twins. A six-year-old human is a noisy animal; two six-year-olds, even more so. Sam and Emma typically enter stomping and banging, chattering and humming, creating their own little unselfconscious cacophony.

The only thing more conspicuous than the racket they make is the absence of it. I dried my apple-damp hands on a towel and walked down the hallway to the foyer so I could investigate.

Alison was there, her head bent toward a bill she had opened.

4

"Where are the kids?" I asked.

She looked up from the bill, perplexed. "What do you mean? It's Wednesday."

"I know. But you sent me a text."

"What text?"

"About the doctor," I said, digging into my pocket so she could read it. "It's right here."

Without bothering to look, she said, "I didn't send you any texts about any doctors."

I suddenly knew what it must be like to sit on a beach when all the water mysteriously rushes away, as happens just before a tsunami. You simply can't imagine the size of the thing that's about to hit you.

"So, wait, you're saying you *didn't* pick up the twins?" Alison asked.

"No."

"Does Justina have them?"

Justina Kemal is the Turkish college student who lives rent-free in our cottage in exchange for a certain amount of childcare each month.

"I doubt it," I said. "It's Wednesday. She—"

My phone rang.

"That's probably the school," Alison said. "Tell them I'll be right there. Jesus, Scott."

Alison was already grabbing her keys from the bowl. The number was coming up as RESTRICTED. I hit the answer button.

"Scott Sampson," I said.

"Hello, Judge Sampson," came a voice that sounded

5

thick, deep, and indistinct, like it was being put through a filter. "It must be nice to have your wife home."

"Who is this?" I asked stupidly.

"You're probably wondering where Sam and Emma are," the voice said.

There was a surge of primal juices in my body. My heart began slamming against my rib cage. Blood raced to my face, roared in my ears.

"Where are they?" I asked. Again, stupid.

Alison had paused, halfway out the door. I was braced like I was about to start throwing punches.

"Skavron," the voice said.

"Skavron," I repeated. "What about it?"

United States vs. Skavron was a drug sentencing scheduled for my courtroom the next day. I had spent the early part of the week preparing for it.

"You will receive your instructions about the verdict we want in a text message tomorrow," the voice said. "If you want to see your children again, you will follow those instructions exactly."

"What instructions? What do—"

"You will not go to the police," the voice continued. "You will not approach the FBI. You will not notify the authorities in any way. Your children remaining alive and unharmed depends on you going about your business as if nothing is wrong. You will do nothing. You will say nothing. Do you understand?"

"No, wait, I don't understand. I don't understand anything."

"Then let me make it clear to you: If we even suspect you've spoken to the authorities, we'll start chopping off fingers. If we know for a fact you have, we'll do ears and noses."

"I got it. I got it. Please don't hurt them. I'll do whatever you want. Please don—"

"Say nothing," the voice warned.

Then the line went dead.

2

The front door was still open. Alison's eyes flared.

"What's happening?" she asked. "What's going on? What do you mean, 'don't hurt them'?"

I couldn't immediately answer her. I couldn't even breathe.

"Scott, talk to me."

"The children . . . They've been"—I had to force myself to say the word—"kidnapped."

"What?" she shrieked.

"This voice . . . He said . . . He wanted a verdict in this case I'm hearing and . . . He said if we go to the police he'll start chopping off"—I involuntarily brought my hands to my face and gasped for air—"chopping off fingers. He said we have to say nothing. Say nothing or . . ."

My heart was thrashing. I felt like there wasn't enough oxygen in the world, even though I swear I was sucking it in as fast as I could. My chest was being crushed by some huge, unseen hand.

Oh God, I thought, *I'm having a heart attack.*

Breathe. I had to breathe. But I couldn't get my lungs to fill, no matter how desperate I was to make it happen. I yanked at the collar of my shirt, which was buttoned too tight. No, wait, it was my necktie. I was being strangled by it.

I brought my other hand to my neck so I could tear away whatever clothes were impeding the flow of blood to my brain. That's when I realized: I wasn't wearing a tie anymore.

My face was a furnace. I was suddenly sweating out of every pore. Pins and needles attacked my feet and legs. They weren't going to hold me much longer.

Alison was screaming at me. "Scott, what is going on? What do you mean they've been kidnapped?"

I watched, with surreal detachment, as the veins in the side of her neck bulged.

"Scott!" she said, grabbing my shoulders and shaking me. "Goddamn it, Scott! What's happening?"

To me, the question was unanswerable. But Alison, apparently expecting some kind of reply, started banging on my chest and raving, "What's happening? What's going on?"

Her fists kept striking me until it occurred to me I should shield myself from the blows. As soon as I brought my hands up to ward her off, she dropped to the floor, hugging her knees and sobbing. It sounded like she was saying, "Oh God." Or maybe she was saying, "My babies." Or both.

I bent over to pull her up—what this would accomplish, I had no idea—but couldn't manage it. Instead of lifting her up, the effort just brought me farther down. I sank to one knee, then both knees. The corners of my vision had gone blurry. I felt myself losing consciousness. I let out a loud moan.

Some dimly functioning part of my brain told me that if I was going to die, I should lie down. I let myself fall to my side, then rolled onto my back. From there, I stared up at

9

the ceiling, gasping and waiting for everything to go black.

Except it didn't. My face was still flushed and I swore the top of my skull was going to erupt from the heat. But it was slowly dawning on me that meant there was too much blood going to my head, not too little.

I wasn't having a heart attack. I was having a panic attack.

Panic attacks don't kill you. I had to will my body to start operating, even if it didn't want to. Sam and Emma needed me. They needed me more than they ever had in their entire lives.

This thought brought me back to my hands and knees. I crawled over to the wall, leaned against it, and managed to hoist myself up. I shut the front door—why, I don't know—then looked down to where I had dropped my phone.

I picked it up and started searching for a number in my contacts. The desire to help my children was suddenly as strong as the desire to keep breathing had been just moments before.

"What . . . what are you doing?" Alison asked.

"I'm calling the marshals."

The US Marshals Service oversees my safety while I'm at the courthouse. Outside the courthouse, I'm the responsibility of the Federal Bureau of Investigation. I didn't have any FBI numbers stored in my phone, but I did have the chief deputy marshal in charge of the courthouse. He, in turn, could call the FBI.

"What?" Alison demanded.

"I'm calling the chief—"

With extraordinary speed, Alison leapt to her feet and

knocked the phone out of my hand. I watched it skitter into the corner.

"Are you out of your mind?" she asked.

"Why did you—"

"You're not seriously calling the marshals service."

"Yeah, I—"

"Absolutely not," she said, a shrill spike in her voice.

"Look, Ali, we need to call in some reinforcements here. We need people trained in negotiating with kidnappers. We need the FBI. They have resources we don't even begin to—"

"*Absolutely not,*" she said again, in case I hadn't heard her the first time. "What did that man on the phone tell you? That if we went to the police they'd start chopping off fingers?"

And ears. And noses.

"They obviously have resources too," she continued. "They have the technology to fake the origin of a text message. They got your cell phone number. They knew to call right after I got home, which means they're watching us right now. What do you want to do? Test them to see if they're really serious? They're serious, okay? We have to assume they're out in those woods"—she pointed in the direction of the approximately ten acres of forest between our house and the road—"and the moment they see a cop car, marked or unmarked, they're going to start carving. I don't want pieces of my children sent to me in the mail."

My stomach lurched.

"I could never, ever forgive myself if something we did resulted in . . . ," she began, but then couldn't bring herself to finish the thought. At least not out loud. What she came up with instead was: "I grew those fingers."

It effectively ended any argument we might have had. Alison and I tell ourselves we are one of those modern couples who share equally in the duties of child-rearing. And that's true. Until we disagree about something. Then it becomes very apparent that, deep down, we are still old-fashioned. When it comes to the kids, Alison calls the shots.

"Okay, so what are you saying we should do?" I asked.

"You said, 'Skavron.' Is that the case they're looking to control?"

"Yes."

"When do you hear it?"

"Tomorrow."

"Well, then you give them what they want—exactly and precisely what they want, whatever that is," she said. "And by this time tomorrow, this will all be over."

"I give them a verdict. They return the kids unharmed."

"That's right."

"And you believe them, because people who kidnap children are known to be so honest?"

Her face went crooked.

"Sorry," I said.

She looked away.

I might have tried to press my point further. But then I remembered something I had once been told about the FBI. In kidnapping cases, agents don't face discipline if the victim gets killed. That's seen as sometimes-unavoidable collateral damage. They suffer career consequences only if the kidnappers get away.

That meant, at this moment, the FBI and the Sampson family had very different priorities.

"Okay," I said. "We'll say nothing."

3

The single-story, wood-sided ranch had been built by a man—now long-dead—whose primary aspiration in life was to be left alone. It was situated in a county so thinly populated it did not have a single stoplight; down a lightly traveled road lined with abandoned farmhouses and corroded trailers; deep in a forest thick with loblolly pines, marshland, and poison ivy.

Its only connection to the outside world, beyond the power line, was a satellite dish that funneled television and Internet from the heavens. Vehicle access consisted of a meager, rutted sand-and-dirt lane with a rusted chain stretched across the entrance and several prominent NO TRESPASSING signs.

It was not the end of the Earth. It just felt that way.

Outside the house, on the small clearing of pine straw that passed for a turnaround, there was a white panel van. Inside the kitchen, two men sat at a circular table. Both had untrimmed beards, protuberant noses, and eyes the color of strong coffee. Both were broad shouldered and well built. It was easy to see they were brothers.

The older one was slightly taller. He was reading a cracked-spine paperback. The younger one was slightly thicker. He swiped at his iPad, playing a game whose end goal was planetary domination.

When they spoke, it was in a foreign language.

"You should feed them now," the older one said.

"Why?" replied the younger, not looking up from his game.

"They're children. They need to eat."

"Let them starve."

"They'll be more docile if we feed them."

"They'll be more docile if we tie them up."

"Our employer said not to."

The younger one just grunted. The older one returned his attention to his book, making no move toward the refrigerator or cabinets. The younger one eventually lit a cigarette, taking drags as he continued poking his iPad.

Situated between them on the table was an Internet phone, a necessity in a place so far from cell tower coverage. When it rang, the older brother answered, pressing the speakerphone button so both could hear.

"Yes?" he said, in accented English.

"I made the call to the judge."

"And?"

"He got the message. I don't think we'll have any problems, but you'll still be keeping an eye on him, yes?"

"Of course."

"First delivery is tonight, right?"

"Yes."

"Good. Don't let him get comfortable."

"We won't."

The call ended. The older brother placed the phone back in the middle of the table. From a satchel at his feet, he retrieved a long-handled, serrated hunting knife and handed it to his younger brother.

"Okay," the older one said. "Time to get to work."

4

Over the next hour, as the horror of what happened lashed into us, Alison and I failed in all attempts to comfort each other. Eventually, we went to our own sections of the house and our own separate hells.

She retreated to the family room, where she pulled a blanket over herself and stared at the wall, lost in her agony. From time to time, I heard the noises of grief: sharp intakes of breath, shudders that became audible, soft groans.

The temptation to do the same was nearly overwhelming. I'm sure if I allowed myself to consider our new reality—that the foundation of our lives had been washed away and there was not a damn thing underneath—I would have found a hollow in which to collapse and capitulate to the breakdown that was surely coming.

But that urge was still there: the desire to do *something* that felt like it would help my children, no matter how futile the gesture was. I kept pacing in manic circles around the house until eventually I wound up sitting at the kitchen table, where we fed the kids, as if that could somehow draw me closer to them. Driving out all the extraneous (and terrifying) thoughts that kept invading my head, I forced myself to focus on Skavron. The people who had my children had to be connected to him. If only I could figure out how.

Up until 5:52 P.M., I would have told you there was nothing particularly noteworthy about *Skavron*. If anything, the case was heartbreakingly typical. Drug sentencings were, by far, the most common cause of action in the federal judiciary, which bears its share of burden from the spectacular public policy failure that is the war on drugs. I handle at least thirty such cases a year.

My staff had given me the case work-up on Monday. I had a call with the probation officer who wrote the presentencing report on Tuesday. I had spent much of this day, Wednesday, in the office, going through that report, which is essentially the defendant's life story.

Rayshaun Skavron had been born in Danville, a down-on-its-luck town in the south-central part of Virginia. His father had never been in the picture. His mother's parental rights were terminated when he was six, after she was arrested on drug charges. He was raised by an aunt. His first arrest was at thirteen, and it was followed by many others. Drugs and guns, guns and drugs—with a few driving offenses thrown in for variety. He was in and out of juvenile facilities for the remainder of his childhood, then graduated to state penitentiaries.

At some point, he drifted over to Virginia Beach, maybe for a fresh start, or maybe for a place where the cops didn't know him as well. There were two years without an arrest, and then he hit the big time: Using information from a cooperating witness and a family member who was tired of his act, the police tied Skavron to a stash consisting of five kilograms of heroin and smaller amounts of cocaine and crack.

To his credit, he had spared the judicial system the expense of a trial, taking a plea deal and agreeing to cooperate with the authorities.

The weight of the drugs was what made the case federal. His deal would help him some, though federal sentencing guidelines bent only so far. With his record and with the crime he had committed, Rayshaun Skavron was going away for a long time.

Except, possibly, if someone wanted to ensure that he didn't.

But who? And why?

My knowledge of the drug world was limited to what I saw in my courtroom. But Skavron seemed to be, at best, middle management. According to the charging documents, he received his product from someone who was listed as UCC No. 1, which stood for Unindicted Co-Conspirator No. 1. He had a few clients of his own but mostly served as a pass-along. He packaged the product and sold it to other dealers/users, who then worked the streets.

The evidence suggested none of this had been particularly lucrative. Before being arrested and detained, Skavron lived in a small apartment, drove an aging Chrysler, and had been working on and off as a cook, most recently at an assisted-living facility that paid him minimum wage. Police had seized some paltry amount of cash—I believe it was two hundred and thirty-eight dollars—from his residence. He had no bank account. He had been unable to post bond or hire a private attorney.

How had someone like that found the wherewithal, from

behind bars, to orchestrate the kidnapping of a judge's children? I thought about the steps involved. First, there had been the text message. The kidnappers needed to make sure I wouldn't pick up the children, and also that I wouldn't immediately be looking for them. So they somehow hacked the phone system and arranged for "Alison" to send me a text.

The next step was the abduction itself, whose particulars were harder to fathom. Sam and Emma were first graders at Middle Peninsula Montessori. It was a tiny school, with only three other first graders. It's not like two children could have disappeared without someone noticing.

Likewise, the staff was not in the habit of allowing students to wander off with strangers. The school kept lists of people who were approved for pickup. Ours included only Justina and Alison's family: her mother, her two sisters, and their husbands. But perhaps that safeguard had been circumvented through some bit of deception?

What that told me, along with the text message, was that whoever orchestrated this was cunning, disciplined, and well organized.

None of which seemed to fit the Rayshaun Skavron I had met in that presentencing report. He must have been assisted by someone far more sophisticated than he was. But whom?

The obvious answer might have been UCC No. 1. This, in theory, was someone who was a little further up the food chain, someone who might want to ensure Skavron's release so that he wouldn't testify in UCC No. 1's case.

Except there was the matter of the *U* in UCC. Unindicted.

Which might as well have also meant Unknown. If there really was a case pending against UCC No. 1, Skavron wouldn't be in my courtroom. The US Attorneys Office would prosecute UCC No. 1 first and Skavron sometime after that. They always landed the bigger fish first.

Skavron probably didn't know one useful thing about UCC No. 1. That's why the cartels have hundreds and thousands of middlemen like Skavron in the first place. Dealing on the streets is a hazardous enterprise, one where it's nearly impossible to distinguish the customer from the undercover cop and/or the snitch. Arrests are part of the cost of doing business. For this reason, the real bosses never deal directly with the consumers. They maintain several layers of insulation, like Skavron, between themselves and the chaos of the streets.

And they keep that insulation clueless. Skavron probably didn't even know which organization he worked for.

The US Attorneys Office could go no higher with this case. From a prosecutorial standpoint, Skavron was a total dead end.

*

Perhaps an hour or two later, I was still shuffling through everything in my mind when Alison entered the kitchen with a loud sniffle. Her eyes were red rimmed.

She didn't stop at the table or acknowledge me in any way. She just went to one of the cabinets and withdrew a water glass.

Even under obvious duress, she moved with easy grace. Alison was also forty-four, though you'd barely know it. Her body has the same slender shape it did when we met, twenty-odd years ago. Her posture is just as straight. Her shoulders—my wife has great shoulders, if that doesn't sound too strange—have not surrendered an inch to gravity.

She was getting a few gray hairs, but they blended easily with her natural ash blond. While I'm acutely aware of my own receding hair and advancing wrinkles, I could swear Alison is barely aging at all. Or maybe I just didn't notice. Love does that.

I'm not trying to hold her out as some kind of paragon of perfection. She binges on chocolate and potato chips. She sneaks cigarettes at work, even though she thinks I don't know. She's a terrible driver.

Nor would I say we have a perfect marriage, inasmuch as such a thing exists only in the imaginations of greeting card writers and the delusions of single people. We have these fights defined not by their noise but by their ferocious silence. We will literally go days where we barely talk, each of us too stubborn to concede on whatever point started the dispute. In the depths of these silences, there are times when I'll think we really are on the brink of divorce.

But, inevitably, one of us caves. And I will say, if we do one thing well, it's finding a way to laugh about it later. We have an ongoing gag about her running back to Paul Dresser— Paul being the high school boyfriend who now grows more dashing, gallant, and rich with each passing year. So after we've made up, she'll say, "Well, Paul Dresser's private jet

22

has been waylaid in the Maldives, so I guess we might as well stay together a little longer."

Beyond that, I can say without question that the initial flame of attraction—that spark that fired my crush on her all those years ago—still burns in me. My wife doesn't believe me when I tell her this, but it's true: If you wiped my memory and I walked into a room with her and a hundred other women, she's still the one I'd want to take home.

So if I took a moment to admire her as she poured herself a glass of tap water, it was only because it had become muscle memory.

She half turned toward me and asked, "Do you want any?"

"No. Thanks."

Alison contemplated the glass in her hand.

"Emma was here, just last night," she said in a hollow voice. "She was so insistent she wanted to help me wash the dishes I let her stand on a chair and do it. All I did was dry. She was being so grown up."

The glass slipped out of Alison's fingers. As it shattered in the sink, she was already sobbing.

"Hey, hey," I said, rising from my chair and walking quickly over to her.

She wouldn't straighten herself or face me, so I bent down and wrapped my arms around her from behind. For a little while, all I did was hold her in that awkward pose, just so she knew I was there.

"I just can't stop thinking about them," she said. "Where are they? What are they doing? Are they hurt? Are they scared?"

"I know, I know."

An unexpected aspect of parenthood was that sometime during Alison's first trimester, my brain developed an extra region that was dedicated to only one purpose: worrying about my children. Even when the rest of me is occupied by something completely unrelated, that part pulses softly.

Right then, it was throbbing.

"I think I'm still in shock," she said. "If I was even processing this at all, I'd just shut down completely."

"Yeah," I said.

In an attempt to steady herself, she was taking breaths so deep they rocked her entire body. I ran my hand up and down her back, hoping that might soothe her.

"By this time tomorrow, it'll be over," I said. "We just have to keep it together, do what we're told, and everything will be fine."

"I know, I know. Without that . . ."

She didn't complete the sentence. I held her some more.

"Scott, if we lose them, I—"

"Shh. We can't think that way. It's not going to help anything."

"I know, but—"

"Shh," I said again, as if either of us voicing the thought would somehow give it power.

We stood there without talking until she found the impetus to push herself away. "I'm sorry," she said.

"Don't be."

She made to move back toward the sink to clean up the broken glass. I blocked her.

"I've got that. Seriously. Don't worry about it."

She paused. "Okay. I think I'm going to go lie down."

"That's a great idea."

"Would it be . . . Would it be weird if I went into one of the twins' rooms?"

"Not at all," I said.

She nodded. I kissed the side of her face, still moist with tears. She departed the kitchen without another word.

I kept expecting, as I delicately removed what had once been a water glass from the sink, that a rage would begin to well inside me, that I would be seized by the urge to strike out at the people who had done this to us, that I would begin to entertain deadly revenge fantasies.

Instead, all I felt as I picked at those shards of glass was supreme impotence.

It was a distinctly foreign sensation for a man of my occupation. Within our democracy, the federal judiciary is the one place that tolerates dictatorships. Federal judges are appointed for life. We do not have to worry about running for office or groveling to our patrons. It takes an act of Congress to remove us from the bench. On a daily basis, we do not answer to supervisors or voters or anything other than our own consciences.

Some lawyers refer to federal judges as Little Caesars, like the pizza chain, except it's not totally a joke. We really do have an astonishing degree of authority. Some of my decisions can be overturned or amended by higher courts, yes, but a surprising number of them are, for all practical purposes, unassailable.

With little more than my own gut to guide me, I routinely make pronouncements that will shape the remainder of people's lives. The wealthiest lawyers in the land kowtow to me. Huge bureaucracies are forced to follow my orders. The most formidable people in our society are but one bad decision away from winding up in my courtroom, begging for my mercy, sometimes literally trembling before me.

I realize it's the position, not the person, that inspires this sycophancy. I certainly do nothing to encourage it. I am something of a reluctant Caesar. The constant fawning embarrasses me.

It comes with the job all the same.

Whether I like it or not, I represent power.

Whether I want it or not, I have power.

Or at least I used to.

5

Around midnight, I went up to our bedroom to begin an ill-fated attempt at sleep. What this soon became was me lying there, with that extra region in my brain—the kid part—in overdrive.

I thought of Sam. Brave, lovely Sam. Alison and I have done our best to eschew gender stereotypes in how we raised our children. Yet Sam is still one hundred percent boy. There's a certain amount of energy he simply has to expend each day. And if he doesn't? Woe to all furniture, walls, and human beings in his path. Sometimes in the late afternoon, when his rambunctiousness is about to overwhelm all of us, we'll send him to run laps around the house.

Then I thought of Emma. Sweet, thoughtful Emma. She also has her share of energy, except she expresses it emotionally, rather than physically. She is incredibly perceptive. If Alison and I have a loud conversation— even if we aren't disagreeing about something, just talking boisterously—she'll ask us to stop fighting. On the rare occasions I've had to reprimand her, I had learned to do so gently, beginning with assurances that I loved her endlessly and forever. Otherwise, one cross look could make her burst into tears and end all hope of discourse.

As I considered some of the questions Alison had

asked—where were they? what were they doing?—I concocted a scenario under which they were safe and unharmed.

Under this wishful thinking, their kidnappers had invented some kind of lie to make the children think the whole thing was a game, so they didn't fully understand what was happening. They were not being fed peanut butter or other tree nuts (Emma was allergic). They were being given the Big Three of a six-year-old's diet—pizza, pasta, chicken nuggets—and allowed to gorge themselves on television.

They knew something was a little strange, yes, but they were basically okay. After all, Sam had his Emma. And Emma had her Sam. On some level, twins are always okay as long as they have each other.

That was the best-case scenario.

The worst-case scenario was something I was fighting desperately to keep out of my head.

Time passed in small increments. Around two A.M., Alison crept into the room, peeled back the covers, and slid under them. We lay, side by side, each of us quiet in our own misery.

The house was dark and still and making all its usual house noises, though none of them sounded right without the twins there. We had been drawn to this place for them, not for us. We bought it because we knew they'd grow to love the river, with its white-sand beach and its gently sloping shoreline; because its ample acreage included a thousand trees to shade their summer days; because it was this big, rambling former farm with a million memories waiting to be made. Alison often talked about how special it was to her that we were giving the twins a childhood that was so different from the usual cul-de-sac existence of most upper-middle-class kids.

But ultimately, we bought it because before The Incident I had been the kind of blithe optimist who trusted in the goodness of my fellow man. After it, having seen the human potential for wickedness, I wanted to raise my children in a place that was as safe as possible. I had thought all those trees and all those acres would act as a kind of fortress; and that our driveway, a dirt road spanning four-tenths of a mile, was long enough to effectively seal out the worst of the world.

It was only now that I understood the falseness of that. Security was a myth, a grand lie we told ourselves to mask the jarring reality of the human condition: that the social contract was written in sand, not stone, and it could be blown away at any time, by anyone with sufficient breath in his lungs.

This was the thought going through my head in a relentless loop as I lay in bed and the night plodded on. I tried to steer my dreams toward the happier times that would come. This would end. Soon. I had to believe that.

Slowly, I felt my body sinking into the mattress. Alison's breathing had become more steady. I was just starting to think I might be able to drift off for a minute or two.

Then someone rang the doorbell.

I was on my feet before the *bong-bong* chiming of the bell had played out. Alison was sitting up. I could see the whites of her eyes, looking wild in the blackness. The clock read 3:17.

Operating without much thought, I was already striding toward the door of our bedroom.

"Wait, where are you going?" Alison asked in a ferocious whisper.

"What do you mean? What if that's the kids?"

"The kids? Just walking up to our door and ringing the—"

"Well, a sheriff's deputy with the kids."

I wasn't waiting around to debate her. I had arrived at the door to our bedroom and was reaching for the door handle.

"Wait," she said, having jumped out of bed and grabbed me by the wrist. "Don't you think the sheriff's office would have called us first? What if it's the kidnappers? What if they have a gun?"

"Just stay here," I said, tearing my arm away.

"Scott," she called after me, but I was already out the door, on my way downstairs.

We own a gun, a Smith & Wesson nine millimeter we bought when Alison was pregnant and I was gone most of the time. She had joked—well, half joked—that her momma-bear hormones were telling her she needed it. Woe to the criminal who tried to take on Alison. She was an army brat whose dad's idea of father-daughter bonding was an afternoon of target shooting. As a kid, she had won a trunkful of marksmanship ribbons. Judging from the way she handled the Smith & Wesson on the range the day we bought it, her skills had not faded much.

Unfortunately, the weapon was currently disassembled, with half in the attic and the other half hidden under the sink in the master bathroom. I had insisted on this after researching the statistics on accidental gun deaths for a bill I drafted. The numbers were clear: A functioning gun inside a house was a far greater danger to children than anything lurking outside it.

This was the first time I regretted that decision. I quickly catalogued the possible weapons at my disposal—kitchen knives, screwdrivers, a fireplace poker—and opted for a golf club from the hall closet.

The absurdity of it—a soft, middle-aged man thinking he could confront armed assailants with a six iron— had not yet dawned on me. I flipped on the switch that controlled the outside lights. Then I skittered around to our sitting room so I could look out the window and at least have some idea of what I was about to face.

Like a lot of southern farmhouses, ours has a generous front porch, one that wraps around two sides of the house. It is decorated with wicker furniture and a series of bird feeders, which had been painted by the kids when Justina had gone on an arts-and-crafts kick the previous summer. Beyond the porch is a front yard dotted with magnolia trees and loblolly pines, and that long dirt road.

Peering out the window, I couldn't make out much. The

porch and the part of the yard that was now illuminated appeared to be absent of humanity. The trees and the road beyond it were mere suggestions in the gloom.

Regripping the golf club, I returned to the front door, which was old and heavy. I unchained it, then eased it open, hiding most of my body behind its bulk in case there was some ambush awaiting me.

There was no need. No one was out there. All I heard was distant yipping from a small pack of semiferal dogs that sometimes patrol our woods.

Then I looked down to see a knee-high cardboard box with a Home Depot logo printed on the side. A line of silver duct tape had been used to seal the top.

I toed the box to get a sense of its weight. Whatever was in there wasn't much heavier than the box itself. I listened—for, what, a ticking sound or something?—but heard nothing.

Then I finally realized I was being paranoid. Whoever was doing this needed me alive, at least until sometime after eleven o'clock in the morning, when I followed whatever instructions awaited me. I let the golf club drop to my side and tore open the box.

Inside were two clear Ziploc sandwich bags, filled with hair clippings. Specifically, my children's hair. Sam's was straight and sun bleached. Emma's was curly and, while still blond, ever so slightly darker.

My hand went to my throat, a classic gesture of vulnerability. A judge spends his life examining evidence. This was all I needed to see to know this nightmare was real. I had to grab on to the doorframe to keep my balance.

Once I steadied myself and took some deep breaths, I saw there was also an envelope. It was small, the kind you might see attached to a bouquet of flowers. I pulled it open. There was a piece of card stock, folded in half. The message it contained was printed in block lettering:

JUDGE SAMPSON,
FOLLOW YOUR INSTRUCTIONS OR NEXT TIME WE'LL
CUT MORE THAN JUST HAIR.
          —FRIENDS OF RAYSHAUN SKAVRON

I gazed out into the darkness one more time. Nothing about it had changed. Except as my eyes returned to the porch, I noticed something strange about the post nearest the steps.

One of the bird feeders was missing.

6

The chiming of the motion sensor was loud enough to wake the younger brother from the easy chair where he had been dozing. He rose and grabbed an assault rifle that had fallen to the floor, then went to the window.

A pair of headlights burst into the clearing in front of the house, then flicked on and off several times.

The all-clear signal. The younger brother stepped back from the blinds and disarmed the security system. It was old, installed by the crackpot who built the place, and no longer connected to central monitoring. But it still wailed plenty loud if anyone opened a door or window. He returned the gun to the hook on the wall where it belonged and was seated at the kitchen table with his iPad when his older brother entered.

"How did it go?" the younger asked.

"Fine," said the older as he rearmed the security system.

"No problems with the delivery?"

"None," the older said. "Any trouble here?"

"Not really. The boy started complaining he needed food. I fed him just to shut him up."

"I told you they'd be more docile that way. What did you give them?"

"Peanut butter and jelly on bread. You said that's what American children like."

"Did they eat it?"

"The boy did. The girl wouldn't touch it."

"She will when she gets hungry enough."

The younger gestured his head toward one of the bedrooms. "The boy has been crying a lot. He keeps asking for his mother and father. It's getting on my nerves."

"Well, then I guess that settles it."

"What?"

"Which one we get rid of."

7

There was no sleep the remainder of the night. Just a lot of tangled sheets.

In the morning, the early-autumn sun rose over Gloucester, Virginia, cruelly unaware of the two agonized lives it was illuminating. Alison was already out of bed. I heard her in the shower and may have lightly dozed to the sound of the water running.

The next thing I knew, she was back in the room, dressing.

"Are you going to work?" I asked.

"God no. I already called in. I'm going to the kids' school."

I propped myself up on my elbow. "You can't. Say nothing, remember?"

"I won't. I just . . . I just have to ask some questions, that's all. I've been thinking about it all night. I mean, what happened? Someone just came and took our kids? I have to understand. Or at least try. For my own sanity. They're going to want to know why our kids aren't in school, anyway. We have to come up with something."

"I'll come with you," I said, swinging my legs down onto the floor.

"It's better you didn't. You being a judge, it intimidates people sometimes."

"Then you do the talking," I said. "I just want to be able

to hear their answers."

"I don't—"

And then she stopped herself. "Okay," she said.

With that concession, I forced myself into the shower. We left quickly after I got dressed. The house was excruciatingly quiet without the twins.

We took separate cars and within fifteen minutes had arrived at Middle Peninsula Montessori. Gloucester was not an especially affluent county, and the school's simplicity reflected this. It was just a small steel building set at the edge of a gravel parking lot. The student artwork that decorated the outside had always made me think of it as a cheerful, welcoming place, this little haven of love and learning where I sent my children each day.

Now it seemed grotesque.

It was a few minutes past eight o'clock when we arrived. The school day would start in less than half an hour.

"I'm doing the talking," Alison said again when I met her at the door of her car.

"Absolutely," I said.

We walked across the parking lot, our feet crunching on the stones. The front door was locked—that was policy—so Alison rang the doorbell.

Suzanne Fridley, the head of school, soon appeared. Miss Suzanne, as everyone called her, was one of those preternaturally calm people who would have been wasted in anything other than an educational environment. She had a simple magic with children.

"Well, good morning, Mrs. Sampson. Judge," she said as

she opened the door. "Come in, come in. To what do we owe the pleasure?"

We were standing in the small school's entryway, which also doubled as a library. I looked at Alison, to make it clear to all she was taking the lead.

"This may sound like a strange question," she said. "But who picked up the twins yesterday?"

Unruffled, Miss Suzanne grabbed a clipboard on a small table next to the door. Every pickup was recorded there. Miss Suzanne flipped a page.

Then her brow crinkled. "Why, you did."

She turned the clipboard around so Alison could inspect the page. Sure enough, at 3:57 P.M., Sam and Emma were recorded as having departed. The "Picked Up By" column had "mom" in it. Next to that were the scrawled initials of a staff person.

I think if it had been me, my mouth would have been hanging open. Alison, to her credit, simply said, "That's Miss Pam's signature, yes?"

"Yes, it is."

"Is she here?" Alison asked.

"One moment, please."

Miss Suzanne walked serenely into the next room and returned fifteen seconds later with Miss Pam, the grandmotherly sort who served as a teacher's assistant.

"Judge Sampson and Mrs. Sampson were just asking a few questions about pickup yesterday," Miss Suzanne said. "Do you remember checking out the twins yesterday?"

"Yes," Miss Pam said blankly.

"Who picked them up?"

"It was . . . Mrs. Sampson," Miss Pam said, eyeing Alison, whose face had flushed.

At this point, I jumped in: "We're just having some confusion. Someone picked up the kids yesterday, but we're not sure who. So I know this is going to sound weird, but are you *sure* it was her?"

Miss Pam's head snapped from me to Miss Suzanne, back to me, then to Alison. "Well, yes, I . . . I think so," she said. "You were wearing a . . . a ball cap and sunglasses, weren't you?"

Alison hadn't worn a baseball hat in public since the days of college all-nighters.

"Did you actually see her face?" I pressed.

"No, I . . . Just the back of her head. She had her hair in a ponytail."

"Did she speak at all?"

"Well . . . no," Miss Pam said.

Which, for me, confirmed it wasn't Alison, who was a please-and-thank-you kind of woman. Someone had obviously impersonated my wife, trusting in the hat and shades to hide the differences between her and another thin blond woman.

"And it was the right car?" I asked.

"Yes, of course," Miss Pam said. She was looking at Miss Suzanne again, a desperate look that said, *Help me out here.*

Finally, Miss Suzanne came up with: "We had that security camera installed last year. If you like, we can look at the video from yesterday afternoon."

"That would be great," I said.

"Come with me," she said.

We followed her into a cramped office that was just off the entrance. She sat at a chair in front of a computer monitor, which was soon filled with a current view of the school. The camera was really aimed at the front door but captured at least a little bit of the parking lot.

"Let me just rewind it," Miss Suzanne said.

She clicked several times. The clock in the upper right corner of the screen started scrolling quickly backward. Morning gave way to night, then to yesterday's twilight, then to an increasingly sunny afternoon.

Soon a succession of cars and trucks, all of them moving backward, flitted across the screen. I wasn't seeing anything of note, but Alison said, "Right there."

"Okay," Miss Suzanne said.

She set the video going forward, at regular speed. The clock in the upper right corner read 15:55.06—military time for a few minutes before four o'clock. For the next seventy-two seconds, nothing happened. Then, at 15:56.18, a gray Honda Odyssey minivan glided into the left side of the frame and came to a stop.

We own a gray Honda Odyssey minivan. We bought it secondhand a few years back so Justina could use it to pick up the kids.

I couldn't say whether this gray Honda Odyssey was our gray Honda Odyssey. The make and model appeared to be identical. You couldn't see the license plate—only the right side of the car appeared on the screen. But I did recognize a

Middle Peninsula Montessori School window decal on the right side of the back window, in the exact spot where we had ours.

This was either our car—stolen from our driveway and then returned, perhaps?—or a painstaking reproduction of it.

The driver was wearing sunglasses and a pink hat with a blond ponytail pulled through it. She stared straight ahead. It certainly could have been Alison. It also could have not been Alison. The footage was too grainy to tell.

At 15:57.13, Miss Pam appeared. The side door to the minivan slid open.

I had to stifle a gasp as my children, my two beautiful children, came bounding out. First Sam, then Emma. I fought the desire to tell Suzanne to pause it just so I could stare at them.

But I stayed quiet as I watched the minivan roll off screen. I looked at the time stamp. It said 15:59.45.

That was all the time it took to rip our lives apart. Two minutes and thirty-two seconds.

"Would you like to see it again?" Miss Suzanne asked.

Alison had lifted her hand to her mouth at some point during the viewing. She brought it down, straightened herself, and tried to retake control.

"No, that's okay," she said. "We've taken enough of your time."

"It's not a problem," Miss Suzanne said, perhaps even more confused than before.

"The children won't be coming to school today," Alison said.

"Oh?" said Miss Suzanne.

"They both came down with a fever last night," Alison said, then added: "My mother is watching them today."

"Well, I hope they feel better," Suzanne said.

"Yes, thank you. We'll see ourselves out."

We escaped to the parking lot. Alison waited that long before the sob she had been muffling crept out. I walked toward her, to put my arm around her. She glared at me.

"Keep walking," she said between gritted teeth. "Don't make a scene."

She had kept her back to the office the whole time. If Miss Suzanne was watching us out the window, she wouldn't have necessarily seen anything.

I'm not sure it mattered. We had just given a performance that could be carried off only by two people who had lost their minds.

8

Alison called me shortly after we pulled out of the parking lot.

"It wasn't me," she said. "I didn't pick up the kids."

"Yeah, I know."

"I can't believe the kids would just hop into the car with a stranger. Did they really not notice?"

"It was just another day on the pickup line," I reasoned. "They didn't have cause to think anything was out of place."

"It's just wild. I"—she interrupted herself with a strong exhale—"I don't know if I can hold it together."

I didn't know if I could either. But this didn't seem like the right moment to admit that. I think it's an unwritten rule of parenting that only one of you gets to freak out at a time.

"Can you imagine how insane we must have looked? 'Hey, who picked up our kids? We're such bad parents, we don't even know.' 'Oh, actually, you did, you lunatic.' "

"Yeah. We must have looked pretty nuts," I said. "But, I have to be honest, I think we have bigger things to worry about."

"I know," she said softly. "I know."

I had just made the left turn to travel south on Route 17, a four-lane decorated by the gaudy ornamentation of American commerce—fast-food joints and chain hotels, strip malls and banks, auto-repair shops and gas stations, all set on an endless loop.

"Okay, I guess I'll let you go," she said. "You'll let me know as soon as you have them, right?"

"Of course. Just sit tight. This will be over soon."

We ended the call. I had just crossed over the York River on the Coleman Bridge and merged onto Interstate 64 when my phone rang again. I thought it would be Alison. Instead, I saw just one name on the screen: FRANKLIN.

*

For thirteen years, Senator Blake Franklin had been my boss. No, more than that. He had been my mentor, my cajoler, my cheerleader, my tormentor, my obsession. He was that rare person who could always tell me how good I was and also how much better I could be, and I would believe him, no matter what he said. As my job titles became more impressive and my responsibilities grew, so did the hours I spent in his service. I typically arrived by six A.M., seldom left before eight P.M., and told myself I was happy to do it. I was, above all, desperate to please him.

Then came this one day five years ago, otherwise known as The Incident. Blake was holding a press conference to announce a much-heralded piece of gun legislation we were calling the Gun Rights and Responsibilities Act.

It was, we felt, a very reasonable law, one designed to appeal to both sides of the aisle. It recognized, in very strong terms, that the Second Amendment guaranteed the individual

44

right to gun ownership—codifying recent Supreme Court rulings on the subject, an important concession to the gun lobby. It implicitly outlawed any efforts to limit the number of guns owned by an individual, another nod to the crowd of lawful citizens who merely wanted the gunpowder-backed instrumentality to resist government tyranny. But it also greatly strengthened background checks and other commonsense measures designed to keep guns out of the hands of criminals, spouse abusers, and the mentally ill.

I had worked on it like a fiend, polishing it to unassailable perfection. Various versions of the bill had been passed around Capitol Hill, and it seemed to have the broad support in both houses necessary to pass. I was proud to be standing just behind Blake as he introduced it.

Then some nutcase—precisely the kind of person the bill was designed to prevent from owning a gun—opened fire.

He squeezed off eight rounds before a police officer tackled him. Blake, miraculously, was not hit. Seven of the bullets bounced harmlessly off the steps of the Dirksen Senate Office Building. One buried itself in the right side of my chest.

The doctor told me later I was extremely fortunate: The bullet struck at an angle and ricocheted off my ribs to the left, exiting out my armpit. Had it gone straight, I would have been in real trouble. Had it turned right, I would have been dead for sure.

As it was, it carried away a chunk of flesh and any notions I might have had about immortality. It is, perhaps, a cliché to say that facing death makes you reevaluate your priorities.

But it's a cliché because it's true. That bullet impacted me far beyond the scars it left behind.

Certainly, it reinforced what my late father had told me about how no man ever lay on his deathbed wishing he had spent more time at work. The twins had just celebrated their first birthday and, in the harsh light of the surgical recovery room, I saw that I had basically missed the whole year, losing it in a haze of fourteen-hour workdays. Sure, a bullet tearing off in a different direction might have made their lack of a father permanent. But I had been depriving them of a second parent long before that bullet arrived.

I knew nothing would change as long as I continued in Senator Franklin's employ. When I told Alison I was thinking about quitting—this, mind you, was before the anesthesia from surgery had even worn off—she wept with joy.

Two days later, still in my hospital bed, I presented my handwritten letter of resignation to Senator Franklin. He was incredibly gracious about it. I'm sure guilt played a role: He knew those bullets had been intended for him. Maybe it also helped that he was Emma's godfather. There was a higher authority telling him this was right for me and my family.

The judgeship had actually been his idea. One of the seats in the Eastern District of Virginia, in Norfolk, had just become vacant. I was, to say the least, an atypical candidate. No one could remember a Senate staffer being appointed to a federal judgeship, and I hadn't regularly been in a courtroom since clerking in the Fourth Circuit Court of Appeals, when I was just out of law school. But I rode my many contacts within the Senate and a strong measure of shooting-inspired sympathy to an 88–0 confirmation.

The twelve senators who opposed my nomination were too chicken to show up and cast their votes. Instead, they got their revenge by working behind the scenes to scuttle the bill I had nearly died for.

Since that time, Blake and I had stayed close. The shared experience of near death had bonded us like something akin to war veterans. We were also just friends who enjoyed gabbing about policy, politics, and the gossip that was in continual orbit around the Senate.

I thought about letting his call go to voice mail. But there was a long time in my life when ignoring Senator Franklin wasn't an option, and ultimately old habits are hard to break.

"Hey, Blake."

"Good morning, Judge," he returned in his gentle southern drawl, an accent that had won him countless votes in the southern and western parts of the state through the years. "You in the middle of anything?"

"Just driving. What's up?" I said, trying to sound casual.

"Well, my press officer just had me chatting with a reporter from *The Wall Street Journal*."

"About the campaign?" Blake was in a tight race for reelection.

"No, son, about you," he said. "You got some big drug case?"

It was all I could do to keep my car on the road. *The Wall Street Journal* was calling about *Skavron*? What was

I missing? What could there possibly be about Rayshaun Skavron that had attracted the attention of one of America's most important newspapers?

"Oh yeah?" I said warily. "What'd you tell them?"

"Oh, the usual: that you gave out child pornography as gifts every Christmas, but that we forgave you for it because you were high on heroin most of the time."

This was, clearly, not the side of Senator Franklin the voters got to see. Ordinarily, I would have invented some equally ribald retort. But not now.

"I just hope they don't find out about all those bribes you've been taking, because—"

And then he stopped himself, because I wasn't playing along, and said, "Hey . . . you all right, buddy?"

I felt myself well up. Blake had this way with people. It was part of his genius. He could be a relentless despot, demanding more-more-more, pushing without end until the moment he realized you were at your personal brink. Then he could flip a switch and suddenly it was like he cared about nothing more in this world than your personal well-being.

And of course, I wanted to pour my heart out to him, like I had so many times before. My parents died within a year of each other when they were in their mid-sixties and I was in my early thirties. Blake had nursed me through that and was now as close a thing as I had to a father.

But I reeled in the nearly overwhelming urge to share my burdens with him.

"Yeah, yeah, sorry, I'm fine," I said. "I'm just a little distracted by this case."

"Well, I could say I understand, but of course I don't. I'm not sure I could go it alone the way you do. It's a lot easier to make a decision when you know there are at least fifty other people to share the blame with you if you screw up."

"Yeah. Thanks," I said, and then just to change the subject, I said, "Everyone in your household okay?"

He prattled on about his wife and kids for a moment—he had two girls, both happily launched into adulthood. He steered the conversation back around to *The Wall Street Journal* so he could assure me he told the reporter nice things about me. He finished with, "And how's my goddaughter doing these days?"

I felt my breathing hitch, then forced out: "She's great, thanks."

"All right," he said before ending the call. "Send Alison and the twins my best."

9

On the morning of a sentencing, my chambers—a suite of offices that occupy the western wing of the fourth floor of the Walter E. Hoffman United States Courthouse—have a different feel to them.

My staff is quieter. The mood is more somber. You would understand why if you had ever been to a federal prison. They are dreadful institutions whose procedures are designed to dehumanize the people they contain. And when you look at our rates of incarceration—roughly seven times higher than those of our peer nations, higher even than the Soviet Union under Stalin—you can't help but feel there is something wrong with a society that feels the need to lock so many of its citizens in cages.

It's part of my job all the same. It's just not a part I relish. My staff knows this and usually affords me some space on mornings like this.

So it was somewhat unusual, as I went toward our small kitchen to pour myself some coffee, that I heard Jeremy Freeland's voice coming from his office.

"Hey, Judge, got a second?"

Jeremy was a handsome man in his late thirties with perfectly groomed sandy-colored hair and clear blue eyes. He ran a minimum of twenty miles a week and remained scrupulously trim. He wore fitted suits and colorful ties that perfectly matched the rest of his outfit.

Between that, his effeminate nature, and the fact that he had never been married, I assumed Jeremy was gay, though we had never discussed it. The lawsuit that struck down Virginia's ban on gay marriage, the *Bostic* case, had been decided in our courthouse. I had made it clear to Jeremy I thought the judge had rendered a very just, very eloquent decision and that it was a long-overdue triumph for civil rights in America. He responded with a dispassionate analysis of the Fourteenth Amendment.

Jeremy's official title was "career clerk," but don't be fooled by the "clerk" part. He is a lawyer, one whose experience had saved me from embarrassment countless times. Many of the rules of procedure in federal court are not codified anywhere. They've evolved over many decades of common practice and I had forgotten most of them when I first came out of the Senate. Jeremy was my secret weapon, making me appear far more competent than I really was.

He had been clerking for a Fourth Circuit Court of Appeals judge who had finally retired, but he agreed to go back down to district court because the challenge—helping a rookie judge who clearly needed a lot of hand-holding—appealed to him. He also did research for me, kept the younger clerks in line, wrote some of my more routine decisions, and acted as a sounding board for the more complex ones. I always told Jeremy he was the best career clerk in the history of the Eastern District of Virginia, and that was not hyperbole.

I stopped at his doorframe. His office was as carefully

maintained as his personal appearance. He had plants he treated like pets. His actual pets—a pair of fish named Thurgood and Marshall, after his favorite Supreme Court justice—were like his children.

"I'm so sorry to bother you," he said. "I just wanted you to know a reporter from *The New York Times* called this morning. I told him you had no comment, but he asked if you could talk off the record. I said no to that, too, but I at least wanted you to be aware of it."

First the *Journal*. Now the *Times*. What about *Skavron* was I missing?

"That's fine," I said. "Thank you."

"I also got a call from a reporter named Steve Politi from a website called HedgeofReason.com. It's some kind of investing blog run by this Politi guy. Instead of edge of reason, its *hedge* of reason, like hedge funds? I clicked on it and it's . . . As far as I can tell, it's just a lot of rumor and innuendo, sort of a *National Enquirer* for the finance crowd. He claims to have more than two million unique viewers a month."

And why did *he* care about *Skavron*?

"Oh. Well. We'll have no comment, of course," I said.

"Of course."

For a long moment, I rubbernecked at the security camera monitor that sits on his desk. You wouldn't know it, but in our courthouse, which was built during the Great Depression and looked like it hadn't been touched since then, there were actually cameras hidden everywhere. For the judges, that meant two or three angles of the hallway outside their chambers. The idea was that if someone was asking to be buzzed in, we could look at the person first. The monitor was in Jeremy's office because my judicial assistant, Joan Smith, hated having it on her desk.

At this moment—like most moments—the hallway was empty. But I stared at it. My head felt pretty empty too.

*

After I mumbled my thanks to Jeremy and got my coffee, I returned to my office and tried to do what I'd normally do: Go through the case one more time, check and recheck my gut about the rectitude of the punishment I was about to mete out.

But on this morning, I couldn't get myself to concentrate. I kept staring out the window at the gap-toothed skyline of downtown Norfolk, which is what I often did when I wanted to ponder something. Except all I could think about was the kids.

I chased away the unpleasant thoughts and settled on something happier. It was the image of the morning routine Sam and Emma had worked out for themselves over the past year or so. Sam was the earlier riser of the two, but he never went downstairs without his sister. He just played in his room, waiting for her to call for him.

That was Sammy's signal to enter Emma's room. He usually cuddled with her a little bit—we used to keep the twins in the same crib, and they've become accustomed to the closeness—until she declared herself ready to go downstairs. Then Sam, who was bigger by two inches and maybe ten pounds, gave his sister a piggyback ride down the stairs to the family room.

The whole thing was so adorable Alison and I didn't want to call attention to how much we loved it. But sometimes we would lie in bed a few minutes longer just so we could listen to their banter, or we'd sneak out of bed, stand near the door to our bedroom, and watch.

I was treating myself to that memory when I felt my cell phone buzzing. I pulled out the phone and read the screen: ALISON.

"Hey," I said.

"Justina has a wig," she said.

"Excuse me?"

"Justina has a blond wig," she said again, emphasizing the last two words, as if the meaning of this should have been self-evident. "I found it in the cottage. In her closet."

"I'm sorry, I'm not following you. Justina has a wig in her closet. So what?"

"Why does she need a *blond* wig?"

Justina was a brunette, though I made it a point not to notice much more about her appearance than that. When you're a middle-aged man with a college-aged woman living on your property, it's in the best interests of your marriage to pay as little attention as possible.

"I don't know," I admitted. "Wait, are you thinking—"

"That she put on the wig so she could pretend to be me when she picked up the kids? Yes."

I considered the possibility of that fooling someone.

54

There was no doubt Justina bore some resemblance to my wife from the neck down. They are roughly the same height and have the same thin build. And while Justina is from a country that straddles two continents, her looks were more European than Asian. Would a wig, a hat, and dark glasses be sufficient to make Miss Pam think Justina was Alison? Just for the few seconds the door to the Honda was open on the pickup line?

"Wait, why would she need to pretend to be you?" I asked. "She's on the list. She picks up the kids more often than you and I combined."

"Yeah, but she knew about the sign-out sheet and she knew if she was listed as having made the pickup we'd ask questions."

"Okay. So talk out the rest for me . . . Why would Justina want to help free a drug dealer she has almost certainly never met?"

"Well, we don't know that for sure. We don't really know what she does or who she associates with when she's not with our kids."

"Fair point."

"I've thought about two scenarios," Alison said. "One, she has a drug problem she's been hiding from us and it's brought her into contact with this . . . criminal element."

I quickly flashed through a mental file of my interactions with Justina. Nothing stuck out as being suspicious, but I had certainly seen ample evidence in my courtroom of how cunning addicts could be.

"The other scenario—and this seems more likely—is that

someone forced her to cooperate by, I don't know, threatening her or her parents or something. I haven't worked out all the details. But think about it: Who else has keys to the Honda?"

I stood up and walked over to the window. Justina's parents were in Turkey, but it wasn't unimaginable that an international drug cartel could reach that far. If Skavron mattered enough.

"Okay," I said. "What do you want to do about this?"

"Well, I already texted her and told her she didn't need to pick up the twins this afternoon. I was thinking we could just deal with it once we got the kids back. In the meantime, I'm going to keep looking through her stuff, see if I find anything else. Like, I don't know, cash or drugs or . . ."

"Okay. Good. Let me know."

We ended the call. I returned to my desk and thought about Justina, who for two years had been a loving presence in my children's lives. I can't say I was ready to convict her of kidnapping and conspiracy on the basis of one blond wig.

But I also wasn't ready to rule anything out.

The building was old and brick and perfectly suited to the brothers' needs.

It was not, as far as the City of Norfolk was concerned, abandoned. But it was unoccupied. And it offered an unobstructed view of the Walter E. Hoffman United States Courthouse. These were the things that mattered most.

The younger brother had scouted it a week earlier. Its street-side windows and front entrance were sealed off from vagrants and would-be squatters by steel cages. But the back entrance, which could be accessed from an alleyway, was protected only by a chain-link fence with a padlocked gate. During that earlier visit, he had snapped the padlock and replaced it with his own.

So now gaining entry to the building was a simple matter of using his own key.

He carried a briefcase and a canvas bag with him up to the sixth floor, which he had previously determined to be just the right height. From the canvas bag, he unfolded a tripod.

After setting it up, he snapped open the briefcase and removed a telescope. Setting it atop the tripod, he aimed it into the fourth-floor courtroom of the Honorable Scott Sampson. The resolution on the device was remarkable, and the younger brother had practiced adjusting the focus until he had become expert at it. He could actually see the strained faces of the defendant's family as they entered the courtroom.

He smiled. They were not part of the plan. They had no idea what was coming.

Pulling out his phone, he called the older brother. "I'm in place," he said.

"Good," he heard in response. "The first text goes out in fifteen minutes."

"Excellent. I'll be watching."

For the rest of the morning, I watched the big hand of the clock on the far wall of my office drag through molasses on its way to eleven.

I kept my cell phone on top of my desk, not wanting to take any chance I'd miss my instructions. I was operating under the assumption that I would be told to set Skavron free, which in this case meant sentencing him to time served—two months and three days, about fifteen years less than he would have gotten under the sentencing guidelines.

There are, of course, exceptions to the mandatory minimums that I and other judges find so wearisome. But they are narrow: The defendant must be a first-time, nonviolent offender who neither used a gun nor played a larger role in a criminal syndicate.

In other words, not Skavron.

I could still rule in whatever manner I wanted, of course—Little Caesar had his throne. My ruling would then be appealed by the US Attorneys Office and reversed by the Fourth Circuit Court of Appeals in Richmond. A new warrant for Skavron's arrest would be issued. By that point, I could only assume he would be long gone, secreted off by whoever was coordinating all of this.

Naturally, it went against everything I believed in and

stood for as a judge. And, just as naturally, I would do it without blinking if it meant saving my children.

By 10:55 no instructions had come. It was time to move out. I slipped my phone into my pocket. Then I donned my robe and went into my private bathroom to perform a quick mirror check, always the last thing I do before heading into the courtroom.

So that's what I was doing—specifically, looking at the bags under my eyes—when I felt a buzz on my thigh.

I whipped out the phone. There was a text message from a 900 number I had never seen before. It had to be the kidnappers. My breathing was short as I clicked on it.

I had to read it three times to make sure I understood it:

Let Skavron rot. Give him two life sentences.
Subsequent, not concurrent.

That was what this was about? Not about getting Skavron out of prison but about keeping him in there until he died? Who benefited from that?

Obviously, it was someone who bore the man significant ill. But I was only beginning to contemplate those possibilities when another text came in:

To signal that you've received our message and intend
to comply, appear on the bench with your hair parted
on the other side.

I felt ice in my spine. The preposterousness of that command struck me less than what it signified: They had someone keeping an eye on me. Someone near enough to be able to spot the subtle difference of my hair going in the opposite direction.

Another text:

Keep your phone with you to receive further instructions.

I waited to see if there was more, but that seemed to be it. I texted back:

I'll do it, of course. But why? Why two life sentences?

Within seconds, my phone buzzed again, telling me I had texted a landline, but for thirty-nine cents I could have my text converted into a message that—

I put the phone back in my pocket. There was no time to make sense of this Gatling-gun burst of dictates. My staff, to say nothing of a courtroom full of people, were waiting for me to make my appearance.

And I had to do it with my hair going in the opposite direction. I had been parting my hair on the left side for as long as I could remember. Did they know that? Were they just trying to shove me as far out of my comfort zone as they could?

If that was their intent, it was working. I wet my hair, took several dozen desperate swipes at it with a comb, then studied the result.

It was me. But not me. I looked like my own doppelgänger.

"Good God," I said to myself.

With one final shake of my still-damp head, I left the bathroom and strode into the reception area, where my staff was waiting for me.

"Everyone ready?" I asked, trying to seem unflustered.

"Jean Ann just called," Joan Smith confirmed.

Jean Ann Sanford was my deputy clerk, a former beauty queen who sometimes acted as though my courtroom were a pageant she needed to keep on schedule. It was her job to make sure all was in place and then phone us to say the show could go on.

Jeremy Freeland was giving me the up and down. We had worked together long enough that he knew something was off, even if he couldn't immediately place it.

"You okay, Judge?" he asked.

"I'm fine," I insisted.

Finally, his eyes settled on my head. "What's with your—"

He stopped himself before he said the word "hair." He knew it wasn't the career clerk's place to comment on the judge's coiffure.

"I'm fine," I said again, a little more firmly.

"Are you sure? Because we can—"

"Let's do this," I said.

The court security officer escorted me down the hallway. He held the door for me as one of my law clerks began the time-honored cry: "All rise! Oyez, oyez—"

What I saw as I passed through the doorway was, in some ways, exactly the same scene that usually greeted me.

Unlike some of the grander spaces on the first floor, with their towering ceilings and magisterial air, my courtroom was more intimate. It had six rows of benches for spectators. They were filled with but a smattering of people. One row was solidly African American, likely Rayshaun Skavron's friends and family. On the other side of the aisle was a middle-aged white couple, nicely dressed but world-weary.

In front of them were the attorneys: the prosecutor to my left, the defense attorney to my right.

To the right of him was Rayshaun Skavron. He was a short, round black man with a blunt head and a forgettable face. He was dressed in a faded orange jumpsuit, standard issue from the Western Tidewater Regional Jail. His forearms and neck were festooned with tattoos.

He looked like so many of the defendants who appeared in my courtroom: righteously beaten, his pride gone, ready to accept his fate.

Near Skavron were two men in US Marshals Service Windbreakers, who had escorted the prisoner into the courtroom. Jean Ann and the court reporter were in front of me. The law clerk, who had just finished the cry, took her usual spot to my right.

That was it. Was one of these people watching me and, somehow, reporting back? A member of my staff, perhaps? Or was some stranger spying on me through the tiny glass slits in the doors in back? Or had they found a way to look into my courtroom through the fourth-floor windows?

All I knew was that somewhere, very close by, there was a person who was part of an effort to kidnap my children, an enterprise crucial to the larger conspiracy of ensuring Rayshaun Skavron never again left prison.

And I was still baffled as to why he was worth the trouble.

*

Wanting to move things ahead as quickly as possible, I raced through the things that needed to be put on the record at a sentencing, all of which I had memorized after four years of repeating them. I was still conscious of my phone, which I ordinarily would have never taken to the bench with me.

Further instructions. What further instructions?

As I continued speaking, I surreptitiously lifted my robe and eased my cell phone out of my pants pocket. Keeping it under my desk, I cupped it against my thigh so I wouldn't miss its vibration.

Then I turned to Will Hubbard, the assistant US attorney. Hubbard had been in my courtroom many times before. He appeared to be just on the appropriate side of bored.

"Thank you, Your Honor," he said, standing as he spoke. "I know you've read the presentencing report, and there's no need to repeat the details. I'd like to note that when Mr. Skavron was first arrested he denied any connection to the drug stash in question. But to his credit, he changed his tune after about twenty minutes and since that time he has been consistent about admitting his guilt. He has cooperated with authorities in this case, and even though that cooperation has not led to any arrests, it ought to be considered all the same. He has also expressed an interest in completing a GED program, which suggests he is at least contemplating a more law-abiding life someday.

"Those are some of the mitigating factors. There are two main aggravating factors. One is that he stored his drug stash and a firearm in an apartment belonging to his cousin. She has three children under the age of ten and was obviously very upset to discover that Mr. Skavron had brought this kind of element into her household. There were originally some child endangerment charges, which the government agreed to nol-pros when Mr. Skavron pled guilty."

Then he turned toward the gallery and gestured toward the middle-aged white man I had seen earlier. He was dark-haired, with a narrow nose and a long head. The woman he was sitting next to, presumably his wife, had an expensive-looking blond dye job.

As the man rose to his feet, Hubbard continued speaking.

"The other factor that the court should consider is that, Your Honor, this was a pretty bad batch of heroin. It came to the attention of law enforcement because it caused several overdoses at Norfolk Academy, including one tragic fatality. The Drug Enforcement Administration ran a sample and found it had been cut with fentanyl, which makes it a lot more harmful because of the reaction of the two drugs."

The white man was now at the waist-high divider that separated the gallery from the rest of the courtroom. He was wearing a light gray suit. Gold cuff links peeked out from beneath his jacket.

"Your Honor, there were a number of families who

were affected by this, but one in particular has been truly devastated," Hubbard said. "And I think it's important you hear from them before imposing your sentence. I'd like to invite Thomas Byrd to address the court."

With his right hand thrust toward the sky, Thomas Byrd swore to tell the truth and nothing but the truth, so help him God.

He sat in the witness box and pulled out some reading glasses, which he perched at the end of his nose. His shaking hand held a piece of paper.

"Your Honor, my name is Thomas Byrd. I was born and raised in Norfolk. My family owns a chain of appliance stores as well as several restaurant franchises. My son's name was Dylan."

Was Dylan. I could think of nothing more wrenching than hearing a parent refer to his child in the past tense.

He reached into his jacket and produced a photograph, which he held up so I could see it. It was a school portrait of a young man with his father's long head and thin nose.

"Dylan was a fine young man. When I say that, I know I sound like a naive father. But he never gave his mother or I any trouble. Norfolk Academy is very rigorous academically, as I'm sure you know, and his report card was all As and B pluses. He was part of the National Honor Society and also played on the baseball team. This past summer he got his own job, painting houses. He could have worked for one of my family's stores or restaurants and they probably would have taken it easy on him. But he wanted to be on his own, which I respected. He worked hard all summer and was able to buy a used truck at the end of it. He was very proud of it. We were all proud of it. If you can imagine a seventeen-year-old boy with a truck paid for with his own money, maybe you know what I'm talking about."

Thomas Byrd took a large swallow. He looked down at his notes again.

"Your Honor, I don't honestly know what my son was thinking when he took those drugs. He wasn't the kind of kid who smoked weed or snuck booze or anything like that. We had talked to him about drugs from the time he was in elementary school. He knew full well how dangerous they were. He was . . . Maybe he was trying to impress a girl or maybe he was curious or, I don't know. And I don't want to make any excuses for . . . for what he did to himself. I can't tell you how many times over the last three months I wished I stopped him from going out the door that night."

A small squeak escaped from Byrd's wife, who then muffled herself with a tissue.

"My wife and I . . . We're going to have to make peace with what our son did. But we're having an even harder time making peace with the idea that the man who supplied him this . . . this poison . . . gets to go on enjoying his life and seeing his family and doing all the things Dylan can't do anymore. Mr. Hubbard said if he didn't do a plea deal there was always a chance this man would go free and, well, I'm not sure we could handle that. So we said, 'Okay, go ahead and do the deal.' And Mr. Hubbard said he'll probably get about fifteen years or so and, well . . . The harsh truth is, my son is still going to be dead in fifteen years."

His voice was trembling. He was fighting a losing battle with his lower lip.

"Your Honor, my wife and I, everyone tells us we need to start moving on. But how can we? Dylan was our only child. He was the center of our lives. This has destroyed us beyond anything I can describe. And I don't know if having Mr. Skavron go to prison for a long time is really going to make it any better. But . . . do you know what it's like to bury a seventeen-year-old boy, Your Honor? It's not something I'd wish on anyone, not even Mr. Skavron here. If someone had let me crawl into that box in my son's place, I wouldn't have skipped a beat. It just . . . I . . . I miss my son . . . I miss my son so much. It hurts all the time. Can you imagine what that feels like, Your Honor?"

Ordinarily, I never would have said a thing. I'm not even sure I knew I was about to talk. But the next thing I heard was my own cracked voice.

"Yes," I said, at a volume just above a whisper. "Yes, I can."

Byrd nodded and looked me square in the eyes. "Then I know you're going to do the right thing. For us and for Dylan. Thank you, Your Honor."

Byrd left the witness stand to a courtroom that had fallen silent. I was grateful—immensely so—that if nothing else good came out of this calamity, I was at least going to be able to give this man and his suffering wife some small measure of comfort by announcing a sentence far harsher than what he or Mr. Hubbard or anyone else in the courtroom could have reasonably expected.

And then I felt my phone buzz.

Hubbard was back on his feet. As he murmured a few words of thanks to Thomas Byrd, I took a peek down. It was the 900 number again:

Change of plans. Let Skavron walk.

*

For the next few seconds, I experienced what I can describe only as vertigo. The courtroom seemed to pitch and yaw right in front of me.

My phone buzzed again: FREE SKAVRON! it taunted.

Then again: FREE SKAVRON!

I let the phone drop softly to the carpeted floor at my feet, then brought both hands up to the desk in front of me to steady myself. I feared I was going to vomit all over its polished cherry surface.

Free Skavron? After what I had just heard? How could I possibly do that to Thomas Byrd and his wife? How could I ever again have a shred of respect for myself as a judge or as a human being?

And yet I already knew I didn't have a choice.

I hated myself for how quickly I came to this selfish, self-serving conclusion. But nothing I did to Skavron could change that Dylan Byrd was dead.

My children, on the other hand, were still alive. They had to come first. And I felt like any parent—even the Byrds— would absolve me for that decision, if only I could tell them the full circumstances.

Mr. Hubbard had resumed: "Part of our agreement with the defense is that Mr. Skavron's offense be reduced from Level Thirty-six to Level Thirty-one, without some of the enhancements that could have been added. He is a Criminal History Category Five. The guidelines call for a sentence range of one hundred and sixty-eight to two hundred and ten months. Given what we've just heard, my recommendation is for the high end of that scale. Thank you, Your Honor."

Hubbard sat. I was still trying to recover my equilibrium. Jail Skavron. Free Skavron. What *was* the agenda here, exactly? And who was behind it? It was like trying to unscramble an egg.

Alan Sutherlin, a lawyer from the public defender's office, was already standing and expecting to be recognized by the court so he could begin his defense. Wearily, I turned to him.

"Mr. Sutherlin?" I said.

"Yes, thank you, Your Honor," he said. "On behalf of my client, I'd like to express my condolences to the Byrd family. And I'd like to thank Mr. Byrd for that moving statement."

Sutherlin shuffled some papers on his desk. I was hoping he might give me something to work with, something that would make me seem remotely justified in the travesty of justice I was about to commit.

He immediately began disappointing me.

"I don't have much to add beyond what appears in the presentencing report," he said. "Obviously, you've read about Mr. Skavron's childhood. He didn't exactly have a lot of breaks in this world. Yes, he's made some poor choices, which he acknowledges. But there were also times when I think Your Honor could recognize he wasn't dealing from the best set of options. I don't need to tell you how hard it can be for an ex-convict to find work, and Mr. Skavron's record would deter even the most forgiving employer. But he was trying, Your Honor.

"As to some of the aggravating factors addressed by Mr. Hubbard, it should be noted that the firearm Mr. Skavron stored at his cousin's house was not loaded and did not have bullets with it, so it wouldn't have been a danger if a child found it. In addition, with the fentanyl, there is no evidence to suggest that Mr. Skavron knew the heroin had been cut with this other product. Mr. Skavron was really just acting as a pass-along here.

"As to the overdoses, these students made statements to the police that they had never used heroin before and that they were looking to experiment with the drug. They were seeking it out. If they hadn't gotten the heroin from my client, they would have gotten it from somewhere else."

They would have gotten it from somewhere else. As legal arguments went, this was like trying to beat a murder rap by arguing, *But, Your Honor, the victim was going to die eventually.*

Then again, what was I expecting? Sutherlin was defending the indefensible.

"So, bearing that in mind, and having reviewed the sentencing guidelines, and taking into consideration Mr. Skavron's continued cooperation, we feel that a hundred and forty-four months is an appropriate sentence. That's just below guidelines, but it's still twelve years. And with all due respect to the statement from Mr. Byrd, I'm quite sure the Bureau of Prisons will see to it my client will not be enjoying his life. Those will be long, hard years. And I know Dylan Byrd will weigh heavily on his mind during that time and for the rest of his life. Thank you, Your Honor."

My mouth had gone dry. But I managed to say, "Thank you, Mr. Sutherlin."

I turned my eyes to the defendant. "Mr. Skavron, is there anything else I should consider before I impose my sentence?"

This was my last shot. In truth, there wasn't much Skavron could say, given the evidence against him. But if he could at least appear human . . .

Instead, the worthless son of a bitch just looked down at the carpet and mumbled, "I just wanted to say I'm real sorry for what I done, Your Honor. I didn't mean to, you know, hurt no one or nothing. And I just want to, you know, throw myself on the mercy of the court."

I waited for more, but that was it.

He had given me virtually nothing.

I looked down to the floor, where my phone was resting. Quickly, I bent and picked it up, hoping it might offer me a reprieve: another text, reversing the reversal. I tapped at it a few times.

But its face contained only the time and date. There were no new messages. I was on my own.

*

This was the moment everyone had come for. A courtroom full of eyes was trained on me. A courtroom full of ears awaited my words.

Having appeared to deliberate on the matter, I lifted my head. I couldn't look at Skavron, much less the prosecution. Certainly not the Byrds. So I gazed out at the wood paneling in the back of the courtroom as I spoke.

"Mr. Skavron, after carefully considering the guidelines and all the factors in thirty-five fifty-three A, the court has now prepared to impose a sentence," I said, and then I forced down the bile in my throat and went on with it:

"I feel you have demonstrated significant remorse for your crimes. I have noted your recent work history and your intent to pursue a GED. I believe you have found the desire to live a crime-free life. You have asked for mercy, and as I consider that, I would like to be very clear: This is your last chance, Mr. Skavron. If you squander it, I will personally make sure any future judge punishes you to the fullest extent of the law and beyond. That said, judges are given discretion at sentencing, and I am going to take the admittedly unusual step of exercising the full extent of that discretion. I hereby sentence you to time served."

I was going to finish by telling him the marshals would need to take him back to jail so he could fill out some paperwork before his release, but there were already outbursts coming from around the courtroom.

The first came from the row where Skavron's family sat. One of the older women, perhaps the aunt who raised him, was loudly thanking Jesus. The man next to her had leapt to his feet and raised his arms in triumph. A younger woman was clapping her hands with joy. Skavron had twisted around to look back at them, so I could see only about a quarter of the disgusting smile already spreading across his lips.

"Your Honor," Hubbard was shouting over the din. "Are you—"

But I couldn't hear him anymore once Thomas Byrd found the use of his vocal cords. The victim's father was standing and pointing at me. "What the hell kind of judge are you? He killed my boy! That scumbag killed my boy and you're going to let him go free? What's your problem? My son is dead. He's dead. Does that mean anything to you?"

His blond wife was tugging on his suit jacket in a fruitless attempt to get him seated. His face was something close to purple.

The court security officer was also yelling, attempting to restore order to a courtroom where none would be found. I was searching for my gavel, so I could at least attempt to quiet things down. But I couldn't find it.

It was bedlam. None of the people who had started yelling would stop long enough for me to quiet things down and finish this farce of justice once and for all.

And then, in the back of the courtroom, the door opened. One of the court security officers from downstairs had appeared. And he was holding the hand of a little boy.

My son.

I leapt to my feet. Dimly aware that I still had a duty to perform, I said something like, "Court is adjourned."

My confused law clerk began giving the cry, which was barely being heard over the other shouting. I was already dashing past the attorneys and the defendant, none of whom had ever seen a judge move so fast. Even the marshals, who were in courtrooms nearly every day of their working lives, just gaped at me.

When I reached the waist-high wall that bifurcated the room, I plowed through the swinging door, passing a stunned Thomas Byrd, who was still gesturing and screaming. I reached Sam, I fell to my knees, and smothered him in a hug.

"I love you," I blurted. "I love you so much."

I buried my face in his silky blond hair and gripped him so hard I was probably knocking the air out of him. There were tears rolling down my cheeks. I smelled his sweet, little-boy scent and felt the tiny muscles in his back.

Then I lifted him and continued right on out the back door. I had to get him out of that noisy, chaotic courtroom. It didn't feel safe in there. Above all else, I had to keep Sam safe.

The CSO followed us out. When we reached the hallway, I set Sam down.

"He just walked up the courthouse steps and asked to see his daddy," said the CSO, who had followed me. "Surprised the heck out of us."

Sam was appropriately bewildered. He didn't understand why Daddy was crying; but, then, he probably didn't understand a lot of what had happened to him over the previous twenty hours or so.

"Are you okay, Sammy?" I said, kneeling in front of him.

I scanned him from top to bottom, looking for bruises or cuts or welts, finding none.

He couldn't seem to summon a response. He just stood there, frozen in his spot. It must have jarred him, seeing me so out of control. Children are emotional mirrors. They reflect their environment.

For his sake, I tried to force an outer calm that I was nowhere close to feeling internally. "Is your sister with you?" I asked.

Still no answer. I grabbed him gently by the shoulders.

"Sammy, buddy, where's Emma?"

A look of confusion and anguish coincided with his first words: "She's still with the men."

"What m—"

And then Sam pulled a small envelope from his pocket. It was identical to the one I had found in the box on my porch and had JUDGE SAMPSON printed on it.

"They said to give this to you," he said.

I grabbed it, then slid my finger under the flap. Inside was, again, half-folded card stock. I flipped it open and read:

THIS IS YOUR REWARD FOR FOLLOWING ORDERS. IF YOU WANT TO SEE YOUR DAUGHTER, KEEP UP THE GOOD WORK. YOU'LL HEAR FROM US AGAIN SOON. AND, REMEMBER, IN THE MEANTIME: SAY NOTHING.

"Is everything okay, Your Honor?" the CSO asked.

"Yes, yes, fine," I said, standing and grasping Sam's hand.

"I'm just going to take him back to my chambers now. Thank you very much for bringing him up here. He . . . I think he just got separated from his mother. But it's fine now. It's fine. Thank you."

"Okay. Glad to help," the man said, with a smile and a parting wave.

As I scooped up Sam and carried him back toward my chambers, the reality of the situation was crashing into me: Rayshaun Skavron had been nothing more than a test, a kind of trial balloon to see if I could be controlled. This had never been about Rayshaun Skavron.

It was about one of the other four-hundred-plus cases on my docket. And at that moment, I didn't have the slightest idea which one.

12

Before my staff could begin asking questions—about why I had inexplicably cut loose an admitted drug dealer, about why Sam was visiting his father at work—I swept us out of the office, mumbling a quick series of apologies and non-explanations that probably only heightened the intrigue.

I held off on interrogating Sam on the way home. Alison was going to need to hear everything he said, and I didn't want to make him relive the ordeal more than once.

She was waiting for us on the front porch when we arrived. As soon as my car emerged from the woods into the clearing outside our house, she leapt off her chair and ran toward us. I had called her on the way home and let her know she was getting only one of her babies back, and she practically tore the handle off my door to get at him.

"Oh, Sammy, my love," she said, hauling him out of his booster seat and squeezing him fiercely. I recognized her experiencing the same bittersweet emotions I did. Getting to touch one of them made you only that much more cognizant of how much you ached to touch the other.

We eventually got him inside and plopped down on the family room sofa. She sat on one side of him, putting a weak smile on her face. I had thought we were going to let him settle in, give him time to acclimatize before we peppered him with questions. Alison was apparently of a different mind.

"Sammy, honey, Momma and Daddy need to ask you some things about what happened to you," she began.

But before she could get going, I interrupted. The judge in me knew witnesses were more forthcoming when they were at ease.

"The first thing we want you to know," I said, quickly flashing my eyes toward Alison, then looking back at Sam, "is that Momma and I may be acting like we're a little . . . concerned. But it's not because we're mad at you. We're very, very happy you're here. And you're not in trouble for anything that happened. Okay?"

Sam bobbed his head twice. He had the saddest little look on his face.

"None of this was your fault," I said. "You didn't do anything wrong. You understand that, yes?"

He nodded again.

"Can you start using your words, buddy?" I asked.

"Yeah," he chirped.

"Okay, good. So we're going to ask you a few questions and you just do the best you can to answer them."

"It's important for Emma," Alison added, and I wished she hadn't. The boy was already under enough pressure.

"No big deal if you can't," I countered, smiling through the strain. "Just do the best you can. Let's start with yesterday when you got picked up from school. What happened? The Honda came and picked you up, right?"

"Yeah," he said.

"Did you notice anything different about it?"

"Yeah, there was *Transformers*."

"Where? On the seat?" I asked.

"No. On the TV."

This would have been noteworthy because, one, *Transformers* cartoons had been banned in our house (too violent), and, two, we turn on the TVs in the car only during longer trips. The kidnappers must have thought—correctly, it seemed—it would be a good diversion so the kids wouldn't notice the stranger in the front seat.

"And who was driving the car, honey?" Alison asked. This had become a subject of some importance for my wife.

The gaze he returned to her was one of innocent childhood confusion. "You were, Momma," he said.

"No, honey, that wasn't Momma," she said immediately. "It was someone dressed up to look like Momma."

To which he replied, "Oh."

"It might have been Justina," she said. "Was it Justina?"

He immediately shook his head. "Oh no, Momma."

Alison furrowed her brow. I felt like we had gotten as far as we could on the subject, so I said, "What happened next? After you got picked up?"

"Well, we drove out on the big road"—this was how Sam described Route 17—"but then we turned off on a little road."

"What little road?" Alison asked.

"I don't know. It wasn't our road. I said, 'Where are we going, Momma?' but you didn't answer."

"Honey, that wasn't Momma, remember?"

"Oh," he said again.

Not wanting to belabor the point, I said, "What came after you turned on the little road?"

"The Honda stopped. And two men came and got us and told us to get in the van."

"Tell me about the men," I said gently.

Sam squirmed in his seat. There was real fear in his eyes. Up until this point, he had merely been recounting a slightly weird drive home from school. This was where it got scary.

Words had left him again. He was just looking back and forth between his mother and me. Alison pulled him up on her lap and wrapped both arms around him. "Honey, I know you don't want to talk about this, but it's really important to Momma and Daddy, okay? Can you please try?"

Wanting to please his mother, and now afforded the protection of her lap, Sam came up with: "They were really mean. I didn't like them."

"Did they hurt you in any way?" I asked.

He didn't reply.

"What is it, honey?" Alison said, encircling her arms tighter. "It's okay. You can tell us anything, even if it's really bad. Like Daddy said, you're not in trouble."

Then Sam looked me right in the eye: "One of them had a knife. And he showed it to me. It was a big, big knife."

Now Alison and I were the ones without words.

"He cut my hair," Sam said. "But he said maybe next time he'd cut my throat. He said he liked to cut people's throats."

I was glad Sam couldn't see his mother. Her face had lost what little color it had.

To keep him from dwelling on the knife, I said, "What did the men look like, buddy?"

"They had scratchy faces"—scratchy faces being how Sam and Emma described beards—"really scratchy. And they talked funny."

"Funny how?" I asked. "Like a different language?"

"Yeah, it was all *gghhh* and *gaaaa*," he said, making sounds from the back of his mouth.

"Did they talk English at all?" I asked.

"Yeah, but it was funny too."

"You mean like an accent?"

"Yeah," he said.

"Did it sound like Justina?" Alison asked.

"I don't know. Not really," Sam said.

Which didn't necessarily mean anything. I'm not sure a six-year-old had enough experience of the world to pin down the origin of an accent. The takeaway was that two bearded, knife-wielding foreigners had come and stuffed my children in a van.

As if that wasn't terrifying enough, they had allowed Sam to see their faces. It was brazen and told of their fearlessness: They knew they weren't going to get caught. They considered whatever plan they had in place to be perfect.

"Tell me about the van," I said.

"It was bigger than the Honda. Sort of like a truck. But it wasn't a truck-truck. They made us get in the back. There weren't any seats, so we sat on the floor."

"Could you see out? Did it have windows?" Alison asked.

Sam shook his head.

"It just started driving," Sam said. "And I'm sorry, Momma, I didn't put a seat belt on because there weren't any."

"It's okay, Sammy."

"How long did you drive for?" I asked, hoping we might be able to get at least some sense of the distance they had been taken.

"I don't know," Sam said. His general awareness of the passage of time was still somewhat imprecise.

"Was it longer than a TV program or shorter than a TV program?" Alison asked.

"About the same," Sam replied.

Call it half an hour, which meant they could have been transported anywhere within approximately a thousand square miles in southeastern Virginia. We could spend the rest of our lives driving around, knocking on doors, and still not find where Emma was.

"Then what happened?" Alison asked.

"The van drove and drove. And then the men grabbed us. They just . . . grabbed us. They were rough."

Sam pantomimed this with his hands, which he curled like a raptor's talons.

"This was when they took you out of the back of the van?" I said.

"Yeah. And then they took us in the house."

"What did it look like outside the house?" I asked.

"Well, there were mostly just trees. Like, a lot of trees. Big ones."

Children being held deep in the middle of a thick forest. It was like something out of a Grimms' fairy tale.

"And then where did they take you?"

"To this room."

"What was it like?" I asked.

"It was little. And the windows had boxes over them"—I took this to mean they had been covered in cardboard—"and there was a TV with *SpongeBob* and *Dora*. I asked them if I could be in the same room as Emma but they said no."

"Did you ever try opening the door?" I asked.

"It was locked," Sam said.

"What happened after that?"

"I kept telling the men I was hungry. And they said, 'Shut up, shut up.' I'm sorry, Momma. I know 'shut up' is a bad word, but that's what they said."

"It's okay, honey," she said, rubbing his leg.

"And then I started crying. I was really hungry. And then one of them gave me food."

"What did he give you, Sammy?" Alison asked.

"Peanut butter and jelly," Sam said.

Alison and I shot each other worried looks. The first—and last—time Emma had been given peanut butter, her eyes and throat swelled up like a blowfish, necessitating a harrowing trip to the hospital. We now had EpiPens stashed everywhere, a precaution I doubted the kidnappers would have taken.

"Did Emma get a sandwich too?" I asked.

"I don't know," was all Sam could offer.

Sam said he cried a lot more and that finally one of the scratchy-faced men yelled at him and told him to go to sleep.

We asked in a variety of different ways whether the scratchy-faced men had hurt them, touched them inappropriately, or anything else. His answers were consistent nos.

He concluded his story by explaining how the next morning, he and Emma were hauled out of the room and into the van. After driving "for a while," the vehicle stopped. He was told when the van doors opened, he should run into the courthouse and ask for me. Which was what he did.

We tried to dredge other recollections out of him, but nothing more had stuck in his sweet little head. Alison finished by asking Sam if he had any questions for us.

"Yeah," he said. "When's Emma coming back?"

Alison and I exchanged desperate, empty glances.

"We don't know, buddy," I said. "We just don't know."

Sam has an incredibly expressive forehead. When something upsets him, the whole thing shifts at least a quarter of an inch downward. When he was a baby, I called it his worry brow. He wore it whenever he was feeling gassy, fussy, or colicky or was generally about to throw a fit.

He was wearing it now.

"But," he started. "But . . ."

Alison swooped in with a redirect. "Sammy, honey, why don't you pick a program on Netflix? Daddy and I need to have some grown-up talk. Then maybe we can all play a game."

"Okay, hang on," Sam said, and then dashed upstairs for a moment.

When he came back down, he was clutching his favorite stuffed animal. Kids acquire a lot of plush toys through the first several years of life, and you never know which one is going to be elevated to the level of beloved family member. For my kids it was a pair of teddy bears given to them by my aunt, a latter-day hippie who lived out in Colorado.

There was just something about the bears' size, shape, and softness that first attracted Sam and Emma when they were maybe six months old. The bears had since become *the* irreplaceable comfort item for each twin, the one you couldn't leave on a long trip without, the one that accompanied each of them to bed at night.

They were now ratty and worn, having undergone several emergency surgeries and as much snotty love as the twins could dish out. Emma called hers Sammybear. Sam called his Emmabear.

Sam returned with Emmabear clutched in his hand.

"Okay, I'm ready," he said.

Alison ran out of the room before Sam could see her burst into tears.

*

After I got Sam and Emmabear settled in front of the television, I went into the living room, where we could both keep an eye on him—I don't think either of us was ready to let him out of our sight—but where he couldn't hear us. Alison was waiting for me on the couch.

"You okay?" I asked, sitting down next to her.

"Yeah. I wasn't ready for Emmabear. It just took the wind out of me a little bit. I'm fine."

"You sure?"

"Uh-huh."

"Okay," I said softly. "So what's this grown-up talk you want to have?"

She grabbed both my hands. "I want to tell my family what's happened," she said.

Alison and her two sisters had spent their childhoods bouncing between army bases, from Korea to Germany to a variety of stateside installations. Their father's last stop was Fort Eustis, in nearby Newport News. Wade Powell had retired as a full-bird colonel, then died of cancer six months later, before he and Alison's mom, Gina, had figured out what would come next. Somehow, that translated into Gina deciding to settle here.

The rest of the family slowly drifted down. Jenny, the middle sister, and her husband, Jason, had been the first to move here. Next came Karen, the oldest sister, with her husband, Mark, and their four kids. Our brood was the last to arrive.

I loved Alison's family, especially since I barely had any of my own left. My parents were dead. I had no siblings. There was a smattering of aunts, uncles, and cousins scattered around the country, all of whom I talked to maybe twice a year. But that was really it. The Powells had become my tribe.

"You want to tell your family," I said, just to stall for time as I formulated a response that was more articulate than *That's a terrible idea.*

"We have no idea how long this is going to last," she said.

"You don't even know which case this is about. We're in it for the long haul here. What if it's one of those cases that goes on for years?"

"We don't do those," I said. And that was true: The Eastern District of Virginia was known as the "rocket docket" in legal circles. It was a district-wide point of pride that we moved matters along quickly.

"Well, okay, so not years. Months. And there's just no way we can hide this from my family for more than, what, a week? We're supposed to be at Timmy's birthday party on Saturday. And the weekend after that, my mother had talked about getting the grandchildren together. And on and on. What are we supposed to do? Say that Emma has the flu the whole time? Stop answering the phone and the doorbell? You know they just drop by sometimes."

She gave my hands a squeeze.

"Listen, we're still not calling the police," she continued. "And we can tell Miss Suzanne we're going to homeschool the kids for a while. She'll think we're nuts, but she already thinks that. But we . . . we have to tell my family."

Her eyes started filling with tears again and she blurted, "I just . . . I need them, okay?"

My opinion was so firm on this point, I was already shaking my head. "We can't, Ali. We just can't. We have to maintain the facade that nothing is wrong. I know that's not going to be easy, but every time we widen the circle of people who know about this, we increase the chance of this getting out somehow. We increase it exponentially."

"My family won't—"

"It's too great a risk!" I said, then rechecked my volume, which had gotten too loud. I returned to more of a whisper. "Look, if it leaks out in any way—just one careless comment that snowballs into something bigger until it catches the attention of someone at the courthouse—they would force me to stop hearing cases. No one would allow a compromised judge to keep rendering opinions. At that point, I'd stop having any value to the kidnappers . . ."

I let that linger out there for a second before finishing: ". . . and Emma wouldn't have any value to them either. She'd just be someone who could testify against them if they got caught."

And they'd kill her without hesitation. But thankfully I didn't have to say that part. Alison seemed to get it.

"Look, let's at least give it a few more days," I said. "I'll probably get more instructions from the kidnappers tomorrow or the next day. For all we know, this might be a case I'll hear two weeks from now. We can keep a lid on this for that long, can't we?"

I thought I saw a nod. It was all I was going to get. Without a word, she slid off the couch. I heard her sniffling as she went up the stairs.

Maybe I shouldn't have been so strident. Maybe I should have considered her emotional needs more. But I had been on the bench long enough to learn at least once crucial distinction between my old job and my new one. A good lawmaker has to be forever willing to change his viewpoint, to consider someone else's needs, to compromise.

A judge has to learn to make a decision and stick with it.

13

Sam and I had settled on the couch and were finishing up his second offering from Netflix. Alison was upstairs, taking some time to compose herself.

Or at least I thought she was until I heard a rhythmic *thwock, thwock, thwock* emanating from behind the house.

I didn't have to rise off the couch to know: Alison was chopping wood.

This was something she started doing not long after we moved to the farm. At first, in typically dense male fashion, I had thought of it as a rustic replacement for her northern Virginia health club, one with eminently practical benefits. We have three fireplaces, and nothing cuts through the chill of a poorly insulated southern farmhouse like a nice fire. I had even stupidly suggested we buy a log splitter.

That's when I learned it wasn't really about the wood. Or the workout. This was her therapy. In the years since we had come down here, I had come to recognize that when she had something to work through, it was going to be with an axe in her hands.

Even if, at a time like this, there weren't enough trees in the world to help her.

Sam had perked up the moment he heard the chopping and was soon slipping out from under my arm.

"Can I do wood with Momma?" he asked.

When Sam asked to "do wood" with his mother, it meant waiting until Alison was taking a break and carrying the split logs to a nearby pile. If it sounds like forced child labor, it shouldn't. Sam thought stacking wood was fun.

I briefly considered the pros and cons—did I really want Sam outside when we knew the kidnappers were watching? should I just let Alison be alone with her axe?—before I decided an activity that felt normal would be good for him. For however much we might have wanted to, we couldn't keep the boy sealed in a bubble.

"Sure, buddy," I said. "Just remember to put on your work gloves."

I followed Sam out to the backyard, where Alison was taking healthy swings at some pine stumps. It was remarkable how proficient she had become over the years. I watched, mesmerized, as she halved, then quartered the logs.

Every time she put the axe down to take a breather, that was Sam's cue to scurry in, pick up a piece of wood, and run it over to the nearby pile. He usually made two or three trips before his mother was ready to resume.

Ordinarily, this was something Alison and Sam did together, while Emma and I would be inside—playing a game, cooking dinner, reading a book. It was an unspoken thing, but we all understood it. Alison and Sam were about action. Emma and I were more like housecats.

Now? It just felt strange, standing around and watching my wife and son work. Not knowing what else to do with myself, I pitched in. I thought I would help Sam keep up with Alison's output, though it quickly became clear I was fouling up their usual patterns. Sam and I kept bumping into each other. Alison had to wait longer for me to clear out of the way, because I was so much bigger than Sam.

We kept working all the same, each of us trying to adjust to a family that had so unexpectedly morphed from square to triangle.

Before long, we were all red-faced from exertion. We had gotten in enough of a groove—each of us so intent on the task, trying to figure out this new three-person dance—that I didn't notice we had a visitor until she had rounded the corner of the house.

It was Karen, Alison's oldest sister.

"Hey, guys," she said, "what's going on?"

She was looking at all of us with bemusement, but at me in particular. I was still wearing my suit pants, wing tips, and a white button-down shirt. Not exactly lumberjack clothes.

We all just stopped what we were doing and stared at her. She was clutching a reusable nylon bag, which she now held up.

"I was just up at Sweet Earth, picking up our share," she continued. "They had so many apples they gave me extra. I thought you guys would like some."

Sweet Earth was a nearby organic farm. Karen had a subscription that entitled her to fresh produce every other week—whatever was in season. She often shared the overflow with us.

She was now looking at Sam. "Don't you have school today, Sammy?"

"Half day," Alison improvised. "Student-teacher conferences."

"Oh," Karen said, now looking around. "Where's
Emma?"

The question seemed to freeze Alison, and I wasn't doing
much better with it. I just couldn't come up with another
ad-libbed answer that would be satisfactory. If I said Emma
was inside playing, Karen would want to visit her. If I said
Emma was sick, Karen would want to comfort her.

It was Sam—who had not been coached to keep his
mouth shut—who blurted out, "She's with the men."

*

This was what led, four hours later, to the convening
of an emergency family meeting. It was called with the
understanding that what was going to be shared had to be
kept in the strictest confidence.

It had certainly occurred to me, during the remainder of
the afternoon, that Karen's visit was less impromptu than
it appeared; that Alison had surreptitiously called her and
instructed her to come over and ask questions until we were
cornered into a confession.

Or maybe Alison had been right. We were never going
to be able to keep this from her family. Whether Karen's
appearance was truly chance or whether it had resulted
from a minor act of sedition on Alison's part, it was only
a hastening of the inevitable. The Powells were too tightly
knit to keep secrets from one another.

As an only child, I am endlessly fascinated by the Powell sisters: three women, born thirty-five months apart and raised almost as triplets, who have remained so close into adulthood.

It's just a complicated dynamic. There are jealousies born long ago—about who got what when, who had it easier or harder, who was given what freedom at what age—that live on. They morph into slightly less infantile form, perhaps. But the scoreboard still exists, somewhere. Everyone still remembers that Jenny was allowed to get her ears pierced at a younger age, that Alison got to go on the high school band trip to England, that Karen took the family's used car off to college.

In some ways, no one is tougher on one another than sisters. Like parents, they're hyperaware of one another's past foibles and faults; but, without the infinite parental capacity for love and forgiveness, they judge one another far more harshly for them.

I swear there are times when they really might kill one another. Until, of course, one of them is in trouble or threatened by an outside agent, in which case they band together into an unbreakable front.

Internally fractured yet externally united. The world over, it's the very definition of sisterhood.

As the kids rambled noisily upstairs, we gathered the adults in the living room. Alison's mother, Gina, was sitting in an easy chair. She obviously knew something was up but had this unflappable grace about her. There is probably no other way to survive all those years of being a military wife.

Alison's two sisters were stationed on the couch, a Queen Anne–style piece that didn't really seat more than two people comfortably.

The oldest sister, Karen—she had taken her husband's last name, Lowe—shared Alison's build and coloring but little else. She was pure firstborn: domineering, a lightning rod for confrontation, highly competent, and fiercely self-sufficient. Ever since Wade died, she had taken over the role of paterfamilias, calling the shots both for her nuclear family and for her extended one. She was a stay-at-home mom, having left a job in benefits administration after her second child was born. Her four kids were neatly spaced two years apart, exactly as planned. The youngest was now six, born eight days after the twins. Karen had talked about rejoining the working world now that her kids were in school, but nothing had come of it yet.

The middle sister, Jennifer—she was still a Powell—looked less like Alison. She was darker complexioned, had rounder cheeks, and was shorter. But, personality-wise, they probably had more in common, to the point where they were more or less best friends. Jenny's family role was that of the peacekeeper, although that meant she had a tendency to go along with things that she found untenable for too long, until the dam holding back her anger simply burst. Like Alison, she had chosen a helping profession, working as an emergency room nurse at a large local hospital. Unlike Alison, she was childless. This made her the de facto "cool aunt," the one with the time and energy to lavish on nieces and nephews.

95

As best I had been able to figure their childhoods, Karen had been a go-getter from the start, a high achiever who was vice president or secretary of half the clubs in school, all while being a National Merit semifinalist and her class salutatorian. Then came Jenny, who was completely disinterested in building her résumé, instead spending her time and energy cultivating a large group of friends at every stop they made. Then came Alison, who studied both of her sisters and decided to be like Karen, albeit a slightly more accomplished iteration—she was president of all the clubs, a National Merit finalist, and the class valedictorian.

In some ways, little had changed over the years. Alison was still the Golden Child, the prettiest of the three, the one who did everything right. Jenny was still the Popular One, amiable, cheerful, and easy to like. And Karen was still the Boss, who ruled with the consent of the other two.

All three had husbands, although I was always a little uncertain as to how we fit into the larger drama that was the Powell sisters. At best, we were supporting cast.

Karen was married to Mark Lowe, a thoughtful, quiet man who worked with computers and seemed content to let his life be controlled by his spouse. That he spent so much time indoors was at least partly genetic. He had red hair—so red, it had actually been orange when he was a kid—and pale enough skin that he slathered on sunscreen before mowing the lawn. He fit certain computer-geek stereotypes, inasmuch as he was the last guy you wanted on your sports team but the first guy you called if your wireless router was acting up.

Jennifer was married to Jason Bundren, a career salesman who was sort of Mark's opposite. He was loud and swaggering, a big, beefy ex-jock who enjoyed his position as the strapping son-in-law whenever Gina needed some heavy lifting done. His latest job involved selling large-scale sewage equipment to municipalities and the military. Without kids of his own, he was stuck in a kind of eternal adolescence, one that revolved around cars, football, and guns. He and Jennifer had actually met on a firing range.

With the family arrayed before her, Alison assumed a position in front of the fireplace. The tension in her face was obvious, as was the strangeness of this sudden emergency meeting. Everyone quieted as she began talking.

Alison laid out the ground rules: They couldn't tell anyone what they were about to hear; they couldn't act on the information, not even in a manner they thought benign or helpful; they had to respect our wishes in how we were going to handle everything; their only role was to listen.

"Is that okay?" Alison asked.

Once she saw heads around the room bobbing, she told all.

Gina was the first to cry, followed quickly by Jenny and Karen. Alison held her composure until she was done. Then Gina and Karen and Jenny mobbed her with hugs and consoling words. I could see Alison gaining strength from being able to share her burden.

It was take-charge Karen, who had a four-hour head start on absorbing this news, who was the first to break from the scrum and move on to next steps.

"So, what's your plan? What are you going to do about this?"

She had aimed the question at me.

"That's just it, Karen. We're not going to do anything," I said, deliberately choosing the plural pronoun. "We're going to follow our instructions, say nothing, and hope this is all over with soon."

"But you don't even know what case they're looking to control," she said.

"It doesn't matter. When these people contact me and tell me what ruling they want, I'll make it. We have no leverage here."

Karen chewed on this for a moment. Almost literally. You could see her jaw muscles clenching. The family, collectively, seemed to be holding its breath.

"We can't sit here and do nothing," she said. "Not while Emma is out there and in trouble."

"Karen," Alison said sharply. "You promised."

"Well, just hold on. I'm not saying calling the cops. I'm just saying"—she groped for an idea—"I mean, do we have any lines of communication open with these people? Can you talk to them at all?"

"No," I said, shaking my head. "The texts have been manipulated to obscure their origination point. And the call came from a restricted number."

"Well, surely, the phone company can tell you what the number was. They've got—"

"Not without a warrant," I said. "And I can't issue a warrant and have it carried out without involving law enforcement."

Karen was unbowed, looking at Mark. "Do you have any friends who could hack the phone company's computers and get information like that?"

Mark seemed a little horrified. "That's not really what I do, dear," he said softly. "I mean, I wouldn't even know where to—"

"Forget it. I'm just trying to think through our options," she said. "What if we put Sam under hypnosis? They say that a good hypnotist can get people to remember all sorts of things they don't realize are in their memories."

I looked at Alison pleadingly. "We questioned Sam as thoroughly as we could," she said. "Even if he could give a sketch artist a flawless description of the men, what would we do with it? It's not like we can put up wanted posters at the post office."

"Okay, okay, I'm just brainstorming here," Karen said, and now turned back to me. "We need to go through your cases systematically. I bet if we crunched it enough, we could narrow down which one it might be."

"I have several hundred cases on my docket. There's no way—"

"There have to be a few that are really desiring a certain outcome."

"It's federal court, Karen. They're *all* desiring a certain outcome. No one goes to court because they want to lose."

"Have you even tried to identify the possibilities?"

"No," I said, trying to keep my patience with her. "Because, okay, hypothetically, let's say I'm able to narrow it down to three or four cases. It's probably impossible to do that, and it would take at least two months to even start, but never mind that for a moment. Let's say I can do it. What do I do at that point, walk up to the six or eight plaintiffs and defendants and say, 'Hi, you're not blackmailing me by any chance, are you?' "

"There's no need for sarcasm," Karen said, bristling.

My mother-in-law was the one who stepped in with: "Karen, honey, this has been hard enough—"

"I know, I know," she said. "If you don't want to do anything, I'll respect that. A promise is a promise. I'm just saying, if it was my daughter, I don't know how I could just sit there and let this happen."

And there it was: Bossy Karen throwing out the challenge to man up.

But I wasn't going to take the bait. There was nothing to be gained from it.

*

Our colloquy broke up shortly after that, and some members of the family peeled off.

Jennifer had a shift at the hospital that night, so she and Jason were first to go. Gina made noises about not wanting to drive at night and excused herself.

That left Karen, Mark, and their mob of children. I was happy they stayed. Sam could use some good cousin time. At the very least, they would keep him distracted.

Turning our efforts to dinner, we ordered pizzas for the kids. Alison and Karen retreated to the kitchen to cook food for the grown-ups. Karen insisted they open a bottle of wine, wearing down Alison's initial objections.

Getting the sense they needed a little sister time, I asked Mark to join me on the back deck. My brother-in-law was adequate company, and I liked him well enough. He was a dedicated husband; a caring father; steady, solid, and dependable in all areas of life. Certainly, he was preferable to Jenny's husband, the lamentably paramilitary Jason.

As we went outside, the September sun was setting slowly behind us, bouncing its colors off the opposite bank of the York River, making Mark's red hair look like it was on fire.

"So," he said, after getting himself settled into a chair. "It seems almost ridiculous to ask, but how are you doing?"

All I did was shake my head. I knew he meant well, but how I was doing couldn't be put into words.

He continued: "I mean, I can't imagine. This is . . . to say it's my worst nightmare come true doesn't even come close."

Mark wasn't chatty by nature. In a group, when it was all three sisters and all three husbands, he almost never said a word. I recognized he was making an effort to reach out.

I just couldn't summon the emotional energy to engage in the conversation he was trying to have.

"You know what? I'm sorry," I said. "If I even try to think about this anymore, I'm going to go crazy. Can we talk about something else?"

"Oh yeah. Geez, I'm so sorry, I was just—"

"Don't worry about it. Seriously. Just . . . distract me, please," I said, groping around for a safe topic. I came up with: "How's work going?"

Eager to appease, Mark launched into what was basically a monologue about his efforts to slay the digital giants. His job involved optimizing computer networks for an investment company called the Whipple Alliance, and I think he was pretty good at it. I didn't really understand the intricacies, but there were instances where the traders— including the boss, Andy Whipple—could make a fraction of a cent more per transaction if it could be completed a few nanoseconds quicker, something that starts to matter when you make millions of transactions a year.

Mark used to work for the Whipple Alliance up in New York City. It was a confluence of events that led him and Karen down here. First, Karen decided to stay at home with the kids, meaning they were trying to survive on one salary, no easy thing in the New York area. Then Wade Powell died and Karen began making noises about wanting to move closer to her widowed mother. Mark was able to convince his superiors he could do his job from anywhere.

In many ways, we were just following the trail they had laid down for us when we came down here five years ago. We had kids. We returned "home" to raise them—home for a military brat being wherever your family was last stationed.

As Mark talked, twilight approached. When our wives joined us, I could tell, from the way they were wobbling, they had finished off the first bottle of wine and had opened a second. It had clearly been a bit much for their empty stomachs to handle.

Some of the substance-abuse counselors whom I ordered defendants to see would say this was dangerous behavior:

self-medicating out of an inability to handle reality. But I didn't blame them. At the moment, reality flatly sucked.

"How's it going out here?" Alison asked.

"I've just been boring Scott with work stuff," Mark said.

"Oh, work." Karen snorted, spilling a little bit of her wine as she flopped down. "Did you tell him you keep letting Gary and Ranjit take credit for everything you're doing?"

Karen turned to me and continued: "Do you know what they've started calling him? Lowe Man. As in, Lowe Man on the Totem Pole."

"That's just a joke," Mark interjected.

Karen ignored him. "These two a-holes up in New York, anything Mark does, they go to the boss—not their direct boss, the boss's boss. And they're all, like, 'Oh yeah, that thing that's allowing you to make millions of dollars? That was totally my doing.' When really it was Mark's. But Mark never says a word."

Mark coughed uncomfortably. "They're not . . . they're not fooling anyone. The truth is in the code. They can see what each log-in has—"

"You think any of those traders understand code? Jesus," Karen snapped. "You know what Andy Whipple understands? He understands making gobs of money and banging strippers. You're deluding yourself if you think he has a clue."

"Andy is a lot more savvy than—"

"Then why don't you ask for a raise like we talked about?" Karen demanded. "Why don't you be assertive for a change? Maybe Scott here could teach you. Judges have to be assertive, right?"

There was finally a pause in Karen's rant. Alison cleared her throat and the glance she shot at me said, *Please make this stop.*

I stood up and offered a meek, "Let's eat."

14

The monitor was thirty-four inches from corner to corner, and it cast a bluish light on the back wall of the bedroom.

"Go back some more," the older brother said. "I want to see when the car arrived."

The younger brother nodded and fiddled with his laptop computer. There were three images on the big screen. One of them was now peeling backward, showing not just one car, but another . . . and a third.

"You should have been watching more carefully," the older admonished. "You play that computer game. We are not here to play games."

The younger brother didn't reply. He was not in the mood to be lectured.

"There," the older said. "Start there."

The younger brother clicked the play button. The picture on the screen was of a farmhouse with a wraparound porch. Between the three views on the screen, the brothers could see a 270-degree wedge of the front and sides of the structure. The middle camera showed a hundred feet of grass and dirt driveway in front of the house. Each side camera, when panned all the way out, captured another broad slice of the grounds, all the way to the edge of the forest.

The lenses providing those images were so tiny that not

even a squirrel climbing one of the tree trunks they were affixed to would have necessarily noticed them. Three small wireless transmission boxes, silently sending their signals to the Internet, were hidden nearby.

The brothers gazed as three vehicles pulled into the driveway over a span of about twenty minutes. A lone woman, who looked to be in her seventies, disembarked from the first. Then came a middle-aged man and woman. Finally, there was a family of six.

"Speed it up," the older said. "I want to see when the first two cars left."

The younger complied. For a time, little about the view changed, except for the gradual setting of the sun. Then the middle-aged couple came back out, soon followed by the older woman. As they caught back up to real time, the family of six was still, apparently, inside.

"Do you think we should make a call?" the younger asked.

The older responded by walking into the kitchen and grabbing the Internet phone. He set it on speakerphone, dialed, and waited.

"This had better be important," came a voice. "I'm in the middle of a meeting."

"The judge has visitors."

"What kind of visitors?"

"Three cars. Nine people in all. Some of them have left already."

The voice was immediately agitated: "Any of them cops?"

"I don't think so. They appear to be civilians."

"Okay. I still think we should send a message. Let them know this isn't acceptable."

"Of course. What are you thinking?"

"Just remind them what's at stake."

15

I was cleaning up the last of the dinner dishes when Alison reentered the kitchen. The Lowes were gone. She had been upstairs putting Sam to bed, having sobered up considerably. The food helped.

"How'd he go down?" I asked.

"A little rough," she said, sighing and coming to a stop on the other side of the kitchen island, where she plopped herself on a stool.

"How bad?"

"Well, I guess it could have been worse. He was crying about Emma not being there to say good night. We talked about how we missed her and how we were scared. Then I rubbed his back. After about five minutes he was out like a light. Thank goodness he was already tired. The cousins ran him around pretty good."

"He's not going to have his cousins around every night, you know," I said.

"I know. Believe me, I know," she said.

I took a dish towel to a salad bowl and tossed out the question that had slowly been working its way to the top of my consciousness. "You know, with what he's been through . . . Should we send him to a children's therapist or something?"

"I was thinking about that. But I don't know how that would work. I mean, he can't exactly tell the therapist the truth. And lying to a therapist seems to negate the whole point."

"Wouldn't the therapist be bound by doctor-patient confidentiality?"

"Not when there's a child in danger. I looked it up. They're required to report that."

The salad bowl was now dry. I frowned at it while putting it away.

"I actually Googled 'post-traumatic stress syndrome in children' this afternoon before my family got here," Alison said.

"And?"

"Well, it's not like there's a test you can administer or anything. I clicked on a couple sites and it seems like some kids get hit with it and some kids don't and there's no real rhyme or reason. We just have to keep an eye on him, give him lots of love and support, listen to him if he starts talking, make him realize what happened isn't his fault, that sort of thing."

"In other words, we have to reassure him even though we're not feeling reassured ourselves."

"Pretty much. They also said—"

She was interrupted by a pair of headlights strafing the trees behind the kitchen. It spoke to our state of hypervigilance that we immediately stopped the conversation to watch.

"Is that Justina?" Alison said.

"Probably."

Alison stood and walked quickly toward the front of the house so she could get a better view. I followed.

From the living room, we could see Justina's car, an aging Toyota, pulling into its usual spot beside the Honda Odyssey, next to the cottage, which was easily visible from our house.

"I'm going to talk to her," Alison said.

"I don't think that's—"

But Alison was already out of the room, then the house. She was walking so fast it was all I could do to catch up to her.

"Alison, wait, let's discuss this for a second."

She was already halfway to the cottage, her shoes scratching urgently against the dirt under her feet. From somewhere in the distance, I heard a member of our local dog pack let loose a howl.

"Just stay with Sam," she said, slightly out of breath.

"Sam is fine. We can see the house from here," I said. "What's your plan?"

"I told you, I want to talk to her."

"Honey, this is not the right time for this. It's after ten o'clock. And you've been—"

Drinking. Though I stopped myself short of saying it.

"You can go home if you want," she said.

Now that I had caught up to her, I could see she had the wig balled up in her fist. She must have grabbed it on the way out. I positioned myself so I was blocking her path.

"Alison. Please. Hold on. Just for a second."

She finally halted, allowing me to say, "You can't just march in there and say, 'Hey, someone kidnapped our children yesterday, and I found this blond wig in your closet so it must be you.' "

"Well, I wasn't the one driving that car."

"That doesn't mean it was Justina," I said. "I'm not saying I've made up my mind about her either way, but think about it logically for a second. She's watched our kids for two years now. She cares for them like they're her own. I think we need more to go on than just a wig."

"Why, because she's hot and you want to sleep with her?"

I was so startled by the accusation, which was so out of character for Alison, I could barely summon a reply. "Oh, Alison—"

"I see the way you look at her," she said, her eyes scorching my face.

"That is completely unfair. I've never—"

"And I see the way she looks at you too. The way she bats her eyes at you. She's got these daddy issues that are, like, a mile wide, and you're . . . her daddy and her idol and she wants to—"

"You're being totally ridiculous right now."

"Oh, am I? When Justina came here, she was premed. Now she's prelaw."

"College kids switch majors all the time."

"She's constantly asking you about legal stuff."

"And that means she wants to have sex with me? Sorry, that just—"

"Then tell me. Tell me you don't want to sleep with her."

"Are we seriously talking about this?" I said. "I shouldn't have to deny anything here."

"Because you know you can't. You know—"

"Fine: I don't want to sleep with her. I don't want to sleep with her because I'm in love with my wife and I have no interest in defiling a girl who is not even half my age."

"Then why are you defending her?"

"I'm not defending her. I'm just trying to point out we need to be a little careful about throwing around accusations when we—"

"What do you want? A video? Oh wait, she's already on video," Alison said, then starting ticking things off with her fingers. "There's that. There's the fact that she's the only other person with access to the Honda besides us. There's the fact that the men who took the kids had foreign accents—"

"Which could be from anywhere in the world, based on what Sam was able to tell us."

"My point is there are plenty of reasons to suspect Justina. It would certainly be enough probable cause for a search warrant, Judge Sampson. If you weren't so busy thinking with your dick, you'd see that."

I was going to refute that, then stopped myself. I might as well have tried to talk to one of the nearby trees. I never knew Alison harbored any suspicion about my intentions toward Justina, nor any hidden animosity toward her. They seemed to have great camaraderie when they were together with the kids, and there were times, after the twins went to bed, that Justina would sit in our kitchen, drink tea, and talk with Alison, using her as a surrogate mother since her own was half a world away. Up until this moment, I would have said there wasn't a whiff of a problem between them.

But having your children kidnapped brings all kinds of slumbering feelings to life.

"Fine, let's go talk to her," I said. "But don't you dare tell her the children have been kidnapped. If she gets it in her head to go to the police—"

"She wouldn't. But fine."

And then she continued her charge, a bull in search of a china shop.

*

When she reached the front stoop of the cottage, she scaled the cinder-block steps and pulled open the rickety screen door. Then she thumped on the main door with the butt of her hand.

Under ordinary circumstances, when Justina didn't have the kids with her, we never intruded on her life. If she chose to be with us—to chat with Alison or to ask me legal questions—we welcomed her. But we were not in the habit of dropping by unannounced.

After maybe ten seconds, Justina appeared, looking mildly surprised.

"Hey, guys, what's up?" she asked. Justina had only a faint accent. And after four years in the States—two in college, plus two in a boarding school before that—she had all the American colloquialisms down pat.

Alison had plastered on a smile that was pure laminate. "We just wanted to talk," she said.

Backing away, Justina opened the door a little wider so

we could enter. "Yeah, sure. Come on in."

Justina had her dark hair pulled back in a ponytail. She wore a tight T-shirt and even tighter jeans, but I averted my eyes, hoping Alison would notice. I looked around the cottage instead. It was the usual scene. Her schoolbooks were piled on the table in the eating area. The couch was in casual disarray, with a few blankets and mismatched pillows cast across it. The bedroom and kitchen were both dark.

"What do you need to talk about?" Justina asked.

"I was hoping you could explain this to me," Alison said, holding up the wig where Justina could see it.

Clenched in Alison's hand, the mass of fake blond hair looked like a piece of sorority-girl roadkill. Justina studied it without comprehension.

"What is it?" she asked.

"Do you recognize it?" Alison asked.

I still wasn't looking directly at Justina—there was no safe place for my gaze to rest—but out of the corner of my eye I could see her glancing toward me for help.

It would not be forthcoming. Alison had enough worries right now without my doing anything to stoke the fear that she also had a philandering husband. I was determined to make it clear whose side I was on.

"No," Justina said.

"Well, it's yours, isn't it?"

I risked a quick look at Justina. She was properly baffled.

"Uh, maybe? Is that a wig?"

"Yes. Were you wearing it yesterday when you picked up the twins?"

"Yesterday?" Justina said. "But yesterday was Wednesday. I don't pick up the twins on Wednesdays. The judge does."

She was again looking to me for salvation, but the judge was no fool. I had absolutely nothing to gain by interceding here.

"Justina, someone else picked up the kids from school yesterday. It wasn't the judge. And it wasn't me. It was someone driving our Honda Odyssey. You're the only other one who has keys."

"But I didn't . . ." Her voice trailed off.

"What, you don't have the keys?"

"No. They're right over there," Justina said, pointing to the hook on the wall by the door. We kept the keys there so if Alison or I needed the Honda for something, they would be easily findable. The keychain was a fist-size brass pendant that was impossible to absentmindedly slip in your pocket—guaranteeing it ended up back on the hook for the next person to use.

"So you're saying you didn't get them yesterday?" Alison asked.

"No. I have class. And then you sent me that text today saying not to pick them up. What's going on? Is everything okay?"

"I think you know it's not," Alison said, her voice smoldering.

I finally risked a glance at Justina's face. It was perfectly blank.

"Just tell us the truth," Alison said, glaring. "We can deal with the fallout later. Right now all that matters is the kids. Did someone pay you off to pick them up? Did they threaten you or your family?"

"What are you talking about?" Justina said.

Alison was standing there, ramrod straight. She took a long breath in, then pushed out an even longer one.

"I'm sorry," she said at last. "I have no choice. You're fired. I want you out of here by the end of the weekend."

"But, Mrs. Sampson, I don't have any other—"

"You can find an apartment closer to school. I'm sure there are plenty of vacancies. I can't have you in the cottage anymore."

"But, please. I haven't . . . ," she started, and then she turned her attention to me. Which was a mistake. I had no power to commute her sentence.

"Judge Sampson, can't you—"

"I'm sorry, Justina," I said, with what I hoped was the appropriate amount of firmness.

*

Later, when we had turned out the lights and gone to bed, a tape measure would have shown we were only two feet apart. It just felt like a thousand miles.

Alison inhaled deeply, like she was going to say something. She stopped herself. Then it finally came out: "I'm sorry about Justina."

I wasn't sure which part she was sorry about—accusing me of wanting to sleep with her or throwing her out—but I wasn't going to turn down a freely given apology. I just said,

"Okay."

"If I'm wrong about her, I'm a horrible person. I know that. But I can't stop thinking that I'm right about her. And I can't deal with having her living so close while I'm wondering if she was the one."

"Okay," I said again.

"After this is over we can bring her back."

"I doubt she'll want to come back."

"You think I'm wrong about her?"

"I don't know what to think right now," I said, in all honesty.

She was quiet for a moment or two, then said, "I'm going in there sometime tomorrow while she's at class and getting something with her fingerprints and her DNA on it."

"That sounds like a good idea." By which I meant: It certainly couldn't hurt.

The HVAC system clicked on, pushing cold air into the room. I pulled the blanket up a little farther.

Then she said, "I'm sorry about . . . about what I said about you wanting to sleep with her."

"Thanks," I said guardedly.

Then she rolled toward me, bridging that two-foot, thousand-mile distance between us in one quick movement. She kissed me on the mouth, quick and hard.

"You're a good man, Scott Sampson. I'm a lucky woman to have you. Even if this thing is making me totally crazy, I still love you."

"I love you too. Don't forget that."

I snaked an arm under her and she leaned her head against

my chest. I pulled her tight against me, suddenly cognizant of my need for human contact. Her warmth was a reminder that I really wasn't alone in this. It was probably the first thing in a day and a half that hadn't felt completely wrong, and I allowed myself to treasure it for a moment.

Then the doorbell rang.

My body reacted instantly. I half pushed Alison off me, getting to my feet, then ran into Emma's bedroom, which faces the front of the house, and peered out the window.

There was only darkness. My eyes swept our front yard, looking for some hint of movement. The scene was perfectly still.

Alison was catching up with me just as I was leaving the room.

"What's out there?"

"Nothing," I said, slipping past her and back out into the hallway. "At least nothing I can see. But just in case, go into Sam's room, lock the door, and don't come out until I tell you it's safe."

Behind me, I could hear her footfalls making their way toward Sam. I quickly descended the stairs and, not bothering to go into the sitting room for a closer inspection of the front porch, turned the deadbolt, slid the chain off the door, and threw it open.

The first direction I looked was out. It was the same scene it always was. The magnolia trees. The yard. The driveway. All undisturbed.

Then I looked down. There was another Home Depot box, identical to the last one, with the silver-metallic strip of duct tape along the top. I tore it off and lifted the flaps.

Then I gasped.

The bottom of the box was covered in curly blond hair.

Emma's.

My hand flew to my mouth. They had shaved her bald. I thought about my poor, sweet girl having her head denuded like that. They probably had to hold her down to do it. I was sure she screamed and cried.

I was shaking as I lifted up the white envelope, which contained a message, written on card stock in the now-familiar block lettering:

THERE WERE TOO MANY PEOPLE AT YOUR HOUSE
TONIGHT. NO MORE PARTIES. WE'RE OUT OF HAIR
TO CUT.

I walked a few steps toward the edge of the porch, again looking out into the gloom beyond. There were a thousand places in the woods between our house and the road that someone could hide if they wanted to. And it wasn't like we had neighbors around to wonder why someone was spying on us. I turned to reenter the house.

That's when I noticed another bird feeder was gone.

16

Somehow, I slept that night. My body had finally reached the point where it gave me no choice in the matter.

By the time my eyes opened, Alison had already left the bed. From downstairs, I could smell breakfast. Coffee. Bacon. Pancakes on a Friday, two full days before Pancake Day.

Summoning the will to drag my still-exhausted, aching self out of bed, I shuffled over to the window. We had an extra-wide windowsill, which Alison had turned into a cozy little cubby. She decorated it with pillows that invited you to take a load off and watch the river go by. The York is more than a mile wide where we live, on the banks of the north shore, just up from the mouth of the Chesapeake Bay. The south shore is visible, though pleasantly indistinct. It was ordinarily a view I loved.

Now it just seemed obscene. So did the sun, which shined down on us from a cloudless blue sky. Nothing should have been allowed to be so beautiful on a day when so much else was wrong.

I pulled myself away and went into the bathroom. I showered. Slowly. I shaved. Mechanically. I dressed. Haltingly. All I really wanted to do was ball up in the fetal position. I was battling inertia the whole way.

Day three of a crisis is a strange time. Day one you're in total shock. Day two is an extended triage session. By day three, your world may be shattered, but you're getting the first inkling that it's still spinning, whether you want it to or not.

Alison had, as usual, reached that realization first. When I got down to the kitchen, she was bustling around, already cleaning up the last of the dishes.

"I saved some for you," she said, nodding toward the stovetop, where a tinfoil-draped shape awaited me.

"Thanks," I said, not making a move toward it.

"Eat it," she ordered. "You need the energy."

She looked up at me, forced a smile from under her dark-smudged eyes. Her drive astonished me. While I was wallowing, she was being the strong one. For me. For Sam. For Emma.

She always was the strong one, of course. When you got right down to it, stripping away all the outer layers of bluster and faux fortitude, I felt like I was made of insubstantial things, all fluffernutter, white bread, and gummy bears. She, meanwhile, was one hundred percent steel-cut oats.

I still remember the moment I first laid eyes on her. We were both sophomores. She was striding along in front of the student center, all youthful confidence, with her great shoulders thrust back, her long blond hair flowing behind her. There was an athletic elegance to how she moved, and the sun was setting behind her, catching her in just the perfect light. It was as if the entire solar system was blessing our meeting. The very simple thought that passed through my head was: *Wow, who's that?*

In the most uncharacteristically bold act of my life, I walked right up to her and asked her what she was doing that night. I couldn't go another second without her being in my life.

In that moment, I might have told you I already appreciated how beautiful she was. In truth, I had yet to see even the slightest fraction of her real radiance. Sometimes I marvel that the twenty-year-old me—an otherwise imbecilic college student who understood so little of the world—ever had the good sense to fall in love with such a remarkable woman.

"You're really amazing, you know that?" I said as she loaded the dishwasher.

"Uh-huh," she said, not stopping for the compliment.

"No, really," I said.

I was trying to say more, to express how grateful I was for her, to say how astonishing I found her toughness, to tell her how much I admired her selflessness. I wanted to explain I was thinking of the entirety of our relationship and all that we had experienced together, from the harried days of our early careers, to the stolen weekends of sex and movies before we had kids, to some of those incredibly long days when the twins were babies and we thought we'd never survive; and now, to this. Somehow, I couldn't find a way to put all that in context, or to unsnarl the traffic jam of ideas in my head. And, for her part, Alison wasn't even glancing up from her work.

"I'm going to check in on Sam," I said. "Then I'll come back and eat."

"Uh-huh," she murmured as I left the kitchen.

Some portion of my sleepless night had been spent thinking about how our boy was coping. I wondered what he had done for a morning routine without Emma. Had he waited for her to call out before realizing it wasn't going to happen?

I found him in the family room, staging an elaborate race scene with some of his cars, making engine noises and providing play-by-play of all the action. Emmabear was perched on the arm of the couch, taking it all in.

"How you doing, buddy?" I asked.

"Good," he said.

"You sleep okay?" I asked, because I knew sleep troubles were a leading indicator of post-traumatic stress disorder.

"Yeah," was all he said.

Like his mother, he didn't look up at me. I watched him play for a little while. He seemed content enough.

"Love you, pal."

"You too, Dad."

Deciding that was as good as I was going to get, I returned to the kitchen, grabbed the plate Alison made for me, and sat down.

"I already called work," Alison said as she wiped down the counter. "Someone needs to stay with Sam and it obviously can't be you. I told them I'm taking an extended leave of absence. It's not fair to just keep calling in sick. They need to be able to make plans without me."

"Okay," I said.

"And I called school and told them the twins are still

sick. That will at least hold us through the weekend. On Monday I'll call and say we've decided to homeschool them. It's the only thing I can think of that won't arouse too much suspicion. We can't exactly send Sam to school by himself."

"Right," I said.

"Also, I went online and found a lab in Williamsburg that will do DNA and fingerprint testing for us. If we pay extra, they'll put a rush on it and we'll have our results in three weeks. I'm going to put some of Justina's things in there so they can be tested against the stuff from that box—just the envelope and other things that wouldn't give a lab person a hint about what's going on. Maybe it's a waste of time, but it makes me feel like I'm doing something."

She smiled weakly at me. That's when I saw just how thin she was stretching herself. This whole thing—getting out of bed, making breakfast, researching DNA testing, moving forward even as this tornado hovered over us—was not the product of some indefatigable reserve of resilience she possessed naturally. It was a huge effort.

"What time did you get up this morning, anyway?" I asked.

"Oh, I barely slept," she said, brushing it off. "Those child PTSD websites I was looking at said it's important to resume normal activity as much as possible. They actually said we should send him back to school but in lieu of that we should help him seek pleasurable activities—trips to fun places, bike rides, things like that. I thought I'd take him to the Living Museum today."

The Virginia Living Museum, in nearby Newport News,

had just enough critters to keep kids entertained, but not so many that you were exhausted by the time you got through it.

"Oh, that's a good idea."

"Karen and Jenny are coming with us."

"Great," I said.

I was thankful that Jennifer worked strange shifts at the hospital and Karen was a stay-at-home mom. It would be good for Alison to have adult company. I was sure Sam would enjoy being lavished with attention from his mother and aunts too.

"I'm going to get ready," she said. "I'll see you tonight."

She walked over, bussed my cheek, and disappeared upstairs.

*

As I tucked into the pancakes, I busied myself with my phone, scanning the e-mails that had come in since my sudden disappearance the previous afternoon.

After scrolling past a couple that could wait, there was one that practically leapt off the screen: from John E. Byers— "Jeb" to those who felt they could address him familiarly. Jeb Byers was the chief judge of the Fourth Circuit Court of Appeals in Richmond. Federal judges don't really have bosses, of course. But if we did, he would be my boss's boss.

As best as I understood, Byers came from one of those old Virginia families where most everyone who was not an evident success—a distinguished public servant, a wealthy businessperson, a boarding school headmaster—at least had the good breeding to revert to quiet shame and alcoholism.

We had met a handful of times. He almost never e-mailed me.

This one had the subject line "Conversation." I had a strong sense of foreboding even before I opened it.

"Judge Sampson," it read. "We need to have a conversation about *US vs. Skavron,* today if at all possible. Would you please suggest a few times when we might talk?" It was signed, "JEB."

I felt a spurt of anxiety. Judges, as a rule, did not initiate conversations about each other's opinions. Even the ludicrous ones. Yes, Judge Byers would likely head the three-judge panel that would reverse my decision in *United States vs. Skavron.* But he would do so without consulting my thoughts on the matter.

There was only one reason I could think he wanted to have this talk, and it was contained in the Judicial Conduct and Disability Act of 1980. Under that law, which regulated the care and handling of malfunctioning judges, all accusations of judicial misconduct were channeled through the chief judge of the circuit.

Most complaints came from convicted felons whose inventive imaginations were surpassed only by the time they had available to make spurious allegations, or from indignant lawyers whose chief grievance was that the judge in question hadn't ruled in their favor. The chief judge typically dispatched those so quickly they might as well never have existed.

But if the chief judge felt there was some smoke from a

complaint, with the possibility of fire beneath it, he began an inquiry. He usually started with a phone call to the accused judge, who would be given a chance to explain himself.

It was a codified politeness as much as anything, a nod to the venerated tradition of judges policing themselves.

It was also the first step in the impeachment process.

17

Throughout my forty-minute commute to Norfolk, I rehearsed various versions of the conversation I would need to have with Byers.

None of them went particularly well. By all rights, Skavron should have just now been settling in for a long stay with the US Bureau of Prisons. There was no question about his culpability, which had been settled the moment he pleaded guilty. There was, likewise, no dispute about the weight of the drugs he was found with, or his extensive criminal history, or any of the factors that might have impacted his punishment. Even his own attorney recommended a twelve-year sentence.

Every time I imagined Byers asking me my rationale for cutting loose such a scourge, I then had to imagine myself babbling and disseminating. Which would only lead Byers toward the conclusion I was sure he, and others, were already considering:

That I had been bought off.

What other possible explanation was there when a judge let an admitted drug dealer walk free?

Well, in this case, there was one other. The truth. But I couldn't tell him that. Not without kick-starting a potentially disastrous chain of events.

I was no closer to figuring out how I'd handle the mess when I arrived at the Walter E. Hoffman United States Courthouse, the impressive gray limestone monument to federal government hegemony where I work each day. As I entered the building, I made a supreme effort at projecting normalcy, trying to remember what I used to look like back when no one thought I was crooked and when I could take for granted that my daughter would be coming home at night.

As the stars of the small galaxy that is a federal courthouse, we judges are under constant—though strangely oblique— scrutiny. Most seasoned courthouse employees have absorbed enough legal education to be the equivalent of roughly two years of law school, so opinions about opinions are legion. When a judge makes a controversial decision, it sets the entire place abuzz.

The thing is, no one dares breathe a word to the judge directly. It's all sideways glances and whispers once they think you're out of earshot. People will talk about you, not at you, making the federal judiciary something like an eighth-grade lunchroom.

I hoped some of the gossips would give me the benefit of the doubt. I always tried to be affable with everyone at the courthouse. There are certainly judges who don't bother with such niceties. They make like divas, acting as if their jobs matter more than anyone else's, wearing their superciliousness with the same gravitas as they wear their robes.

Which I never fully understood. To me, all of us there— whether we were sweeping the floors or rendering the verdicts—were, on some level, merely fellow laborers at the justice factory. Each of us was needed to keep the assembly line running properly.

More to the point, we're all equal in the eyes of the law. And it has always struck me that a judge ought to act accordingly.

That meant smiling at folks. And calling them by name. And knowing as much about them as they did about me.

I can tell you, for example, that Ben Gardner, the amiable CSO who has stood guard at the employee entrance for roughly half a millennium, is an inveterate fan of University of Alabama football. I know that Hector Ruiz, the excitable janitor who cleans our floor, bursts with pride because his daughter is now in law school. I know that Tikka Jones, who works in the main clerk's office, enjoys when people compliment her hair, because she spends hours in the chair at her local salon, having it braided or having extensions put in.

Would any of those friendships, however superficial they were, matter now? Would they stick up for me? Or would they turn on me like everyone else?

It made merely walking through the doors and falsifying good cheer feel like an enormous undertaking. After my first "good morning" to Ben Gardner, I almost turned around and went home. It felt like I was betraying Emma, putting up this smiling front, making small talk about Alabama's defensive secondary. Somehow, I maintained the facade all the way through security, up the elevators, and to the door of my chambers.

My immediate staff consists of just five people. Their jobs are all intricately tethered. It results in a certain groupthink, to the point where the staff's mood tends to resemble a school of herring: multiple organisms that act as one.

Normally, they moved in easy concert. I was sure today they would be on edge. Whereas I was spared the direct frontal assault from the rumor mill, they would be a locus for all the incredulous questions and petty gossip the courthouse could churn out.

As I pushed through the door, I took a deep breath and put on my bravest face. They needed to see me looking confident and unbothered by all the spurious talk.

"Good morning, everyone, good morning." *Nod and smile.* "I'm fine, thank you, and you?" *Smile and nod.* "Give me twenty minutes; I just have to make one phone call."

I made it through the door to my office, which I closed behind me. I set down my briefcase, hung up my jacket, and took my phone off the hook to make it seem like I was on a call.

Then I collapsed in my chair and buried my face in my hands.

When I brought my head back up, my gaze fell on a framed picture we had taken of the twins at Busch Gardens two years earlier. They were four at that point, having recently mastered a host of new tricks—dressing themselves, peeing without being told, speaking in full and surprising sentences, etcetera—thus freeing their parents to enjoy them as the tiny human beings they were. It was glorious weather. Everyone was in a good mood. We reveled in train rides and ice cream and the Land of the Dragons kids' area.

The photo on my desk came from the merry-go-round. I caught them as they were whirling around from the far side. The angle was just right, with Sam barely ahead of Emma, exactly as it had been on the day of their birth. Their faces wore the pure, unadulterated joy of children having the time of their little lives. Their tiny hands gripped the poles; their spindly arms bravely battled the centrifugal forces.

A few of Emma's curly locks were flung out to the side as if they, too, had been caught in the exuberance. Sam was all wild-eyed, his mouth open in a yell.

It was when I studied Emma more closely that I noticed something I had never quite caught before. She wasn't looking off into the distance like Sam was. She was looking straight at Sammy. *Her* fun was based on the fact that *he* was having fun. That's how twins often go, of course: When one laughs, the other can't help but join in.

Except it wasn't that way now.

Now she was trapped in a tiny bedroom, shaved bald, her brother nowhere to be found. She had no one to laugh with, no one whose presence could reassure her. She was being held captive by people who did not value her life as anything other than a high-stakes bargaining chip.

She was utterly alone.

I turned away from the photo, then put it in a drawer, unable to bear looking at it any longer. After a trip to my private bathroom to splash cold water on my face, I returned to the office and put the phone back on the hook. It was time to face the world again, even though it was the last thing I wanted to do.

Then I realized I had received a text message. It was from the same 900 number that had texted me the day before. And it said:

Interesting article in the Journal today, don't you think?

18

I had, up until that moment, forgotten that *The New York Times* had called my chambers and *The Wall Street Journal* had sought comment about me from Senator Franklin.

Scrambling over to my computer, I Googled "Judge Scott Sampson Wall Street Journal." The top result was a story with the headline BIG PHARMA EYES TURN TO VIRGINIA COURTROOM.

It was about a patent infringement case called *Palgraff vs. ApotheGen*. The name of the man claiming his patent had been violated, Palgraff, meant nothing to me. The defendant, on the other hand, was instantly familiar: ApotheGen's products could be found in half the medicine cabinets in America.

The *Journal* called Palgraff "a heretofore little-noticed case, quietly filed in the Eastern District of Virginia, that has the potential to be the largest patent lawsuit in US history."

"Little-noticed" was an understatement. I had no memory of seeing it on the docket. This wasn't necessarily unusual. Cases typically didn't come to my attention until I had to make some kind of preliminary ruling on evidentiary matters; or, at the very least, until there was a meeting between the litigants and my staff. To the best of my knowledge, that hadn't happened yet.

The wheels in my head were already spinning so fast—a patent case? this was about a patent case?—I had to force myself to slow down and actually read the article. The dispute, I quickly learned, centered on the next generation of statins, the cholesterol medicine taken by roughly twenty-five million Americans, with many more to come as baby boomers aged. Statins diminished the body's ability to make LDL, the so-called bad cholesterol, while also clearing the way for a modest increase in HDL, the good stuff.

The future of statins involved something known as a PCSK9 inhibitor. Scientists had figured out that certain unlucky people with chokingly high cholesterol—the type of people who often had their first heart attacks in their thirties or forties, even though they were in otherwise good shape—had an abundance of the PCSK9 protein in their bodies.

On the flip side, a small group of people were born with a malfunctioning or severely hampered PCSK9 gene and therefore had little or no PCSK9 in their systems. They had shockingly low LDL levels and almost never suffered heart attacks, despite any number of other risk factors, from smoking to diabetes to obesity.

The science had become clear: If you could find a way to remove or reduce PCSK9 from the body, you could send LDL levels plummeting and all but eliminate the risk of heart disease, the number one killer in America.

This discovery set off a fevered race in the pharmaceutical industry. Companies were pouring millions into the effort and tooling up their factories so they were ready the moment their research teams shouted, "Eureka!"

ApotheGen claimed to have gotten there first, trademarking the drug as Prevalia. It was now in the final stages of clinical trials. FDA approval was expected within a few months.

The *Journal* called Prevalia "the next coming of Lipitor, the bestselling prescription drug in history with $125 billion in sales before it lost patent protection in 2011." Like Lipitor, Prevalia was projected to be a maintenance drug for millions of Americans, who would take it every day for as long as they lived. With a well-worded patent, the company was guaranteed twenty years of reaping billions from a legalized monopoly.

"The statin market had been all but dead to Big Pharma after the last generation of those drugs lost patent protection, leading to their manufacture as low-cost, low-margin generics," the *Journal* reported. "In Prevalia, ApotheGen could, with one little pill, not only reinvigorate the statin market but dominate it for a decade or more."

The company CEO, Barnaby Roberts, still thought it would. "This suit is wholly without merit and we will defend ourselves with all the legal resources we can muster," Roberts told the *Journal*. "The plaintiff is nothing more than a dreamer and gold digger. We are not going to let one man's frivolous fantasy stop us from bringing this lifesaving product to the marketplace."

The only mention of me was far down, toward the end. It chronicled my employment with Senator Blake Franklin and, of course, The Incident. It noted that my four years on the bench had not included any cases as prominent as this one.

"Scott Sampson is an outstanding judge who has proven himself to be very evenhanded," Blake was quoted as saying. "I have no doubt the verdict will be fair and just."

I remembered the conversation Blake and I had the previous day. When he asked me whether I was distracted because of a "drug case," I thought he meant *Skavron*. He assumed I knew he was talking about *ApotheGen*.

And, certainly, it was not a faulty assumption. If I had actually gone through with Karen's plan to systematically study my entire docket and look for a case that cried out for blackmail, it would have been hard to come up with a more fitting candidate.

Having completed the *Journal* article, I went next to HedgeofReason.com, the website whose reporter had called. According to Jeremy, it specialized in the down-and-dirty tabloid take.

I got that and more. Steve Politi's story was headlined NO APATHY ON APOTHEGEN: JUDGE IN MASSIVE PATENT LAWSUIT IMPRESSED WITH PLAINTIFF'S CLAIM.

The words were like a slap. I was impressed? How was that possible? Up until a few minutes earlier I hadn't even *heard* of the plaintiff's claim, much less been impressed by it.

I continued reading to learn that "a source close to Judge Scott Sampson" was saying I was "ready to rule for Palgraff" and that I was pushing ApotheGen to settle "given the near-inevitability of the plaintiff's chances of success."

This supposed "source" could only be Politi's own gift for fiction.

There was a burn starting in my stomach. I swore at the

computer screen. People were now going to be watching me even more closely, believing that I had a leak in my office and was sharing inappropriate thoughts with that leak, whispering things I shouldn't have been divulging to anyone. This at a time when I was already under scrutiny for the *Skavron* hearing.

Then it got worse. At the end of the post, there was an update, or, rather, an UPDATE!!!

"ApotheGen shares are down sharply on this news. ApoG started the day trading at $92.72 and is already down $6.44. That's seven percent, kids! Kudos to any of you who sold short!"

Politi didn't bother explaining the mechanics at work. As with all stocks, expectation was everything. ApotheGen had been valued in a manner that factored in Prevalia's anticipated success. Analysts were now troubled by the possibility of having to share that bounty. It galled me that the imaginary stories Politi was concocting were being used to gain and lose real money in the real world.

I was so angry at being grossly misrepresented—and yet was correspondingly so powerless to do anything about it without bringing more notice to myself and to this muck-mongering blog—I punched the monitor's off button, as if Politi himself could somehow feel the blow.

For a minute or two, I sat there, feeling hatred toward the man. Then I released the breath I had been holding and turned the monitor back on. Getting furious at a website would do nothing to help my daughter.

I also had one more story to check out, one that would

have a lot more eyeballs and influence. I went back to Google and typed "Judge Scott Sampson New York Times."

While the *Journal* focused on the financial implications of *Palgraff vs. ApotheGen*, the *Times* went for the human angle, casting the case as "a modern-day David and Goliath."

I knew all about Goliath already. David was Denny Palgraff, a self-employed chemist who drove an old station wagon that he converted to run on used vegetable oil, which he personally collected from restaurants in and around the central Pennsylvania town where he lived. A science prodigy, he applied for his first patent when he was thirteen. He graduated from college at seventeen and had his PhD by age twenty-one.

He went on to work in research and development for several pharmaceutical companies, but he chafed at their corporate strictures. Finally, he set off on his own, creating a home laboratory where he could try out his iconoclastic ideas without the meddling of bosses. When he felt he was close to a breakthrough, he often worked thirty-hour shifts.

Everything he came up with, he patented. He then tried to get companies interested in using his creations in products they brought to the marketplace.

His most successful patent to date had been an enzyme that was used to create hypoallergenic baby food. That gravy train had come to a stop two years ago. The company that had licensed the patent switched to another enzyme.

But while he was searching for a new jackpot, he came to realize he was already sitting on one. Six years earlier, he had been toying with the PCSK9 protein. Theorizing it might play a role in diabetes, he slapped together a PCSK9 inhibitor and quickly patented it. He turned out to be dead wrong about PCSK9's link to diabetes and forgot about it until Big Pharma's PCSK9 sweepstakes became news a few years earlier.

He might have stepped in and immediately declared himself the winner. Except Palgraff knew he didn't have a viable PCSK9 inhibitor as far as the marketplace was concerned. He had no idea how to mass-produce it and, besides, his version needed to be injected directly into the bloodstream. All he really had was a patent that said he was the first person to create a PCSK9 inhibitor. So he had just been lying in wait, ready to sue the first company that got its PCSK9 inhibitor into clinical trials.

In patent law, it doesn't matter how you intended your invention to be used. If you create something you envisioned as a butterfly net and someone else wants to market it for fishing, it's still your patent. When ApotheGen entered Phase III clinical trials—the large-scale testing of a drug that is its last step before receiving FDA approval—he went ahead with his lawsuit.

Midway down the article, there was a picture of Denny Palgraff, gazing at some faraway object through circular, John Lennon–style glasses. His long gray hair was held back in a ponytail and his beard went down to his chest, beneath which his stomach protruded.

Palgraff was not interviewed for the story. The only quotes came from his attorney, Roland Hemans, a partner with Cranston & Hemans in Chesapeake. It was a roughly fifty-lawyer firm that specialized in patent law and filed most of its cases in the Eastern District of Virginia because of the rocket docket. Generally speaking, plaintiffs in a patent case liked things to move fast.

"We're very pleased that Mr. Palgraff's discovery will help millions of people stave off the ravages of heart disease," Hemans said. "But ApotheGen cannot bring this drug to the marketplace while conveniently ignoring the simple fact that Mr. Palgraff got there first."

The *Times* did not interview the ApotheGen CEO. It went, instead, with a canned quote from a spokesperson: "ApotheGen categorically denies any patent infringement and plans to vigorously defend itself against this spurious claim. There will be no settlement."

They were the last words of the article, and my eyes rested on them as they churned in my head.

There will be no settlement.

Which is why someone reverts to the desperate measure that is kidnapping a child. Because they know it's the only way to ensure the outcome they desire.

The enormity of my situation was now pounding me in hurricane-force waves of understanding. This was a massive case, with billions of dollars—to say nothing of the future of heart disease—at stake. It was, personally and professionally, the most consequential matter that would ever appear in my courtroom.

A multitude of news-gathering organizations, from niche websites to the largest media outlets, would be monitoring every step of the process. The country would be watching.

The world would be watching.

That huge audience would expect me to be the impartial, cool-headed arbiter; the robe-wearing symbol of authority; His Honor the judge, firmly at the helm.

Yet I wasn't really in control of anything. The kidnappers had already proven their dominion over something as small as which way I parted my hair. If they ordered me to appear in court naked, I'd have to do that too. I was a puppet, with unseen hands yanking my invisible strings.

And if I failed to respond properly to just one little twitch, it could cost my daughter her life.

*

For a while I was so paralyzed by the size of the thing confronting me—and so daunted by the task of facing it— all I did was sit in my chair with my arms wrapped around me. I wasn't sure I could get up anyway. My legs were too weak.

I tried to remember a meditation from a long-ago yoga class but found I was too nauseated to concentrate on my breathing; and my mind, which I was supposed to be trying to clear, was like a crowded intersection at rush hour, hopelessly jammed, with far too many ideas trying to push through it at once.

If I allowed myself to think about Emma—and how, for whatever I was experiencing, she was having it ten times worse—I feared I would be incapacitated altogether.

Instead, I focused on Alison.

I thought of her attacking a pile of wood, achieving catharsis one swing at a time. I thought about how strong she had been that morning, of the effort she was exerting for our family, of how she was refusing to surrender. She was surely having all the same dreads and doubts yet was still summoning the resources to move on.

My eyes went to another picture that was framed on my desk. It was my favorite picture of my wife from our wedding day. It wasn't the traditional bride-and-bouquet pose. She was sitting in front of a mirror, getting ready. It was shot from behind, but someone must have just called her name or said hello, because she had turned toward whoever called out. The camera caught half her face directly. The other half was reflected in the mirror. Both halves showed, from slightly different perspectives, this incredible hope and optimism on her face. Here on her wedding day, the first day of the rest of her life, the future was boundless and wonderful.

The woman in that photo could conquer anything. Surely, the man she chose to marry could do the same.

Compelling my arms back up to my computer, I clicked off my browser and went over to the case-management system to see what I could learn about *Palgraff vs. ApotheGen* that was not already in two large newspapers and one irresponsible website.

It was scheduled for a Rule 16B Conference on Monday. That, finally, was a piece of good news. It meant the case was further along than I thought.

There are several steps that precede a Rule 16B Conference—none of which happen under my purview, which was why the case hadn't hit my radar screen yet. Obviously, a complaint had been filed by Palgraff. It had then been answered by ApotheGen. Next, the parties' lawyers had convened on their own for a Rule 26F Conference, where they began to discuss what was in dispute (usually everything) and what they agreed about (usually nothing). They also tried to reach an accord on what they would disclose to each other as part of discovery: what documents and computer files they would turn over, who would be made available for depositions, and so on.

Then it was on to the Rule 16B, where a schedule for trial would be set. I usually let Jeremy Freeland and Jean Ann Sanford take care of those details. Big patent cases typically took a year, even with the rocket docket.

The specter of Emma being away from us that long was sickening.

My arms still felt leaden as I scrolled through the complaint, then the answer. I already knew where the case was heading. Patent cases like this one often hinged on something called a Markman hearing.

The term comes from a landmark Supreme Court decision in the mid-1990s, a case called *Markman vs. Westview Instruments*. The question before the Court was whether the scope of a patent was a matter of law or fact. It's an important distinction because within our legal system, juries decide matters of fact (did the accused kill the guy?), while judges decide matters of law (is it legal to kill someone?).

In *Markman*, the Supreme Court ruled that patents

are essentially laws that guarantee inventors the right to exclusively sell their products for a given period of time. Therefore, a judge must interpret what is or isn't covered by an individual patent. Each side tries to convince the judge how to construe a certain set of claims, essentially tutoring the judge on their way of thinking.

The judge's decision, now known as a Markman determination, has a huge impact on the rest of the case—often ending it, for all practical purposes. If the determination goes in favor of the plaintiff, there is a settlement. No sane defense lawyer would let his client go to trial under those circumstances, where the client was almost guaranteed to lose and lose badly.

If the Markman determination is favorable to the defendant, on the other hand, the plaintiff sometimes simply gives up, realizing the case is now facing an extremely expensive, likely unwinnable battle.

The good news, for me and for Emma, was that the Markman hearing happened early in the process, well before the trial date.

The battle lines were now clear to me. Both sides were convinced of their righteousness. Both had what they felt were compelling arguments. Both desperately needed me to decide in their favor, and one had gone to drastic measures to make it happen.

But which one?

It wasn't much of a stretch to cast the big, bad pharmaceutical company as that kind of evil entity. In a corporation as large as ApotheGen, there were probably any number of people, from the CEO on down, who would feel enormous pressure to ensure the unimpeded successes of a vital new product.

I hunched back toward my computer and, after a few keystrokes, found Roberts' *Wikipedia* entry. He was English, with degrees from Oxford and Cambridge on his résumé. The picture with the entry showed a grandfatherly sort with snow-white hair, though it was still cut like that of the British schoolboy he had once been. He had been ApotheGen's CEO for twenty years, which made him one of the longest-tenured chief executives in the Fortune 500.

He hardly looked like a kidnapper. But he surely hadn't lasted so long without being a strong, decisive leader, the kind who could anticipate problems and address them proactively. With the stock in a tumble, I could imagine the company's largest shareholders calling him in a panic, demanding, *What are you going to do about this, Mr. Roberts?* And he would assure them, *Don't worry, I've got it under control.*

And then he would contact whatever trusted lieutenant had arranged the abduction of my children, just to make sure all was going to plan.

On the other side, it was a little harder to envision Denny Palgraff—the bearded scientist bungling along in the vegetable oil–fueled station wagon—as a would-be kidnapper.

His lawyer, however? Well. I can't say I fell easily into believing the stereotype of the sleazy lawyer, because so many of the attorneys who appeared in my courtroom were honorable people. Yet there was no doubting the type existed. A one-third share of a multibillion-dollar fortune, which awaited the plaintiff's attorney in a case like this, was temptation enough for anyone.

I didn't know Roland Hemans and he had never appeared in my courtroom, so I set my Internet browser to work on him. There was no *Wikipedia* entry, but I did find a profile of him in *Virginia Lawyers Weekly,* with two pictures of him alongside.

In one, he filled up the doorframe of his law office. He was a giant, at least six foot eight. He had ebony skin, bushy black eyebrows, and an enormous hairless head. His shirtsleeves were rolled up to reveal sinewy forearms. He was pure alpha male, and he stared down on the camera like it was one more thing he was looking to dominate.

In the other, he had his arm around his wife, a woman who was as rotund as he was muscular.

According to the article, he had played basketball for the University of Virginia in the eighties and claimed to have entertained an offer to play professionally in Europe, which he turned down in favor of law school. His sporting passion turned to golf, and he once came within two strokes of qualifying for the US Open.

As a lawyer, he had long specialized in patent law and had gained a reputation for taking on complex, highly technical cases and translating them into language that lay judges and juries could understand.

"When I played basketball, I was fortunate to have outstanding coaches," he was quoted as saying. "They were really teachers. They could explain their concepts in a way that made sense, so the players couldn't help but buy into the system. A trial is the same thing. I'm coaching the jury to buy in."

There were a few personal details. In addition to his wife, he had two teenage children; he lived in Newport News; his vacations consisted of hunting and fishing trips. Mostly, the story was a chronicling of his many courtroom triumphs. The Virginia Black Attorneys Association had named him their Lawyer of the Year a few years earlier.

But it was a funny thing. While it was a glowing article, I could feel Roland Hemans' yearning for something more: He played college ball but wasn't good enough for the NBA; he could beat anyone at the country club, but the pros had him by a few strokes; even his legal victories, while solid, had this not-quite-there feel to them.

Now here he was, finally, after many years of hard work, poised over a huge score, one that would put him in the big leagues for all time.

Would a guy like that pull out all the stops?

Oh yes.

Yes, he would.

I would keep an eye on Barnaby Roberts. But in Roland Hemans, I felt like I had my man.

19

I was just settling in to learn more about Hemans when Joan Smith rang me from the next room.

"Yes, Mrs. Smith," I said.

"Judge, I'm sorry to bother you, but it's Judge Byers' chambers calling from Richmond. He wants to know if you're available to talk right now."

My anxiety surged. I had yet to have one useful thought about how I would explain my utterly inexplicable ruling to the chief judge of the circuit.

And yet there was no putting the man off further. He had e-mailed me. And now, having not gotten an immediate response, he was calling. He would not be denied. I probably wouldn't have been either if I thought one of the judges in my district was on the take.

The weakness I had felt before was back. Except now, instead of just hitting my legs, it was affecting my whole body. Even the phone seemed too heavy.

"Judge, are you there?"

"Yes. Yes, of course. Put him through," I said.

"Okay. Hold on, please."

Mrs. Smith went away from the line and I waited for Byers. Most of what I knew about the man came from rumor and Google. He was a former federal prosecutor who was now known as a judge's judge, one who stuck up for the sanctity of the position and battled fiercely for judicial independence. An avowed enemy of mandatory minimums, he once famously testified before a congressional subcommittee that they turned judges into "punishment-dispensing vending machines." He was bright, straightforward, and well respected in all corners of the federal judiciary.

"Hello, Judge Sampson. Thank you for taking my call," he said in a voice well suited to a Vuh-ginia gentleman.

"My pleasure, Judge Byers," I said, trying to affect an external calm with my voice that I absolutely did not feeling internally. "What can I do for you today?"

"I sent you an e-mail last night. I'm not sure if you had a chance to—"

"I saw it. I was actually just about to call you."

"Well, thank you. I'm hoping you can maybe . . . ," he started, then changed course. "Now, look, I understand better than most that a judge often has explanations for his decisions that are not obvious to the lay public or to anyone who isn't . . . privy to all the things we're privy to. So I was hoping you could walk me through your thinking with this *Skavron* case."

God bless him. Byers' respect for a judge's dominion over his own courtroom was so complete, he still couldn't bring himself to directly challenge my ruling.

"Certainly," I said. "Can I ask why you're asking?"

It sounded every bit as defensive as it was.

"Well, yes, of course. I . . . There was apparently a father who made a statement at the sentencing yesterday, a father who—"

"Thomas Byrd," I said, because his performance was not easily forgotten.

"Yes, that's right. Thomas Byrd. Well, it seems Mr. Byrd is rather well connected at Norfolk Academy. He's on the board of trustees and whatnot. And it seems his son—"

"Dylan."

"Yes, right, Dylan. It seems Dylan was a popular boy at Norfolk Academy, and one of the boys he was friends with is the son of Michael Jacobs."

I nearly dropped the phone. Michael Jacobs, I did not need to be told, was a Republican representing the Second District of Virginia in the United States Congress. He was cut from the pugnacious, blunt-talking, take-no-prisoners cloth that had taken over the House. He was an ex–Marine sergeant from the Midwest who settled in the area after his enlistment was up and made a bundle of money on a chain of car washes. He was relentlessly pro-defense and pro-veteran, important stances in a highly competitive district where no small portion of the electorate was current or former military. He burnished his everyman image by shaving his head bald and riding to campaign events on his Harley.

"The boys were on the same baseball teams growing up and it seems the fathers were close as well," Byers said. "I think it's fair to say your ruling, ah, significantly angered Mr. Byrd. He put in a call to Congressman Jacobs, who immediately called his good friend Congressman Keesee."

I felt myself shrinking further. Neal Keesee, also Republican, was the chair of the House Judiciary Committee. The Constitution has any number of checks against judicial power built into it. Keesee was one of the biggest ones going. All recommendations from the US Judicial Conference about impeachment went through him.

"And then Keesee called me to make sure this matter received my full attention," Byers said. "Now, of course, I don't want you or anyone to get the idea that I would allow the politics of the situation to influence the process or enter into my thinking."

"No, of course not," I said. Even though we both knew that was a lie.

"And I should stress that, at this point, this is just a preliminary inquiry," he said in that way people did when it was evident something much more than preliminary would soon follow. "But that doesn't change that, at least outwardly, there would seem to be . . . I'm sorry, I should say, that some further explanation might help everyone understand what happened here. I was hoping you could give me the insider's perspective on this thing."

"Right," I said, still trying to absorb this new information.

Jacobs and Keesee were powerful enemies. And Byers was now my primary line of defense against them. Under the aforementioned Judicial Conduct and Disability Act, the chief judge alone decides whether to pursue a complaint by forming a special investigative committee—which is basically a Spanish Inquisition performed by a team of judges. The committee forwards its recommendation to the

US Judicial Conference, also comprised of judges, which votes whether to send it to Congress.

Or the chief judge could dismiss the matter. Which was the outcome I badly needed. I just had to come up with some kind of story that would push enough of the man's buttons.

"Well, I realize it was an unusual ruling," I said in an effort to start convincing Byers I hadn't lost my grasp on reality. "And it's not something I intend to make a habit of. I've never . . . I can't think of another time when I've deviated from the guidelines so much. So I understand the attention this is generating. And . . . How many years have you been doing this, Jeb?"

It may have been slightly overfamiliar, slipping his nickname into the flow. But I had to establish that we were pals. And colleagues.

"I think in October it'll be twenty-two."

"And in those twenty-two years, did you ever just get a feeling on the bench? Just a feeling deep in your gut about someone or something?"

"Of course."

"Well, then maybe you can understand what happened to me yesterday. I know from the outside it wouldn't seem to make much sense. I just . . . I was looking at this defendant"—I didn't want to use his name, lest it seem like I was overly invested—"and I was really moved by his . . . his earnestness. He said some things that—"

I interrupted myself, because it occurred to me Byers might look up the transcript and see just how pathetic Skavron's elocution had been.

"It wasn't so much what he said as the way he said it," I continued. "There was . . . I can't explain it. There was real sincerity in the man, Jeb. I felt like if he just had one more chance to get it right he'd—"

This was sounding flimsy even to me. I needed it to get better in a hurry.

"Look, I realize the man has had a lot of chances already. But there was something about him that was really striking in how closely it reminded me of . . . Well, he reminded me of someone in my past, someone who took a second chance and really did something with it."

"And who was that?" Byers asked.

"Oh, it doesn't matter."

"Well, now, I think maybe it does. This is just the sort of thing that people don't always understand about what we do, about how something that can seem impersonal can really become quite personal."

Byers was clearly engaged. I could practically feel him leaning into the phone. This was my chance to lay it on thick. *No one understands how hard this job is sometimes, Jeb. We judges, we're people, not vending machines.*

"Well, it was a long time ago. It was a young man I worked with. This was when I was in Senator Franklin's office, before the shooting," I began, trying to wring whatever mileage I could out of my tragic past, which Byers would certainly be aware of. "The senator encouraged us to be active in the community whenever possible, and I was volunteering as a mentor with the Boys & Girls Club. There was a young man they teamed me with—"

"What was his name?" Byers asked.

My mind was momentarily blank. I opened a file that had been sitting on the corner of my desk. It was some kind of class action complaint. The first name listed among the plaintiffs was "Acton, Keith."

"Keith," I said.

The second name was "Bloomenthal, Rodney."

"Keith Bloom," I continued. "He was . . . he was a very good athlete, a football player, but he came from one of those neighborhoods in Anacostia where young men face a lot of challenges. He had gotten himself in some trouble with the police—and he was eighteen, so he wasn't a juvenile anymore. Keith and I talked a lot about what had happened and he understood the seriousness of it. I convinced Keith to spill his heart to the judge who was doing the sentencing. I think it was clear to everyone that this was the moment where life was going to go one way or another for Keith. And the judge, he . . . he showed Keith some mercy, even when the guidelines said he shouldn't. Keith was able to go on and get a college scholarship for football. He's now a math teacher and a high school football coach, making a difference in the lives of kids just like him, doing a lot of good. And I guarantee you, if he had ended up going to prison—"

"He would have learned some very different skills than he did in college," Byers interjected.

"Well, exactly. But that judge, he didn't just see another troubled young black man in front of him. He saw a man of great potential. And Keith ended up vindicating that confidence the judge showed in him. I think most of the time, I don't . . . I don't see a lot of Keith Blooms in my courtroom. But yesterday, I saw something in this defendant. His whole family was in court with him. He had been working steadily at the time of his arrest. I got this feeling that if I gave him a chance, he would end up vindicating that decision in the same way Keith did."

"So you'd say it was a matter of conscience?"

"Yes, exactly. A deeply personal one."

Clearly moved by the story, with several of his buttons firmly pressed, Byers voiced his approval until I was confident he didn't plan on taking any immediate action against me.

As we said our polite good-byes and hung up, I considered the events I had just set in motion.

It was possible the chief judge of the circuit, now convinced of my good intentions, would run interference for me until Michael Jacobs and Neal Keesee tired of this cause and went elsewhere to find a new chew toy. If that was the case, I had just dodged a hail of bullets: I would get to keep my judgeship long enough to deliver the ruling that would save Emma's life.

It was also possible Byers would discover Keith Bloom was one hundred percent fiction.

In which case every one of those bullets would hit me right between the eyes.

I didn't even try to make it to the bathroom. I simply pulled the wastebasket under my chin and vomited until my stomach was empty.

20

Perhaps half an hour later, having done my best to clean up both the remnants of my purge and the acid it left behind in my mouth, I was still sagging in my chair, completely enervated, when I heard a soft knock.

It wasn't Joan Smith—her knock was much more forceful. And there was only one other person in our little suite who felt entitled to disturb me when my door was closed. So I said, "Come in, Jeremy."

Jeremy Freeland came into my office, hiding behind an enigmatic smile.

"Sorry to bother you," he said. "There's just been so much going on, I wanted to check in, see how you were doing."

"Thanks," I said, hoping he couldn't smell any of the sickness lingering in the air. "Please, sit down."

He complied, crossing his legs and folding his hands on his knee.

"I heard Judge Byers was calling for you," he said.

He tossed it out in a typically coy, noncommittal fashion. Jeremy had surely done the math—controversial decision plus call from the chief judge equals trip to the woodshed—and wanted to see how much of his boss's hide was left.

"We had a nice chat," I said. Then, just to sate Jeremy's curiosity a little, I added, "He wanted to talk to me about the *Skavron* sentencing, of course. We discussed how we follow the guidelines most of the time, but every once in a great while there comes a decision from deep within our gut that really catches us by surprise. *Skavron* was one of those for me."

I could tell Jeremy wanted to ask why, but his sense of decorum forbade it. And I was thankful I didn't have to repeat the Keith Bloom story. The more people tugging at the strings of a lie like that, the more quickly it would unravel.

Jeremy moved on, instead, to what was clearly his larger concern. "You think Byers understood where you were coming from?" he asked.

Translation: Is the trouble over, or should I start putting out my résumé?

"He's been doing this a long time now. He's had a few *Skavron*s in his time."

"Well, that's good," Jeremy said. "Shifting topics, I take it you saw those articles about *Palgraff* this morning?"

I nodded.

"Including that investing website?"

Now I was rolling my eyes. "God. That thing."

"Oh. So that's not—"

"Jeremy. Don't tell me you thought that was legit."

"Well, I mean, I know *you* didn't talk to him. But I thought maybe you, I don't know, accidentally let something slip around someone else or . . ."

Lord help me. If my own clerk thought it was possible HedgeofReason's post was based on real information, what did everyone else think?

"Absolutely not," I said firmly. "Whatever that man reported was a figment of his imagination. I didn't know the case existed until this morning."

"Yeah, about that. I'm so sorry I let it sneak up on you like that," he said. "I had seen it on the docket but I didn't realize it was such a big deal or I would have—"

I help up a traffic-cop hand to stop him. "Not your fault. You were still one step ahead of me. I hadn't even seen it on the docket."

"It's just, you see patent case, you see Cranston & Hemans, you think, 'Ho hum, here comes another one.' If I had even realized it was Roland Hemans I would have stopped and looked at it a little more carefully."

The moment he said the name "Hemans" it pricked my curiosity. Sensing an opening to learn more about the man, I said, "Oh, have you worked with him before?"

"He had an appeal with us in Richmond a few years back. I was going to look it up this morning just so I could remember the details a little better. That was . . . six, eight years ago?"

"What did you think of him?"

"He was fine, I guess."

"I saw pictures of him in *Virginia Lawyers Weekly.* He looks like he's huge."

"Yeah, he's a big one, all right."

"What else? I'm just trying to get to know the personalities involved here."

Jeremy hefted a sigh. "It's been a while, but . . . I guess you could say he's pretty aggressive about going after what he wants. I mean, what plaintiff's lawyer isn't? And obviously he likes to use the press as a weapon. But I guess you've seen that by now."

"True," I said, then paused, because I wasn't sure how to word the question I really wanted to ask. I came up with: "Based on what you've seen of him, do you think he would ever do anything . . . unethical to win a case?"

Jeremy's face squeezed as he contemplated the question.

"Oh, I don't know," he said. "I mean, he'll push things right up to the line. But he's also smart enough to never cross it. Are you . . . worried about something in particular?"

"No, no. Nothing specific. I was just—"

I stopped myself because Jeremy was biting his lower lip. It was a nervous tic of his.

"What's wrong?" I said. "Something on your mind?"

There was more lip biting. "Is it okay if I speak honestly with you for a second? Not like judge and career clerk but like Scott and Jeremy?"

"Of course."

He looked up at the ceiling, then down at the floor, then finally blurted it out:

"I was wondering if you would recuse yourself from this case."

It was such an unusual request and I was so taken aback, I just sat there for a moment. Jeremy had never begged off a case before, never expressed the slightest preference about my caseload one way or another. He took on everything— the big ones, the small ones, the ones you couldn't even categorize—with the same cheerful determination.

All I could manage was: "Why?"

"I just . . . I have a bad feeling about this one."

So did I. More than he could ever know.

"Can you be more specific?" I asked.

"Not really."

"But is it . . . a conflict of interest you're worried about?" I pressed. "Or something about the merits of the case or—"

"No. No."

"The publicity, then?"

"Well, a little. I just . . . I have a bad feeling and . . . Especially after the *Skavron* ruling and Judge Byers calling, and I . . . There's talk in the courthouse that Harley-riding pig Michael Jacobs has put Neal Keesee on the warpath against you. Is that . . . is that true?"

There was no point in denying it. "Yes. But as I told you, I think Byers is going to go to bat for me. So I wouldn't worry about it too much."

"Even still, I feel like we need less attention on us, not more. Let's just give everything with *Skavron* a chance to blow over before we take on something big like this. No one would think any less of you if you recused yourself. You could say you weren't comfortable with the science and you felt like another judge would handle it better. There's a Rule Sixteen on Monday. Now would be the right time to get rid of it, before we've gone down the road too much."

I leaned back and studied him. It was such an odd request. Clerks didn't ask judges to recuse themselves from cases because they felt vaguely queasy about the publicity surrounding them.

He fixed me with a blue-eyed stare: "Please. It would mean a lot to me."

"Okay. I'll think about it," I lied.

"Thank you. Thank you so much."

I smiled at him as he rose from his seat, feeling empty again. Jeremy had been nothing but loyal to me during the four years we had worked together. And I could neither grant his request nor be honest about why.

As he departed the room, I began composing an e-mail telling him I respected him and valued our working relationship but that I couldn't shirk what I felt like was my judicial duty. I set the message to go out at 8:37 the next morning.

That way it would at least look like I had slept on it.

*

About half an hour later, there was another knock on my door. This time, it was a Joan Smith knock.

Mrs. Smith was a fastidious lady who never met a blouse she couldn't button all the way up to her neck. Her husband had left her many years earlier, long before we started working together, and her children were grown and off in other cities. Whenever I asked about her weekend, she usually told me about her pastor's sermon. If she was in a good mood, you might hear her humming a gospel tune her choir had sung that weekend.

She had been my judicial assistant since the day I was sworn in, yet she had never once called me by my first name, despite my repeated entreaties that she do so. I think, as far as she was concerned, my first name *was* "Judge." I eventually surrendered my efforts to entice her into more familiar address, but I did even the score in my own way: If I was always going to be Judge Sampson, she was going to be Mrs. Smith.

So I answered her knock with, "Come in, Mrs. Smith."

"I just thought you'd want to know there was a filing in *Palgraff*," she said. "It's an emergency motion for preliminary injunction from the plaintiff."

I felt a jolt the moment she said "Palgraff" but tried not to show my alarm. "Thank you," I said.

"Would you like me to print it out for you?"

"No, I'll just read it on-screen. But thank you."

She left without another word, closing the door behind her.

Since this was an emergency filing, I would be expected to respond within hours. My first instinct was to call in Jeremy, because I almost always consulted him about this sort of thing. But I couldn't now. He would use this as another reason why I should shove the entire case off on another judge.

I was on my own to ponder how it fit into the larger picture and what it told me about the strategy being pursued by the plaintiff.

The timing was certainly curious. Hemans could have easily filed for a preliminary injunction when he submitted his original complaint.

Instead, he waited. Perhaps it was an attempt to ratchet

up the pressure for a settlement. His first move had been to file the complaint. His next was to leak it to the newspapers. Now here was another arrow from his quiver: the request for injunctive relief. If it was successful, it would send the stock tumbling even further, bringing Barnaby Roberts into more shareholders' crosshairs.

All of which suggested Hemans might not be responsible for the kidnapping. Why attempt to force a settlement when you knew you had the judge dancing at the end of your marionette strings?

What I didn't fully understand was why ApotheGen hadn't already settled. Why not just dangle fifty million bucks in front of Denny Palgraff's face and be done with this? Because, really, to a Fortune 500 company like ApotheGen, fifty million dollars was little more than a third-quarter write-off that would be forgotten by Christmastime.

And yet that hadn't happened. Perhaps because a few select people at ApotheGen knew they had the judge firmly under their control.

As I scanned the document, I saw Barnaby Roberts had, perhaps unwittingly, supplied Hemans with some of his fodder. One of the claims contained a portion of the CEO's quote from the *Journal*: "We are not going to let one man's frivolous fantasy stop us from bringing this lifesaving product to the marketplace."

That was the basis for requiring emergency relief: The defendant, by his own admission, fully intended to continue infringing on the plaintiff's patent.

By granting a preliminary injunction, a judge is saying

there is some probability of success on the merits of the case. It's a tip of the hand from the judge, a sign to all parties that the plaintiff has a fairly valid claim.

I was just getting wound up to go through all the case filings—and actually consider those merits—when I stopped myself. I had a duty as a judge, yes.

But my duty as a father was far greater.

The last thing I wanted to do was grant the injunction. Without knowing which side had Emma, I had to stick with the basic assumption that ruling for the plaintiff would make ApotheGen more likely to settle. And a settlement would render the judge—and therefore the judge's child—a moot point.

There was no point in pondering the matter further. With clear eyes and steady hands, I began crafting my denial of Roland Hemans's request.

I was nearing completion when I felt my phone buzz. It was the 900 number:

Grant the motion for an injunction at exactly 3 p.m. or someone is going to get stabbed in the eyeball.

21

The younger brother had been stuck at level 28 for several hours. And now, having broken through to level 29, he was lost in the challenge of conquering a new foe.

It was after lunchtime when the older brother walked into the kitchen and, his hands on his hips, peered down with a scowl.

"Has it been too quiet in there?" he asked.

"She's probably sleeping," the younger murmured.

"When is the last time you heard from her?"

"Maybe an hour," he lied. It had been several. "She was crying for a while. But it finally stopped."

The older brother looked toward the door to the little girl's bedroom. "We should check on her."

Neither man moved.

Finally, the older brother, shaking his head, walked over to the door. He thumbed the lock, which had been switched to his side—its goal being not to keep people out of the bedroom but to keep the occupant in. He swung the door open.

The room was dark, as usual. He didn't see the little girl anywhere. He knew she couldn't escape. There were only two ways out: the door, which was locked, and the window, which was painted shut. Besides, if the window had opened, the alarm would have sounded.

Then he heard something. A soft wheezing sound. Coming from the other side of the bed.

The older brother illuminated the flashlight on his phone and crossed the room in three long strides. The little girl was flat on the floor. Her face was red and blotchy. Her eyes were swollen almost entirely shut.

He called out to his younger brother, who soon joined him in gawking at her.

"What did you do to her?" the older asked.

"Nothing. It was probably that," he said, pointing to the peanut butter sandwich, still on the dresser but not untouched. The crusts had been torn off. He added, unnecessarily, "I think she's allergic."

The older brother bent down over the girl and listened to her labored breathing.

"She needs a doctor," the younger said.

"Not a chance."

"But what if—"

"If she lives, she lives."

"If she dies?"

"It won't change things. We can still offer proof of life."

The younger brother seemed confused, so the older added, "You can cut the fingers off a dead child just the same as you can a live one."

22

It was getting hard to keep my thoughts straight, and this latest dictate had only disoriented me further. Whoever had my daughter already knew they were going to get the end ruling they desired. Why bother granting an injunction? Why manipulate any of the intermediate steps between now and the Markman determination?

As I typed up the new decision, I felt like my head wasn't quite attached to my shoulders. I finished with about an hour to spare before I had to file and, with a desire to ground myself in something that felt more real than this game of legal ping-pong I was trying to play with myself, I called Alison.

"Hey," she said, in a hushed tone that told me she was likely somewhere in public.

"Hey. I was just calling to check in. How's it going?"

"Good," she said, then hastened to correct herself: "I mean, you know."

"Yeah. Believe me."

"We're just at the Living Museum."

"How's Sammy doing?"

"He's fine," she said.

"That's good. Can I say hi to him real quick?"

"Uh, you could, but I actually don't know where he is right now."

"What do you m—"

"Relax," she said quickly. "He's with Jenny and Karen. I'm just in that little cafeteria by the entrance, grabbing some coffee."

"Oh, okay. Sorry."

"It's fine. Everything's fine."

"Are you in a spot where you can talk?"

"Yeah. What's up?"

She didn't know about *Palgraff vs. ApotheGen* yet. So, over the next fifteen minutes or so, I filled her in. She listened well and asked questions, only some of which I could answer. She clearly wasn't giving up on the notion that Justina had something to do with it. But, at the same time, she didn't dispute the notion that Roland Hemans was also a highly likely suspect.

I finished by telling her about the injunction, though I left out any mention of eyeball stabbing. It was bad enough one of us had to know about that.

"So you're going to file your response at three?" she asked.

"Yeah. It's already written," I assured her. "I'll just be watching the clock between now and then."

"There's a group of moms who just walked in," she said, lowering her tone even further. "I have to go."

"Got it," I said. "Love you."

In a louder, false-cheerful voice, she finished the conversation with: "Love you too, honey. See you at home tonight."

As promised, I kept scrupulous tabs on the clock for

the remainder of the hour. The moment my phone's screen changed from 2:59 to 3:00, I sent the motion to the clerk's office.

No more than fifteen minutes later, Mrs. Smith alerted me that Steve Politi at HedgeofReason was calling. I told her I would, of course, have no comment. But before I left the courthouse that afternoon, I logged on to HedgeofReason. com to learn what I was supposedly thinking about the Palgraff case.

Sure enough, the lead item was headlined: JUDGE SLAMS ApoG IN PATENT LAWSUIT.

"As you first read here on HedgeofReason, the judge in the blockbuster *Palgraff vs. ApotheGen* case has it out for the defendant," it began. "And now we have the proof: Federal District Court Judge Scott Sampson has granted Palgraff's request for a preliminary injunction. It's another sign pointing in the direction of the plaintiff, and that could end up costing ApotheGen billions. With a *B*. Yes, kids, it is time to sell, sell, sell!"

So there it was again. Steve Politi asserting I was pro-plaintiff, something he couldn't possibly know, since I didn't know it myself.

I considered the possibility that Politi really *did* have a source, someone who was close to me, someone who could convince Politi I was whispering in his or her ear. But who could that possibly be?

Jeremy? It couldn't be. Jeremy wanted me to drop the case altogether.

Mrs. Smith? I couldn't begin to fathom her motive.

One of the law clerks? That seemed unlikely. What reporter would believe a lowly law clerk had access to a judge's inner thoughts?

It left me with the same conclusion I had reached before—that this source was Politi's own invention—and the same indignant burn that not only was this charlatan misrepresenting me, but everyone in the free world seemed to be believing him.

The UPDATE! confirmed it. ApotheGen stock had slid another three dollars and seventy cents. This was on top of losses it had already suffered. All told, it was down more than twelve dollars from its fifty-two-week high, which was posted shortly before the lawsuit became public.

There were 578 comments on the post. I looked at only the first few. They were by users thanking Steve Politi for his quick and incisive reporting and bragging that they had either gotten out before the slide or had contracts for short sales that were growing more valuable by the day.

I shut off my screen, disgusted, and snarled a few choice words at Politi and his readership. It felt like they were feasting on misery—mine and others'. For every investor making free money off these fake revelations, there was someone being cheated.

On my way out of my chambers, I mumbled my good-bye to Mrs. Smith. At the exit to the building, I skipped the mindless football talk I would have normally exchanged with Ben Gardner and got my car pointed in the direction of the farm.

I was just past the Hampton Roads Bridge-Tunnel, still slogging through a halting procession on Interstate 64, when my phone rang. It gave me a start, and I was relieved when I saw FRANKLIN.

"Good afternoon, Senator."

"Good afternoon, Judge," he returned. "Am I interfering with important judicial matters?"

"Not unless I've started hearing cases on Interstate Sixty-four."

"Ah, good, good . . . Heck of a story in the *Journal* today."

"Yeah. Thanks for the quote."

"You're welcome. I thought about telling them you beat up orphans for sport, but I decided to keep that between us."

"I appreciate that."

"So this thing has a real shot, huh?"

"Oh, I don't know," I said, and didn't add more. I knew he was just making harmless conversation, but it wasn't proper for me to share my thoughts about *Palgraff* with anyone. Not even the Honorable Blake Franklin.

"Well, you granted the injunction, didn't you? I saw it on the Bloomberg wire just now."

"Yeah, well," was all I said, because I didn't have any other words.

"Barnaby Roberts must be crapping a golden brick."

"You know him?"

"A little. He's testified before HELP a couple times."

HELP was the Senate's Health, Education, Labor &

Pensions Committee, of which Blake was a part. It was something of an unwieldy amalgam of topics, but I had always enjoyed the work I did with it for that exact reason.

"What's your impression of him?" I asked.

"Well, he's a CEO. Aren't they all the same? He's a megalomaniac who will try to rob you blind, usually while he's patting you on the back and smiling."

"Noted."

"Anyhow, I didn't realize this, but it turns out I have a fund-raiser in Newport News Sunday afternoon. If you and Alison wanted to come out, I'd be delighted to have you."

Alison would not tolerate a public appearance under these circumstances. But knowing I had to play along, I said, "Oh yeah? What's it gonna cost me?"

He just laughed. "I haven't gotten that desperate yet," he said. "But if my so-called party doesn't start kicking in a little more, I might have to."

As a genuine centrist, Blake was an unusual political creature in this hyperpartisan era. He started his career as a Reagan Republican and then switched to the other side of the aisle when he felt the GOP had drifted too far from its socially moderate roots. The end result of this was that while Republicans regarded him as the worst kind of traitor, Democrats didn't entirely trust him either. Their support had always been lukewarm.

He had managed to get himself reelected twice anyway. It helped that he had been on both sides of the Senate aisle and had swapped favors with nearly everyone in that august chamber. It made him a champion at the kind of horse trading that got things done in Washington. He also had a gift for retail campaigning. Few did a whistle-stop tour better.

But now, seeking his fourth term, he had hit up against a political buzz saw: a wealthy, staunch conservative entrepreneur who had whipped the far-right base into a frenzy while managing to appeal to the center with talk of job creation. Between his opponent's seemingly endless cash reserves and the strong anti-incumbent sentiment sweeping the nation, Blake was in the fight of his political life.

"Have your secretary e-mail me details and I'll see what I can do. I have no idea what Alison has planned for me this weekend, but I'm sure she'd love to see you."

The first part was true. The second wasn't. Alison had never much liked Blake, either before or after The Incident. Her resentment had faded some now that I wasn't spending most of my waking hours in the man's service. But sometimes old rancor dies hard.

"All right," he said. "Well, you behave yourself, you hear?"

"You do the same," I said, and ended the call.

*

When I arrived home, Alison's car was not in the driveway. It was a little before five. She and Sam must have still been in thrall to the Virginia Living Museum.

The only person on our twenty acres—at least the only one I saw—was Justina. As I rolled by the cottage, I caught

174

a glimpse of her carrying a box out to her car. I still hadn't made up my mind about her. But Alison was right about at least one thing: As long as we suspected she was involved, it was untenable having her live next door.

After parking my car, I marched straight up to our bedroom, where I put on jeans and a threadbare flannel shirt. Then I went down to our liquor cabinet, where I poured a large gin and tonic.

I took it out to the back deck so I could look out at the river. Ordinarily this would have been a treat—a Friday afternoon, a stiff drink, the setting sun sparkling on the water. I realized it was too much to expect anything resembling the relaxation I might normally experience from this setup. But if I could at least get a little bit of a break from reality . . .

Instead, I reached the bottom of the glass without feeling even the slightest bit of relief. So I went for a reload. This time even stronger.

Somewhere in the middle of that second drink, the doorbell rang. I lurched to my feet and stomped heavily through the kitchen and into the foyer. I hadn't been able to stomach much lunch—this after vomiting—so the booze had gone straight to my head. I was aware I had lost some control of my body and my inhibitions, enough that I didn't bother to check to see who was there before opening the door.

It was Justina. She was wearing a tank top and formfitting black yoga pants, clothing that fit the laborious task of moving. The exertion of carrying all those boxes had left her with a light sheen of sweat.

"Oh hi," I said, my voice thick from the drinks.

"Hi, Judge," she said. "I just wanted to let you know I was leaving now."

She had already entered, the front door closing behind her.

"I wanted to give you my keys, too," she said, holding them out for me until I accepted them. "I left the key to the Honda on the hook in the cottage."

"Thanks. That's great."

"Are Mrs. Sampson and the kids home?" she asked.

I was thankful she said "kids"—plural. It told me nothing about our strange behavior the night before had led her to suspect anything regarding Emma.

"They're out," I said.

"Oh," she said. Maybe she was expecting me to elaborate, but I didn't.

"Anyhow," she said. "I guess this is good-bye."

"Uh-huh."

"Please tell Sam and Emma I said good-bye too."

She was obviously looking for some kind of closure after what was, if she was actually innocent, quite an ordeal: being summarily dismissed from a job she had held for two years and losing her place of residence in the process. But she wasn't going to get it from me.

"Thank you for dropping off the keys," I said.

"Thank you for everything," she said, and I realized her eyes were getting moist. "I'm really going to miss it here."

She took a step toward me. I might have been imagining it, but she seemed to have arched her back, subtly—or not so subtly—thrusting her breasts in my direction. Her bra, lacy and black, peeked out from under her shirt. The sweet smell of her was suddenly everywhere. Was she wearing perfume?

"You've always been so kind to me," she said.

Her right hand was suddenly resting against my left shoulder. The next thing I knew she was narrowing the gap between us. Her other arm was tracking toward my opposite shoulder. She was rising on her tiptoes.

And really, truly, I don't know what her intentions were. This could have just been a hug—a purely platonic exchange between two human beings who had spent two years in close quarters, sharing a duty of care for two boisterous children.

Or she was trying to seduce me.

If that was the case—and, really, I was too buzzed to decide with any accuracy—it certainly begged the question why. I didn't flatter myself into thinking a beautiful twenty-one-year-old college student was actually attracted to a lumpy forty-four-year-old judge. Was she trying to save her job? Or was she after something bigger? To steal something or plant a listening device in our bedroom or perform some other task at the kidnappers' behest?

I didn't have time to ponder it. All I could do was extricate myself from the situation, and I did so. Clumsily. Drunkenly. In my haste to avoid contact, I stumbled backward. Her momentum kept her coming toward me, and she sort of mashed into me. The whole thing couldn't have been more awkward.

"Yes, well, okay then," I said, gently pushing her away. "Thanks again for the keys."

I inched in the direction of the front door, which I held open for her, making it clear I intended for her to exit. As I followed her out onto the front porch, Alison's car, a Lincoln MKX, appeared in the driveway. I watched, dumbly, as it came to a stop. Then I turned my attention back to Justina, so I could continue escorting her out.

But Justina wasn't leaving just yet. She was waiting for Sam, who had just gotten out of the back of the car.

"Hey, *bebişko,*" she said, using her Turkish nickname for Sam. "Come here for a second."

She had her arms open. And Sam, bless his little heart, was going to accept her hug, just as he had a thousand others from Justina—until Alison, tearing around from the driver's side of the car, started yelling.

"Don't you touch him," she snarled. "Sam! Up to your room, now."

Sam stopped short, looking appropriately confused, casting his eyes between the two women who had been his most frequent caregivers over the past two years—which to a six-year-old might as well have been forever.

"Now, Sam!" Alison barked.

His chin dropped and he followed his orders, his little legs churning quickly as he passed by me on the porch.

"Where's Emma?" Justina asked. "I'd like to say—"

"Good-bye, Justina," Alison said firmly. "It's time for you to leave now."

"But can't I—"

"*Good-bye,*" Alison repeated, accompanying it with a glare that forced Justina's retreat.

Alison watched her go, her hands on her hips, then joined me on the porch.

"What was she doing in the house?" Alison asked.

"Just dropping off her keys."

Or maybe more. But I wasn't going to mention that theory, half-baked as it was.

"Did you let her in?"

"Well, yeah. I mean, she knocked."

Alison was eyeing me. "Have you been drinking?"

"Yeah, I had a couple of cocktails when I got home."

She didn't reply. But the look on her face made her disapproval plain as she stormed past me into the house.

23

We didn't talk much that night. Alison slept in the guest room, saying she didn't want to disturb me with her tossing and turning.

When I awoke in the morning, it wasn't quite yet dawn. I had been in the middle of an anxiety dream where I was waiting to testify before a Senate committee, only I didn't know what I was being called in to talk about. I started reading from a white paper, but the words on the paper disappeared. I tried to consult a colleague who was with me, who turned out to be Jeremy—even though I didn't know Jeremy when I was in the Senate—and he wouldn't tell me what was going on despite my repeated entreaties.

One of the senators kept asking me questions and I couldn't really see him, not until I started hearing gunfire. Then I realized the senator was Blake Franklin, and he was shooting at me. And I couldn't make myself duck. I couldn't make myself move at all. My body wouldn't respond to my commands. And so the bullets kept slamming into me, one after another. I couldn't even scream. All I could do was watch my torso get torn into bloody shreds.

It was not my first time having some version of that dream, although it was worse than usual. The shooter was usually faceless. It had never been Blake before.

Ordinarily, when I emerged from that dream, it was with the relief that it wasn't real. Except now I was awakening to a reality that was far worse than anything my subconscious could dish out. Dread washed over me in waves that only amplified with each beat of my racing heart: *Emma's gone, Emma's gone, Emma's gone . . .*

It was still early, but I didn't even attempt to go back to sleep. My bed might as well have been hot coals. Besides, I had made up my mind about something during my long, lonely evening: I couldn't sit idly by while Emma was out there somewhere. I had to start to do something, and the something that felt most productive was to learn more about Roland Hemans.

I redressed in the same clothes I had been wearing the night before, grabbing an old baseball hat. I left Alison a note saying I would be out for a little while following a hunch, then climbed into my Buick Enclave, the sensible crossover SUV I drive every day. Google Maps was soon pointing me toward the Newport News address I had found in LexisNexis for Hemans.

A few turns off Interstate 64, I arrived at Hemans' subdivision. His house was big and boxy, with all kinds of incongruous rooflines and stone facing that was supposed to keep it from looking cheap but somehow had the opposite effect. The driveway had a circular turnaround area with a basketball hoop in it.

The land was flat, as is typical of the tidewater, so I was able to park down a curving street and still enjoy a clear view of his premises. I have often heard testimony in my courtroom about FBI stakeouts lasting days or even weeks, so I yanked my cap low and steeled myself for the long hours of nothing that were to come.

Instead, it wasn't more than thirty minutes before the man himself emerged. Hemans was every bit the giant he appeared to be in his picture. The golf bag he had slung over his shoulder looked small against his massive back. He moved with the easy grace of an athlete and still had a muscular trimness about him. The magazine profile put his age at fifty, but as he passed near the basketball hoop, I imagined he could still dunk if he felt the urge.

He tossed the clubs in the back of a gold Lexus SUV that had a vanity plate that read PTNTLAW. As in patent law.

Maybe he was going out for a Saturday-morning round of golf.

Or maybe he was going to visit the two bearded men who had kidnapped my children.

He was soon backing down the driveway. As his car passed mine, I ducked down. When he was nearly out of sight, I began slinking after him. He eventually merged on Interstate 64 in the direction of Norfolk. There were any number of golf courses that way. But there were far more places you could stash a child.

I stayed three or four cars back, though he wasn't particularly hard to keep up with. After thirty minutes, he departed the interstate at Tidewater Drive.

That was one of the exits for downtown Norfolk. I was no expert on the local links scene, but I wasn't aware of any courses in that vicinity. There also weren't any forests, which was a problem. Sam had said they were held in the woods somewhere.

I continued my tail all the same, winding through the city streets as he neared a neighborhood known as Ghent. Then he slowed and turned into a small strip mall.

Following him into the parking lot would have been too conspicuous, so I set up in a spot just beyond. I twisted my body and looked through my rear window just in time to see him exit his SUV and enter a florist shop.

After five minutes, he reemerged carrying a white paper sheath with a few blossoms poking out the top. He poured himself back into his car and resumed driving.

We soon entered an area of older homes, some of them with historic signs. The streets had gotten narrower. After a few more blocks, the SUV was again slowing. It turned into a large, gated condominium complex off Princess Anne Road called Kensington Mews.

I eased past the turnoff but did not tug my wheel. I didn't know how I'd get past the guard. Hemans didn't have the same problem. After he rolled down his window and uttered a few words, the gate swung open.

There was street parking alongside the fence of the complex, so I hastily veered into one of the slots, killed the engine, and departed my car just in time to get a glimpse of Hemans. He had parked his car and was unfurling his rangy frame from the driver's side, with the flowers clutched in one hand.

This, clearly, was not where Emma had been detained. But I was still curious about what was going on as Hemans strode away from his car, covering ground quickly with his long strides until he disappeared around the corner.

I ran up the street, trying to get a better view of where he was going. But he was blocked by landscaping and other buildings. So I returned to my Buick, where I could keep my eyes on Hemans' Lexus.

Now with time to kill, I considered what I had likely just witnessed. A man had told his wife he was going to play golf. He then went to a place that was not a golf course, stopping at a florist shop on the way. He took those flowers into someone else's place of residence.

It wasn't a hard conclusion to reach: Roland Hemans was having an affair.

That, in itself, was hardly shocking. Lots of men stepped out on their wives. And Roland Hemans had that hypersexual air about him.

But there was potentially more to this, something I couldn't be sure of, something that was taking a little longer to work its way to the top of my thinking.

Kensington Mews was a familiar name. I had heard it mentioned around the office. Someone on my staff definitely lived there. And I was reasonably certain that someone was Joan Smith, my pious, divorcée judicial assistant.

Was it possible that Roland Hemans was cheating on his wife with Mrs. Smith?

24

The little girl nearly died overnight.

The younger brother thought they were going to let her. But the older brother—not sure how their employer would respond to their accidentally killing their captive—went out and bought some liquid antihistamine that he managed to pour down her throat.

Now the older brother was looking forward to a quiet morning, a hope that ended when the Internet phone rang at a quarter after ten.

"Yes?" the older brother said.

"The judge is out of pocket," came the voice of their employer.

"What do you mean?"

"He left the house early this morning. Didn't you see it on the cameras?"

"It looked like he was going out on an errand. I didn't think it was of consequence."

"Well, I'm telling you it is of consequence," the voice said. "He needs to return home."

"Why? Do you think he's meeting with law enforcement?"

"No, no. The woman wants him home."

This was not the first time their employer had referenced "the woman" he was working with. The woman wanted this. The woman wanted that. The woman was the reason they weren't allowed to tie up the little girl, even though it would make their lives easier. The older brother was getting annoyed with this woman's demands.

"Do I work for the woman, or do I work for you?"

"Just get the judge back home. Now."

25

My plan had been to stick around, in case Kensington Mews was merely Roland Hemans' first stop of the day. But my surveillance ended when I got a text from Alison:

> There's something I need to tell you and it has to be in person. Can you come home, please?

There's something I need to tell you. Could she be any more vague? Nevertheless, there wasn't going to be that much more to see here. And if she really did need me . . .

I texted back:

> In Norfolk. Leaving now.

Casting one last glance in the direction of the love connection currently under way, I started up my car, pulled a U-turn, and got pointed back toward the farm.

Forty uneventful minutes later I was rolling down our long driveway, kicking up a plume of dust that I could see billowing in my rearview mirror. Sam was lying on the front lawn, his skinny arm supporting the weight of his blond head.

As I got out of my car and walked closer, I could see he

was digging a small hole with a broken shard of tree branch, building up a pile of dirt next to it. He was also wearing his classic worry brow.

Before the kidnapping, I would have told you that Sam was as agreeable and even-tempered as kids came. He was like an engine that just needed the right mix of elements to keep motoring cheerfully along—but instead of oil, gas, and oxygen, it was food, sleep, and Emma.

His sister was that critical as a component of his happiness. Literally from the moment of their conception, they had been constant companions. Before Thursday, they had never spent a single night under different roofs.

And now, deprived of her presence, he didn't know what to do with himself.

"Hey, buddy, what's up?"

"Nothing," he said morosely.

"You're thinking about Emma, aren't you, pal?"

"Yeah," he said, eyes still downcast.

"What would you be doing right now if Emma was here?"

"Probably playing Acorns."

Acorns was a complicated barter game whose rules I had never fully understood. Still, I offered, "I'll play Acorns with you."

"No. It's not the same without Emma. You don't know how to do it."

I couldn't argue with him there.

"Do you want to go roaming?" I asked. What Sam called "roaming" was really just a walk in the woods on our property. It was referred to as roaming because you didn't have a destination. You just rambled around, exploring fallen trees, dry streambeds, and whatever animals—or evidence of animals—you might bump in to.

Ordinarily, it was one of his favorite things to do. But this time, he just said, "Nah."

I thought back to what Alison said about helping him seek pleasurable activities. "All right. Well, I'm going to go in and talk to your momma about something for a few minutes. Why don't you think of something fun we can do together?"

"Okay," he said.

I left him to his digging and walked inside. It felt too jarring to yell for Alison, so I walked softly around the house. I discovered her in the mudroom, where she was looking out the window at Sam while clutching a pink dress of Emma's, which she must have just pulled out of the washing machine. It was a dress Emma cherished, refusing to let it be relinquished to Goodwill even though it was getting so short it barely covered her little butt.

Seeing it gave me this harrowing vision of the future, where we became one of those tragic couples who trudged through their lives in perpetual disbelief, maintaining their missing child's room as a shrine, as if Emma was going to come back to us any second. In the meantime, everyone tiptoed around us, not wanting to tell us the truth—that our daughter was gone and we needed to move on—but also not understanding that we weren't even there anymore. Our bodies were heedlessly and stubbornly continuing with the motions of life even though, on the inside, we were already dead.

I was still staring at the dress when Alison looked up.

"Hey," she said, giving the dress a brisk snap and positioning it on the drying rack.

"Hey," I said.

She went back into the washing machine for more wet clothes.

"You needed to tell me something?" I said.

"What are you talking about?"

"Your text. You texted me you needed to tell me something."

She whipped her head away from the laundry. "I didn't send you a text."

I almost pulled my phone out of my pocket to show her that, yes, she did. But, of course, that was a pointless exercise.

"What did it say?" she asked.

"Just that you wanted me to come home because you had something you needed to tell me in person."

"Nope, definitely not from me."

"So, obviously, they sent it," I said, not needing to explain who "they" were. "The question is why?"

Before Alison could offer any speculation, the answer suddenly became obvious to me. "Oh my God, they must have known I was camped out on Hemans. And they wanted to get me off his tail."

"What do you mean, 'camped out on Hemans'? Was that this so-called hunch you were following?"

I told her how I had spent my morning, which prompted her to make a sour face.

"What?" I asked.

"I don't know. Do you even know what you're doing, following someone around? It's not like you're trained as a private investigator. I mean, what if they spotted you?"

"I was careful."

"Still. It's too much risk. If they found out and punished Emma for it—"

"You're right, you're right," I said. "I'll stop. I just . . . I got tired of doing nothing."

"I understand. Really, I do. As a matter of fact, you remember that lab in Williamsburg?"

"Yeah, what about it?"

"They said DNA would be a waste of time, but that they might be able to get fingerprints off some of the things that came in the boxes from the kidnappers. For matching purposes, I gave them two objects that we know have Justina's prints on them—the Honda's keychain and the toaster. But they still need your fingerprints and mine, to rule us out. There are kits in the kitchen. I picked them up after the Living Museum."

She expelled a loud sigh.

"What?"

"I was just thinking about the Living Museum again. Karen and Jenny were . . . I mean, I know they were trying to quote-unquote take my mind off things and quote-unquote act normal. But Jenny was bitching about her work schedule, because in her perfect, consequence-free life she has nothing else to bitch about. And Karen was just going on and on about the usual stuff—about how she and Mark are still upside down with the house, about how Mark doesn't have the balls to ask for a raise, about how much things have changed in the benefits world and she can't convince anyone to hire her after so much time on the bench, about how unfair the world is to women who have children, and blah, blah, blah.

"And, yeah, they were just trying to keep me distracted from Emma. But it was also just, like, really? Really? You're going to just sit here and pretend like . . . like these things matter? I mean, I'm sitting here, feeling like I can't even breathe, like I just want to bury myself in a hole somewhere. Except I can't, because I still have a son and I'm trying to keep him sane, and . . ."

She signified her disgust by making a scoffing sound.

"Karen called me this morning and actually apologized because I think she realized they had been sort of tone-deaf," she said. "But it was, like, still."

"Yeah," I said as she draped another dress on the drying rack. "Did Sammy at least have a good time?"

"Yeah. By the way, before I forget, something came up during my conversation with Karen this morning that I wanted to run past you."

"Oh?"

"She pointed out that we've now gotten two late-night deliveries, and she thinks we'll probably get a third at some point."

"Yeah? And?"

"Well, she wants to keep watch over the house at night. She thinks we can catch one of them in the act of dropping off a package, and then maybe we can pressure the guy we catch into telling us where Emma is. She's proposing she, Jenny, and Jason take turns."

"What? Like sitting on the front porch with a shotgun?"

"Maybe a little less obvious than that. But something along those lines, yeah. What do you think?"

I leaned against the doorframe, trying to think of ways that could backfire. Nothing immediately came to mind.

"Yeah. I guess that would be okay."

"That's what I said," Alison said. "It sounds like they're planning to start tonight."

"Great," I said.

"Okay. Hey, would you mind doing that fingerprint kit now? I just want to be able to get it off my mind."

"Sure."

"Follow the instructions carefully. I didn't get extras."

*

After leaving impressions of all ten of my digits in the designated boxes, I returned outside. Sam was now filling back in the hole he had made, using his digging tool to smooth the dirt.

"Hey, buddy," I said. "You thought about what you want to do?"

Without looking up, he said, "We could maybe go fishing."

I looked out at the water. It was nearing noontime, the tide was at its midpoint, and the wind had roiled the waves into a decent chop. In conditions like that, nothing would be biting. We might as well toss our lines onto the front lawn.

But anyone who thinks fishing with your child is about actually catching something well and truly does not get the purpose of the sport. Especially now.

"That's a great idea," I said. "Let's go get our stuff."

Sam scrambled to his feet. We were soon equipped and making our way down to the water. We have a short pier that has somehow withstood the various hurricanes and nor'easters that have battered it through the years. Standing on the end, you can cast out and, under different conditions than the ones we were currently experiencing, catch croaker, spot, red drum, maybe even the occasional rockfish.

I chopped off a piece of squid, which Sam immediately grabbed. This was our big accomplishment for the summer: He and Emma could now bait and cast without my help. He had his line in the water before I did.

And then we sat and waited. Sam has become more patient over time, resisting the urge to check for a fish every time he felt the slightest tug.

"So what did you do this morning?" I asked.

He shrugged. "Nothing," he said.

"Did you watch TV?"

"Yeah."

"What did you have for breakfast?"

"French toast."

His gaze was fixed out at the river. The wind tousled his fine hair.

"Yeah? And how was the Living Museum yesterday?" I asked.

"Good."

"Did you see the sharks?"

The Virginia Living Museum has a saltwater tank that contains a few species of small sharks. Sam can kill half an hour—an eon in six-year-old time—watching them do laps. Alison always pretends to be scared of the sharks, and Sam tells her there's nothing to be afraid of because they're behind the glass.

"Yeah."

"Did you tell Momma not to be scared?"

And then, in his guileless little-boy way, he said, "Momma wasn't there."

"Because she was getting coffee?" I asked.

"No. She didn't go with us. Aunt Karen and Aunt Jenny took me."

"You mean Momma was never at the museum at all?"

"Yeah," he said, like he was relieved I finally understood.

"So where was she?"

"She went on a little errand," he said.

"What kind of little errand?"

He shrugged and mumbled an "idunno."

"Are you sure, buddy?" I asked. "Momma really wasn't there?"

"Nope," he said. And that was it.

I turned my attention back to the water and my empty line. But I wasn't thinking about fishing.

26

Throughout the remainder of the afternoon and into the evening, I kept replaying the exchanges Alison and I had had about the subject of the Living Museum.

The first was at breakfast the day before, when she said, "*I* thought *I'd* take him to the Living Museum." And, yes, there was a mention of her sisters. But as joiners. Not as surrogates.

Then there was the phone conversation we had, which allegedly took place while she was in the Living Museum's cafeteria.

Finally, there was earlier this morning, when she seemed to go out of her way to insert into the conversation how she was peeved with her sisters about their behavior at the museum.

Never in any of that did she mention errands, or separating from Sam, or anything of the sort. It was possibly just an unintended omission. And I might have written it off to, I don't know, the stress we were under or having more important things to talk about.

But what *had* she been doing during that time? What was important enough that she would leave him when he was still so fragile?

I kept looking for a chance to ask her about it without making it seem like a big deal, an opportunity that arrived after dinner. Sam was in the family room, having been permitted to watch one more program before bath time. Alison and I were doing the dishes.

"So Sam was telling me about the Living Museum while we were fishing," I started.

"Oh yeah?" Alison replied.

"He told me he spent a lot of time watching the sharks."

"Like usual."

I didn't know how to take her "like usual." Because you could say "like usual" whether you were there to watch it or not. I had to press further.

"Did he tell you not to be scared of the sharks?" I asked.

"Uh, I don't remember."

Was that true? Or was she being intentionally evasive?

"Well, could you try?" I asked.

"Why?"

She had stopped drying a pan to look at me. I came up with: "It's just, you know, you said we needed to keep an eye on him with this post-traumatic stress thing and it struck me that if he told you not to be afraid of the sharks, like he always did before, maybe it shows he's coping okay, still being able to reassure his mother that something isn't dangerous, rather than fixating on the danger. Do you follow me?"

"Yeah, I guess."

"So did he tell you not to be scared? Come on. It's important. Think about it for a second."

As she complied, her eyes shifted up and to the right—a classic sign of deception, according to an FBI profiler I once heard at a judicial conference.

And then she said, "Yeah, I guess he did. 'Don't worry, Momma, the sharks are on the other side of the glass.'"

"You're sure he said it like that?"

Up and right. "Yeah," she said.

I nodded, like I was satisfied, and returned my attention to the sink so she couldn't see the devastation on my face. I had to get out of that kitchen. I had to get out of her presence. Something was crumbling inside me.

Though I had allowed my wife to explain herself and given her every chance to correct the record, she had not merely continued to feign ignorance, nor had she nibbled at some small deceit. She sank her teeth into a lie and then, with great gusto, swallowed it whole.

And what was I to make of that? In the twenty-five years we had been together, had she ever lied to me?

Well, of course she had. With the cigarettes. Alison had been a smoker during our twenties. She wasn't a pack-a-day girl or anything, but she'd smoke when we went out to bars—this was before the indoor smoking ban—or at parties when other people were smoking, or now and then when she was feeling stressed about something.

She supposedly quit cold turkey once we started trying to get pregnant. And I would have told you she had stopped for good. But there was this one time—this was maybe three years ago—when I came to surprise her at work and take her out for lunch on our anniversary. When I pulled into the parking lot, I caught a glimpse of her in the designated smoking area on the side of the building, just as she was exhaling a big lungful of smoke. As soon as she saw my car, she immediately extinguished the cigarette and fled inside. When she came to greet me in the lobby three minutes later, she smelled like hand soap and toothpaste.

A few months later, when I was at the school for a fund-raising event, I found an almost-full pack of cigarettes in her desk at work. Curious, I crushed the corner of it. A week and a half later, I created an excuse to be in her office while she wasn't there. It was the same pack, now half-full. She was sneaking a cigarette a day, probably at lunchtime.

Over the past three years, there had probably been half a dozen times when I'd taste just a hint of cigarette on her breath or catch the barest whiff of tobacco coming off her clothes. I never mentioned it to her. It seemed like such a little thing. A woman is allowed to have her secrets, right?

Except, of course, it now made me wonder: Having gotten away with that small lie, did she think she could get away with a much bigger one?

*

Making the excuse that I felt a headache coming on and wanted to lie down, I escaped the kitchen as soon as I could.

For the sake of my children—and my own sanity—I had to pull myself together and think about this. But not like a husband. Husbands are too prone to emotion, to letting their feelings get in the way of drawing a logical conclusion.

I had to think about this like a judge.

What if a defendant accused of kidnapping came into my courtroom with the kind of evidence Alison currently had against her? And let's just say it was a bench trial, where the defendant waived her right to a trial by jury and was instead asking me to make the determination of guilt or innocence. How would that trial play out?

Prosecution Witness No. 1: A very credible grandmother type with absolutely no motive to lie—Miss Pam from the Montessori school—had identified Alison as picking up the children from school. This was beyond the kind of eyewitness ID you might get from a stranger. Miss Pam knew Alison well. And it was part of Miss Pam's job to note who was driving the car. She had even been able to add details like the ball cap, the sunglasses.

Prosecution Witness No. 2: A little boy, while somewhat shaky on the stand, also identified his mother as the driver of the vehicle. And, yes, he had been shredded on cross-examination, eventually admitting that he had mostly been paying attention to the television screen. But still.

Prosecution Exhibit No. 1: A video of a car identical to one owned by the defendant, with the children getting into the car at exactly the time Miss Pam had noted. It showed a woman who certainly looked like Alison driving.

Then came Prosecution Exhibit No. 2: Transcripts of text messages from the defendant's cell phone to the father of the kidnapped children. The first one said she would be picking up the kids. Another one said the father should come home instead of trail a potential suspect.

And, oh, how the defense attorney had tried, during pretrial motions, to keep the transcription of all the text messages out of evidence. He said there was no evidence they really came from the defendant's phone. And the prosecutor had countered by pointing out there was also no evidence they *hadn't* come from the defendant's phone.

Any judge would have no choice but to allow Exhibit No. 2 into evidence and give the defendant the opportunity to testify she had never sent the messages. And she seemed credible enough while doing it.

Except there were other parts of the defendant's testimony that were deeply troublesome. For one, she had insisted—*insisted!*—that neither she nor her husband would involve law enforcement. And isn't it always the guilty person who wants to stay away from the cops?

Second, she had been caught in a lie about going to the Living Museum with her son. The prosecutor didn't even need to harangue on the subject, because judges didn't have to be told: Witnesses who lie about one thing are often lying about a lot more than just one thing.

There was also the unanswered question of what she had done during that time. Had she, perhaps, met with her coconspirators? Or visited her daughter?

And, sure, the defense tried to get fingerprint testing done. It had also testified about its efforts to set up a guard at the house. But that was starting to feel like an elaborate, O. J. Simpson–style dodge: We'll stop at nothing to find the real killer! And, of course, the guards wouldn't catch anyone and the science would neither prove—nor disprove—anything.

After that, the defense rested. That's all I had on which to base my verdict. And where did that lead me?

To a totally absurd thought. But it was one I couldn't

help but having anyway. Did Alison have something to do with this?

The overly emotional husband in me was screaming: No! Absolutely not! No mother—much less a mother like Alison—could subject her children to that kind of terror. She birthed those children. She nurtured them through infancy, toddlerhood, and now childhood. She loved them with a selfless ferocity.

And what possible reason would she have to do something like this? Because she wanted Denny Palgraff to have his patent? Because she wanted to protect ApotheGen's shareholders? There was no motive that made a shred of sense.

But what did the logical judge in me think?

The judge would have known the prosecution was not required to prove motive. The judge would have looked at two witnesses, a video, and text messages all pointing to the same conclusion.

The judge would have convicted her and then slept very well that night.

27

Unable to extricate the husband—or the father—from the judge, I slept terribly.

Part of it was simply the pain: the roiling in my gut, the inability to catch my breath, the bone-deep ache that came from a stress beyond anything I had ever experienced. Thinking about strangers kidnapping my children, as I had for the past four days, had been agony enough. Thinking about that kind of betrayal coming from the person I shared my life with—my partner, my soul mate, and the mother of my two children—was a visit to a chamber of hell I never knew existed.

If it was true. And I was still deeply divided on whether it was. As the night wore on, I cycled through every interaction and every sentence Alison and I had shared over the past week, month, and year, looking for some indication in either direction, finding none.

There were times when I lay there, just staring at her in her sleep, battling the temptation to shake her awake and confront her with what I knew. But I knew I couldn't. If she really had done it, all I would be doing was inviting another fabrication. If she hadn't done it, merely making the accusation would tear something essential in our relationship, something that couldn't be mended. Some lines cannot be uncrossed.

Sometime in the middle of the night, I slipped out of bed. I had become convinced that, no matter how careful she might have thought herself, she had to have left some trace of her activities behind.

My first stop was her phone. I checked her texts and found nothing out of the ordinary. Then I went to her sent and received calls. It was mostly, "Karen Cell" or "Mom Home" or "Work" or other names that linked to her contact list. There were only two foreign numbers. But when I Googled them, they turned out to be our doctor's office in Gloucester and the forensics lab in Williamsburg. Nothing suspicious there. Her e-mail was also clean.

Though, of course, all of that could have been sanitized. Or she could have a second phone she used to contact her coconspirators.

Next I went through her purse, thinking there might be something incriminating: a receipt, a note on a scrap of paper, whatever. But, again, I came up empty.

I thought hard. What would be the kind of small thing where she *wouldn't* think to cover her tracks? I went to my laptop and accessed our E-ZPass account, trying to see if there was any unusual toll activity on any of the bridges or tunnels in our area. Nothing seemed out of place.

But at that point, being that I was already on the computer, I hopped over to her Facebook account. Alison rotates between three passwords, so it wasn't hard to guess which one she used.

Once I was in, I scrolled through six months' worth of updates—mostly cute posts about the twins or family photos—then through her friends list, to see if there was anyone I didn't know. Nothing popped. Then I went over to her messages.

The first few were benign. But then, from about a month back, there was a message from none other than Paul Dresser, Alison's high school beau.

He was writing to say he had changed cell phone numbers and was giving her his new one, along with the suggestion that it had been too long since they had spoken, that he had some news he wanted to share, and they really needed to catch up.

Alison's reply: "Definitely. I'll call you tomorrow."

I tried to tamp down the brief—and surely irrational—rush of jealousy that greeted this message. Yes, Paul Dresser had been her high school boyfriend, her first love. They had been together for two hot-and-heavy years while their fathers were stationed at Fort Bliss, outside El Paso. But then, the summer after graduation, her father was reassigned. Then his was. So not only were they heading off to college; they wouldn't even be able to see each other during semester breaks. They called it off rather than attempt an untenable long-distance relationship. Alison had once told me it took her all of freshman year to get over it.

But that was, what, a quarter century ago? Surely, I was being ridiculous.

Just as surely, I clicked over to Paul's profile. I went to the pictures first. I had never met him, but there was no doubt he was a good-looking guy: a head taller than me and broad shouldered, with the chin of a movie star. A photo of him at the beach—with the simple caption "Tahiti!"—showed off a toned physique and an impressively flat stomach. Another showed him skiing in Aspen. In yet another, he was rock climbing in Switzerland. The man's life seemed to be one fabulous vacation after another.

I thought back to all the times she had joked about Paul Dresser: how Paul was going to sail by our dock in his yacht and sweep her away from her humdrum life, how Paul would buy her jewelry and cars, how Paul would take her on fabulous trips. The constant theme was that she was only biding her time with me until Paul came back along.

They *were* jokes, right?

None of the photos showed him with a wife or children, so I went over to the "About" section to see if he was in a relationship.

He wasn't. His status was listed as "Single."

He was also listed as living in Alexandria, Virginia, which I found a little disturbing, inasmuch as globe-trotting Paul was now within easy driving distance.

But there was something else in the "About" section that was far more menacing, something that filled my body with a dread chill. It was under "Work."

There, Paul Dresser listed his employer as "ApotheGen Pharmaceuticals."

*

Even as my head pounded, my hands shook, and my racing heart felt like it was going to rupture, it was not difficult to put together a scenario that now seemed, if not probable, at least nightmarishly possible.

I could imagine Paul sitting in a meeting where the lawsuit was being discussed—what else would people at ApotheGen be talking about?—and discovering the judge in the most important case in the company's history was none other than his ex-girlfriend's husband.

He likely shared this fact, and the other executives had urged him to reach out to Alison. Maybe Paul—hunky, glamorous, dimple-chinned Paul—could rekindle with his old flame to some advantage for the company. Or at least he could reach out to her to see if he could learn anything.

And maybe that's where it started. Just a ruse to get close to me and the case. But when he had contacted Alison, they hit it off. Obviously, there had been attraction there once. First loves have a hold on us that way. I know: Alison was mine.

It wasn't hard to imagine Paul being wowed all over again by Alison. She was, in some ways, more beautiful at forty-four than she had been at eighteen, if only because she had aged so well in comparison to peers who had not been as genetically fortunate.

But was Alison similarly taken by Paul? It wasn't out of the question that she had never truly gotten over him. He had always been her what-if, the guy taken from her by fate and circumstance. And now these two star-crossed lovers found themselves orbiting each other once again.

Was the kidnapping—in addition to having enormous professional benefits for Paul—merely stage one of a plan where Alison and Paul ran off together with the kids and started a new life together? A life that started after I rendered my verdict and they found some convenient way to dispose of me?

It was bizarre to even ponder. And yet it was also strangely prosaic. I remembered reading not long ago about a church in New Jersey that forbade its deacons from signing up for Facebook because the pastor was tired of counseling couples whose marriages had been imperiled by cheating that started with old relationships renewing on social media.

I tried to calm myself down, to remind myself this was pure speculation. All I really had was one Facebook message; the phone call that seemed to have followed it (though Alison's call log didn't note one, she could have used our landline or a burner phone); and the fact that he worked for ApotheGen.

An hour's worth of Internet searches did little more to clear things up. Paul Dresser was definitely employed by ApotheGen Pharmaceuticals. He seemed to be in sales and marketing. But neither ApotheGen's website, nor LinkedIn, nor a page for a professional association he belonged to, would tell me his exact title or explicate his role in the company.

But those were just details. The more fundamental question was—and this, truly, was the world war–size conflict raging between my ears—would Alison really do something like this?

Up until a few days ago, I would have told you that while

I didn't necessarily know much, I did know my wife. She was at the core of whatever epistemology I thought I had. We had been together for twenty-five years—basically, our entire adult lives. I had a hard time remembering when there hadn't been an us.

After The Incident, when that bullet ripped me open in so many ways, one of the first conclusions I reached was that Alison had been the one source of perpetual good in my life. From our days as undergraduates, through law school, through my clerkship, through the workaholism that nearly consumed me during my time with Senator Franklin, she had done nothing but love me.

Even when I didn't necessarily deserve it. Or understand why. I had come to accept that, for me, her love was like the speed of light: a mathematical constant true throughout my universe.

So how could I create any order out of a cosmos that included a betrayal this depraved?

Something a divorced friend told me kept coming to mind. He talked about that shocking moment, as his marriage was fragmenting into tiny pieces of accusation and hatred, when he realized his wife was essentially a stranger to him; that her behavior had become so inexplicable within the context of what he thought he knew, he had to acknowledge the person he thought he knew didn't exist.

Was that now happening to me?

The cruel irony was that the person I most wanted to discuss this with—Alison—was essentially unavailable to me. I couldn't say anything to her until I was sure. And it was difficult to have a real conversation with her while I still suspected her.

All I could do was watch her. And pray like hell this wasn't so.

28

The next morning, Alison made two suggestions I found immediately alarming.

Part one, she asked if she could go to church. Alone.

The church part didn't strike me as being strange. The alone part did. One of the main reasons we had become churchgoers since coming to Gloucester was for the family aspect of it. We didn't want to push religion on our kids— what they did when they became adults was their own business—but we did want to at least expose them to faith. And we did that as a unit.

Her explanation for wanting to go by herself was that we couldn't very well go as a three-person family when we were normally four; but that she, going solo, could offer the explanation that I had been under the weather and she didn't feel like dragging the kids by herself.

Besides, she said, she had a lot to pray for.

Then she presented the second part of her plan: that I should go to Blake's fund-raiser.

Apparently, his secretary had e-mailed both of us the details about it. Alison, as predicted, had absolutely no desire to attend. But she thought it would be a good distraction for me, a chance to escape the unrelenting pressure of home and work. "Just go out and have a good time with Blake and try not to think about things," she said, as if that was possible.

In truth, I didn't like any of it. But I agreed to her proposal, mostly because I didn't know how to explain my objections. In the meantime, it only fueled my dread.

Was her desire to go to church strictly spiritual?

Or was this another excuse to slip away and visit Paul and Emma?

I spent the morning splitting my time between Sam and my nascent efforts to either prove or disprove this awful thing I suspected, making no further progress.

At one point, as I made Sam's breakfast, I flipped on the small television we had in the kitchen. It was tuned to CNN, where Andy Whipple—my brother-in-law's boss's boss's boss—was being interviewed about his charitable works. From what Mark had told me, Whipple had become something of a celebrity in his world when he anticipated the bloodbath of 2008, pulling out all his investments at the right time and plowing the money into safe havens. As others took a pounding, the Whipple Alliance's largest fund returned an astonishing twenty-eight percent, cementing his legend.

For a supposed master of the financial universe, he didn't look like much. He was small statured and round middled, with receding hair he had chopped short and one chin too many.

He was donating twenty-five million dollars to an inner-city Boys & Girls Club, for which the interviewer was lauding him. I watched his mouth move as he spoke, but I wasn't really hearing him. I was fantasizing about his money.

If I had twenty-five mil, would I be able to buy myself out of this current mess? Could money get Emma back?

This led to more daydreaming about whether Mark might be able to connect me to Whipple, who might then offer me a loan that I would happily spend the rest of my life repaying if it ensured Emma's safe return.

Or would twenty-five million not do anything? Would Whipple, with all his monetary resources, be just as helpless as I was, with all my judicial resources? Were there really things neither money nor power could buy?

*

After Alison arrived back home from church, we had time for only a quick check-in about Sam—what he had eaten, what we had done together, whether he seemed to be okay— before I had to get ready for the fund-raiser.

Sunday with the Senator: An Intimate Afternoon with Blake Franklin was being held at a yacht club in Newport News. Blake might have now been a Democrat, but he still raised money like a Republican.

When I arrived, I was given a name tag that read JUDGE SAMPSON. I knew his staff was just being respectful. But if I had some Wite-Out I would have used it. I didn't mind being "Judge" in the courthouse. Elsewhere, I preferred to be Scott.

The crowd was more intimate than I thought the "intimate afternoon" would be, which told me it was also more expensive than I realized. A thousand bucks a ticket?

Five? I probably didn't want to know. As the policy wonk on his staff, I had always isolated myself from the grubbier details of campaign finance.

As I walked into the country club's ballroom, I spied the senator locked in an earnest conversation with a pair of would-be donors. Blake was barrel-chested and just over six feet. He had fantastic hair, still thick and wavy even though it was now fully gray. It sat atop the kind of big head and strong features that gave him a larger-than-life aura and looked great on television.

Blake had relentless energy, and it had pushed him a long way in this world. He had been a blue-collar kid, the son of a Newport News shipyard worker and a homemaker. He put himself through college, then, with seed money he cajoled out of a few rich friends he had cultivated, started his own real estate development company. He made a small fortune during the 1980s buildup, when Hampton Roads was booming with military spending, then sold out before the cold war ended and the bubble burst.

He entered politics because he wanted to make sure his kind of up-by-the-bootstraps personal narrative stayed possible for the next generation. It was a line that appealed to Republicans and Democrats alike.

I watched as Blake moved on to delighting a small group of older folks who sort of reminded me of china: fragile and expensive. Over the years I worked for him, I started off thinking his seemingly effortless schmoozing had to be fake, or at least affected. I assumed it was something he did out of necessity, because he understood politics, like so much of life, was about relationships. And that therefore it made sense to invest in them.

It turned out he was far less calculating about it. He simply enjoyed the pressing of flesh, the telling of stories, the connecting and reconnecting with friends new and old. His enthusiasm was genuine.

Perhaps a minute after walking in, I was approached by a waiter carrying flutes of champagne on a tray. He looked at me expectantly, like I should have been happy to see him. And that was when I realized I had made a huge mistake in coming here. Champagne? How the hell could anyone be drinking champagne when Emma was in danger? When Alison might have been scheming behind my back? When all I really wanted to do was crawl in a hole and die?

The mere thought of it was revolting. It made me feel like smashing the whole tray on the floor.

The waiter smiled at me. I knew I was supposed to be doing the same. Everyone around me was. I just couldn't.

I had to get out. Immediately.

"No, thanks," I said, and turned to leave.

Which was when Blake surprised me from the other direction. He swiped a champagne flute from the tray and simultaneously put his arm around me while sticking the glass in my hand.

"Great to see you, great to see you," he said. "Thanks for coming."

From somewhere nearby, I heard a camera clicking.

"My goddaughter behaving herself?"

He removed his arm. With the photographer still lurking,

I felt compelled to force a smile. "As much as she ever does," I said.

The camera clicked a few more times. Blake ignored it. I found it unnerving.

"Good, good," he said, then pulled me close again. "I've got to do my thing here, but stick around so we can catch up later, okay? We can grab dinner or something."

Then he was off. I studied the champagne, now in my hand. Moved by an impulse I can't explain, I drank it in one gulp, feeling it burn my esophagus. I didn't even like champagne. I signaled the waiter for another.

Maybe Alison was right. Maybe I should try to take my mind off things, take a break from the stress. I was putting on a show all week at the courthouse. I could continue the act around Blake.

I still couldn't bring myself to talk to anyone, but I downed the second glass, then a third. By the time it was announced the senator would be making some remarks, I was flush-faced. I wobbled to a seat just in time for Blake to give a short version of his "Bullish on America" speech, which I had heard many times before, even if the details always changed slightly. It was a talk that played well with this crowd: It stood to reason that if they could drop a few thou on an afternoon at a country club, they were pretty bullish too.

He then spoke about the election at hand, about the importance of scrapping for every vote. Virginia had leaned Democratic in its last several statewide elections, but only by the narrowest of margins. Polls now had Blake trailing, not that he mentioned that part.

Toward the end, he got around to recognizing his hosts and some of the other local folks who had helped put the event together. I wasn't paying particular attention until suddenly I heard my name.

"... who was a member of my staff for many years and was nothing short of the best policy guy in Washington. I can't tell you the number of times he made me look smarter than I really am," Blake said, getting a polite chuckle. "He now serves his country on the federal bench here in the Eastern District of Virginia. Some of you may have seen his name in *The Wall Street Journal* and *The New York Times* this week about this big ApotheGen case, so now he's a celebrity. Judge Sampson, can you wave to everyone?"

I wasn't sure whether I was supposed to be the dog or the pony in this show, but I waved, feeling embarrassed.

"Thank you. And now that y'all know who he is, those of you who lost a bundle on ApotheGen stock this week know who to lobby so you can make your money back."

There was a big grin on his face when he delivered the line, and the room, as if following audience cue cards, erupted in laughter. Outwardly, I laughed with them, trying to appear to be a good sport. Inwardly, I seethed.

He had no right to call attention to me like that. And to even suggest I was somehow susceptible to lobbying or could have my opinion influenced by a conversation at a cocktail party? It was a huge insult to my integrity.

And, yeah, sure, maybe some of my reaction was because I knew just how thoroughly my integrity had already been compromised, but I left as soon as I could find a way to make an unobtrusive exit.

He could find someone else to have dinner with.

29

The older brother held a piece of paper in his hand as he twisted the handle of the door of the little girl's room.

The lock sprang open, making a pinging sound, and he walked in. He didn't immediately see her, not until her head popped up from the other side of the bed.

"What are you doing over there?" he asked.

The little girl stood up.

"Nothing," she said quickly.

He walked over to where she was standing and looked down at her. Children were terrible liars. She was up to something. He just couldn't tell what.

"Show me your hands," he said.

She held out her palms so he could see they were empty. The older brother narrowed his eyes. He still didn't believe her.

He wished, again, that they could keep her chained to the bed or restrained in some meaningful way. Then they wouldn't have to worry about what she was or wasn't doing.

But there was the matter of the woman, whoever she was, and her orders.

No matter. He had a task he needed to accomplish. Grabbing the little girl's arm, he led her into the bathroom, where she squinted in the light. He handed her the piece of paper.

"Hold this," he said.

"Why?"

"Just hold it."

"What is it?" she asked.

"Stop asking questions."

The older brother took his phone out of his pocket and jabbed at it a few times until he got the camera app going. Then he looked up at her.

"No, not like that," he said, repositioning the paper so the words on it were facing him. "Like this."

The little girl did as she was told. But now she was studying the sign.

"No, no. Don't look at the sign. Look at me."

The little girl ignored him.

"Don't make me spank you. I'll spank you if you don't look at me."

Their employer said not to hit the children. The woman had apparently been quite insistent on that point.

But she wasn't around. The older brother would do what he needed to do.

"Now," he barked.

Finally, the little girl turned toward him.

"That's good," he said. "Now look at the camera."

As soon as he was sure he was capturing the lost look on her face, he started snapping pictures.

30

I was still simmering at Franklin when I returned to the house, and I was set to spend the evening ignoring Alison— or at least avoiding meaningful contact—until, as I brushed past her in the foyer, I smelled something.

Cigarette smoke.

There was just a hint of it. But there was no question in my mind, or in my nose, about what it was.

"Hey," I said to Alison, who was already on her way back to the kitchen, where she had some pasta boiling for Sam and chicken in the oven for us.

"Yeah?" she said, turning back toward me but staying in place.

I walked up to her until I was basically on top of her, trying to suck as much air in through my nostrils as I could.

"What?" she said, taking two steps back.

"Have you been smoking?" I asked.

"No," she said. Though not convincingly.

"Then why did I catch a whiff of cigarette smoke as I passed you?"

She smelled her clothing, one shoulder, then the other.

"I don't know," she said. "Sam and I were at the grocery store before. I walked past a smoker on my way out. Maybe it . . ."

I crowded her again. We were in the kitchen now, where the cooking aromas masked whatever it was I had been able to detect in the foyer.

"Let me smell your hand," I said. Alison was a right-handed smoker. Always had been.

"What?"

"Hold out your hand. I want to smell it."

"No," she said, protecting the hand with her other arm.

"If you haven't been smoking, there should be nothing for me to smell."

"Scott, this is ridiculous."

"So you deny it. You deny that you've been smoking."

"Yes, I—"

"Because you quit before you got pregnant with the twins, is that right?"

"Stop it," she said. "You're being weird. Why are we even talking about this?"

"Because I know what I smelled."

"What are you, the high school principal?"

"Just tell me you smoked a cigarette. You're a grown-up. You're allowed to smoke if you want to. Why are you trying to hide it?"

"I'm not . . . This is stupid," she said, then pointedly turned away from me and returned to her cooking.

"I know what I smelled," I said, one last time.

She ignored me. And I let her. There was no point in continuing with this charade. Her reaction was telling enough. The denial. The deflection.

I knew it shouldn't have mattered much. If, during this

horrible chapter of our life, my wife wanted to continue with a relatively harmless cigarette-a-day habit—to relieve stress, to find a few seconds of escape—she was certainly entitled to.

But why did she have to lie about it?

It was just one more thing making my head spin as I went to bed that night. I had turned in early, in the hope of getting a good night's sleep so I could be well rested for the Rule 16B Conference that was scheduled for the next morning.

But that wasn't happening. I was thinking back to that pack of cigarettes in her drawer at work; to the sight of her hanging out by the side of her workplace, smoke pouring out of her mouth.

There's a famous theory in policing known as broken windows. It's the notion that if the police ignore petty crimes—like vandals who break windows—it will lead to a sense of lawlessness that allows bigger crimes to occur.

If I had confronted her about her cigarettes way back then, would Paul Dresser be happening now?

Or was Paul Dresser an unstoppable force the moment he chose to step back into her life? Had I always been some kind of consolation prize? I was now playing back all the times through the years she had referenced him. Even if she was being facetious, it now seemed obvious to me he had been on her mind an awful lot for a guy she hadn't been with since high school.

After an hour or two of thrashing around in bed with these kinds of thoughts playing in my head, the incessant anguish of it all got to be too much. I went into the bathroom, where

I found the sleeping pills that had been prescribed to me after The Incident. Back then, one pill usually helped me when the pain in my chest and armpit was making it difficult to drift off. They were, of course, long since expired.

I didn't care. I took three of them.

So I wasn't really aware of it when I finally slipped into a slumber. Nor did I realize that Alison had joined me sometime later.

I just know what woke me up:

The unmistakable thunderclap of a gunshot.

*

The sound waves were still echoing off the trees as I leapt out of bed.

"What was that?" Alison asked, sitting upright.

I was already striding toward the door of our bedroom, groggy as hell but determined.

"Don't you dare go outside," Alison brayed. "For the love of—"

"Just go be with Sam. He's probably scared."

I didn't wait around for her response. I barreled down the stairs, flipped on the outside lights, and, with nothing more than pajama bottoms and a T-shirt to protect me, threw open the front door. I was hoping to catch a glimpse of the shooter before he fled.

Instead, the shooter was stalking around from the edge of the porch. I froze. I had been at the wrong end of a gun once in my life. That was more than enough.

The gunman wasn't looking at me, though. His rifle was pointed toward something in the front yard. His finger was still on the trigger. He had what looked like night-vision goggles strapped to his head, with the lenses flipped up. He was covered from head to toe in jungle camouflage and what I could see of his face was obscured by black paint.

Then, despite the paint and goggles, I recognized it was Jason, my brother-in-law. Karen's night watchman had been doing his duty.

"Jason, what the—"

Then I heard a moan, coming from just beyond the steps. I walked to the edge of the porch. On a thin patch of grass and pine straw, perhaps eighty feet from the house, was a man. He was young. And scrawny. He was clutching his leg and unleashing every curse word he knew.

"The assailant may still be armed," Jason said in my direction. "Just stay there until I determine the threat level."

Looking at this kid as he writhed on the ground, banging it occasionally with his palm, I felt a twinge in my armpit. I would remember forever how it felt in those first moments after that bullet struck me. The pain was indescribable.

And incapacitating. Forget what you've seen in action movies, where the gun-blasted hero bravely fights on. When you've been shot in real life, all you can do or think about is the searing hotness of ripped flesh, how you would give anything to make it stop, and how you're quite sure anything that hurts that bad must be fatal. Striking back doesn't enter your thinking.

"I'll put one in his head if I have to," Jason announced loudly.

Between bursts of profanity, the kid said, "Come on, man. I swear, I ain't armed or nothing, I swear."

He was sucking air in and out with ferocity. Jason reached him and, with the barrel of the gun pointed at the young man's head, ordered, "Let's see those hands, punk. Hands. Now."

The kid lifted his hands away from his wound. He held them up in the air. His arms shook.

"Higher," Jason said, then strode up to him and gave his now-exposed midsection a savage kick with a boot that was heavy, black, and probably steel-toed.

The kid squealed and curled his body, bringing his good leg up for protection. The lame one was still straight. He was whimpering: "Please, oh please, oh sweet Jesus, please, it hurts so bad."

Jason had finally stopped pointing the gun at his target but was now raising its stock chest high, like he was going to bludgeon the kid. Maybe in the leg. Maybe in the head.

"Jason, stop, *now*," I said. "He's had enough."

I ran toward them, yelping as my bare foot struck a pinecone. I slowed only when Jason brought the gun back down. He reached into his vest—was it actually body armor?—and I thought maybe he was going to pull out a handgun to finish the kid off. Instead, he extracted a flashlight, which he turned on and shined down on his prey.

The boy was in his early twenties. If that. He had a scruff of hair on his chin. He was wearing a tank top that exposed several tattoos, including a large one that looked like the Little Mermaid, albeit without her shells. His skin was pimply and sallow. My courtroom had seen its share of crystal meth addicts. This kid reminded me of several of them. He certainly didn't look like any kind of criminal mastermind capable of kidnapping my children.

He squinted and turned away slightly from the light, which Jason had shined in his eyes.

"What are you doing here, boy?" Jason demanded.

"Jason, I've got this," I said, putting a hand on his shoulder. Then, not that I wanted to, but because I felt it would calm Jason a bit, I added, "Thank you. You can stand down."

I knelt by the young man. His jeans were dark with blood. The bullet had caught him in the thigh, leaving a surprisingly neat hole. I couldn't see the wound underneath. It was difficult to tell how much blood he was losing.

"What's your name, young man?" I asked.

"Bobby," he said quickly. "Bobby Rowe, sir."

"Okay, Bobby Rowe. Now, please tell me: What are you doing on my property?"

"A guy gave me five hundred bucks to put an envelope on your front porch. I swear, that's all, sir."

An envelope. It had to be from the kidnappers. "Where's the envelope?"

"I don't know. I think I dropped it when that"—and here he offered an indelicate description of my brother-in-law—"shot me."

Jason bristled at the word and made a move like he was

going to kick the kid again. "Just take it easy," I told him. "Give me a second to look for the envelope."

A minute or two of diligent searching turned up nothing. Jason still had the flashlight shining bright. It ruined my night vision and made it difficult to make out anything else that might have been lying nearby on the grass.

"Okay, forget the envelope for now," I said. "You said a guy gave you five hundred bucks. What guy?"

"I don't know. He wasn't from around here. He sounded like he was, I don't know, Russian or something. And he had a beard."

An accent. A beard. That sounded like one of the so-called scratchy-faced men Sam had described.

Bobby grunted and grasped at his leg again.

"Do you think we should call an ambulance?" Jason asked.

I was about to list all the reasons we couldn't—EMTs who would call sheriff's officers, ER doctors who would be required to report a gunshot wound—when Bobby piped up.

"No, sir, please, sir. If my probation officer hears about this he'll bust me back to prison. I got, like, five years hanging over my head. I can't go back there. I'll be fine."

He put his hand back on the wound, squeezing his eyes shut.

"Do you think we can get the bleeding stopped?" I asked Jason. "I don't want this kid dying on my front lawn."

"I wasn't using hollow-tipped rounds or anything," Jason said. "It was a bonded bullet."

"Meaning what?"

"Meaning it probably passed right through."

Jason said this with the breeziness of someone who had never been shot, as if bullets that pass through don't hurt as much.

I looked down at Bobby, his chest heaving in and out.

"Jason, can you do me a favor and run into the mudroom? There are some old sheets above the washing machine. They should be clean. Tear them into strips for me. If Alison asks anything, just tell her to stay with Sam."

Jason, always happy to follow orders, trotted off.

"All right," I said. Then, more to reassure myself, I added, "You're going to be okay, Bobby."

He nodded, then closed his eyes. Jason had taken his flashlight with him, leaving only the lights from the porch to illuminate us. My night vision was slowly returning. I still couldn't see the envelope. I would have to look for it again once the sun rose.

"Take me through this again," I said. "Start from the top: Some man with a beard and an accent wanted you to put an envelope on my porch."

"Yeah. I was just, you know, coming out of Walmart and he was, like, hey, kid, how'd you like to make a thousand bucks?"

"A thousand. I thought you said five hundred."

"It was five hundred to put the envelope there, and another five hundred if I came back with a bird feeder. He said"—he gritted his teeth and clutched at his leg—"he said you had a bunch on your porch."

That explained the two previous missing bird feeders, which had been snatched by two previous deliverymen, neither of whom was Bobby Rowe. The kidnappers had obviously been familiar with the decorations on our front porch. Returning with a bird feeder was tantamount to proof of delivery of the package.

"So you're supposed to grab a bird feeder and meet this guy back . . . where? At the Walmart?"

"Yeah," he said. "He said he'd be waiting for me."

Sure he was. If I was a kidnapper, would I really hang around a Walmart parking lot, fully exposed, waiting for some twenty-year-old tweaker to deliver a bird feeder to me so I could give him money?

Not a chance. I would burn rubber to get out of that parking lot, knowing that someone else on my team was watching the house and would see the delivery completed.

"You can go back there if you want," I said. "But I'm telling you it will be a wasted trip. That guy is long gone."

Jason had returned with the sheets.

"Okay, let's do this," I said. "Lift his leg for me."

Bobby groaned.

"Shut up," Jason said. "Kidnappers are nasty people, boy. You should have known better than to mess with them."

"Kidnappers?" Bobby chirped. "Y'all are kidnappers?"

"No. That's not . . . Just mind your own business." I was furious at Jason for saying too much. This was the kind of loose talk that could have dire results for Emma.

I fixed Jason with a stern look and said, "Keep a lid on it."

We kept at our task and soon had the wound bound tightly

enough that there was only the slightest dapple of blood on the second layer of sheet. Jason and I gave him a ride out to his car, then sent him away.

*

I relieved Jason from duty, then returned to the house. Alison was asleep in Sam's bed. They were curled up together, the boy as safe as could be, wrapped in the embrace of his momma bear.

It was the kind of sight that made me think there was no way—no possible way—Alison had any culpability in this, cigarettes or no cigarettes, Paul Dresser or no Paul Dresser.

Retiring to our bedroom, I lay on top of the bedspread for a while and closed my eyes. I figured after all the adrenaline wore off, the pills would kick back in.

In reality, I was still far too keyed up. I soon gave up, went down into the kitchen, brewed some coffee, and waited for the sun. I shut off all the lights, both inside the house and out, to allow my pupils to dilate fully.

After a cup and a half, I had the sense that the blackness outside was no longer total. It was more of a smudgy gray now. Dawn was on its way. I finished the last half a cup, sipping deliberately, then went outside.

It didn't take long to find what I had come outside for. Maybe twenty feet from where Bobby Rowe had bled on my grass, there was the slim manila envelope he had been paid to deliver.

The outside was blank: none of the block-letter writing

231

like the previous correspondence. It had a stiffness to it, like there was a piece of cardboard inside.

I took it back into the kitchen, turned on a light, and tore it open. Inside was a piece of cardboard, which served as a backing for a piece of photographic paper. I slid out the paper.

It was a picture of Emma. Her hair was gone, mowed down to a blond stubble. It made her head—all of her, really—look small and strange, almost embarrassed. Her shoulders were slumped, her face dejected. She was holding a printed sign in her doll-like right hand.

The sign said, RULE 16B? SPEED IT UP, DADDY. MY LIFE DEPENDS ON IT.

I sagged against the kitchen counter. Emma's feelings were all over her face. Just one glimpse at her fright, confusion, and torment was more than I could bear. I buried my head in the crook of my arm and wept. It was only after a few minutes that I willed myself to look at the picture again, to study it for any clues about her location or her captors.

There were none. They had photographed her standing against a backdrop of beige drywall that could have been the house next door or somewhere in the Southern Hemisphere.

I went back to staring at my daughter's desolate little countenance. She had been reading since kindergarten. There was no question in my mind that she could make out the words on the sign she held.

What her six-year-old mind would make of a death threat, I couldn't say. But the way she stared at that camera, coupled with the dour downturn of her mouth, told me she had parsed its message quite accurately.

We all eventually figure out that life is a gift, not a guarantee, and that there's only one way it ends. This epiphany, however, is usually saved for some time after the first grade.

I wanted to reach out and hug the photo. I wanted to rail at its callousness. I wanted to reassure my daughter that her daddy would find a way to protect her. I wanted to strip the thorns off the world so they couldn't tear at her. I wanted to do what daddies the world over were supposed to be able to do: make things okay.

Speed it up, Daddy. I could do that, of course. But why did Emma's captors want it? Ordinarily, in patent cases, speed favored the plaintiff, yes. It was why the rocket docket got so many of them.

But if this was the work of Roland Hemans or someone else on the plaintiff's side, why would he even need the extra advantage? He already had the ultimate edge: a judge in his pocket.

Or did the captors simply not want to draw this thing out any longer, knowing that every day brought risk with it? Risk that Emma might escape. Risk that they would be discovered.

And, yes, the chance of something going awry on any one day was small. But with every day that passed, it added up. That was why they wanted this to speed up. It was one area in which our interests were, for once, aligned.

I wanted this to be over far more than they did.

31

I was barely functioning later that morning as I showered, dressed, and girded myself for work.

Alison had demanded a full recounting of the night's activities. Then I showed her the picture. She was full of anger and tears, just like me, and I wanted to believe the mini collapse she suffered was so unscripted and so visceral that it had to be genuine. No actress could have faked the way her fists balled, the way her body shook.

Or was I just allowing myself to be manipulated? If she knew I was about to find that picture, because she was the one who ordered it to be sent, could she have practiced how she would respond?

I was no closer to making up my mind about any of it by the time I reached the courthouse.

The only person in my chambers when I arrived was Joan Smith. She was bustling about with a watering can in her hand, giving some of our office plants a drink.

After what I had seen at Kensington Mews on Saturday morning, I was looking at Mrs. Smith in a new light. Was this woman—wearing a skirt that went midway down her calf, the world's most sensible flats, and a sweater set—really the object of Roland Hemans' desire? Or was her allure simply that she could give him access to the judge who would decide the biggest case of his life? Had she, knowingly or unknowingly, supplied him with details about my life that aided the kidnappers?

"Good morning, Judge," she said as she drained a few last drops on top of a ficus plant. "Saw a picture of you in the paper this morning."

"Oh?" I said.

"It's on top of my desk if you want to look."

I wandered over to see a photo of Blake Franklin and me on the upper right corner of an interior page of the *Daily Press*'s local news section. It was a candid photo of us talking. He had his arm around me. I was even holding a glass of champagne, which made me cringe a little. It just made the whole thing look clubby and elitist. Associating with politicians was one thing. Hobnobbing was another.

The photo was one of three under the heading, "Senator Franklin Hosts Newport News Fund-raiser." There was no story, just a caption.

"Thanks," I said, taking a moment to gather myself before I tossed out a casual: "And how was your weekend, Mrs. Smith?"

"It was fine, thank you," she said, getting herself seated, having finished her watering. "Pastor is doing Matthew."

I waited for more. Nothing came.

"Did you . . . have any visitors or do anything social?" I asked.

She looked up. I had just gone outside the bounds of our normal Monday-morning conversation.

"I went to my sister's for Sunday dinner," she said.

"Oh. And how was that?"

"Fine, just fine."

Again, nothing more.

"You live in Kensington Mews, don't you?"

"That's right." She was looking at me really strangely now. I continued as if I didn't notice.

"It seems like that would be a nice place for entertaining," I said, really groping.

"I suppose it is."

She wasn't going to volunteer anything more. If Joan Smith was maintaining an intimate relationship with Roland Hemans and not saying anything about it, she'd know it was, at the very least, a breach of ethics. I had to push the conversation to see if I could prompt a glimmer in her eye with the right question.

"Mrs. Smith, do you by any chance know an attorney named Roland Hemans?"

She didn't hesitate. "Not that I'm aware of."

"He's representing the plaintiff in *Palgraff.*"

"Oh," she said.

And, again, that was it. There was no glimmer. Mrs. Smith wasn't giving me anything.

"Well, off to work," I said.

"Mm-hmm," she said.

As I closed the door behind me, she was already humming the first few bars of a hymn.

*

Maybe twenty minutes later, I was making my run toward our little kitchen for coffee when I saw that Jeremy Freeland had arrived and was sitting in his office.

I stopped myself short and tapped softly on the frame to his door. I had sent that e-mail turning down his request for us to recuse ourselves on Friday—well, technically, Saturday at 8:37 A.M.—and I wanted to make sure it was sitting okay with him. I really couldn't make it through a case of this magnitude with a disaffected career clerk.

"Hey," I said. "Got a second?"

"Yeah, yeah, of course," he said.

There was a slight flush to his skin, which told me he had probably gone on a long run before work. I softly clicked the door shut behind me.

"Sorry to bother you," I said.

"Not at all, Judge," he said. "I was actually about to come see you."

I took one of the chairs in front of his desk and briefly glanced at the security camera monitor. The thing was sort of hard to take your eyes off, even when it showed nothing.

Clearing my throat, I said, "About the e-mail I sent you Saturday morning—"

"Let me go first," he said, waving me off. "Look, I was thinking about it Friday night and Saturday morning, and even before I got your e-mail, I realized I was being silly. I was actually about to e-mail you saying, 'never mind,' when I got your e-mail."

"Are you sure?"

"Absolutely. I think I just . . . Sometimes I feel like these guys"—he pointed to Thurgood and Marshall, swimming aimless circles behind him—"like we're in a fishbowl all the time. It's just us in this little office suite, isolated from the rest of the world, and we render our decisions and who knows what everyone thinks? It's not like there's a comments box in the back of the courtroom. And then along comes a case like *Skavron* and suddenly we really *do* know what everyone is thinking, because they're all talking about us behind our backs—sorry to say it, but you know it's true.

"And then you add that to this *Palgraff* thing, which is obviously going to be very high profile, and it's like that fishbowl has gotten really small. And I think it just . . . it just messed with my head a little; that's all."

"Okay," I said. "I understand."

And I did. A little. Frankly, the whole thing was pretty curious. But I didn't have any leftover energy to ponder it.

At the moment, I had to focus on the Rule 16B Conference. Ordinarily, a judge might only pop his head into such a gathering and then pop back out, letting his staff handle the details. After the late-night delivery to my house, I would clearly need to be more hands-on.

"So are we ready for the Rule Sixteen this morning?" I asked.

"I think so. Jean Ann's got us set up in two-fourteen"—a conference room down on the second floor—"though I'm not sure if there are going to be enough chairs."

"Why not?"

"Did you *see* the list of attorneys on the docket? I didn't dare print it out. They'd have to kill a whole rain forest just to supply the paper."

I wasn't surprised. Defendants with essentially unlimited pockets, like ApotheGen, treated lawyers like so much parade candy, throwing them at the case in liberal handfuls. With good reason. More attorneys are usually able to prepare a better case. And a better case usually wins. Money talks in every aspect of life. It just tends to be that much louder in a court of law.

"I hadn't looked yet. What's the tally?"

"Well, it's Roland Hemans and two associates for the plaintiff. For the defense, Vernon Willards is in-house counsel for ApotheGen, but a man named Clarence Worth is sitting first chair. He's a senior partner with Leslie, Jennings & Rowley in New York."

Last time I checked, Leslie, Jennings & Rowley was either fifth or sixth on the Am Law 100 list of the legal field's largest firms.

"Who else?" I said.

"Well, Clarence Worth is part of a six-lawyer team for LJR. Then you've got three from Graham, Fallon and Farley from D.C. I'm assuming they're there for the FDA stuff. They've got McDowell-Waters doing their patent work. That's another four, I think. And then they've got two from Edgerton, Alpert & Sopko to round it out."

Edgerton, Alpert & Sopko was a local firm in Norfolk. Their role would be to smile a lot and try to wrangle favors out of my staff. They were hired out of legal necessity—someone representing ApotheGen had to be admitted to practice in federal court in Virginia—and on the presumption they might be able to wrest some small piece of home-field advantage from the plaintiff.

It was, all told, fifteen defense attorneys, not including in-house counsel. Given their rates for litigation, we were probably looking at about ten thousand dollars an hour worth of high-powered legal representation. If you were Roland Hemans, with his two associates, it was a lot to have stacked against you.

Just another reason why it made sense that Hemans might go about ensuring the outcome in a different manner.

"Sounds like a full house," I said. "And what were you and Jean Ann thinking about doing with them?"

"Could we just lock them in the room and tell them not to come out until they settle?"

He was joking, though I had known judges who had done something close to that. Obviously, I couldn't allow it here.

"Probably not," I said. "How's discovery looking?"

"Well, Hemans wants to depose the entire world—seventeen scientists, along with ApotheGen's division head, the CFO, and the CEO, Barnaby Roberts. He's also asked for a pile of documents and notes and things like that. I'm sure Worth will try to whittle it down, but ultimately I think we're going to have to give Hemans most of it."

"Okay. And what kind of schedule were you and Jean Ann thinking about proposing?"

"We were going to say six months for discovery, knowing Worth would probably ask for more. So we'll probably give them eight. Then we'd schedule the Markman for another two months."

Ten months without Emma. It was unthinkable.

Still, I said, "Got it. All right. I think we're set, then."

"Are you going to be joining us?"

"Yeah," I said. "I'll stop by for a little bit to say hello."

And then I would turn the entire case on its ear.

32

I waited a full hour into the proceeding before tapping lightly on the door to Room 214. I figured by that point they would be deep into it.

I followed the door in as Jean Ann was opening it, allowing me to glimpse the room before anyone inside realized the judge had arrived. There was a long conference table with room for eight chairs on each side. The defense had obviously gotten there first, because it had chosen the side with the windows at their backs, following that bit of pop psychology that said people with a large open space behind them appear more powerful than people who are backed up against the wall.

All eight of the chairs on the defense side were full, with another eight or nine people lurking behind them. I was sure I didn't want to know about the negotiations that determined who sat and who stood.

On the plaintiff's side, there was Roland Hemans, his two associates, and Denny Palgraff. I would have said they looked pathetic by comparison, except Hemans was such a physical presence. And he had exaggerated it by spreading himself out, filling three chairs' worth of space. *The New York Times* had called this case David vs. Goliath. Maybe that was true, but Hemans still made for one hell of an imposing David.

As I fully entered the room, whatever conversation had been going on immediately stopped. Everyone stood, delighted to be in my presence. This is an inescapable part of being a judge: People suck up to you all the time.

The introductions were a series of too-broad grins and forced laughter. Hemans actually stooped, using the full length of his arm to keep himself at a distance, not wanting to loom over me. He understood what impact his size and skin color had on many people. He didn't want to intimidate the little white judge.

On the defense side, the man who led the charge was Clarence Worth, the first chair from Leslie, Jennings & Rowley. He was a slim white man, a shade over six feet tall, with a polished, well-bred air about him.

Then came Vernon Willards, ApotheGen's in-house counsel. The names after him were a blur—other than that none were Paul Dresser. I was aware some of them had no real purpose in a Rule 16B Conference. They had traveled to Norfolk from New York, Washington, or wherever primarily for the three seconds they would have their hand pressed to mine.

It was stupid. But as far as they were concerned, it was part of the game. And, besides, ApotheGen was footing the bill. I made it all the way around the table until I reached the last person, a distinguished white-haired gentleman whose face I had seen before.

"A pleasure to meet you, Your Honor. I'm Barnaby Roberts," ApotheGen's CEO said in a polished Oxford-and-Cambridge accent, such that the first syllable, "Bar," came out in a rich, broad "Bah."

It told me everything I needed to know about the importance of this case to ApotheGen that the chief executive would drop everything and attend what should have been a routine scheduling meeting.

The only person in the room who didn't try to ingratiate himself was Palgraff. He stuck out his chest and thrust up his nose as he shook my hand, making it as clear as he could that he did not consider me his intellectual equal. After all, had I applied for my first patent when I was thirteen? Did I have a PhD at twenty-one? No. As long as towering genius Denny Palgraff was there, we were all just vying to be the second-smartest guy in the room.

"Take a seat, everyone, take a seat," I said, and all who actually had a chair assigned to them made use of it. I remained standing and said, "I trust Mr. Freeland has been taking good care of everyone this morning?"

Jeremy beamed. The lawyers smiled.

"Excellent. And how are we coming with a discussion of a settlement? Any progress?" I asked, because it's what a judge had to say in such a setting.

Hemans, the alpha male, immediately jumped on the question. "Your Honor, I've given the defendant every opportunity. They haven't been interested."

"Your Honor," Worth said, already sounding exasperated. "The plaintiff has asked for either a fifty percent share of all Prevalia profits for the life of the patent or a onetime payout of fifty *billion* dollars. We don't see how we can talk about a settlement with someone who is being so unreasonable."

"Unreasonable?" Hemans boomed. "You want to take my client's patent and—"

"Thank you, Mr. Hemans," I said, and Hemans quieted. "It sounds like we're fairly far apart on a settlement. Where are we with discovery?"

I pretended to listen as the two sides bickered back and forth. The gist of it was that Worth thought seventeen scientists was excessive. Ten, in his mind, was sufficient. Also, he was balking at turning over many of the documents and e-mails Hemans requested, saying it would be compromising too much of ApotheGen's proprietary information. I let it play out, then asked about scheduling, which prompted another round of pointless conversation.

"Okay, okay," I said, acting like I was losing my patience with their squabbling. Which, in a way, I was. "There doesn't seem to be a lot of agreement on anything here."

I surveyed them as if they were a room full of unruly truants. "Ladies and gentleman, I am aware of the importance of this case and of what's at stake," I said. "And I could send these disputes to a magistrate judge, but I'm going to save us all a lot of time and expense and tell you how I want this to go."

There was a lot of leaning forward in chairs around the room as I continued.

"First of all, on the matter of discovery, I agree with Mr. Worth that seventeen depositions seems excessive. I'm going to cut it to ten. Mr. Hemans, you can choose which ten are most important to you."

Worth allowed himself a brief, smug look of triumph, which I quickly stamped out:

"However, I think Mr. Hemans' document and e-mail requests are all very reasonable. We'll keep them good and sealed so ApotheGen doesn't have to worry about its competitors nosing around in them. I don't have any concerns about Mr. Hemans' discretion. And we'll have Mr. Palgraff sign an aggressively worded nondisclosure agreement as well. Does that sound fair?"

Neither side would have dared disagree. It was, so far, the kind of Solomon-like baby splitting for which judges were notorious. But I wasn't done.

"Now, as to the scheduling. As I'm sure you're all aware, I granted a preliminary injunction on Friday. Given Mr. Roberts' public comments about bringing Prevalia to the marketplace regardless of potential patent impingement, I felt I didn't have a choice."

Roberts flushed. I went on: "That said, I am deeply concerned about delaying the rollout of a drug that could potentially prevent millions of premature deaths. The law calls on me to weigh the greater good in decisions such as these, and in this case the public interest is very clear. I refuse to let this court stand in the way of such an important drug any longer than it absolutely has to. Therefore, you have two weeks from tomorrow to complete discovery. And we'll have the Markman hearing the Friday after that."

Into the orderly world of civil procedure, I had just thrown a concussion bomb. One of the lawyers from Graham, Fallon and Farley actually had his jaw hanging down. Another one—from McDowell-Waters, I think— made a sound like he had been punched.

246

It was Worth, the seasoned trial lawyer, who recovered first, albeit haltingly.

"But . . . but . . . Your Honor . . . with all due respect, you're talking about completing a year's worth of work in . . . in . . . less than three weeks?"

"Yes, I am, Mr. Worth," I said evenly. "So I suggest you get busy."

"But I don't know how—"

"Oh, stop sniveling," Barnaby Roberts declared, standing and pointing his finger at me. "This is outrageous. Not even three weeks to prepare for a case this intricate? It's ludicrous. You can't do that!"

Worth began the delicate task of trying to soothe his employer with: "Mr. Roberts, we'll be fine. If you could—"

"No, we will *not* be fine. This is . . . this is absolutely unacceptable! There have to be rules against this. We're filing an appeal. Now."

"Mr. Roberts, you can't appeal this," Worth said through clenched teeth.

"This is ridiculous," Roberts said, pointing at me some more. "Who do you think you are? What kind of kangaroo court is this?"

"Barnaby, *shut up*!" Worth yelled, then turned to me: "I'm terribly sorry for my client's outburst, Your Honor. Of course the court is right. And of course we'll comply with your schedule, providing Mr. Hemans can cooperate."

"Mr. Hemans will be just fine," the big lawyer said, not bothering to suppress a smug grin.

"Very good," I said. "I think we're done here."

The kidnappers wanted speed? They now had it. And then some.

The room was silent as I walked to the door. As soon as it clicked behind me, the shouting began.

33

In what remained of the workday, I buried myself in paperwork, which the federal judiciary excels at creating and which made for an excellent excuse not to have to talk to anyone.

That night, I returned to the emotional minefield that was my home. I had a brief conversation with Alison, making inquiries about her and Sam's day. To Alison, this would have seemed like a mental health evaluation—how was she? how was Sam? what did they do? But as soon as she wasn't around, I checked all the details with Sam. At least on their day, their stories corroborated.

After a quiet and strained meal—alongside an empty spot at the dinner table it hurt too much to look at—I fell asleep in front of the television. I was too exhausted from several nights' worth of interrupted and nonexistent sleep to even make it to Sam's bedtime.

At some point, I woke and shifted to the guest bedroom, a fact Alison and I did not discuss the next morning before my departure.

As I commuted in, I was looking forward to a genuinely uneventful day at work, a hope that was dashed as soon as the limestone edifice of the Walter E. Hoffman United States Courthouse came into view.

A line of news vans had formed on the street outside the main entrance. I saw the logos for the local affiliates of ABC, CBS, NBC, and Fox. On the sidewalk, a coterie of camera crews was setting up shop. This clearly wasn't a business-as-usual morning.

I turned into the judges' parking lot, around the corner from the commotion. Then I hurried out of my car, already apprehensive even though I wasn't sure I had a reason to be.

"What's going on out there?" I asked Ben Gardner as I passed through security.

"Press conference," Gardner said.

"Who called it?"

"Our esteemed congressman, Mr. Jacobs."

My body reflexively stiffened. Gardner was grumbling about how they weren't given any warning and weren't properly staffed for it.

"Does anyone know what it's about?" I asked, trying to seem nonchalant.

"Who knows? Maybe he just wanted some attention. You know those politicians. All I heard is it starts at nine. I hope it's over by 9:02."

I tried to smile, even if it probably came out more as a grimace, then quickly made my way upstairs. We had a small television mounted on the wall of our kitchenette. I flicked through channels until I found CBS, which had a morning news program.

It was only quarter of nine. A bottle redhead was talking about a high-pressure system. I took out my phone and did a Google news search for "Judge Scott Sampson Congressman

250

Michael Jacobs." Nothing pertinent returned.

At the top of the hour, the screen switched to a feed outside the federal courthouse. Soon the bald, bullet-shaped head of Michael Jacobs appeared. He was scowling from behind a temporary podium covered in logoed microphone boxes. His short-sleeve polo shirt revealed forearms with a set of Marine Corps tattoos. He probably had consultants, mindful of all those military voters in his district, telling him to keep them exposed whenever possible.

"Good morning and thank you for coming," he said in a gruff, drill sergeant's voice. "Last Thursday, in this courthouse, a travesty of justice was committed. A lifelong drug dealer named Rayshaun Skavron, who had pleaded guilty and should have spent no less than fifteen years in prison for his crimes, was set free. This was no ordinary drug dealer. This was a menace to the community, a man whose disregard for our laws resulted in the death of a very fine young man named Dylan Byrd."

The screen immediately flashed to a picture of Dylan. My stomach twisted as I remembered his father's words. *I miss my son so much. It hurts all the time. Can you imagine what that feels like, Your Honor?*

But I also felt no small measure of disgust at Jacobs and his bloodlusting communications staff. They had obviously provided that picture ahead of time to all the local television stations, who had agreed to embargo it until the press conference. This was a choreographed political event, one designed to show a public servant battling for his constituent—and the side of righteousness—against an out-of-control, out-of-touch federal judge. It had been planned and executed to maximize its dramatic potential in front of an electorate who, a mere seven weeks from now, would get to choose whether Congressman Jacobs kept his job.

I recognized all the tricks being pulled, because I had seen them from the other side so many times.

"The judge who rendered this ruling is a man named Scott Sampson," Jacobs continued, and now my official portrait had replaced Dylan's face. "He is hired by the taxpayers to send men like Rayshaun Skavron to prison. Instead, Judge Sampson has released this man back into our neighborhoods and into our schools, where he can continue to harm our children and our most vulnerable citizens."

The screen returned to the front-of-the-courthouse tableau, albeit from a slightly wider angle than before. I could now see Thomas Byrd, the aggrieved father, had been strategically stationed just behind Jacobs' right shoulder.

Jacobs gestured broadly. "I can't begin to tell you why Judge Sampson did this. You'll have to ask him that yourself. It is certainly worth questioning when a high-ranking member of a notorious drug cartel has been allowed to walk away scot-free. I think we all know how justice works in Mexico. What I cannot accept is Mexican justice here in the United States of America."

I balled my fists. Jacobs had managed to plant the suggestion I was corrupt while keeping his comments general enough to sidestep outright slander. He had also turned Rayshaun Skavron, a low-life nothing, into the next coming of El Chapo.

Jacobs wrapped up his harangue against me by introducing Thomas Byrd. The victim's father gave a more polished version of the statement he delivered in my courtroom, one that seemed—at least to my ears—to go lighter on his son's culpability and heavier on his outrage and injury about my decision. But if that made him less sympathetic, it was only by a matter of one or two degrees. His agony was still plainly genuine.

Midway through, I received a call from Alison, who must have been alerted to what was happening. I silenced the ringer and let it go through to voice mail.

Byrd broke down toward the end of his words, though not before he managed to deliver at least five perfect, emotion-drenched sound bites that would undoubtedly run on multiple newscasts throughout the day. Jacobs deftly handed him a handkerchief—a masterful piece of theater the cameras ate up—then gave Byrd a back-pounding hug.

Once back at the podium, Jacobs went for the big finale.

"The US Attorneys Office assures me it is going to do everything within the law to appeal this egregious decision and get this drug dealer back behind bars, where he belongs," Jacobs said. "But we cannot allow the judge who delivered this sentence to continue on the bench. I have attempted to go through proper channels with my complaint. But the chief judge of this circuit told me this ruling was a quote-unquote matter of conscience on the part of Judge Sampson, and he would not pursue the matter further."

At this point, Jacobs arched an eyebrow—*can you believe that crap?*—and whatever gratitude I felt toward Jeb Byers for coming to my defense was swamped by my loathing for the congressman.

"I have no choice but to publicly call for Judge Sampson's resignation. If he does not resign immediately, I will call on my friend and colleague Neal Keesee, the chairman of the House Judiciary Committee, to begin impeachment proceedings."

He lingered over that pronouncement for a moment, then finished: "Mr. Byrd and I will now take any questions you might have."

I clicked off the television, unable to tolerate any more of the Michael Jacobs Show. In a way, nothing he had said—and nothing he could do to me in the short term—truly worried me. It would take months for any investigation that might lead to impeachment to even begin.

The more immediate problem was that there was now a horde of reporters digging into my business, wanting to know why Judge Scott Sampson rendered this strange sentence. True, it might save my job if they learned the truth.

But it would be a death sentence for my daughter.

*

The first phone call asking for comment came in to Mrs. Smith's desk twenty minutes later. I told her I would have none. More requests flooded in quickly thereafter.

The press conference had obviously broken up. Outside my window, I could see several of the news crews had moved operations to the sidewalk outside the judges' parking lot. I knew exactly the footage they were looking to capture: me coming out, looking terrified and guilty; reporters shouting loaded questions at me, as if they were actually interested in "my side" of the story.

I wasn't going to give them that satisfaction. I could wait them out. I'd hide in the courthouse all day and halfway through the night if I had to.

What I couldn't duck was a phone call from Jeb Byers, which arrived shortly thereafter. I barely had time to register the quickening in my pulse as the chief judge of the circuit's voice entered my ear.

He did not bother with a greeting, starting instead with: "I take it you are aware of the spectacle outside your courthouse just now?"

"Yes, unfortunately."

"I wish I could say it surprises me, but it doesn't. Keesee and I spoke on Monday and I told him that while your sentence was unusual, I didn't think there was anything untoward about it. Keesee made it pretty clear to me he didn't think Jacobs was going to drop the issue."

"I can see that," I said, then added, "Thanks for your confidence in me, Jeb. I really appreciate it."

"You're welcome. I have to be honest, I'm not sure I understand the decision you made. But I'll defend to the death your right to make it. I won't stand for one of my judges being bullied, especially not by the likes of a second-rate lawmaker who is just trying to gin up a controversy for the evening news."

"Amen."

"But I have to tell you," he said, putting in an ominous pause, "I think the media is going to ask some rather pointed questions."

He didn't need to stoke my dread on that front. "I'm sure it will," I said.

"I think it would be wise to issue a statement. This thing is in the public and political sphere now. It doesn't reflect well on the judiciary to let a claim of this nature go unanswered. I don't like it when people accuse us of hiding behind our robes."

I was shaking my head, even though Jeb couldn't see it over the phone. "With all due respect, Jeb, I don't know if that's the best idea. I sometimes dealt with the media while I worked for Senator Franklin. The press is sort of like a parasite: The more you feed it, the bigger and hungrier it gets. The only way you can make it lose interest and drop away is by starving it."

"I understand where you're coming from, and ordinarily I might agree with you. But I think you need to come out swinging. My father taught me a long time ago the only thing a bully really understands is force. I think you have to issue a statement where you talk about Keith Bloom."

This was heading toward a disaster in a hurry. A statement about Keith Bloom would invite a level of scrutiny it couldn't withstand. I could imagine a handful of enterprising reporters trying to interview a high school football coach who didn't really exist. How long would it take them to realize they were chasing a figment of my imagination?

I had to get Byers off this public relations strategy, and

unfortunately there was only one way to do it: lie some more, essentially doubling down on what was already a losing bet.

"Well, Jeb, I'm not sure I can do that . . . to Keith. He's got a career and a family and a community he serves that doesn't need to know about his past unless he chooses to tell them about it on his own terms."

Byers didn't immediately respond, so I added, "It's not his fight. It's mine. It's not fair of me to drag him into this."

"Are you still in touch with him?"

"No. Not for years now."

"Well, what if you contacted him and told him what you were going to do?" Byers suggested. "Get his permission to use his story. I bet he talks about his youthful transgressions all the time with the young people he mentors now. He'd probably be proud to know his story inspired you and would want it to inspire others."

"I . . . I don't know, Jeb. It feels like a terrible invasion of a man's privacy. Knowing Keith"—I had to force the words out of my mouth—"he might feel compelled to help me out as a kind of quid pro quo for what happened when he was a teenager. But that still wouldn't make it right."

"I have a friend who's a reporter at the *Times-Dispatch*. He's very good. Very fair. What if I slipped him the name Keith Bloom off the record and let him chase it?"

The line fell silent as I tried to quell my rising panic. A reporter from the *Times-Dispatch* wasn't the answer to my problem. It was the personification of my biggest fear.

Byers was waiting for a response, and I came up with: "That feels like trying a case in the press. I'd rather just

257

ride this thing out. If Congress wants to investigate me and appoint a special prosecutor, that's fine. They won't find anything. It's not like I have a secret offshore account with a million dollars in it."

More silence. I felt like I was winning. And then Byers hit me with:

"Are you sure you should continue hearing cases while this thing is cleared up?" he asked.

As chief judge of the circuit, Byers chaired our circuit's Judicial Council, which could issue an order that would immediately strip me of my entire docket. Yes, it would take a vote of the entire council, not just Byers. But he wielded an enormous amount of influence.

The moment *Palgraff* was assigned to another judge . . .

I tried not to let my voice betray the mad thumping coming from my chest. "I hear what you're saying, but I worry it would be taken as an admission of guilt. It would be letting the bully have his way. You have my word I won't allow any of this to be a distraction."

He chewed on this for a moment, then said, "Okay. We'll see how things progress."

"I think that's a good plan."

"Let's keep in touch," he said.

"Absolutely. Thanks for everything, Jeb."

I hung up the phone, then buried my face in my hands.

34

The story—of the congressman who rode a Harley trying to impeach the federal judge who had once been shot—had enough hooks to it that everyone wanted a piece of it.

As the morning wore on, I watched in horror as Jacobs' quotes and Byrd's sound bites spread across cable news and the Internet, flying at the speed of scandal. Friends from college, law school, the Senate—people I hadn't heard from in years—were e-mailing and texting, either with offers of moral support or because they had been contacted by a reporter and wanted to know how to respond. Senator Franklin called twice.

I let everything go to voice mail. Even the calls from Alison. Especially the calls from Alison.

And yet, clearly, avoiding her wasn't going to work forever. On her fifth or sixth attempt, I finally picked up.

"Hey," I said.

"Oh my God, why haven't you been answering?" she said in a high-pitched voice.

"I've been a little busy," I said, perhaps too brusquely.

"I take it you saw that . . . that . . ."

"Press conference?"

"Yeah. I guess. If you want to call it that. Can that jerk really do that? Just stand up there and accuse you of . . . of . . ."

"Being corrupt? Apparently he can. If you think about it, I sort of am. Just not for the reason he thinks."

"But is he really . . . I mean, can he get you impeached?"

"Look, you just worry about Sam. I'll worry about my job."

In the background, I heard our landline ring.

"That's probably another reporter," she said. "They've been calling nonstop. I thought we were supposed to be unlisted."

"Reporters have ways of getting phone numbers."

"What about our address? Are they going to start coming to the house?"

"I don't think so. They'll be able to get our PO box, but that's it."

After The Incident and my appointment to the bench, I had taken measures, aided by a friendly helpmate at the Department of Homeland Security, to make sure our physical address did not enter the public record. I prayed I had succeeded. I didn't know what the kidnappers would make of a line of news vans coming down our driveway.

"What should I do if someone does come?" she asked.

"Tell them they're trespassing on private property and to get the hell out."

"Can you . . . can you come home? I'd feel better if you were here."

"I'm a little trapped here at the moment," I said, casting my eyes in the direction of the window. "And that might backfire if some reporter was able to follow me home. Why don't you go to your mom's house? Or Karen's? Pack a bag. Spend the night. Spend a few nights."

It would keep them safe from reporters. It would also spare me having to talk to her. And she wouldn't be able to rendezvous with Paul Dresser as long as her family was around, would she? I couldn't imagine Gina or Karen going along with something that insidious.

"Yeah, I guess we . . . Hi, honey," Alison said with sudden warmth in her tone. "I'm just talking with Daddy."

Sam had obviously walked into the room. I could hear him talking but couldn't really make out his words. Only Alison's.

"No, honey, Momma is just fine."

He said something else indistinct.

"You're a sweet, sweet boy. Why don't you go back downstairs and put on another program? I'll get you a corn dog just as soon as Daddy and I are done talking."

She waited, presumably for him to leave the room, then came back in a whisper: "He said I looked upset and asked if I was okay."

"That boy loves his momma," I said, and the thought of it choked me up. For however screwed up everything was, and for however much he hurt, Sam was still looking out for his mother.

Alison continued speaking in a hush. "Scott, I'm freaking out here. What if one of these reporters learns about . . . about why you really made that ruling?"

"They won't. The only people who know that are the kidnappers, and I don't think they'll be holding any press conferences."

"But what if some reporter goes to school and learns we've pulled the kids out? Or what if one of my sisters gets cornered by someone with a microphone and decides to defend you?"

"Oh God help us. You have to tell them not to talk. It is totally imperative that they—"

"I know, I know. My point is, there are a thousand ways things could go wrong. It's just . . . Everything is getting out of control."

You're just now noticing? I wanted to blurt. But a flip comment like that wouldn't help. Instead, I went for brutal honesty.

"Look, I know I'm supposed to be offering you comfort and reassurance here, but I just don't have any to give you, okay? You're right. This is out of our control. It's been that way all along. There's noth—"

I was about to say *There's nothing we can do,* until this thought hit me: Was she just panicking now about the lack of control because she actually had been in control before this? Was there a risk of exposure now that hadn't been there previously, something she and Paul hadn't planned on? I finished my sentence by switching pronouns:

"There's nothing I can do."

"Yeah, I . . . I know. Okay. I guess . . . I guess Sam and I will head to my mother's. We'll plan to stay the night. Maybe tomorrow night, too."

"I think that's a good idea," I said. "I'll call you later."

"Okay. Love you."

I took a deep breath, reminded myself I still had nothing

more than a half-cocked theory about my wife's involvement, and said, "Love you too."

*

One by one, the news crews packed up and left. Some lasted only until a little after lunchtime. Others waited until I was supposed to have come out at the end of the workday. The last of them didn't depart until the sun went down.

I gave it another hour after that, and still I hurried out, braced for an assault of shouts and klieg lights.

None came. On the drive home, I called Alison. She asked me to join her at her mother's house, but I declined. I told her it was because I wanted to keep up a show of normalcy for the kidnappers.

I talked with Sam for two minutes—which was about as long as I could get him to stay on the phone—then spent the rest of the trip, and the remainder of the evening, in lonely despondency.

The next morning, I made a quick drive-by of the judges' parking lot to see if there were reporters waiting there for me. But there were none. I hoped that meant I was old news for good.

After entering the building, I told Joan Smith I had some files to read and didn't want to be disturbed unless it was an emergency. I then lay down on the couch in my office, pulled out my phone, and told myself that spending a few minutes looking at pictures of Emma would be a comfort.

This quickly led to my weeping in silence. My brain didn't

buy the trick I was trying to pull on it. Yes, the little girl in the pictures was happy, smiling, and safe. But the little girl in real life was scared, alone, and in mortal danger.

And not doing anything about it was killing me.

For as much as I continued to be tormented by images of Alison on the beach in Saint-Tropez with Paul Dresser, my more reasonable thoughts told me Roland Hemans was still the most logical suspect.

Ultimately, ApotheGen was going to bring Prevalia to the marketplace—and Paul Dresser would still have a job there—whether the company had to pay off Denny Palgraff or not. If it won the case, it would make more money, yes. But it was still going to make *some* money, and its stock would still be worth *something*.

Which was not true for Hemans and Palgraff. For them, this was all or nothing.

I couldn't make Palgraff as the culprit, especially now that I had met him. Palgraff's arrogance would be such that he believed he would win because he was right. What's more, he would want the trial to take place: The long-withheld vindication of his genius, and the recognition for having discovered the PCSK9 inhibitor that changed the narrative of heart disease the world over, was every bit as important to him as the money it brought.

Hemans wouldn't care about any of that. He knew he was up against an armada of attorneys who were all but unbeatable—unless he could compromise the judge, in which case he could guarantee the payday of a lifetime.

Tailing Hemans, as I had attempted before, could lead to

disaster. He knew what I looked like now. Half of Hampton Roads now knew what I looked like, after Tuesday's media blitz. I had to maintain a low profile. And, as Alison had pointed out, I wasn't trained as a private investigator.

But—and I don't know why it took so long for this to come to me—I could hire one.

35

His name was Herbert Thrift of Herbert Thrift & Associates.

I picked him out of the Yellow Pages not because his ad claimed he had twenty-five years of experience with the Gloucester County Sheriff's Office or because he promised reasonable rates. It was because the word "confidential" was the largest of the several adjectives he used to describe himself.

His first available appointment was at noon on Thursday. His office was about ten minutes from the courthouse, on Northampton Boulevard, in a shabby colonial that was one of several in what otherwise appeared to be single-family homes.

As I walked up his front steps, I got the sense there were still sleeping quarters upstairs. This was not only the home of Herbert Thrift & Associates; it was Herbert Thrift's actual home.

After being buzzed into the foyer, I heard a man's voice call out from a room beyond, "I'm back here. Come on in."

I followed his instructions and was soon shaking hands with a thin, graying, bespectacled man in his fifties who, from the smell of his clothes, still lamented the indoor smoking ban.

"Herb Thrift," he said in a high, soft voice.

"Hi. Carter Ross," I said. It was a name I had gotten from a novel I enjoyed.

"Have a seat. What can I do for you, Mr. Ross?"

"Well, for starters, my name isn't really Carter Ross. Is that okay with you?"

If he said no, I would be out of his office and on to another PI before he was done with his next cigarette. But he showed no reaction.

"That's fine. I've had a number of clients start out that way. Eventually, most of them trust me with their real names, when they realize how seriously I take their privacy. As long as you pay for the work up front, you can use any name you want."

He spoke quickly, with confidence and competence. I already had the feeling Herb Thrift was my man.

"Not a problem," I said.

"So what can I do for you, Mr. Whatever-You-Want-Me-to-Call-You?"

"I want you to follow an attorney named Roland Hemans. Do you know him?"

He shook his head. "I've worked for a lot of attorneys. Not that one."

Which made sense. Patent lawyers didn't have much call for PIs.

"Do you have a picture of him?" Thrift asked.

"You can Google him. An article in *Virginia Lawyers Weekly* will come up. There are two pictures with the article."

He started typing. "And why do you want me to follow him?"

"Can I not say?"

"Sure," he said easily. "Sometimes it helps to know what I'm looking for. Like, if you think he's sleeping with your wife and suddenly he's—"

"It's not infidelity. Well, actually, I'm pretty sure Mr. Hemans is cheating on his wife, but it's not with my wife. His sex life is really not my chief concern."

"All right. So you want me to"—and here, his screen must have popped up with the article, because he interrupted himself—"Whoa. Big sucker, isn't he?"

"About six-eight, give or take," I said.

"I guess I don't have an excuse for losing him, then," Thrift said, then smiled.

I didn't.

"Anyhow, how much following do you want me to do?" he asked.

"Can you do twenty-four-hour surveillance?"

"Sure. If you really want me to. I'll tell you straight off you're probably wasting your money. Most people don't—"

"I'm not worried about wasting money," I assured him. "I'm more worried about whether you can do it without being spotted."

"That's my job."

"Seriously. It's more important to me than I can possibly explain to you that Hemans never sees you. He can't know he's being watched."

"I understand."

"And you can handle doing it round-the-clock?"

"Yes, sir. I'm not married, so it's not like someone is waiting for me at home. I'll do most of it myself. I'll probably use subcontractors for the overnight, but that's it."

"Subcontractors. Those are the associates in Herbert Thrift & Associates?"

"You got it. I only have a few, but I trust them. They're all good."

He leaned back and crossed his legs, resting an ankle on his knee. He wore well-beaten black loafers. They were shoes with a lot of miles on them.

"Okay, so how does this work, then?" I asked.

"Well, you pay in advance for a set amount of work. From there, you're the boss, so it can work any way you want it to. All I request is that you sign a standard agreement saying you understand there are no refunds and that you agree to the terms of service."

"I can do that. What comes after that?"

"Well, if there's something specific I'm looking for—some behavior or some person the subject is associating with—then I can contact you the moment I see it. If you really want this to be completely open-ended, I write a report, summarizing everywhere the subject has gone, what they've been doing, and who they've been with. I'll take pictures, of course. There are obviously limitations to that. Once they're in their home or office, all I can see is what my telephoto lens allows me to see."

"And you'll be able to tail his car. So if it's going to the same place a lot"—like the place where Emma was hidden—"you'll be able to tell me?"

"That's what I do."

"Terrific. When can you start?"

"Immediately, if you like."

That was a good answer. "And what do I pay you?"

"My rate is seventy-five an hour plus expenses. If you really want twenty-four-hour surveillance, that's eighteen hundred a day."

I think maybe he expected me to balk or backtrack at that point, but I said, "Great. It's now Thursday at twelve"—I paused to look at my watch—"thirteen. As far as I'm concerned, the clock started ticking the moment I walked in here. How about we meet again this time Monday?"

That would give me a trace on Roland Hemans during both workdays and weekend days. I trusted that would be a large enough sample size to catch him.

"I can do that."

"That's four days of twenty-four-hour surveillance, which will cost me . . ."

I paused to do the math. He did it for me: "Seventy-two hundred dollars."

"That's right. Seventy-two hundred. Can I pay you in cash?"

He smiled. "Since you're not giving me your real name, I'm afraid I have to insist on that."

"Great," I said. "Let me run to the bank. I'll be back in half an hour."

It turned out to be less. I found a branch of my bank five minutes away. We kept about fifteen thousand in our checking account. So I was able to return twenty minutes later with seventy-two crisp, new hundred-dollar bills, which made for a surprisingly thin stack.

Herb Thrift had me sign his agreement, a one-page document that "Carter Ross" didn't bother reading.

Then I handed him the money. Maybe I was wasting it. But it was exhilarating all the same. It made me feel like I was actually doing something. And that, in turn, made Emma feel closer.

It was worth any amount of money I had.

*

I was closing back in on downtown Norfolk, getting hung up in a few lingering strands of lunchtime traffic, when my phone rang.

It was Alison. We had spoken once on Tuesday night, when I called to tell her I would be spending the night at home, and once Wednesday afternoon, when she confirmed she was going to stay at her mother's again. Neither conversation had been long.

"Hey," I said.

"Hey. Are you alone? Do you have a second?"

It sounded like she was outside, near a road. She was speaking loudly, to overcome the background noise of what I assumed was traffic.

"Yeah, I'm just finishing up my lunch break," I said. Technically, that was true.

"Sam and I just went back home. There was a cop's business card stuck in our front door."

"A cop?" I repeated.

"A detective from the Gloucester County Sheriff's Office.

He left a note on the card saying, 'Please call me.'"

"Oh Jesus," was all I said, because I couldn't come up with anything more insightful.

"What's going on?"

"I have no idea," I said.

And I really didn't. Was this because Congressman Jacobs had convinced someone to arrest me? Or because my brother-in-law had shot someone on our property? Or because of something relating to Emma? It was difficult to guess which had caught up with us first.

"Can you call this guy?" Alison said. "This is your area, not mine."

"Absolutely," I said.

I pulled over so I could write down the contact information for Harold Curry Jr., detective sergeant, Gloucester Sheriff's Office, which Alison dictated to me. She ended the call by saying she was heading back to her mother's.

She didn't even bother saying what we were both thinking. Our instructions from the kidnappers had been quite explicit: Do nothing. Say nothing.

And we knew they were watching the house.

What had they thought when they saw Detective Sergeant Harold Curry Jr. stick a business card in our door? Even if the car was unmarked and the detective was in plainclothes, they would see him and be able to guess what he was. Cops just weren't that subtle.

I dialed the number for Harold Curry and, two rings later, heard a clipped voice say, "Sergeant Curry."

"Hi, Sergeant Curry. This is Judge Scott Sampson. You

left a card at my house?" I didn't hesitate on the "judge" part. I might as well use what pull I had.

"Oh, hello, Judge. Thanks for calling me back," he said.

"Not a problem. What can I do for you?"

"Are you at home? Could I stop by in ten or fifteen minutes?"

"No," I said. "I'm at work. My wife told me you left a card and asked me to call."

"Oh, I see. Is there a time I could pay you a visit tonight?"

"What's this about?"

"Well, nothing, probably. I'm just doing my due diligence about something."

"And what's that?"

"I'd rather just come out and see you," he said. "We can clear up this whole thing in a right hurry. You have ten minutes for me tonight after work?"

"We have plans tonight."

"How's first thing tomorrow, then? My shift starts at six A.M. I could come out before you left for work."

"I'd really rather you didn't," I said. "Look, what's this about?"

There was a pause. "Judge, I'm afraid I need to search your residence."

"And why is that?"

I heard him sigh.

"I can't . . . I can't say, sir."

"Well, then I can't let you search my residence."

"Look, Judge, I'm sorry about this. I really am. It would just be a lot easier if I had your cooperation."

"You're not going to get it."

He paused again. "I can get a warrant if I have to."

Even a man in my position could do nothing to challenge a warrant. The sheriff's office needed only to have probable cause, which is defined as the reasonable belief a crime has been committed. It is an incredibly low legal standard. Sam reasonably believes Santa Claus is coming down our chimney this year. Sheriff's deputies are sometimes every bit as credulous.

"It sounds like we have nothing more to talk about, then," I said, then hung up.

As I got my car back under way, I phoned Mrs. Smith to tell her I had come down with something and would not be returning for the afternoon.

There was no doubt Curry would secure a warrant. It was now crucial I got to the house before he did. I had to deliver a message to the kidnappers.

I pushed my car well past the speed limit on my way home, inventing stories in my head about judicial emergencies in case I got pulled over. As soon as I was back at the farm, I went straight to the closet where we kept arts-and-crafts supplies and unearthed items that would serve my purpose: several large pieces of poster board and a thick, black permanent Magic Marker. The kind whose lines could be seen from a distance.

With the marker, I scrawled WE SAID NOTHING on one piece. On the next, I wrote THEY GOT A WARRANT. WE HAD NO CHOICE.

It might not make a difference. But I wanted it to be as

clear as possible that Detective Sergeant Curry's visit was not an invited one. I made three more copies, then attached one set each on all four sides of our house with duct tape.

After finishing that task, I went to the front yard, to see if there was any evidence I needed to obscure.

Three days after Bobby Rowe had lay bleeding on my grass, there was no trace to suggest it had ever happened: no stains, no spots where the pine straw look disturbed. Satisfied, I took up a post on the front porch and waited for the cops with a sick feeling in my stomach.

I was thinking of Emma. And her fingers.

36

The older brother had noticed something different when he passed the screen on the way to the bathroom. Now he was frowning at the pixels, still uncertain of their significance.

Two large pieces of white, rectangular paper had been attached to the front of the house. The other cameras confirmed the sides had been similarly decorated.

This was the first new development since early Monday, when that kid he had sent with the envelope had been shot. That had been at least somewhat expected: They had seen the guards the previous two nights, prowling around the house.

This, on the other hand, was unexpected.

"Hey, come in here," he said into the kitchen.

The younger brother appeared in the door, starved for activity. "What?"

"Look at that," he said, pointing at the screen. "Can you read what it says?"

The younger brother sat down and clicked a button that looked like a magnifying glass. Soon the camera was zooming in on the pieces of paper.

" 'We said nothing. They got a warrant. We had no choice,' " the younger brother said, in English, before switching back to his native language. "What does that mean?"

"I don't know. Something must have happened. Can you rewind?"

"Which image?"

"All three."

The younger brother backtracked the footage until the image of a woman in a Lincoln SUV flashed into view.

"Stop there," the older brother instructed.

The brothers watched as the woman parked her car and walked up to the front porch with two bags slung over her shoulder. The boy who had once been their captive followed her. When she reached the front door, she appeared to pull a small piece of paper out of the crevice and read it. Then she returned to her car and departed.

"Keep going back," the older brother said. "I want to see who left that note for her."

The younger brother rewound farther until another vehicle appeared.

"Okay, start there," the older brother said. "Show me the middle camera."

The car on the screen had two tailpipes. Which meant police. The man who got out was bald and African American. He wore a blazer and slacks. No badge was visible, but the brothers recognized a detective when they saw one.

He walked up to the front porch and rang the doorbell. When no one answered, he circled the house, taking his time, looking in windows. Then he returned to the front porch, where he pulled a card out of his pocket and wrote something on it before leaving.

"What do you make of it?" the older asked.

"I don't know. Should we make a call?"

"We don't have a choice," he replied, and retrieved the Internet phone.

When he had completed the description of what had unfolded, the voice on the other end was firm. "I think it requires a response," it said.

"What kind of response?"

"I'm sure you'll think of something."

"What about the woman? The one who says we can't hurt the girl?"

"She's not your concern," the voice said. "She's mine. Do what you have to do."

37

I left the signs up for an hour, figuring that would be enough time for their message to be delivered.

Then I took them down. I didn't need the detective asking questions.

Perhaps an hour after that, at about half past four, I heard the low purr of a motor coming up the driveway.

There were actually two of them: a marked car being driven by a beefy, baby-faced deputy who couldn't have been more than twenty-three, and an unmarked Ford Taurus being driven by a black guy with a shaved head, who I assumed was Detective Sergeant Curry.

I walked down the front steps to greet them as they got out of their vehicles. This was not meant to be a friendly gesture. I wanted them off my property as quickly as possible.

"Do you have a warrant?" I asked as soon as Curry was out of his car.

He reached back into his front seat and produced an envelope, which he handed me.

Search warrants have to be very specific about what they are searching for and where they are permitted to search. Otherwise, crafty defense lawyers are well practiced at convincing judges like me that the evidence produced by the warrant must be excluded at trial. At a mere fifty-four words, the Fourth Amendment, which protects citizens against unreasonable searches and seizures, could be printed on a napkin. Yet the amount of case law it has generated could probably fill an aircraft carrier.

This warrant was reasonably well done. It gave the detective the right to search "the primary domicile, along with all other buildings, dwellings, or structures, whether temporary or permanent, whether sided or unsided," on my property, whose dimensions were described not with an address but with the block and lot number from the tax assessor's office.

It was what they were searching for that threw me.

"Evidence of kidnapping?" I said. "You guys think I kidnapped someone?"

"Judge, if you could just let us get this over with," Curry said, sounding more tired than anything.

"Go ahead," I said, knowing I didn't have a choice.

I led them back up the front steps to the porch, then held the front door open for them. Curry entered first. The beefy kid went second.

As I trailed them, Curry made a cursory pass through the first floor of the house. He descended into the basement, spending no more than a minute down there. Then he walked upstairs, briefly eyeballing each room.

"Is there an attic?" he asked.

I led him to the string that controlled the pull-down stairs. "Up there," I said.

He climbed halfway up, just enough to be able to poke his head up through the hole. Then he came right back down.

"Okay, I'm good," he said. "Sorry to have troubled you, Judge."

I was more confused than ever. "Can you tell me what this was about?"

"Do you know a young man named David Montgomery? David J. Montgomery?" Curry asked.

"No," I said.

"You'd remember him if you met him. He's got this tattoo on his arm he's very proud of. It's . . . well, it's a topless mermaid."

I did my best not to let the recognition show in my eyes. David Montgomery was Bobby Rowe. The kid had given me a fake name.

"I've never heard the name David J. Montgomery before," I said, because that was true.

"Yeah, I didn't think so," Curry said. "David is what you might call one of our frequent fliers. He has a bunch of charges pending against him right now, and he's pretty desperate to make them go away. As I understand it, he approached his probation officer early this week with some wild story about two guys living at this address who had kidnapped someone. I think he got it in his head he could get some consideration from the prosecutor. I can only assume he was high at the time."

I thought back to Bobby Rowe, yapping about us being kidnappers after Jason had been unable to control his mouth.

"Drugs are a scourge on the community," I said, trying to sound appropriately judicial.

"The probation officer had to report it to us. And on

the one-in-a-million chance David Montgomery was telling the truth, we had to check it out. I don't think anyone thought . . . Well, like I said, due diligence. I really am sorry to have disturbed you, Judge."

"Not a problem," I said, even though it was.

I showed them out, hoping—praying, really—that the people who had Emma didn't see any of it.

As they drove away, the memory of something that happened to Sammy when he was a toddler leapt into my head. This was maybe a few months after his first birthday. He was at that hell-on-wheels stage where he just tore around, oblivious to the dangers that lurked everywhere. It was exhausting to even try to keep up with him—much less him and his sister.

The two of them had wandered into our bedroom in our town house in northern Virginia. I probably wasn't paying as much attention as I should have been. They were playing, mostly agreeably, near the door. Then Emma closed the door on Sam's hand. In his panic, he ripped his hand away— leaving the nail on his pointer finger behind.

On some level, I knew I was supposed to be the calm, collected grown-up, reassuring and steady. Certainly, if had been my own finger, I would have just cursed, bandaged it, and moved on.

But seeing my son's blood gush, my body actually went into shock. I had to call a neighbor to come over and dress the wound. This was when I learned something most parents eventually come to realize: It's far more distressing when something happens to your kids than when it happens to you.

I thought of that now as I looked down at my hand, which I opened, clenched into a fist, and opened again.

*

Before I got myself totally rattled, I called Alison to let her know it was safe to come home. She didn't answer her cell, so I rang Gina's landline instead.

It was not Gina but Karen who answered with an officious-sounding, "Powell residence."

"Oh, hey, Karen, it's Scott. What are you doing over there?"

"Just brought the kids over to play with Sammy after school."

"Everyone getting along okay?"

"They wrecked the kitchen, then we shipped them outside before they could move on to the rest of the house."

"Sounds like a perfect afternoon at Grammy's," I said. "Is Alison there?"

"She's napping," Karen said apologetically. "She was tired when she got here, so we sent her off to the rack."

The rack. Short for barrack. Alison had long ago told me she hadn't been born into the Powell family. She had been enlisted.

"You want me to wake her up?" Karen volunteered.

"Absolutely not. Just let her know I called and that everything is fine and she and Sam can come home whenever they like."

I heard Karen lower the phone and say, "It's Scott"—

presumably because Gina was inquiring—and then she returned with, "What was up with that business card anyway?"

"Nothing. Just . . . tell Alison it was fund-raising for the Fraternal Order of Police, that the cop came to our house in civilian clothes, and that there's nothing to worry about."

"Is any of that true?" she asked.

"Not really. But I don't want her stressing out any more than she already is."

"Jason told me about the other night," she said. "Did it have something to do with that?"

"Yeah. Sort of. The cops came and searched the house. They went away, but—"

"But now you're worried there's going to be a delivery tonight," Karen finished for me.

"Yeah. And if it's bad, it might be something they'd feel compelled to deliver themselves, without using a courier. Maybe you should think about adding some manpower?"

"I hear you. Thanks."

"I mean, there's a chance they won't—"

"But there's a chance they will," she said. "Don't worry. I'm on it."

38

There were still rings under Alison's eyes that the nap hadn't fully erased when she and Sam arrived home early that evening.

We hadn't seen each other since Tuesday morning. She looked tired. More tired than I remembered. The other thing I noticed as she walked into the kitchen, where I had been making a salad, was just how loose her blouse seemed—except where it was tucked into her waist, which was even smaller and tighter than usual. She had lost weight. Food just hadn't been a priority for either of us lately.

As far as I knew, she also hadn't chopped any wood recently, not since the day Sam had returned to us. My tireless wife had lost the energy.

She crossed the room and sagged into me. Her bones had never felt closer to the skin.

Being able to feel this physical manifestation of her stress—she was, without exaggeration, wasting away from worry—was another argument against thinking she had anything to do with Emma's kidnapping. You couldn't deceive your own body, could you?

"Hey," I said. "How was your mom's house?"

"Fine. She's worried about us, of course. But everything there was fine."

"How's Sam been doing?"

"Okay, I guess. It's always better when he's with his cousins or at Grammy's. Around here, all there is for him to do is dwell on Emma being gone. At least somewhere else he's a little distracted. The cousins are great for that. And Grammy keeps him busy with games when it's just the three of us."

"Well, that's good. How was your nap?"

She separated from me and yawned. "I think I'm actually more tired now."

I looked back at the carrot I had been slicing and suddenly didn't have the energy for even one more chop. Mindful of the need to stuff some calories in my wife, I said, "Do you want to do Chinese tonight? I really just don't feel like cooking."

"Me neither," she said wearily.

"Great. I'll make the call on the way," I said, already walking out of the kitchen.

"No, I'll pick it up. Why don't you spend some time with Sam? He misses you."

I missed him too. So I said, "Okay, good idea."

Alison soon departed. After cleaning the remains of my stunted salad preparation, I wandered into the family room, where Sam was setting up an elaborate ramp system for racing his Hot Wheels.

"Hey, buddy," I said. "Give your old dad a hug."

He complied. It felt good to be able to hold him again, for however briefly he allowed it before he wiggled away.

"Do you want to race cars?" he asked.

"Sure, pal."

"Okay. Let me just finish the track."

He set to work on a particularly harrowing-looking loop, pouring his concentration into linking a series of orange plastic pieces together. For a while, I just watched him, mesmerized by the sureness of his movements.

Then, knowing Alison would be gone only so long—making this my best chance to talk with him alone—I began my routine scrutiny of his activities.

"So how was your day, buddy?" I asked.

"Good," he said. And not necessarily because it had been. Sam had this tendency to seize a monosyllabic answer whenever it was available.

"What did you and Momma do?"

"We went to Chick-fil-A," he said, not looking up from his work.

"The one next to Walmart?"

"Yeah."

"And then you went to Grammy's house?"

"Yeah."

"How was that?"

"Good."

"What did you do?"

"Grammy and I played Uno. Then the cousins got there and we played outside."

"I heard about that from Aunt Karen," I said. "It was nice of you guys to let Momma nap."

Sam, still with his eyes on his track, said, "Momma didn't nap."

"Oh?" I said, the now-familiar alarms going off in my head. "So what was Momma doing while you were outside?"

"She wasn't there."

Again.

I tried to make like it wasn't a big deal, like my ears weren't perked up, like this wasn't reawakening every doubt about my wife I had, mere moments earlier, been convincing myself I could suppress.

"Where did she go?"

"I don't know," he said, having put the finishing touches on his track. "Do you want to race now, Daddy?"

"Yeah, hang on a second, though. Momma wasn't at Grammy's house with you?"

"Well, she was. Then she left."

"Where did she go?"

"I dunno."

"How long was she gone?" I asked.

"I dunno. A while."

"Like, an hour?"

"Maybe."

"Two hours?"

"Yeah, maybe. I don't know."

I nodded, unsure of what else to ask him. My wife had once again disappeared in the middle of the day. And, given the opportunity to tell me about it, she had maintained the lie that she had taken a nap at her mother's house.

A car door slammed outside. Alison was back. I had to shut down the questioning. Not that I even knew what to ask.

"Dad, can we just race cars?" Sam asked insistently.

"Sure, buddy."

"Pick a car. I'm going to be red. Red is superfast."

The front door opened and Alison announced her return. As I settled in to give the yellow Hot Wheels a go down the track, something else occurred to me: Karen had covered for her. And Gina had overheard her doing so.

So not only had Alison snuck off again—to be with Paul? to see Emma?—her family was complicit.

*

I ate the Chinese food without really tasting it, sitting across from my wife without really looking at her.

She made a few attempts at conversation, but the tumult in my head drowned out whatever she was saying. Eventually she gave up and turned her attention to the food she kept pushing around her plate. The only sound coming from our dinner table was the occasional scrape of a fork.

I just couldn't reconcile the discrepancy between the Alison I saw—and felt with my own hands—and the Alison who seemed to be operating the rest of the time. That Alison was this shadowy figure, darting in and out of view in the hazy distance. And my only real lens on her was a six-year-old who barely understood what he was seeing.

It made me feel more estranged from her than ever. Whether she was involved with Emma's disappearance, whether she had rekindled with Paul, what role her family was or wasn't playing—that stuff was all, in some ways, potentially nothing more than supposition. The very real, very nonsuppositional impact was that my suspicion, and the silence it brought with it, was playing hell on our marriage. At a time when we should have been falling in on each other for support, we were instead falling apart.

I might have attempted to talk to her about it, even in a way that didn't directly challenge this latest lie, except my head was hammering from the possibility of that dreadful delivery that might have been on its way. And the aspirin I was gulping didn't even dent it.

After we got Sam to sleep, I lay down on our bed with a *National Geographic*, hoping pictures of faraway places could transport me somewhere else. Alison, who had no idea what might be coming, slipped away into the bathroom, where she took a leisurely shower.

Then she spent a long time with the hair dryer going. She had done this many times before: sit on the floor, allowing the air to rush over her and the white noise to soothe her. It was her version of meditation.

When she emerged, she was wearing only a towel. She walked over to my side of the bed and put her hand on my hip.

"Hi," she said.

I looked up from my magazine without a word.

"Do you think we could . . . ," she said, and began running her hand along my side.

"Oh," was all I could manage. To say sex had been the last thing on my mind was a huge understatement.

"I just . . . I need you right now. I need to feel you,"

she said quietly. "I miss you. We're . . . I mean, we're barely talking, Scott. And I get it. I really do. Words are . . . they're just impossible sometimes. But I still want to feel like we're connected somehow. Even if it's just for a little while."

In the twenty-five years we had been together, I had never denied one of her advances. Why would I? I loved being with her, loved every inch of her. I firmly believed that couples who kept talking, laughing, and having sex would never have to worry about divorce. The first two had been dangerously disrupted, so shouldn't we at least keep the third one in place?

But there was just no way. Not with her lies. Not with the thought the sex might be another smokescreen, a piece of artifice designed to distract me. Not with Jason, Karen, or Jenny outside the window. Not with the Gloucester County sheriff's detective having been in this room a few hours before. Not with Paul Dresser dancing in my nightmares. Not with Emma, possibly in the worst pain of her life at this very moment.

"I'm sorry," I said. "I just don't think I—"

She looked away for a moment. When she turned back, her eyes had welled up.

"Can I just . . . Can I just lie here with you for a second?"

I couldn't say no. I scooted over and she curled up next to me.

"Can you hold me?" she asked, her voice even smaller than before.

I draped an arm over her. I could feel her body shaking.

She was crying, but she wasn't making a sound. I knew I should have been weeping along with her.

If only I was convinced it was real.

39

Once I was sure Alison was asleep, I covered her with a blanket, then rolled off the bed.

I crept into the guest room, where I didn't bother peeling back the bedspread. There was no point in dirtying sheets with the act of not sleeping. I waited with the light off, keeping myself braced for the sound of a gunshot outside.

Perhaps an hour later, I heard a different noise on the nightstand. It was a buzzing, coming from my phone. I picked it up, swiped at it.

There was a text message. From Alison. Or, I should say, "Alison," since the real Alison was in the other room, asleep.

The message read, NO MORE POLICE. There was a video attached.

My heart was thumping as I hit the play button. For twenty tormenting seconds, I waited for it to load.

Then it started. The screen was perfectly black, like someone had covered over the lens.

There was audio, though: a high-pitched whimpering, albeit muffled—like an injured animal making noises with its throat.

Then the volume suddenly spiked. The noise had a human grunt mixed into it. Which was how I knew it wasn't an animal. It was Emma. And she was hurting. Badly.

I brought my face closer to the phone, but there wasn't anything to see. There was only the horrible sound of my daughter yelping with pain.

Pain and maybe shock. It was the kind of noise you never wanted to hear any child make, much less your own.

Adrenaline coursed through my body. I couldn't keep the phone steady. My breath had grown short. I recognized another panic attack coming, and I willed it to stay away.

"Oh God, please help her," I moaned quietly. "Oh God."

Her screams died down for a moment, to be replaced by the same whimpering sound as before. What was happening to her? And who was doing it?

Another round was coming. Emma's cries were building, like she was anticipating something terrible. I could make out a pleading, "No, no, no, no—"

Then there was another shriek. It was so sharp it momentarily overloaded the phone's simple speaker.

Then, suddenly, there was video. And it made me wish the screen had just stayed black.

It was a close-up of Emma, lying on a dirty linoleum floor in what appeared to be a bathroom. She had been hog-tied. I couldn't see her ankles and wrists, because they were somewhere behind her, off screen. But it was apparent that the ropes were tight, because her tiny body had been forced into a backward C. She was sopping wet. She wore only a pair of panties. She was shivering. And twitching.

Her face was bathed in blood. There were smears of red on the floor near her stubbly head. She was clearly bleeding from somewhere on her head or face, though there was so much of it I couldn't tell where the wound originated.

There was also blood pouring from her mouth. Like maybe she had bit through her tongue. That wasn't the worst part, though. It was her eyes, which were wide and terror filled. Just seeing them made me want to scream myself.

Then it ended.

All told, the counter on the bottom of the screen told me the video lasted for thirty-eight seconds.

It aged me a hundred years.

*

The next several hours disappeared into a haze of despair. I couldn't even pretend my thoughts had any logical order to them. I didn't watch the video again—I'm quite sure it would have short-circuited what little connection to sanity I had left. Yet portions of it kept replaying in my mind.

Around two A.M., I went into my office and opened my laptop. Desperate to plant different images in my head, I started scrolling through old family photos: Emma at Halloween, dressed up as (what else?) a Disney princess; Emma on our beach, covered in river mud; Emma baking muffins with her mother; Emma in her Easter dress, waiting to go to church, making funny faces at the camera; Emma in front of the US Capitol during a recent family trip to D.C.

Eventually, I settled on a video from the previous winter. As the action began, Emma was bundled up with so many layers under her jacket her arms stuck out from her sides. There was a knit hat that looked like a kitty cat, pulled low over her forehead. She was lying faceup in a thin dusting of snow that hadn't quite covered the grass tops.

"What are you doing, Ems?" I heard my own voice ask.

In response, she began flailing her arms and legs, flattening the snow.

"I'm an angel, Daddy! I'm an angel!" she sang out, her voice high and clear and innocent.

"You're my angel, all right," I said.

This stopped her. "Am I really, Daddy?"

"Emma Grace Sampson, you will *always* be my angel," I assured her, which prompted her to happily continue her scissoring motion, a blissful smile on her face.

I played it again, then a third time, watching through tears. When I returned to the guest room, I hoped I'd be able to keep that happy picture in the forefront of my thoughts. But it didn't work. A vision of her on that bathroom floor kept coming back, like some relentless invading army.

What came in behind it was what I recognized as the full range of my new emotional spectrum. The despair was followed by feelings of supreme impotence, soon to be replaced by rage, then heartache, then hatred, then anxiety, then rage again, then . . . Well, I'm not sure there's been a word invented that adequately captures what it is to be a parent whose child is being put through a pain that you can observe—and even feel yourself—but are powerless to stop.

I lay in the darkness and watched the window as an inky, starless sky gave way to a blue-gray dawn. Soon, an orange sunrise told me it was time to rise and start pretending some part of my soul wasn't on fire.

40

Alison seemed to be giving me extra space as I lugged myself through a prework routine that eschewed breakfast but included an extra cup of coffee.

At some point during the evening, I had considered whether that horrifying footage ruled out any possibility of Alison's being connected to what was happening to Emma. It was beyond unconscionable to think she would sanction Emma's torture.

But I also had to concede there was a possibility the video had been doctored in some way. I never did see the car battery, or whatever it was they used to administer what I presumed was a series of shocks to her body. Maybe what I had seen and heard was nothing more than high-tech fakery. Maybe that was just what I prayed for. And it left me in the same place I seemed to be stuck in regarding my wife's potential duplicity: I just couldn't be sure.

Either way, I already knew I wasn't going to tell her anything about the video. It was bad enough one of us had to see it.

I soon shoved myself out the door and, after facing some extra traffic in the Hampton Roads Bridge-Tunnel, trudged through the entrance of my chambers, slightly later than usual.

Mrs. Smith was sitting there, as prim as ever. I thought of Herb Thrift and his telephoto lens, wondering if perhaps he had already captured her having a secret rendezvous with Roland Hemans.

"Good morning, Mrs. Smith," I said.

"Good morning, Judge. How are you feeling?"

Could she tell I hadn't slept that night? Was it that obvious? Then I remembered: I had called in sick the previous afternoon.

"Much better, thank you," I said, aware I probably didn't look it. "Everything go okay yesterday?"

"Just fine. Back to normal, really. Only a few calls from the media."

"I guess they're finally getting that no comment means no comment."

"You did get one call this morning, though," she said. "From that man who keeps calling. Steve Politi at HedgeofReason."

"You can give him the same no comment."

"I did. I just wanted you to know."

"Thank you," I said.

And then she uttered a sentence that woke me up:

"There's been a filing in *Palgraff*."

"Oh," I said, even though I wanted to ask, *What now?*

"I printed it out for you," she said. "It's on your desk."

"Thank you," I said again.

I walked slowly to my door and then, as soon it was closed behind me, sped across the room and went straight for the document that was sitting squarely in the middle of my desk. It had been filed by Roland Hemans on behalf of Denny Palgraff. And I nearly choked on my own spit when I read the words "Motion to Recuse."

Roland Hemans wanted me off the case.

The core of his complaint was that I had a conflict of interest because ApotheGen Pharmaceuticals was a major financial supporter of Senator Blake Franklin. And Franklin was not just my "former employer and close associate"—as he asserted in one of his numbered chapters—but also "the godfather to one of Sampson's children."

How did Roland Hemans know about *that*? It was far from common knowledge and had not been reported in the press after The Incident. It hadn't even come up in my confirmation hearing, and those things dig up everything.

I kept reading. ApotheGen had, according to Hemans, given "in excess of $2.1 million to efforts aimed at electing Blake Franklin, both in direct contributions to the Committee to Reelect Blake Franklin and indirectly, through activities of Forward Health America, a Political Action Committee controlled by ApotheGen CEO Barnaby Roberts."

Barnaby Roberts had also made "more than $150,000 in personal contributions to the campaigns of Blake Franklin, the maximum allowable under the law."

To put the allegation in more plain language: Blake Franklin was bought and paid for by ApotheGen—and, therefore, it owned me too.

One of the exhibits was a scanned newspaper clipping of that clubby photo taken of us at his fund-raiser, the one of me holding that ridiculous champagne flute. His arm was wrapped around me. I looked, for all the world, like his lickspittle.

But it was one of the other exhibits that really caught my eye. It was a photo of Blake and Barnaby Roberts sharing a meal together. Even more curious was the caption that ran with it on the Associated Press wire. The picture was three weeks old. It had been taken three Fridays earlier.

The *Palgraff* case had already been filed at that point. It had already been assigned to my courtroom, even if I hadn't been aware of it yet. Jeremy Freeland and my staff had been working on it. It had almost certainly come to Roberts' attention. I wondered if Roberts knew about my connection to Blake at that point.

Had they discussed the case? Had Blake promised to try to subtly (or not-so-subtly) lobby for a certain outcome on ApotheGen's behalf? Say what you will about the influence of money on the political process and you probably can't understate it. I just knew two-point-whatever million dollars bought a lot of it.

So they had broken bread. And a week and a half later, my children were snatched.

I couldn't make Blake out as a kidnapper. He loved my kids. He was Emma's godfather. He would never knowingly harm her.

But had he told Barnaby Roberts certain things about me and our family—where we lived, where the kids went to school, what our patterns were? Had my mentor, in essence, sold me out?

That was one of the reasons I could feel my jaw tightening.

The other was the realization that was sinking in: Roland Hemans had nothing to do with Emma. He wouldn't want a judge he controlled booted off the case.

Likewise, Palgraff wasn't a suspect. Hemans would never file a motion to recuse without his client's knowledge and permission.

So if it wasn't Hemans or Palgraff, it had to be someone at ApotheGen. Like Barnaby Roberts. Or Paul Dresser.

The only problem was—and this accounted for the re-newed sense of helplessness now settling over me—I didn't have an inkling of what to do about it.

*

The central paradox of a motion to recuse is that it must first be filed with the very judge you are looking to boot off the case—a judge who has, theoretically, already reviewed the matter and determined himself to be an acceptable arbiter. In order to avoid any appearance of impropriety, the judge will sometimes ask another judge to rule on the motion.

With that in mind, I asked myself: If this was one of my colleagues being described in this motion, how would I rule?

It wouldn't even be a close call. I'd order the judge to recuse himself.

Which was not an option here.

I still had to file a response, of course. The many lawyers copied on this document would be waiting for it—probably with bated breath, since they were desperate to slow down the breakneck pace at which I had insisted discovery would proceed. I picked up the phone, tapped in Jeremy's extension, and, when he picked up, said, "Will you come in here, please?"

Two minutes later, he was sitting before me. I didn't need to ask if he had read the motion. He was already biting his lip.

"I'd like us to file a ruling on the motion to recuse today," I said.

"Absolutely. Might as well get this case off our plate."

"No," I said firmly. "We're going to deny the motion."

And then Jeremy Freeland, the steadfastly loyal career clerk who had never questioned a single one of my rulings in the four years we had worked together, said, "Judge, really?"

"Yes, Jeremy."

"Judge, with all due respect, I just don't see where you have a choice. You *have* to recuse yourself. It's the only proper course of action. With this on top of the accusations from Congressman Jacobs? It's too much. I mean, think about what Judge Byers—"

"What about Judge Byers?"

Jeremy had stopped biting his lip.

"Listen, clerks talk," he said softly. "I heard that Judge Byers suggested you stop hearing cases until the impeachment thing worked its way through. You know he could force your hand. The Judicial Council would fall in line with him. This is the time to show him how reasonable you are. And what a reasonable judge does with a motion like this is step aside. I'm not saying it's true, what Hemans is alleging here. I'm just saying you need to think about how it looks."

I just stared at him, with his neatly tailored suit and his crisply knotted tie, feeling resentful of—or maybe just angry at—him and his heedless insouciance. This was all so theoretical to him. Just another neat, bloodless decision whose only ramification was what chatter it would create among the other clerks.

And I hated him for it. He didn't understand even one-one-hundredth of a percent of what was on the line here.

"Judge, please," he continued. "Can't you just, I don't know, sleep on it over the weekend or something? Or ask some other judges what they think?"

"Why?" I snapped. "Because you asked me to recuse myself from this case last week and I wouldn't do it? Because you still have a bug up your ass you won't explain?"

His mouth hung open.

"Jeremy, for whatever you or Roland Hemans or anyone else thinks, I don't have a problem with this case. ApotheGen gave my ex-boss some money. So what? It's totally immaterial to my ability to make a fair decision. And I'll happily explain that to Judge Byers if I have to. Now, I'm asking you to write a ruling denying this motion. Will you do it or not?"

"Judge, I just—"

"Get the hell out of my office."

He was too stunned to move.

"Go. Now," I barked. "I've got work to do."

Without another word, he rose from his seat and departed my office, clicking the door shut softly behind him.

41

I could feel the rage radiating from my face. Before I even knew what I was doing, I pulled out my phone and punched the shortcut for Blake Franklin.

"Hello, Judge. I was actually gonna call you today, see how you and your new girlfriend, Congressman Jacobs, were getting along."

"This isn't about Jacobs," I said tersely. "I am right now looking at a complaint filed by the plaintiff in the *ApotheGen* case. It says that ApotheGen and Barnaby Roberts have been major contributors to your campaigns over the years. Is that true?"

"Well, yeah, probably," he said.

"Probably?"

"Okay, definitely. Why do you sound surprised? I get money from ApotheGen and probably every other major pharmaceutical company. I'm on HELP, for goodness' sake. You know the *H* stands for 'Health,' right? Didn't you ever look at my donor list?"

"That wasn't my area."

"Okay, well, yeah, I'm sure I've taken money from ApotheGen."

"Several million dollars' worth," I said.

"I don't know if it's *that* much, but it's all public record, son. You can look it up if you want. Why do you have a bee in your bonnet?"

"Blake, for the love of God, they're the defendant in the most public lawsuit to ever hit my courtroom. Don't you think you could have, I don't know, mentioned at some point that they're one of your biggest contributors, if not your biggest?"

He stayed quiet for a moment. Then he said: "I don't mean to be dense, but why?"

"Why? Don't you think that looks like a little bit of a conflict of interest?"

"But you don't work for me anymore. You haven't for, what, four, five years now? What's the statute of limitations on how long you have to keep lugging around my baggage?"

"It doesn't matter, Blake. You appointed me. You still invite me to your fund-raisers. You're Emma's godfather. We're friends. Everyone knows it. You've been in Washington long enough. The appearance of a conflict is just as bad as an actual conflict."

"Aw, hell, son. You're starting to sound like *The Washington Post*."

"Stop it, Blake. You've been calling me, asking me questions about the case. As soon as I granted that injunction, you were on the phone to me, trying to pry stuff out of me. Did you call Barnaby Roberts as soon as you hung up or did you wait two minutes to let the smell clear?"

"Now, what are you suggesting? I don't like—"

"I'm not suggesting it. I'm saying it: You've been in

305

Barnaby Roberts' pocket for a long time, and now you're doing his bidding."

"Hang on just a second here. You're out of line right now. I take money from Barnaby Roberts and ApotheGen because I have to. That's politics. Do I really have to explain that to you? But if I even thought for a moment that money came with strings, I'd tell them to shove it right back up their asses. You know that. Did you really work for me that long, thinking money could bend me?"

"I'm not sure *who* I worked for anymore."

"Well, then let me put your mind at ease: I'm not in his pocket or anybody else's and I resent—"

"Did you or did you not have a meal with Barnaby Roberts three weeks ago?"

He took a moment. I heard his breathing coming through faintly.

Then, at a lower volume than the one he had just been using, he said, "Yeah. Three weeks ago. A month ago. Something like that. How . . . how did you know about that?"

"Someone from the Associated Press snapped a picture of the two of you. It was one of the exhibits in the plaintiff's filing."

There was more silence on his end. I filled it with: "I asked you about Roberts last week, and you said you didn't know him well."

"I don't. Jesus, Scott, we had breakfast, not sex."

"Did you discuss the case?" I asked.

He didn't say anything.

"Did you discuss me?" I asked.

Still no immediate answer.

Then he said, "It's none of your damn business, what we talked about. But I'll tell you anyway. The subject of the lawsuit never came up, and neither did you. We were talking about some regulatory issues and it was a very proper, aboveboard conversation that I would have in front of *The Washington Post* or the damn Federal Election Commission. You may or may not be aware of this, Judge, but the First Amendment guarantees citizens the right to petition their government."

"Some more than others," I said.

"Aw, listen to you. Look, are we done here? I have better things to do than be accused of . . . whatever the hell it is you're accusing me of."

"Yeah, we're done."

"Good," he said, then hung up.

42

By the end of the day—which was itself at the end of a hellishly long week—my anger had given way to simple exhaustion.

As I departed the courthouse, I retrieved a voice mail from Alison saying Karen had invited us over to their house for dinner and that she would see me there.

"Or you can skip it if you want. We'll just see you at home whenever," she concluded.

There was a gentle tone to her voice. Underneath, I could practically hear the eggshells she was walking on around me. I was tempted to accept her offer, if only because it would spare me an evening of doing calculus: What role was her family playing in the cover-up? Did a glance from Karen or a gesture from Mark have something else behind it?

But, ultimately, I decided I had a certain duty to Karen and the rest of the night watch. My perhaps-paranoia and trust issues aside, they needed to understand—for their own safety—that even though there had been no actual delivery the previous night, there had been a virtual one. The threat level had not subsided but had, in fact, increased.

Besides, I missed Sam.

So I pointed my car toward the Lowe residence, which was located in a subdivision filled with nearly identical houses, all of them well over four thousand square feet. The Lowes' place always had a too-big feel to me. There were large expanses of empty carpet everywhere you looked. A year ago or so the heat pump broke, and the unit they needed to replace it was so monstrous, they didn't have the cash on hand to buy it. Alison and I loaned them the money.

Still, there were benefits to having at least one house in the family with that much interior real estate: There was space for everyone to sprawl out, which was sometimes the only thing that kept a family functioning properly during the high holidays.

I found the children outside the house, tearing around with great velocity but no apparent direction. I grabbed Sam just long enough to extract a sweaty hug, then let him continue in his aimless careening.

When I reached the front door, I didn't bother knocking. I just went in and let the smell of caramelizing onions draw me into the kitchen, where all four Powell women—Gina, Karen, Jennifer, and Alison—were wearing aprons and busily creating several savory somethings.

"Hey," Alison said warmly when she saw me. She walked over and kissed me. "You look worn-out," she added, stroking the back of my head.

"Yeah, I feel it."

"You want to take a quick nap before dinner?"

"No, I think that'll just make things worse."

"Okay," she said. "We've negotiated a we-cook-you-clean treaty with the guys, so they're out on the deck, having a drink. Do you want to get a beer and join them?"

"Sure," I said. Then I spied the empty wine bottle, which gave me an idea. The Lowes had one of those floor-to-ceiling IKEA wine racks in the corner of their laundry room.

"Actually, I think I'd rather have some wine," I said. "Karen, would you mind helping me pick a bottle?"

"Just grab whatever," she said.

"I don't want anything too expensive," I protested. "You know I'm not a wine guy. It'd be wasted on me."

She glanced up at that point, which allowed me to give her the kind of meaningful look that told her this wasn't about wine.

"Okay, hang on," she said, blotting her hands on a towel.

She followed me to the laundry room. There, in a hushed voice, I told her about the video. She asked if she could see it and I told her she really didn't want to. But she insisted.

So I queued up the video and handed her my phone. Then I excused myself, shutting the laundry room door. I really couldn't handle seeing the thing again.

When she was done, she opened the door. Her face had lost some color.

"Now you know why I said you didn't want to see it," I said.

She was shaking her head and sucking air through her teeth. "Those bastards," she said, then swore again. "If I could get my hands on them . . ."

Her look was faraway, her thoughts fixed on vengeance.

Then she came back to me. "Look, I know you're not asking my opinion, and I know I agreed to do this your way. But can you at least think of taking this to the FBI now?"

"Are you nuts? No way. What would that accomplish?"

"Don't you think they'll be able to trace the origin of this and bust those guys? A video like that isn't like some little text message. It's a lot of data to transmit. I bet between the IP addresses and the cell towers, the FBI can figure out—"

"No," I said firmly. "These guys are too careful for that. I'm sure they covered their tracks. It's easy to obscure IP addresses. The kiddie-porn guys do it all the time. And we . . . we just can't risk it. This is what they did to her after the cops visited us for a grand total of maybe ten minutes and I made it as clear as possible I wasn't cooperating. I don't want to think about what they'd do to her if they figured out we were working with the FBI. They're obviously watching us at home. They're probably watching me at work. I just . . . no."

"Okay. I'm just saying if it was my daughter—"

"But it's not. Alison and I have already settled on how we're doing this," I said, invoking the higher authority that was her sister. "I'm only telling you about this because I feel you have a right to know given your . . . nocturnal activities. But you have to respect our wishes on this, okay? Please."

I looked at her imploringly. With her hand, she combed away a strand of blond hair that had come loose. The gesture reminded me of Alison.

Then Karen's face softened a little. The skin under her eyes was loose and baggy. I had been so focused on my own exhaustion, I wasn't taking the time to recognize everyone else's. Spending every third night—or more—outside my house with a rifle in her hands was wearing on her.

"Okay," she said finally. "For the record, I disagree with you. But okay."

She grabbed a bottle off the rack at random and we returned to the others.

*

I soon joined the husbands out on the porch, where they were sipping beers and sitting in deck chairs, staring out at the woods that backed up against the rear of the property. Mark had his feet up on the railing. Jason was a bit slumped. He had to be getting tired too.

"Evening, gentlemen," I said.

"Hey," Mark said, with a nod of his carrot-topped head.

"No offense, dude," Jason said. "You look like hell."

"No offense taken. I feel it."

I slid the door closed behind me. As I sipped my wine, we started talking. I sensed they had just changed conversation topics and were now trying to keep things light, for my sake. This translated into Jason talking about his fantasy football team. He stopped only when the sliding door opened again.

It was Alison, still with her apron on. Her eyes were blazing and she steamed toward me. Jenny was just behind her but couldn't seem to reach her. Jenny, in turn, was trailed by Gina and Karen. They were also trying to slow Alison down, only they couldn't reach her in time.

She pointed at me and screamed, "*You absolute son of a bitch.*"

And then the woman I loved, the woman who had spent

more than half the nights of her life sleeping at my side, charged at me and started flailing at me. Not knowing what else to do, I pulled up my arms to shield my face, in essence going into duck-and-cover mode.

"Is *that* why you didn't want to have sex with me last night?" she yelled. "Because you were spent from banging your girlfriend?"

Her hands, which had been open at first, balled into fists, which she slammed off my shoulders and upper back. Finally—and it was probably no more than three seconds— Gina and Jenny managed to pull Alison off me.

"What the hell are you talking about?" I managed to say.

Alison's eyes still had that crazy look about them. She was separated from me now by her mother and sister, but she was straining against the arms that were holding her back. If they weren't there, she would still be pounding me with everything her 112-pound body could put out.

"Tell him, Jenny," she demanded. "Tell him what you told me."

Everyone turned toward Jenny, who, for her part, looked sheepish.

"All I said was that I saw Justina at the mall . . . and . . . and that she was wearing a really nice jacket."

"A nice *leather* jacket," Alison corrected, as if the material changed everything. "Is that what the money was for, Scott? A leather jacket? Or was it a leather jacket and an apartment? Or was it a leather jacket, an apartment, and all the blow jobs you could handle?"

All eyes were now on me.

313

"Honey, I have no idea what you're—"

"You miserable liar! You think I'm that stupid? I told myself I should give you the benefit of the doubt, thinking you'd explain it to me later. But now I get what that money was for."

"What mo—"

"I went to the ATM today, genius. Did you really think I wasn't going to notice the balance in the checking account was so low? Did you really think I wasn't going to find out about a seventy-two-hundred-dollar *cash* withdrawal? Seriously, couldn't you have at least tried to hide the money you're spending on your whore? Siphoned it off the kids' college funds or something classy like that?"

"Alison—"

"I mean, my God, how did I not see it? You had her living right next door for years until I went and screwed it up for you. But you couldn't stop seeing her, now, could you? No, you had to—"

"Would you shut the hell up and listen?" I roared. "I'm not sleeping around on you. I hired a private detective, okay?"

This news had at least some impact on Alison. Her arms were still up, like she was going to throw more punches, but she was no longer trying to push through her family to get at me.

I continued: "You remember how I spent last Saturday following Roland Hemans, the plaintiff's lawyer? You told me I was being an idiot, and you were right. So I got a private detective to follow him instead. His name is Herb

314

Thrift of Herbert Thrift & Associates. He's in the Yellow Pages. You can call him if you want to. Tell him your name is Mrs. Carter Ross, because that's the alias I used."

By this point, Alison's arms had fallen by her sides.

"Oh," she said.

Everyone was just standing there, not wanting to say anything as the emotional charge slowly drained out of Alison.

"It's okay," she said to her mother, who let her pass through to me.

"I'm sorry," she said, putting a hand on my shoulder. "I'm really sorry."

"It's okay," I said, and she hugged me.

"I'm just done," she said. "I'm so done."

I understood all too well what she meant.

*

That night, shortly after we got home, my body finally shut down on me. I barely remember falling into a deep, dreamless sleep. In the morning, I still couldn't pull myself out of bed. Every time I tried, I drifted back off again.

By the time I got myself upright it was after nine o'clock. There was cold French toast and bacon waiting for me in the kitchen. Alison had left a note saying she and Sam were roaming in the woods.

It made it as good a moment as any to call Herb Thrift. There was no point in wasting any more of the man's time—or our money—on Roland Hemans.

After three rings, I heard: "Yes."

"Yeah, hi, it's Carter Ross."

"Hello, Mr. Ross."

"How's it going?"

"Fine. I'm inside a condominium complex right now."

"Is it called Kensington Mews by any chance?" I asked.

"That's right."

Give Hemans and Joan Smith this much: At least they were consistent.

"How did you get past the gatehouse?" I asked.

"Mr. Ross, give me some credit. I do this for a living."

I thought of Thrift's high-mileage black loafers.

"Yeah, I guess you do," I said. "Well, for as much fun as I'm sure you're having in that parking lot right now, I wanted to call you off the tail."

"Sure. Can I ask why?"

"I just . . . I was mistaken about something."

"Not a problem."

"The way I see it, you've been on the job for close to forty-eight hours now. That's thirty-six hundred. Okay if I just stop by the office on Monday to pick up what's left of the money?"

"I'm sorry, Mr. Ross, but the agreement you signed said no refunds, remember?"

I didn't, actually. "Oh. Right," I said.

"Would you still like to see the report?"

"Yeah, I guess so," I said. I had paid for it. I might as well get something for my money.

"How can I get it to you?"

"I'll set up a Gmail address and send you a note. You can just reply to that."

"That's fine," he said. "I'm sorry again about the no-refunds thing. Sometimes that's just the way the dog hunts."

"Hey, I signed the form." Well, Carter Ross did, but it hardly seemed like a moment to split hairs.

"If you want me to follow someone else for two days, I'd be glad to."

I didn't know if he really meant it or if it was supposed to be a throwaway line. But, without giving it too much thought, I seized on the suggestion and rolled with it. I probably should have realized it the moment Roland Hemans filed that motion, but now it was blazingly clear to me: I was having Herbert Thrift follow the wrong person.

It was time to put him on someone who just might be the right one.

"Actually, that would be great. Could you?"

"You paid for it, Mr. Ross."

"Okay. You wouldn't need to watch this person twenty-four hours. Ten hours a day would be fine. Say, eight A.M. to six P.M. You can start Monday morning if that works for you."

"Sure thing."

"I'll e-mail you a picture and an address," I said. "The subject's name is Alison Sampson."

43

The younger brother was up to level 42 now, steadily mowing down a new adversary. The older brother was off . . . somewhere. The younger brother hadn't even bothered asking.

A cigarette smoldered in the ashtray nearby. He had just brought it to his lips and was taking a deep drag when an earsplitting wail filled the air.

He stood up so forcefully he knocked the chair over. It was the alarm, obviously. But why?

From where he was standing, he could see both the front door and the side door. Both were closed. Then his attention went to the door of the little girl's bedroom, and enough synapses finally made their connections for him to realize:

The little girl was trying to escape.

He threw open the door to her room to find her standing at attention against the wall, frozen with fear. The nightstand had been shoved next to the window, which was open perhaps a foot. She must have hopped down as soon as the alarm sounded.

"Hey, hey!" he barked. "What are you doing?"

The little girl shrunk away from him, into the corner.

"Don't do that," he said.

He looked at the window. He had thought the thing was

painted shut. But upon further inspection, he saw abrasions around the edge of the window. She must have found some piece of metal and scraped the paint away.

Now he'd have to find some plywood and nail it to the other side of the window to make sure she couldn't get out. It was work that would keep him from attaining level 43.

"You're a bad girl," he said. "And this is what happens to bad girls."

He grabbed her wrist. Then he plucked the cigarette from his mouth and jabbed the lit end against the inside of her arm.

44

Knowing what I had set in motion made it difficult to make eye contact with Alison for the remainder of the weekend.

There was part of me that felt awful about it. Really: What kind of man hired a private investigator to tail his own wife? Was that really what I had become?

But there was a much larger part of me that was convinced it was the right decision. At least I would soon know what was really going on.

Alison seemed to keep looking for opportunities to connect with me, which I continued to deflect. I poured my attention into Sam instead. He appeared to have adjusted, at least somewhat, to Emma's absence. He had developed games he could play by himself. He didn't mope quite as much.

That said, I still saw the worry brow come out a lot more than it ever used to. And there were constant reminders she was not far from his thoughts. Sometimes, he would talk to Emmabear as if it were his sister. Other times, he would do—or conspicuously *not* do—something Emma would have enjoyed. Or there was Sunday morning. I was making pancakes and asked him if he wanted one in the shape of an *S*.

His reply: "Actually, Daddy, could you make *E*'s?"

I ended up making those pancakes with a lump in my throat.

Those kinds of small moments aside, we survived the next two days. Before I knew it, I was face-to-face with Joan Smith, doing our usual Monday-morning routine—which I now knew more than ever to be a farce.

"How was your weekend, Mrs. Smith?" I said as I entered the office.

"Very good, thank you. Pastor finished up Matthew."

I smiled and said, "That sounds wonderful."

Then I went inside my office to view the evidence that would someday—after the attention from ApotheGen had subsided—lead to her quiet dismissal. I had set up an e-mail account under the name Carter Ross and sent Herb Thrift a note on Saturday. His reply was waiting for me:

Mr. Ross/Mr. Sampson,
Enclosed is my report on your previous subject. I will consider this matter closed unless you tell me otherwise.

I have performed some preliminary surveillance on the new subject property. Or I should say your property. Next time you try to hide your identity from a private investigator, don't drive your own car to his office.

However, now that I know the subject is your wife, I am hoping you can give me permission to enter your property. Your house is a long way from the road, and it will make it easier for me to track her movements.

Thank you for allowing me to continue to serve you.

Sincerely,
Herbert Thrift
Licensed Private Investigator, Herbert Thrift & Associates

I sat at my desk, drumming my fingers for a minute or two, until I decided it didn't really matter that Herb Thrift now knew who I was—not as long he was as confidential as advertised. I tapped out a quick e-mail, telling him he was welcome to enter my property as he pleased, just as long as he didn't alert my wife. Then I turned to the large PDF file that came with his e-mail.

The document began with a log, tracing the movements of Roland Hemans, who was referred to only as "subject." Each entry began with a time, and it was, as one would expect, fairly dull:

> 9:17 a.m.— Subject arrives in offices at 214 West
>   Brambleton.
> 12:33 p.m.—Subject leaves 214 West Brambleton,
>   travels on foot to Subway restaurant.
> 12:41 p.m.—Subject leaves Subway restaurant,
>   returns to offices at 214 West
>   Brambleton.

I quickly got bored with the narrative and went straight to the pictures. It was page after page of Roland Hemans getting into and out of cars, walking into and out of his home and office.

The only excursion he made on Friday was a trip to the Marriott in downtown Norfolk, where Leslie, Jennings & Rowley had set up what its lawyers were referring to as their "war room." They had taken the unusual step of flying scientists in for depositions—normally, lawyers traveled to the deposed, not the other way around. It was the only way they could get them all done, given the extremely compressed timeline I had insisted on.

None of the photos were all that interesting until I got to Saturday morning. That's when I saw Hemans leaving his home, stopping at the floral shop, then entering through the gates of Kensington Mews.

It was exactly as he had done the Saturday before. I clicked onto the next picture, of Hemans parking. Then came the photo of him getting out of his car with the flowers.

Herb Thrift was closer than I had been, with a much better angle, having wormed his way into the complex. And so he was able to give me a superior view of what came next.

There was a shot of Roland Hemans walking down an exterior hallway and then a shot of him standing outside a door.

And then there was a shot of the door being opened.

But not by Joan Smith.

By Jeremy Freeland.

*

The photo that followed was the real clincher, quite literally: It showed Roland Hemans hugging Jeremy.

Then, to eliminate any shred of doubt, there was one of them locking lips as the door closed.

That was the last photo. I went back and looked at the log. The time for Hemans' entry to Kensington Mews was listed as 8:12 A.M. Then, at 9:17 A.M., there was: "Client phones, cancels surveillance of subject."

But, really, I had already seen more than enough. Roland Hemans *was* having an intimate relationship with a member of my staff. Just a different one than I thought.

I probably sat there for five minutes, staring at that picture, wondering how I had gotten it so wrong. Certainly, I had misjudged Roland Hemans, falling into the stereotype that there was some correlation between masculinity and heterosexuality.

The other part of it was I simply hadn't known Jeremy lived in Kensington Mews. I was reasonably sure he hadn't when he first started working for me. He must have moved at some point, perhaps after overhearing Mrs. Smith talk about what a nice place it was.

As I scrolled through the pictures again, a few things started making sense. First was Jeremy's initial request that I recuse myself from the case. He knew he couldn't participate in a case where he was sleeping with the plaintiff's attorney, but he also couldn't tell me he and Roland Hemans were having an affair. I assumed Hemans—the married-with-children Virginia Black Attorneys Association Lawyer of the Year—was in the closet, deep enough he felt he couldn't risk anyone finding out about him.

In Jeremy, he had found a careful, quiet lover, one happy to continue having their Saturday-morning trysts. The relationship had probably been going on for quite some time. How long ago did Jeremy say he had met Hemans? It was during a matter heard in the appellate court, obviously before he started working for me, so it had to be at least four years. I think he had said something like six or eight.

By now their romance had to be . . . well, almost like a marriage.

I thought back to the way Jeremy had sidled into my office that day he asked me to recuse myself, biting his lip the whole time. He had known from the moment *Palgraff* appeared on the docket that he was going to have to get us off the case. But he thought he had more time.

Then the thing exploded into the public eye and it was too late to do it quietly. When he couldn't get me to drop the case voluntarily, he and Hemans came up with the plan to file the motion for recusal. Jeremy had fed Hemans most of the information for it. That was how Hemans had known Senator Franklin was Emma's godfather.

Once it was filed, they figured I would drop the case and they wouldn't have to worry about, say, Hemans winning a huge judgment then having it overturned when his relationship with Jeremy became public. Nor would they have to worry about Jeremy being fired at some future time when they chose to live more openly as a couple.

Their plan was sturdy. They just happened to throw it against a judge whose desire to hang on to the case was unyielding.

Now there was the question of what I was supposed to do with this sloppy bundle of newfound knowledge—these facts I couldn't unlearn and pictures I couldn't unsee. If I was operating under the guidelines of any ethics book ever written I'd call Jeremy into my office and fire him on the spot.

But ethics were not my top priority at the moment. Emma was.

Even if Jeremy accepted his termination and went away without a fuss, it would attract attention. That was the last thing I needed more of, whether it was from Congressman Jacobs, Jeb Byers, or anyone in the press. Furthermore, I couldn't risk the reason for Jeremy's dismissal becoming public. That would also lead to a forced recusal.

So it was decided. Once the Markman hearing was done, I'd deal with this. In the meantime? I had to bring this issue to a close. I couldn't have Jeremy and Roland Hemans coming up with new and increasingly creative ways to get me off the case.

My computer screen was still filled with the final page of Herb Thrift's PDF, the one that had the two most damning pictures on it. I hit the print button, then dialed Jeremy's extension.

A minute later, he was in my office. Without a word, I grabbed the top sheet off my printer and slid it across the desk. "Look at that, please."

Jeremy's face, normally so symmetrical, went askew for a moment. He recovered it quickly enough. He had been sneaking around for six, eight years now. Perhaps he always knew they would be discovered someday.

"How did you get this?" he asked quietly. "Did you take this picture?"

"No."

"Who did?"

"That's not your concern," I said.

"But how did—"

"Look, there's only one thing you need to know. And it's that this ends. Now. There will be no more attempts to get me off this case. Tell your boyfriend the same thing."

His head was down as he studied the photos again. "Okay," he said.

"You can go," I said.

He didn't. Instead, he brought his gaze up, nice and level with mine.

"Why aren't you firing me?" he asked.

The question startled me enough that I almost answered it honestly. Then I got ahold of myself and said, "Just go."

45

Back in our old life, which now seemed as distant as an ice age, Monday night would have signaled it was time for our weekly round of Hats and Dancing.

The straightforward mechanics of the game were part of its charm. We had this bin of hats. Before the music started, everyone selected one piece of headwear—or more, if they were feeling especially silly. Once the song started, you danced in whatever manner the hat-music combination inspired in you. When it ended, you picked a new hat.

Since the invention of the game several years earlier, I don't think we had missed a single Monday night. Yet this now marked the second consecutive Monday night no one dared touch the hat bin. Just like Sam and I wouldn't have thought about doing Swim With Dad. By unspoken consent, we had decided most of our family rituals would be suspended until Emma's return.

So that night, we passed the time as had become our custom of late. Alison and I ignored each other, pretending to be busy, while Sam watched far more television than was ordinarily tolerated. Then, when one of us decided his face had been infused with enough high-definition plasma, we engaged in some brief family time.

We had just finished up Battleship. Alison was upstairs,

pushing Sam toward bedtime. I was in the kitchen, washing dishes, when I heard this pitiful noise.

It was coming from Sam. In the prekidnapping epoch, I probably would have allowed Alison to handle whatever small drama was transpiring. Not now. I flung down my pot scrubber and charged up the stairs two at a time.

"What's going on?" I asked, a bit too loudly, as I entered Sam's room.

There I found Sam, his head damp from his bath, his pajamas half-plastered to his still-wet body. He was standing in the middle of the room, sobbing.

"Emmabear is missing," Alison said in a soothing tone.

Sammybear and Emmabear were such frequent—and itinerant—playmates that we typically had to put out an AMBER Alert for one (or both) at least twice a week. Ordinarily, it was a sign of business as usual, not a crisis.

It felt different this time. Way different.

"Well, okay, there's no reason to panic," I said, my voice rising. "Where did you last see her?"

Between gasps and anguished cries, Sam said, "I . . . I . . . d-don't . . . know."

"Come on, buddy, think. Where were you last playing with her?"

Sam wilted a little more. Alison said, "He doesn't know, Scott. Give him a break."

"I'm just trying to help here," I said, my patience already fraying.

"You're making it worse. It's like you're interrogating a witness."

329

I threw up my hands. "I'm just asking if he has any idea at all where the damn bear is. That's not interr—"

Sam started crying even louder. This wasn't one of those calculated tantrums kids sometimes have. This was a pure, nuclear meltdown. His little arms were squeezed by his sides. His mouth had a hideous downward curl to it, like a horrified jack-o'-lantern.

"I j-j-just w-want Emma-b-b-bear," he moaned.

"I told him we could find Emmabear tomorrow," Alison said. "It's late."

Sam responded to this pronouncement with a renewed burst of anguish. He had been so brave—maybe too brave—keeping things bottled up. This was clearly about more than the bear. At the same time it wasn't. Sometimes, with kids, you can accomplish an awful lot by focusing on the simple fix.

"He wants the bear," I said. "Let's find the bear."

"Tomorrow."

Sam bayed even louder. It was like a metal rake on my cerebral cortex.

"No," I said, trying—and failing—to keep my tone measured. "We are going. To find. The bear."

"Scott, it's not—"

"Are you helping or are you not?" I asked, already looking under the bed. Then I moved on to behind the dresser, another frequent Emmabear hideaway. Then I rifled through his sheets (she sometimes got tangled up in them) and plowed into the pile of stuffed animals in the corner (where Emmabear had been known to hide in plain sight).

Alison was just gaping at me. Sam was rooted to his spot in the floor, still pitching a fit.

"Come on, buddy," I said, kneeling and grasping his bony shoulders. "Give me some help here. Last place you saw Emmabear. You've got to have some idea."

After another couple of desperate gulps of air, he said, "I think may . . . may . . . maybe the family room."

I tore out of the room and down the stairs, barely touching the steps as I went. The family room was awash in Lincoln Logs, Hot Wheels, and Legos. We normally required the kids to clean up a toy before they moved on to the next one. We had gotten lax about enforcement lately.

After a cursory scan of the obvious spots, I looked under furniture. I lifted the coffee table, the sofa, the easy chair. Then I got into the sofa cushions and tossed them haphazardly about.

Next I spied the hat bin. That had to be it: Sammy wanted Hats and Dancing so bad, he and Emmabear had done their own imaginary round of it. I would find Emmabear underneath a fez or tucked beneath a beanie.

I emptied the bin, hat by hat, flinging each one on the floor until I reached the bottom of the pile. No bear.

The planters in the corner. Perhaps she was hidden in that houseplant jungle? I roughly slid each pot a foot or so to the side, which did not reveal Emmabear but did slosh dirty brown water onto the hardwood floor.

I moved to the entertainment center next. There were dozens of little nooks and crannies there, created by the television, the cable box, the speakers, the wireless router, the cable modem. Any one of those places could easily harbor a little teddy bear, and I was determined to leave no spot unexplored.

Failure wasn't an option. The bear was somewhere. It had not simply ceased to exist.

I was getting warm from the exertion of pawing through so much stuff so quickly. I didn't care. I was already on to the large cabinet where we kept our games. Surely, Sam had come to retrieve Battleship and left Emmabear in there by mistake.

Pulling on the handle, I unwittingly unleashed an avalanche of games. Trouble. Sorry. Candy Land. Chutes and Ladders. Monopoly. Some of the games had landed on their sides, splitting open. An array of dice, sand timers, plastic widgets, and game cards spilled across the floor. I no longer cared. Emmabear was all that mattered.

But she wasn't in the cabinet. Or any of the drawers underneath. I checked each one meticulously, making sure there was not a single square inch that escaped my scrutiny.

My line of sight moved next to the built-in bookshelves on the far wall. Sam sometimes liked to fling Emmabear around. She could have landed on top of some books, then fallen behind them.

Systematically, starting high on the left and moving down and to the right, I began removing row after row, one double-handed scoop at a time, creating stacks on the floor. With each new attack, I told myself: This was the one. Emmabear was hiding here. I would move the next load and there she would be, with her little sewed-on smile. I visualized not only that success but then the satisfaction of presenting the bear to my weary son, whose tears would quickly give way to a grateful smile.

I was several hundred volumes into that effort when I heard Alison, speaking to me from the entrance of the room.

"You can stop now, Scott," she said softly. "Sam's been asleep for twenty minutes. I scratched his back and he dropped like a stone. He was just tired. We'll look for Emmabear in the morning."

I didn't stop to acknowledge her. I had work to do.

"That bear is not your daughter," she said. "Finding Emmabear is not the same as finding Emma."

Another row of books was now at my feet on the floor.

"Scott, look at this room. Stop. And look."

She gently grabbed my wrist before I could scoop up another load. It snapped me out of whatever trance I had been in. I had one of those rare moments where I was able to pull myself out of my body and take a good long look at the guy who inhabited it.

What I saw was a stooped, balding, desperate middle-aged man. He was sweating. His shirt had come untucked. The room around him was thoroughly demolished, like it had been tossed by burglars. His wife was looking at him like she was frightened. He was coming unhinged.

I sat heavily on the floor, leaning against the nearly empty bookshelf. There were stacks of books on either side of me. Alison crouched nearby and patted my shoulder.

"It's okay, honey," she cooed. "It's okay."

"I'm sorry," I said.

"It's okay," she said again.

I think she wanted to get closer but it was difficult, what with all the books. She rubbed my thigh instead.

And then I just lost it. I was suddenly weeping with my whole body. My stomach contracted involuntarily. My shoulders shook. I let it happen, not that I could have held it back if I wanted to. I spent all day pretending to be normal and I couldn't do it anymore.

Alison moved a pile of books and knelt next to me, shushing me and wrapping her arms around me. The woman who had unknowingly spent her day being followed by a private investigator—a man I had hired—was now mothering me with all the tenderness that she had just used with her own child.

When I finally got some control of my abdomen back and wasn't quite as hunched over, she pulled my head next to her chest and let me cry into her blouse.

Her boys were having a rough night.

We ended up finding Emmabear the next morning, sitting in Emma's seat at the kitchen table.

Right where Sam had left her.

46

As his Wednesday began—which did not happen until sometime in the midmorning—the younger brother was completing his routine check of the previous night's surveillance footage.

Tuesday night had been like all the others. Now and then, he would catch sight of the person whose turn it was to keep guard—either a man or one of two women. But otherwise it was quiet. Just like the night before. And, really, like every night for more than a week.

He was now making sure the cameras were all the way zoomed out, ready to capture another day of nothing, when he saw, well, something.

It was a man, one who probably didn't belong prowling in the edge of the woods beyond the judge's house. He was far enough away and small enough that it was difficult to make out much detail about the man, other than that he had gray hair and appeared to be standing very still behind the trunk of a tree, as though to stay hidden from the front of the house. He was smoking a cigarette.

"Hey, hey," he called. "Come in here. There's something you have to see."

The older brother appeared immediately.

"Look at camera three," the younger said.

He bent toward the screen. "Who is that?"

"I don't know. I haven't seen him before."

"What's he doing?"

"He seems to be watching the house."

"Can you zoom in on him?"

"He's too much on the edge of the screen. If I zoom in, I'll lose him."

"Do you think he's police? FBI maybe?" the younger asked.

The older shook his head. "He's alone. The FBI works in pairs."

"We *think* he's alone. Maybe there are more we can't see."

The brothers watched the man who was himself watching the house. None of the three moved.

"Should we make a call?" the younger asked.

"No. We don't know enough yet. Why don't you go out there and see what's going on?"

The younger brother didn't need to be asked twice. He was relieved just to have something to do.

47

After the Emmabear episode, I forced myself to wait until Wednesday morning to call Herb Thrift. It took all the patience I could muster. Throughout Tuesday, whenever I had a moment of downtime, I thought of little else: What was Alison doing right now? What surprises was my private investigator capturing on his camera? Were she and Paul Dresser conspiring at this very moment? Would this be our last day together functioning in any way as man and wife?

My hands were shaking slightly as I dialed Thrift's cell number that Wednesday morning. They didn't stop when I got his voice mail. I left him a message. Then I called his office and recorded a message there too.

I kept my cell phone out on my desk, where I wouldn't miss its ring, as I continued my lukewarm efforts at work. We had a sentencing the next day—another drug case, sort of like *Skavron,* except it had not attracted the attention of the kidnappers. They had already made their point.

It was sometime after my midmorning conference call with the probation officer who had written the presentencing report when Jeremy knocked on my door.

In an office suite as small as ours—and working as closely together as we did—it was impossible for us to avoid each other completely. But in the two days since our run-in over the Hemans photos, we hadn't really spoken. We had merely exchanged businesslike e-mails and nodded at each other when we passed in the hallway.

He was, I assumed, either going to clear the air or forge some kind of detente. We couldn't continue this way.

"Come in, Jeremy," I said.

But there was nothing placatory about him as he entered. He strode quickly across the room to the edge of my desk, where he remained standing.

"I just got a call from a roomful of lawyers on speakerphone," he said. "Denny Palgraff didn't show up for his deposition this morning."

I felt my head tilt to one side. "What do you mean he didn't show up? He's the plaintiff."

"I don't know what to tell you. He was scheduled for nine o'clock at the Marriott. He never came. They tried calling him. No answer. They went to the hotel where he was staying. He's gone. He's completely AWOL."

"But . . . why?"

Jeremy turned up his palms. "Indigestion? How should I know?"

I looked at the time on my computer screen. It was 12:08. I could imagine a conference room with too many lawyers breathing too little air, arguing over what to do, deciding that if they didn't hear from Palgraff by noon they'd call my chambers—because maybe Judge Sampson would have an idea.

My unreasonable deadline for the completion of discovery was the next Tuesday, now less than a week away. I had seen their schedule and it was packed. There was no room for delay. And they couldn't very well finish discovery without a word or twelve thousand from Denny Palgraff.

I cursed.

"I've got them on hold," Jeremy said. "I told them I'd talk to you. What should I say?"

"Tell them to keep trying to find him. Maybe he just freaked out and is hiding in a coffee shop somewhere. If they can't produce him, I want Roland Hemans and Clarence Worth sitting right here at five o'clock."

I pointed to the two chairs in front of my desk.

"Okay," Jeremy said. "You got it."

*

I looked at the clock on the far wall of my office a few hundred times that afternoon. A missing plaintiff—and the delays his absence threatened to cause—accounted for some portion of my angst. A nonresponsive private investigator made up the rest of it.

Even swiping through pictures of Emma on my phone didn't help my addled mind settle down. Because, inevitably, some portion of the pictures had Alison in them. And that would make me wonder: Was she already planning something when this photo was taken? Can a camera capture the malice lurking in someone's heart?

Only Herb Thrift could tell me for sure. I might have rationalized that he was so occupied with tailing my wife he hadn't checked his phone messages. Except surveillance work entailed an inordinate amount of downtime, when you had nothing better to do than check for messages. Over and over. Just to pass the time.

I called several more times that afternoon anyway. Both home and cell. No answer.

Was what he had seen *that* bad? Could he simply not find a way to tell me that Alison was involved in kidnapping her own daughter? Or was he not calling back because he suspected that was the case but didn't want to make the accusation until he was sure? The uncertainty was consuming what little I had left of my wits.

By a few minutes before five P.M., when I started to hear the noises of lawyers arriving at my chambers, I still hadn't heard back from the man. My feelings about it had transitioned from wonder to outrage: How could he leave me twisting in the wind like this? Didn't he realize a man who had his wife being tailed would be slowly dying inside the whole time?

I did my best to put it out of my mind and focus on mediating the mess at hand. Out in the reception area, I could hear Mrs. Smith doing her hostess routine, offering the lawyers water and coffee. I suspected they all wanted something a lot stronger.

There were three of them: Hemans and Worth, whom I had requested; and Vernon Willards, in-house counsel for ApotheGen, whom I had not.

I invited them into my office, along with Jeremy. We were all appropriately grim-faced as we shook hands. With five people, sitting in front of my desk was going to be unwieldy.

So I pointed us over to a small conference table by the window.

"All right. Let's get to it," I said. "Could someone please talk me through what has happened today?"

Worth, his slender fingers crossed, nodded toward his opposing counsel and said, "He's your client. Go ahead."

Hemans straightened himself in his chair. Even without the benefit of his legs, he was half a head taller than anyone else at the table.

"Speaking plainly, Judge?" he said, his voice deep and resonant. "My guy was supposed to come at nine this morning for his deposition, and he didn't."

"Did you have any indication he was going to be a no-show?" I asked. "Was he nervous?"

"Judge, I'm not comfortable discussing my client's state of mind in front of the—"

"Cut the crap, Mr. Hemans," I said. "We're not in court right now and we're not on the record. Just answer the question."

He actually recoiled a little. I'm sure outside a courthouse, no one would have dared bully Roland Hemans. But the fact was, inside the limestone walls of the Walter E. Hoffman United States Courthouse, I was the six-foot-eight stud.

"Well, yeah, I'd say he was nervous," Hemans said. "Shouldn't he be? He's a scientist, not a lawyer. He's never been deposed before. He's never been involved in a lawsuit. And the defense has, what, fifty-two lawyers?"

"It's less than that," Worth said primly.

"You get my point, Judge. Yeah, he seemed like he was a

341

little anxious. And he's a weird guy to start with. But I didn't have any indication he had something like this in his head."

I sighed testily. Judges sometimes played up their impatience, simply to compel action out of a justice system that wasn't designed with speed in mind. In my case, the display wasn't affected.

"All right, so he didn't show up for his deposition and I assume he hasn't answered his phone," I said. "Please tell me you've had people looking for him."

"I sent one of my associates over to the hotel where he was staying—he was at a Motel 6 near the highway. We're not on a Marriott budget on the plaintiff's side, Your Honor. I thought maybe he overslept or was having car trouble. But he wasn't there and neither was his car."

"The vegetable-oil car?" I asked.

"That's right."

"Okay. After that?"

"Well, my associate called me, reported what she had found. At that point, I told Mr. Worth what was happening and he was kind enough to volunteer some of his people to help us look."

"As an officer of the court, I felt it was my duty," Worth interjected, pleased with himself for the points he felt he was scoring with me. "We've had approximately twenty people fanned out around the city looking for Mr. Palgraff today; that's along with"—he looked toward Hemans—"five or six from Mr. Hemans' firm. We thought for sure Mr. Palgraff would be . . . Well, let's just say we thought he'd be findable. We're now assuming he's not in the area."

Yes, with twenty-odd people looking for him, a fat, bearded, John Lennon–bespectacled scientist riding around Norfolk in a vegetable-oil-burping station wagon should have been easy to spot.

I turned my attention back to Hemans. "So what you're telling me is that, at this moment, you have absolutely no idea where your client is?"

"That's right, Judge," Hemans said, slouching a little more.

I let that settle in for a second as I tried to stanch the explosion of temper I felt coming on. If I could have found Denny Palgraff, I'd let him give his deposition. But first I'd choke him.

It was Vernon Willards who broke the silence.

"Your Honor, under the circumstances, I think it's only right to delay the completion of discovery. As a matter of fact, my client would like to see the whole discovery schedule thrown out and have—"

"Mr. . . . Willards, is that right?" I cut him off.

He nodded. I wanted to choke him too.

"I don't recall asking you to come here today. And I don't recall asking for your opinion. But now that you've given it, let me set you straight: There will be no delay in this case. There are millions of people out there whose lives could be dramatically extended by this drug. Are we understood?"

"Yes, Judge," he said.

"Now, as for you, Mr. Hemans, I'm going to make this very simple. You have exactly forty-eight hours to produce

343

your client and get him seated for a deposition, or I'm holding you in contempt. You will find Mr. Palgraff or you will spend the weekend in jail. Am I clear?"

"But, Judge, how am I supposed to—"

"Would you like to be held in contempt right now?" I asked. "I could have the US Marshals Service arrange accommodations for the evening. If you think the Motel 6 is a step down from the Marriott, you should try the Hampton Roads Regional Jail."

It was a naked and blatant abuse of my authority. And I hated myself for resorting to it. But I also wasn't going to back down. And Hemans must have known it, because he said, "No, thank you, Judge. I'll find my client."

"Very good," I said. "Now, I think you've all got work to do. Get to it."

The three lawyers shuffled out. Jeremy, who hadn't said a word the entire time, sat quietly until they were gone.

"What?" I finally said. I could barely look at him. He, on the other hand, wasn't letting his gaze drop.

"I could ask you the same question."

"There's a compelling public interest to keep this lawsuit on schedule and to get it resolved quickly."

"Uh-huh," he said. "I know."

I got tired of being stared at, so I left the conference table and returned to my desk, where I sat heavily and pretended to busy myself with my computer screen. My tantrum now over, I felt a little shaky.

Jeremy eventually stood and walked over.

"Judge, what's going on?" he asked. "Seriously. This

isn't . . . None of this is like you. It's Wednesday. Why aren't you swimming with your kids?"

I pretended to busy myself with my phone, where there was a photo of Emma from the summer. She was on our little beach, wearing a new bathing suit we had just gotten her, pleased as pleased could be, posing like a beauty queen. I can remember thinking when I snapped the picture: *Where do little girls learn how to stand like that? Do they learn it from watching other women? Or from Disney princesses? Or is it just in the air they breathe?*

"Hello? Judge? Maybe I can help?"

"Just go," I mumbled.

Then I got up and went into my bathroom. I stayed in there until I was sure he had left.

48

There was no reason for my continued presence at the office, but I spent the next half hour at my desk anyway, pretending to prepare for the sentencing the next day.

Finally, I admitted to myself that I was stalling and the reason for it: I wanted to visit the home/office of Herbert Thrift & Associates to see why the man wasn't returning my calls. I couldn't go through another night of guessing at what he was witnessing.

Alison would be expecting me at home any minute, which wasn't going to happen. So I called her on our landline.

"Hello?"

"Hey, it's me."

"Hi," she said. There was a clipped edge to her voice. I could hear cartoons in the background.

"I've gotten hung up here. We're having a little crisis."

"How soon can you wrap it up?" she asked.

"I don't know."

"Because I . . . I'd really like you to come home."

"Is everything okay?"

"Hang on," she said. The sound of the cartoons grew faint, then disappeared.

In a hushed voice, she said, "I heard gunfire earlier today.

It sounded really close. I'm sure it was on our property. I'm scared to let Sam out. I'm scared to go out myself."

"It was probably just hunters."

"There were two shots," she went on, ignoring my suggestion. "They were maybe five seconds apart."

"One shot to bring the animal down and then another to finish it off."

"We have NO HUNTING signs posted."

I couldn't very well suggest she call in a complaint to the game warden. "Look, I don't know what to tell you. I'll be home as soon I can. There's just one thing I need to finish up. I'm sorry."

She signaled her feelings about this by hanging up on me.

It was now twenty minutes to seven. Herb Thrift had ended his surveillance of Alison at six. If he went straight home, that would put him back at six forty-five.

I collected my things and was soon out into the early evening, with my Buick rolling toward Herb Thrift's place. Ten minutes later, I pulled off Northampton Boulevard and into the small client lot by the side of his shabby old house. I walked up the front steps and pressed the buzzer three times without an answer.

Where was this guy? Why was he ducking me? I swore loudly and tromped around to the back of the house. If Herb Thrift was anywhere on this property, I was by God going to find him.

At the end of the driveway, there was an old, detached garage. I peered in through a cracked windowpane. There was a small pickup truck parked there.

347

So was he actually home? Had he even been following my wife at all? I swore again.

The back side of the house had its own entrance. I stomped noisily up the steps and knocked on the door. From inside, I could hear voices. It was either a television or a radio. I knocked again, harder.

"Mr. Thrift?" I said loudly, and stood on the landing, my fists jammed into my sides.

No answer.

This time, I pounded on the door with the butt of my hand. "Mr. Thrift, this is getting *very* aggravating," I hollered. "I paid you *in cash*."

From next door, a gray-haired woman briefly appeared on her deck and fisheyed me.

"Mind your own business," I snarled.

She retreated back into her house. I gave the door another thumping and hollered his name again.

Fuming now, I stalked back to my car, went into my briefcase, and tore a sheet off a legal pad. I hastily wrote, "Mr. Thrift—CALL ME." I underlined it three times, then added my name and phone number.

I returned to the back door and wedged the note into the crevice just above the handle, where he couldn't miss it. Then I drove off in a righteous huff.

49

It was well after dark by the time the older brother saw headlights on the driveway.

They did not blink twice to signal all clear, like they were supposed to. But it was clearly the van, clearly being driven by the younger brother. And nothing seemed to be out of order.

The older brother disarmed the security system and waited impatiently by the door for the younger brother to stumble in.

"Where have you been?" the older brother demanded. "You've been gone all day."

The younger brother was bearing a large Tupperware container and a small grin.

"You were supposed to call me," the older said. "I was worried."

"I was fine," he said. The smile grew a little wider.

"Why do you smell like whiskey?"

"I stopped at a bar."

"What? Are you out of your mind?

"I'm tired of being cooped up. You get out all the time and leave me here."

"We are being well compensated for our work," the older admonished. "That should be enough."

"I was just celebrating a little."

"It was a stupid risk. What if someone recognized you?"

The younger brother just laughed. "You think any of these rednecks"—he used the English word—"search the Interpol website for pictures of fugitives?"

The older brother grimaced. "Anyhow, what happened out there? Who is this man lurking in the trees?"

"He's nothing to worry about."

"What do you mean?"

He handed over the Tupperware. The older brother lifted the lid then immediately closed it and handed it back. "My God," he said.

The younger brother smiled some more, then placed the container in the refrigerator.

50

As of Friday afternoon, two things had not yet happened.

One, Herb Thrift had not called me, despite several more messages imploring him to do so. And, two, Roland Hemans had not found Denny Palgraff.

The second item was, according to my earlier threat, supposed to lead to the defense counsel's detainment for the weekend. But when Jeremy Freeland begged for more time on his lover's behalf, I acceded. From a practical standpoint, Hemans was going to have a hard time finding his client if he was surrounded by fifteen-foot-high razor-wire fences.

As for Herb Thrift, he had seemingly gone on walkabout. Maybe it was for the best. I had continued my gentle interrogations of my son throughout the week, and there had been no discrepancies between his accounting of each day's activities and Alison's—no unexplained absences, no unaccounted time with aunts, no naps that weren't. My continued stalking of her Facebook account also yielded nothing noteworthy.

My final judicial act of the week, scheduled for two o'clock that afternoon, was a revocation hearing. This meant a felon out on supervised release had done something—or, often, several somethings—he shouldn't have, and now the government was pressing to have him sent back to prison.

I would have called it a routine matter, except of course there's nothing routine to the man whose freedom is at stake.

The defendant was bald and white and weathered, a hard character like so many I had seen before. He had a private lawyer, a man in a bad suit who was a newcomer to my courtroom.

The prosecutor was, once again, Will Hubbard. As court was brought to order—normally a time when assistant US attorneys stood at attention and submitted themselves to the pomp and circumstance of the moment—he had his head down, like he was trying not to look at me. I was quite sure I didn't want to know what he had told Jeb Byers about my Rayshaun Skavron ruling.

After beginning the proceeding with as few words as possible, I turned it over to Hubbard, who still wasn't making eye contact as he said, "Thank you, Your Honor."

Hubbard launched into a recitation of the allegations against the defendant, namely, that he had already flunked two drug tests and then refused to take a third; and also that he had been hanging around people he had been ordered to stay away from—allegations that put him on a path back toward prison in several ways.

He still had to prove it, of course, so he put the probation officer on the stand. Her testimony was all very pro forma, things she had said—and things I had heard—at least a hundred times before. The way the woman flicked her hair reminded me a little of Alison, and I found myself thinking about, of all things, potpourri.

Sometime in the past week, little bowls filled with dried flowers and other assorted perfumy things had shown up in all the bathrooms in our house. It puzzled me at first. Alison wasn't really a potpourri kind of gal.

Then came Thursday night, shortly after dinner. I had gone into the downstairs bathroom, and underneath the fragrance of lilac, cinnamon, and who knew what else, I caught another, far less inviting odor.

Vomit. The anxiety was playing such hell on her stomach, she hadn't been able to keep her dinner down. Upon further investigation, I also found a can of air freshener—another product that had never been in our house before.

Beyond that, just looking at Alison, I could continue to see the physical toll this was taking on her. She had dropped more weight. Her eyes seemed to be permanently sunken. The girlishness that once defined her movements had been replaced by this creaking hesitance. It was like she had gotten old all at once.

You couldn't fake that, right? And these kind of extreme stress reactions wouldn't be happening if you knew your daughter really was safe and sound, being fed nutritionally balanced meals and kept away from peanuts and dangerous men's knives.

I was somewhere in the midst of this thought when a noise from the defendant's lawyer brought me back into the courtroom.

"Objection," he yelped. "I fail to see how any of this is material to the matter at hand."

Hubbard parried with: "It shows a pattern of risk-taking

behavior on the defendant's part."

"It is incredibly prejudicial, Your Honor. It's well outside the scope of a revocation hearing. And once it's out there, you can't put the genie back in the bottle. I can think of at least three cases right off the top of my head that speak to this: *Bennett, Brown,* and *US versus Feller.*"

I stared at them dumbly, clearly caught flat-footed. I shot a glance at the court reporter, wondering if she might take the cue that I was lost and read back the testimony that prompted this sparring match. But she was just looking back at me expectantly, waiting for me to say something.

Because that's what a judge is supposed to do.

I could feel my ears getting hot. My law clerk was craning her neck to get a look at me. The court security officer shifted his weight uneasily.

It was Hubbard who spoke first.

"Your Honor, you have no idea what we're talking about right now, do you?" he said.

He threw up his hands to show his exasperation. No other attorney would have dared such a demonstrative gesture, except Hubbard clearly felt entitled to it, given our recent history.

That he was actually right to feel that way was now beside the point. I had to get control of this situation, if only to save what little face I had left.

"Mr. Hubbard, you're out of line right now," I said, trying to put some conviction behind it. "You will show this court the respect it is due. Are we clear?"

He sneered at me, but he muttered, "Yes, Your Honor."

"Good," I said. "Objection sustained. Now, move on."

Hubbard's mouth had a nasty set to it. And although he managed to restrain himself from saying anything that would escalate the situation, he was probably already formulating his complaint to Jeb Byers. *Judge Sampson's behavior is unbefitting his position and discredits the Eastern District of Virginia* . . .

What he couldn't have known was that I was at least twice as furious with myself as he was with me. For however prosaic this hearing was to me, it was still the most consequential thing in this defendant's life. Felon or not, he deserved better; so did the entire system I had sworn an oath to faithfully represent.

It went to something one of my new colleagues told me shortly after I was confirmed: Judges don't get to have off days. Every time we take to the bench, what we do matters.

I was still embarrassed and irritated with myself by the time I formally dispatched the defendant, sending him back to the cell he so richly deserved to inhabit. I returned to my chambers, practically tearing off my robe before depositing myself roughly in my chair.

There was a new pile of papers on the corner of my desk, where Mrs. Smith put things that required my attention. Sitting on top was a FedEx package with a slight bulge to it. The words PERSONAL AND CONFIDENTIAL jumped off the side of the envelope at me.

I frowned at it, then picked it up. That's when I saw the sender's name.

Rayshaun Skavron.

There was an address and phone number, all certainly fake. And I'm sure any attempt to trace its origin—or lift fingerprints off it, or get anything else useful out of it—would have led nowhere. The kidnappers had already proven their caution when it came to this sort of thing.

I tried to hold off the by-now-familiar feeling of another panic attack setting in as I grasped the plastic strip at the top of the envelope and tore it open.

Then I immediately felt the bottom drop out of my stomach.

Resting at the bottom of the envelope, neatly sealed in a Ziploc sandwich bag like a lunchtime carrot stick, was a human finger.

51

It wasn't Emma's. It had clearly belonged to an adult, likely a male.

But whatever solace I could wrest from that over the remainder of the afternoon—after I buried the finger at the bottom of the Dumpster outside the courthouse—was otherwise overwhelmed by abject horror. I could come up with a thousand scenarios to explain how that digit had been separated from a human being and wound up snuggled in a plastic bag at the bottom of a FedEx package. All of them were ghastly.

When I got home, I made noises about a bad day, a headache, indigestion, and every other excuse I could think of not to have to perpetuate the guise of human interaction. There was no way I was telling Alison about what had happened. My vomiting wife clearly didn't need more stress.

As I tried to fall asleep—an enterprise that was an exercise in wistful fantasy—I was having a bad case of the self-absorbed why-mes. I had done everything right in this life. Or at least I had tried. I worked hard. I obeyed traffic laws. I was faithful to my wife. I had done my best by my children. What had I possibly done to deserve having a finger sent to me in the mail?

I was so happy to see the night end that I sprang out of

bed and made breakfast for Sam so Alison could sleep in.

After I tidied the kitchen, Sam suggested we go roaming in the woods. It struck me as an excellent idea. Since Monday, when he had his meltdown, I had been especially cognizant of the fact that, even though he might not always be showing it or voicing it, he was still hurting from Emma's continued absence. The busier we kept him, the better.

We spilled out of the house to find a crisp morning, the dew silvery on the grass. Fall comes late, and gradually, to our part of Virginia. This was the first hint that it might visit again this year.

I let Sam set our course, inasmuch as we even had a course, and stayed far enough behind him that when he crashed through branches or brambles, they didn't snap back and whack me in the face.

Sam's monologue was punctuated with its usual degree of marvel, and I loved that he felt compelled to share his discoveries. It was like some kind of adorable existential crisis where what he was seeing didn't become real unless I also saw it. Hence, I heard an endless stream of "Dad, look at this spider! . . . Dad, three trees, one root! . . . Dad, deer tracks!"

As we got deeper into the woods, I was mostly just enjoying his chatter and his joy at living in a world punctuated by exclamation points. I wasn't paying particular attention to the content until I heard:

"Dad, check out those vultures!"

Sure enough, there was a small flock of hook-beaked, bald-headed buzzards clustered tightly around some carrion.

"Oh wow," I said, because that was what he wanted to hear.

Sam halted in his tracks. I closed the gap between us until I was side by side with him. I draped a protective arm on his shoulder. We were still roughly two hundred feet away. The birds were having a fine time with their breakfast, which was large enough to feed seven or eight of them.

I was assuming it was a deer, because nothing else out here was big enough to attract such a crowd. But you couldn't really see what they were pecking at. Not at first, anyway.

Then one of the birds hopped to the side.

That's when I saw a pair of battered black loafers.

*

It took me about a quarter second to wheel around and block Sam's view.

"Okay, Sammy," I said, picking him up and pointing us in the opposition direction. "Time to head back to the house."

He squirmed against me, giggling a little because he thought it was a game and that I was just roughhousing.

"But, Daaaad."

"Momma is going to be waking up soon. We didn't leave a note. She'll get nervous."

"Because of Emma?"

"What do you mean, 'because of Emma'?" I said, even though I knew exactly what he meant.

"Ever since Emma," he said, referencing his sister as if she were a historical event, "Momma gets a lot of nervous when she can't see me."

"Yeah, bud, because of Emma."

The walk back was slow, with Sam's fifty-something extra pounds weighing me down as I picked through the underbrush. As soon as we were out of the forest, I hoisted him on my shoulders and covered the ground back to the house with rapid strides.

"Why don't you race cars for a little while?" I said, depositing him in the family room.

Alison was in the kitchen. She was still in her pajamas, making herself a fresh pot of coffee, moving stiffly, as if she hadn't woken up yet.

"I need you to keep Sam in the house," I said, still breathing heavily.

"Is everything okay?"

"No, it's not. Just keep him in the house."

"What's going—"

"Alison," I said fiercely, then I drew close so I could whisper. "There's a body out there. Those two shots you heard yesterday? They hit a man. He's dead."

"Oh my God," she said, bringing her hand to her mouth.

I pulled away, with the intent of going back outside, but she grabbed my shirt. "Wait, wait. Is it . . . Who is it? Do you know?"

"No clue," I lied.

"Oh my God," she repeated. "Do you think the kidnappers did it?"

"It's the only thing that makes sense. Some poor guy

must have bumped across them and they . . ."

I made a shooting gesture with my hand.

"So what are you going to do?"

"What do you think? I'm going to bury the body."

"But—"

"What? You want me to call the sheriff's department? We'll have cop cars, the county coroner, the state medical examiner's office. It'll be like a law enforcement picnic. You want that?"

She didn't reply.

"Just keep Sam away," I said. "I'll be back in an hour or two."

She released my shirt. I turned and went out the back door, stopping in the garage to get a shovel. Retracing my steps, I found where the vultures were still huddled. Once I was close enough, I broke into a run, swinging the shovel and yelling until they dispersed.

I closed in on Herb Thrift's corpse, now fully visible. The scavenging was actually fairly superficial. The majority of the damage was human inflicted.

A big chunk from the top half of his head was missing. He also had a gaping exit wound in his chest. That accounted for the two gunshots Alison reported hearing on Wednesday.

But those wounds weren't all. The body had been mutilated. The fingers were missing, which explained the delivery that had showed up at my office the day before. The teeth also appeared to have been ripped out. The killer had done some fairly gruesome work to impede the identification of the remains.

It all added up to a mess of meat. As a judge, I have seen my share of crime scene photos. And I thought, therefore, I could handle this. I was wrong. I went to one knee and retched. Then again. I kept going until I was dry heaving.

This death was not, in the legal sense, my fault. I hadn't pulled the trigger. But morally?

I had led Herb Thrift to a slaughter. And I hadn't even explained to him what danger he was facing. He came into contact with armed killers with nothing more than a camera to protect him.

"I'm sorry," I said several times, as I tried to regain my composure. "I'm really, really sorry."

Was I saying it to Herb Thrift? Or to the trees? Or to whatever God I had apparently pissed off in the worst way?

The thing that brought me back to my feet was the same force that kept me going through all of this: Emma. If someone else found this body and called the authorities, she'd suffer terribly for it.

I found the shovel where I had let it drop, and started digging. I chose a spot maybe ten feet from where Thrift was lying—far enough away that I wouldn't have to look at him, close enough that I would be able to move the body into the hole I was creating without too much trouble. I kept my back to him as I shoveled.

One scoop at a time, I made his grave and assembled the story of how it was he came to need one.

It started when he received permission to be on my property. The problem was, there had been someone else on my property—without my permission. I knew that. I just hadn't, somehow, been thinking about that when I asked Herb to follow my wife.

I could picture Herb, crouched in the woods, using the zoom lens of his camera as binoculars, keeping an eye on the house. Then I imagined his surprise when he came across one of the kidnappers—or, perhaps, two or three of them—doing the same thing.

Herb turned and ran. The kidnapper shot him in the back. It was probably enough to kill him, but the kidnapper had wanted to make real sure. That's what the head shot was for.

Then the body had been dragged here, to the approximate middle of the ten-acre wooded patch that separates our house from the road.

The kidnapper had quickly butchered the remains, in case someone stumbled across it. But, really, the hope was that forest critters would find the corpse and dispose of it first.

I continued digging until my soft judge's hands were getting blisters on the palms and my body was drenched in sweat. Once I deemed the effort good enough, I used the shovel as a lever to roll the body toward the ditch I had created. I got it settled in the bottom of the depression, facedown, then covered it back over with dirt.

Then I scattered leaves over the dirt, leaving little trace that Herb Thrift had ever been there.

Before I left, I said a prayer. For his soul. And, selfishly, for mine.

52

Alison and I took turns keeping Sam distracted all weekend, trading him back and forth every few hours—basically, every time one of us reached the limit of our ability to feign serenity.

Otherwise, there was a kind of gloom that settled over us, layering itself on top of the pall that had already been there. Death was creeping closer.

Herb Thrift's mangled body was on the backs of my eyelids every time I closed my eyes. So was the smell of him. I took a shower when I returned to the house, then another a few hours later when I felt like the odor hadn't fully left me. But it was like a few molecules of his essence had crawled up my nose and were refusing to depart.

The impact on Alison was more profound. She had not seen the torture video, nor did she know about the finger. For her, this was the first piece of definitive proof of just how violent these men could be. She seemed to sink into a fatigue even deeper than before, creaking around the house. All the energy and vitality she had shown early during this ordeal were now gone. There was no more wood chopping, no more dashing around trying to solve everything. Every time she'd hand off Sam to me, she'd sag as soon as she knew our boy couldn't see her.

Saturday night, unsurprisingly, I had a nightmare of gothic proportions. I was running through our woods with my shovel in hand and the knowledge that Emma was somewhere in the woods. They were our woods, except they looked different—more sinister, more foreign.

The first part of the dream consisted of my tripping on roots, bushes, and vines, all of them impossibly thick and thorny. They would appear, seemingly out of nowhere, to impede my frantic search for Emma. At times, I knew exactly where I was on the property, only to get lost again a moment later.

In the second part of the dream, I had found Emma, but she was buried alive. I could hear her screams from underground. When I tried to dig, my shovel would break. And then it would regenerate, only to break again. Or I would think it was a shovel and I would look down to see I was actually holding a garden hose. I finally started digging furiously with my hands, but the soil had become impenetrable, the forest floor baked into hardpan. Emma's screams grew weaker and I knew I was running out of time.

Alison woke me because, in addition to my shouts, I was clawing at the bed.

The dream was so vivid it stayed with me through much of the day. It was probably still lingering—somewhere in my chest, it felt like—late Sunday afternoon when my cell phone rang.

I didn't recognize the number. It came from the 917 area code, which meant a New York area cell phone. I might not have answered it, but Sam was elsewhere, and I couldn't rule out that it was one of the kidnappers.

So I brought the phone to my ear and offered it a tentative: "Hello?"

"Judge Sampson?"

"Yes."

"Hi, this is Steve Politi from HedgeofReason."

I was so taken aback, I couldn't even speak. He added, "We're a website that serves the financial community."

"I know who you are," I blurted, once I found my voice. "You've been calling my office for weeks now. How did you get this number?"

"I've got a source," he said, like it was no big deal, like calling a federal judge was something he did every other day.

It told me something about his source: It was real. My cell phone number is not exactly a state secret—it's listed on everything from the parents' directory at my kids' school to the emergency staff contact list at the courthouse—but it's still not something that Steve Politi could conjure from his imagination. He knew someone in my life.

"Look, I know you can't comment on the record," he said. "So this is strictly off the record. I just want us to be able to talk a little bit."

"Absolutely not. It's totally inappropriate for me to have any kind of conversation with you. I should hang up right now."

"Yeah, but you're not going to, because I know your secret."

My entire body seized up. This was what I had been

fearing for weeks now, ever since Michael Jacobs had first started yammering from that podium: that some reporter would learn about Emma and expose everything.

Then I thought it through a little more. If any journalist were to figure it out, it wouldn't be Politi. He was in New York and trafficked in financial gossip. This was not his kind of scoop. He was just posturing, wasn't he?

"And what . . . and what secret is that?" I stammered.

"I have a source that says this case has already basically been decided, that you already know how you're going to rule."

Oh God.

"That's ridiculous," I said. "Who told you that?"

"Can't say."

"How am I supposed to refute something when you won't even tell me where it's coming from?"

"So you're denying you know how you're going to rule?"

"I'm not . . . I'm not even having this conversation."

"Of course you're not," he said. "But tell me something. That motion to recuse. What was the deal with that? Because I've been following this case pretty closely and you've been a plaintiff's dream. Why would Roland Hemans want a different judge?"

I actually chuckled, even though I didn't find any of this funny. The guy was playing me. Or, rather, I was allowing myself to be played.

"Uh-uh, no way," I said. "I'm not talking with you."

"Yes, you are. Because I know things about this case that you don't know."

It was both a challenge and a tease, and I couldn't help myself. He dangled that hook with that big, fat, juicy worm wrapped around it, and I chomped down hard. "Oh really? Like what?"

"Did you know that Denny Palgraff is in talks to take his patent to another pharmaceutical company?"

I didn't. I didn't know anything about Denny Palgraff—not even, at the moment, where he was. Was that why Palgraff disappeared? He was negotiating with other companies?

"Yeah," Politi continued. "My source says Palgraff has gotten so pissed at ApotheGen in general and Barnaby Roberts in particular, he's planning on taking his patent to Merck or Pfizer. He's going to start a bidding war between the two of them and leave ApotheGen out of it."

"Is that what your source says, huh?"

"Why? Is it not true?"

"No comment," I said. What I really could have said, of course, was: *No clue.*

"Well, I'm posting it pretty much as soon as I get off the phone."

"Congratulations," I said.

"All right, now it's your turn. What's the deal with Hemans? Why does he want to get rid of you?"

"I'm hanging up now," I said.

"I know your secret," he said again.

"You don't know anything," I said.

Which had to be true. If he really knew my secret, he would have already outed me.

Still, I stored Steve Politi's number in my phone. The fact

was, he did seem to know things about my case that I didn't know. And that, at some point, could be valuable.

*

Not being possessed of a tremendous amount of investing savvy, I didn't really understand the full implications of what Politi had told me about until Monday morning. I was driving to work, listening to WHRV, the local National Public Radio affiliate, when suddenly the announcer was teasing a segment about ApotheGen.

"Coming up next: What happens when a pharmaceutical giant pins everything on a blockbuster drug—only to potentially lose it to one of its competitors? We'll talk about the fallout of this morning's rumors regarding ApotheGen Pharmaceuticals."

Then another voice said: "It's the most devastating thing you can imagine. There's no silver lining here."

I turned it off. I really didn't need to hear more about how bad things were for ApotheGen. I had more pressing matters, starting with Denny Palgraff still being unaccounted for.

When I got into my chambers, I looked for Jeremy, who hadn't arrived. I asked Mrs. Smith to have him visit me when he got in. Not knowing what else to do with myself while I waited for him, I went into my office and clicked on HedgeofReason.com, just to get a firsthand look at the piece that was right now creating financial carnage.

The item was brief and snarky, playing up HedgeofReason's "exclusive source," who had been "dead accurate on the details of this lawsuit *from the beginning*."

At the end, there were several UPDATE! items that had been appended.

The first was, "UPDATE!: Steve Politi is going to make an appearance on Fox Business this morning at 7:45."

That one was followed by a YouTube link of Steve Politi. I had assumed Politi was an aggressive, just-out-of-college kid looking to make a mark. But the screen grab showed a middle-aged man with a round head and no hair. He looked like an aging Charlie Brown.

The next was, "UPDATE!!: HedgeofReason credited with breaking this news on MSNBC!"

The picture below that was a close-up of MSNBC's crawl, which led with, "HedgeofReason reports ApotheGen may lose blockbuster next-generation statin."

Finally, there was one more UPDATE!!! This one had been posted mere minutes earlier.

"The Street is not yet convinced about Merck or Pfizer but ApoG is getting slammed, down a whopping $14.37 on heavy, heavy trading! For those keeping score at home, that's $27.84 off its 52-week high, a thirty percent drop. We might see a dead cat bounce later this afternoon. But unless you're planning to hang on to your ApoG until sometime next century, run don't walk to your local broker or online trading account, kids! It only gets worse from here once this news is confirmed."

There were 935 comments, a number that astounded me because I knew what it represented. For every person who had commented, there were at least a thousand who had read it without commenting. It was a huge audience for one post.

I could imagine how well this was playing out at ApotheGen headquarters, where Barnaby Roberts was hearing from an army of irate shareholders who were ready to stage an insurrection. Had he called Paul Dresser to make sure things were still under control?

There was no way Roberts would survive with his job if Denny Palgraff carried through on his apparent threat. His board of directors might be able to tolerate having to share the golden goose. Having Palgraff sell the goose to the farm next door was unforgiveable.

But that was only, of course, if Palgraff had a patent he could sell. Meaning *Palgraff vs. ApotheGen* was now a winner-take-all affair for both sides.

What that meant for Emma I could no longer even guess. It was so hard to differentiate the signal from the noise.

All I could really do was keep my eye on the one thing I could control: the Markman hearing, which was still set for Friday. I assumed I would get my orders that day. I would carry them out. And then we would get Emma back.

I allowed myself to briefly daydream on that thought: Emma running to my arms, squealing, "Daddy, Daddy, Daddy"; Alison back to her normal self, smiling real smiles again, smothering her daughter in hugs and kisses; me no longer having to suspect my wife of trying to destroy us; Sam getting his best friend and other half back; our family, whole again, going on picnics, doing Hats and Dancing, returning to the simple joy of Swim With Dad.

It was enough that, when Jeremy Freeland knocked on

my door, I had to wipe tears from my eyes and compose myself before I said, "Come in."

He entered with a steely air of attempted indifference, like he wasn't still angry with me.

"You wanted to see me?" he asked in an inflectionless voice.

"Yeah. Has Hemans heard from Palgraff?"

"They finally spoke on Saturday. He's giving his deposition tomorrow."

"Oh. That's good news."

Jeremy offered nothing in response.

"Do we know what caused him to hightail it out in the first place?" I asked. "Was it because he was negotiating a deal with Pfizer or something?"

"I don't know."

I stared at Jeremy, clearly wanting more. "Didn't you ask?"

"I did," Jeremy replied. "Roland said the less I knew, the better."

"That's probably true."

"Yeah," Jeremy said. "There seems to be a lot of that going around."

He turned around and left without another word.

53

The scream jolted the younger brother out of the midmorning semislumber he had fallen into.

It was coming from the little girl's room.

The older brother was out, getting groceries, leaving only the younger brother to investigate. He rose from his easy chair and went over to her door. There was no other sound. He was going to leave it alone when she screamed again.

"What's going on?" he said.

"It's a spider," she shrieked.

"So kill it."

"I caaaan't. It's too scary."

"Use some toilet paper."

"I can't reach it. It's too high."

The younger brother rolled his eyes. He performed a quick analysis—which course of action would result in the least amount of bother?—and decided it was easier to spend thirty seconds killing a spider than to listen to the girl carry on for the next few hours.

He twisted the handle of the door. The lock made its pinging sound.

The little girl backed away as he entered the room, cowering like she had ever since he burned her with the cigarette. He should have done that earlier. She was more manageable when she feared him.

He closed the door behind himself. But, of course, he couldn't lock it. Not without locking himself in.

"Where is it?" he asked.

"There," she said, pointing in the bathroom. "Above the toilet."

He moved across the room and into the bathroom, where there was a little wisp of a spider in the corner. He unrolled a length of toilet paper, then stepped on the toilet lid and took aim.

Except as he reached for it, he heard the rasping of the door handle being turned. He leapt down and scrambled into the bedroom, now empty.

"Hey," he shouted. "Hey, come back here!"

He ran out into the hallway. There was no sign of her. The younger brother cursed. The alarm was armed, and it had not sounded. So he knew she was still in the house somewhere. But where?

"Come back here!" he bellowed. "Come back or you're going to be in big trouble."

54

That afternoon I was supposed to be engaged in the relatively mindless work that was moving documents to their next bureaucratic station, trying to bury myself in the task. What this turned into was me staring out the window at the skyline, searching it for answers that wouldn't come.

The case was now just a muddle in my mind. I had already ruled out anyone on the plaintiff's side as being responsible for Emma. But if it was the defense, why not simply order me to dismiss the complaint and be done with it? If you were Barnaby Roberts, with Paul Dresser doing your dirty work, why allow ApotheGen stock to continue this precipitous plunge?

Beyond that, there was the constant ache from being without Emma, and the constant terror of thinking about what might be happening to her at any given moment— both of which were incapacitating, when I gave myself over to them.

So I can't say I was being interrupted midway through the afternoon when there came a knock at my door. It wasn't a Jeremy Freeland knock or a Joan Smith knock. I hadn't said a word in reply when my door was already opening.

From behind it, there came a familiar little blond head.

"Hey, buddy!" I cheered.

With permission to enter granted, Sam shouted, "Daddy!" Then he charged across the large expanse of carpet between the door and my desk and buried himself in my waiting arms like he hadn't seen me in months. Six-year-olds' imperfect sense of the passage of time has its benefits.

I enjoyed the hug for the brief moment it lasted; then he wrestled himself free.

"Good to see you, pal," I said, mussing his hair a little.

Alison had entered my chambers as well, closing the door behind her. "Hey," I said when I saw her.

"We were just down here, hitting the zoo again," she said. "Before we went home, we were thinking maybe we could run some stairs."

The courthouse has this old stairwell, replete with marble steps and cast-aluminum railings. For reasons perhaps only a six-year-old could understand, Sam loved to run up and down them.

"Can I, Dad, can I?"

"I don't see why not," I said, eager to have the distraction. "Let's go."

"Actually, I was thinking Mr. Freeland would want to take Sam," Alison said, adding one of those looks that mothers know how to make sail over the heads of their offspring. "Do you think he would be willing to do that?"

"Oh, yeah, Dad, could he? That'd be awesome."

At the moment, Jeremy probably wasn't in the mood to do me any favors. There was also the problem of his noticing that Alison and I suddenly had only one child. But I could finesse that.

"Sure, buddy, let's go ask," I said.

Sam took my hand and dragged me toward Jeremy's office.

"Hi, Mr. Freeland!" he squeaked as soon as he was within view.

"Why, hello, Sam," Jeremy said, appropriately surprised.

"Emma is with her grandma, doing girl stuff," I explained, before Jeremy could ask. "But Sam here is hoping to run up and down the stairs. And he wants to go with Mr. Freeland. Would you mind?"

Sam's smile was lighthouse bright. Jeremy returned it. He wasn't going to take out his frustration with me on my son.

"Sure, let's go."

I smiled thinly at Jeremy. "Thanks, Mr. Freeland."

He ignored me.

"Can I feed the fish first, can I?" Sam asked.

"Okay, but only a little."

"Thanks again, Mr. Freeland," I said.

I received no reply. As I left, I heard Sam cooing, "Heyyyy, Thurgood. Thurrr-goooood."

When I returned to my office, Alison was sitting on the edge of one of the chairs in front of my desk.

"What's up?" I asked, resuming my seat.

"I heard from the lab today."

"The . . . lab," I said, clearly lost.

"The lab in Williamsburg. The fingerprinting."

"Oh yeah. Right."

"You were right about the boxes and bags and envelopes that showed up on the porch. There were no fingerprints."

"Sorry," I said.

"But they did find something interesting on the keychain."

"The keychain?"

"To the Honda? Remember how I sent that along with the toaster so they could lift Justina's fingerprints?"

"Yeah."

"Well, they got her prints off the toaster pretty easily. But when they were looking at that big brass keychain, they saw two sets of prints. One matched the prints from the toaster, making it Justina's. But the other wasn't yours or mine."

"So whose was it?"

"That's the point. Whoever's print is on that brass keychain is probably the person who drove the Honda— in other words, the person who took the kids. The only problem is, this is a private lab. They don't have access to law enforcement databases."

"Oh right," I said.

"But the US Marshals Service does," she said, then pulled that brass keychain—ensconced in a plastic bag—from her purse and placed it on my desk. "You know a thousand of those guys. One of them will do you a favor on the hush-hush, right?"

It is the judge in me that immediately thinks of the counterargument. "Of course, you realize, that database only has about a hundred million entries. That means two out of three Americans aren't in there."

"But criminals are," she pointed out. "Them, federal employees, and anyone like me whose dad made all his kids get fingerprinted."

378

I sat there for a moment, trying to think of the flaws in this plan. I turned it over a few different ways and decided that the risk was small compared to the potential benefit.

Maybe nothing would come of it. But as long as I was careful, it couldn't hurt.

"Okay," I said, taking the bag off my desk and sliding it into my pocket, where it made a lump in my suit pants. "I'll get it tested."

*

Once Sam had exhausted himself on the stairs, I walked him and Alison out to her car, which was in the lot down the street—no preferential parking for judges' spouses.

I returned through the employees' entrance, where Ben Gardner was on duty, alone.

Which was just how I hoped he might be.

"How'd your boys do against Ole Miss?" I asked as he got to his feet.

"Chewed 'em up," he said. "Good day for the O-line."

In his desire not to hassle us, Ben calibrated the metal detector at a setting that might or might not have alerted if you dragged a whole scrapyard through.

Not even the big chunk of brass in my pocket made the machine go off. But after I passed soundlessly through, I turned back toward Ben. He was already settling back into his chair, expecting that I would just keep hustling on toward my chambers like I always did.

"Hey, Ben, you got a second?"

"Yeah, sure, Judge, what's up?" he said, getting back on his feet. He was medium height with gray hair and an easy smile. His blue court security officer blazer only partially hid a belly that was as round as an ice-cream scoop. He reminded me of an owner of a mom-and-pop hardware store, a guy who just wanted to help you find the right pipe fitting.

"I need a favor. A big one, actually. And part of the favor is that you can't tell anyone you're helping me."

"What did you have in mind?" he asked.

"You CSOs are pretty friendly with the US Marshals Service, yes?"

"Well, yeah."

"And the marshals service has access to the FBI's fingerprint database, right?"

"Sure does."

I held out the plastic bag. "I need to have the prints on this keychain run through the system. There's a print that belongs to a young woman named Justina Kemal. She's Turkish and here on a student visa, so I don't think she's on file. But I'm not worried about her. It's the other prints I'm curious about. I want to see if there are any hits."

"Okay. Is this for a . . . a trial or . . ."

"No, no. Nothing like that. It's personal. We had it taken to a private lab but, of course, they don't have access to the FBI database. We think . . . Alison and I, we think someone is stealing from us. But we want to be sure before we, you know, take action."

All of which was basically true.

He smiled. "And you don't want to fire the cleaning lady when it might not be the cleaning lady?"

"Yeah, something like that. I'd bother the chief deputy marshal, but I'd just like to keep this real quiet. It's not a huge deal or anything, but you'd really be helping us out."

"I gotcha."

"And as long as I'm pushing my luck, I need it done, like, yesterday."

"The missus wearing you out?"

"You know it," I said, smiling that beleaguered-husband smile.

"You got it. I can probably get it to you by the end of the week."

"That would be terrific. Thank you."

"Roll Tide," he said.

"Roll Tide," I confirmed.

55

They turned the house inside out. The older brother had joined in the search—after berating the younger brother for his stupidity, of course—but he had been no more successful in finding whatever tiny hole the little girl had disappeared into.

They had gone through every possible hiding spot, haphazardly at first, then systematically. The closets. The bedrooms. The bathrooms. The ventilation system, even though they couldn't figure out how she would have been able to climb up there. Then they repeated the process, to no greater success.

After a while, the younger brother got tired of being cursed at, so he started cursing back. It didn't help.

Long after darkness fell, they were still at it, when finally the older brother said: enough. The little girl would get hungry and thirsty eventually. Then she'd come out.

In the meantime, they just had to make sure she didn't escape the house. They dragged their air mattresses against the two exterior doors. The older brother lay down on the one barricading the front door. The younger brother took the side door. They slept in their clothes.

And that was where they still were, both snoring, when the alarm shrieked.

The younger brother bolted upright, looking around wildly until his vision locked on the one moving object in the room: the upper half of the little girl's body just before it disappeared out of the window above the kitchen sink.

"Hey!" he yelled.

He ran toward the window—a stupid impulse, since he couldn't slither out of it like the little girl. Then he went back toward the side door, opening it and throwing on the outdoor floodlights in time to see her slipping into the woods.

56

It's peculiar how certain phrases can just stay with you, attaching themselves to the inside of your skull.

At first, maybe, it seems like there's no good explanation for it. Then you start to wonder if there's some deeper reason why one particular arrangement of words has gotten to be so sticky.

The thing that kept going through my head—all through what turned out to be another long and mostly sleepless night—was Ben Gardner's Alabama twang asking me, "The missus wearing you out?"

And, well, was she?

Was this whole keychain business some kind of make-work assignment to keep my eye off the ball? Was it another O. J. Simpson–like piece of subterfuge, Alison's equivalent of the bloody gloves? Was Paul whispering in her ear, telling her she just needed to keep me distracted a little while longer?

It was the next morning, while I was having these thoughts, when something Alison said during breakfast entered my ear canal at an odd angle. I had asked her what she and Sam were planning to do that day.

Her reply had been: "Oh, it's Aunt Karen to the rescue. She has those friends who run that organic farm, and she got them to invite us over. They've got pigs and goats and chickens and hay bales. Sam ought to have a blast."

I had strung together the expected reply about how that sounded great. But all the while, I was thinking about how that was the exact setup she had relied on the last couple of times she had left Sam alone. There was always something— a museum, a game, and now a farm—to distract him. And there was always Aunt Jenny, Aunt Karen, or Grammy to provide backup.

Was this another one of those days when she was going to visit Emma? To see Paul?

There was no hiring another private investigator to answer those questions. Not in anything resembling good conscience. Even if I told the PI not to go on my property and to watch his tail wherever he went . . . No. I was never going to forgive myself for Herb Thrift. If the new man found tragedy, it would be something far worse.

But maybe I could follow Alison myself. Just this once.

Then I'd know.

My plan was already forming as I finished breakfast, knotted my tie, and prepared myself for launch. I could play hooky from work—at least for the morning, which was when the organic farm visit was allegedly taking place. The *Palgraff* lawyers weren't going to need me. There were no other matters pending before the court that would require my immediate presence. I could do this.

I kissed Alison and Sam good-bye, like absolutely nothing unusual was about to take place. But as I drove up our driveway, I dialed Mrs. Smith's number and left her a voice mail informing her that a judicial errand was taking me out of the office that morning.

Then something Herb Thrift had written in an e-mail came back to me: *Next time you try to hide your identity from a private investigator, don't drive your own car to his office.*

I thought about the big, rolling box of conspicuousness that was my Buick Enclave and pointed myself toward an off-brand rental car place a mile or so away.

Fifteen minutes of paperwork and one credit card swipe later, I was back on the road in a slightly used and perfectly anonymous Chevy. I silently thanked Herb Thrift for his teaching.

Then I settled into a parking spot in the strip mall that was on the southwest side of the intersection where our road met Route 17, and I waited for Alison to make her appearance.

*

By nine forty-five, I was worried that perhaps the rental had taken too long and that I had missed Alison and Sam as they slipped out on their way to the organic farm. I was starting to wonder if I should just return the rental car and try this another day.

Then I saw a vehicle emerge from around a curve in the distance. I took a moment to be sure, but as the grill plate came into better view, I was sure it was Alison's Lincoln MKX.

She applied her brakes to stop at the light, which was red, coming within maybe twenty feet of where I had parked. But her eyes were fixed straight ahead. As soon as she passed me, I started the engine and got moving.

She turned left to head north on Route 17, and I followed. Once in the flow of traffic, I eased back a bit. After the Walmart shopping center, then Walter Reed Hospital and the cluster of buildings around it, the businesses started to thin out, as did the spacing of the lights. We soon passed into Middlesex County, our more rural neighbor to the north. I started wondering how long a trip I was in for.

But it turned out to be not much of one. From the other side of the pickup truck that I was keeping between us, I saw her turn signal flash. She was taking a right.

This was where shadowing her got riskier. I lagged farther back. After a mile or two of farms and forest, the road forked and she bore to the left. Before long, she was going to hit water—most of these offshoots to the east side of Route 17 dead-ended at a variety of Chesapeake Bay tributaries.

Soon, she was slowing. I was about two-tenths of a mile back and decelerated to a commensurate degree.

She disappeared into a gravel driveway on the left. I stayed straight as I passed a thin dirt lane with a sign next to it that read SWEET EARTH ORGANIC FARM.

As I cruised past, I managed to make out some hoop houses, a chicken coop, a barn, a smattering of goats. Definitely a farm.

A few hundred yards down, I found a spot to turn around. I crept back up the road just a little, then pulled off in a spot to the side where I could just see the farm's entrance.

And that was where I stayed. Really, the duration of my wait would tell me everything I needed to know. If Alison was there for two, three, four hours, then all was exactly as it seemed: a mother and son making a trip to an organic farm; nothing to see here.

If it was otherwise, Alison was up to something. It was really that simple.

I made it a point to mark the time on the Chevy's small digital clock. It was 10:04 A.M.

57

The younger brother was well beyond infuriated.

He had seen the *exact* spot where the little girl had vanished into the forest. He went in after her, sure his longer legs would catch her in no time.

The older brother had shut off the alarm system less than a minute later, then bellowed for quiet. It was dark. They had to use their ears, not their eyes, to find her.

Sure enough, the younger brother heard some rustling, coming from . . . where exactly? It was hard to tell. Whatever made the noise was too big to be a raccoon and too clumsy to be anything else. It had to be the little girl.

He had trained his ears toward what he thought was the spot. There was no further sound. She had obviously hidden somewhere.

That had been, what, three o'clock in the morning?

They waited and listened until dawn, knowing they were close, knowing if she moved they would hear it. They called for her, offering her every kind of inducement they could think of—chocolate, ice cream, dolls. Then they switched to threats.

Once the sun rose, they started looking for her in a more orderly fashion. They calculated how far a little girl might be able to run in a minute, then doubled that amount, then used that distance to form a search grid. When they still didn't find her, they doubled its size.

There was no trace of her. It was like she had vanished into the forest floor.

Finally, after several hours, they convened at the center of the grid.

"This is not getting us anywhere," the older brother said. "It's time to be smart about this. You stay here. Do *not* leave this spot. She's somewhere very nearby."

"Where are you going?"

"Out. We need some technological help."

"Why do you get to go?"

The older brother fixed him with a withering look and stomped off.

The younger brother stood rooted to his spot for a while. He wished he had his iPad game to help pass the time. Maybe he could sneak into the house and retrieve it. Surely, there was no danger in that.

58

Exactly twelve minutes after Alison had turned into the farm, the nose of the Lincoln appeared at the head of the driveway. Alison paused briefly to look to her left, then hit the gas, her tires kicking up gravel.

Like she was in a hurry to get somewhere.

She had been at the farm just long enough to get Sam introduced and settled in with Karen. Then she hightailed it out. Was there any doubt now?

"Oh, Alison," I moaned.

As I gave chase, back in the direction of Route 17, I could feel the betrayal, like someone was unspooling a roll of barbed wire in my veins.

How could Alison do this to Emma? To Sam? To me? I was already thinking about the trial that would result. Kidnapping. Times two. In the hands of an aggressive prosecutor, that was life in prison.

But was that what I wanted for the mother of my children? To be put in one of those inhumane cages forever? To have Sam and Emma go through all the milestones of their lives, big and small—everything from losing their first tooth to having children of their own—without the woman who birthed them?

A memory leapt into my head unbidden. It was from when

I was in my early thirties. I had contracted a particularly virulent strain of the flu that was making the rounds in Washington.

I kept working from home all the same. I was crafting some legislation for Blake that I was convinced was mission critical. And so—heavily dosed on acetaminophen, ibuprofen, and self-importance—I kept taking phone calls, typing e-mails, and dashing to the bathroom.

Alison came home when I was in the midst of this ridiculous act. Without a word, she removed the phone from my hand and slid the computer off my lap. Then she said, "You're allowed to be sick, Scott. The US Senate doesn't give perfect attendance awards."

The award became something of a running gag after that. When she got pregnant, I made it a point to be at every ob-gyn appointment and ultrasound. After the last one, she presented me with a framed plaque that contained a certificate for perfect attendance.

"This one," she told me, "is the only one that really matters."

That was Alison. She kept the big picture in focus. She knew family—not running off with your ex-boyfriend—was at the core of everything.

Where was that Alison now? And what made her think she was going to get away with something like this?

It was all too surreal, and I was still trying to make any sense of it when I realized Alison's Lincoln was slowing. We had just reentered the more well-developed part of Gloucester.

Alison slid into a left-turn-only lane that channeled traffic toward the collection of low-slung white buildings that comprised Walter Reed Hospital. There were also some buildings behind it—medical offices and whatnot.

She didn't go toward the main entrance for the hospital. She forked off to the right. According to the directional signs, she was pointed toward employee parking, deliveries, and a few other destinations whose names I couldn't quite read. The signs were passing by too quickly.

After a few hundred feet, she took a left. The road sloped down, past a retention pond, then back up. On the left, there was a building labeled WALTER REED MEDICAL ARTS.

Had they somehow stashed Emma there as a patient? It was baffling. And I was so determined to catch my wife red-handed, so narrowly focused on the alternate reality I had constructed for her, so myopic in my view, that I couldn't consider any other possibilities.

That changed the moment Alison turned away from the Medical Arts center, taking a right turn toward another building.

It was labeled CANCER CENTER.

59

The younger brother did not retrieve his iPad. As tempted as he might have been, they were getting a hundred-thousand-dollar bonus upon successful completion of this job. World domination could wait.

He stayed within the search grid, sometimes giving it another pass in case he'd missed something, sometimes staying put in hopes the silence might lure the little girl out.

Two hours later, he heard the van coming up the driveway. When his older brother got out and glanced his way, the younger just shook his head.

"Stay there," the older ordered.

The younger answered with an obscene gesture.

The older disappeared into the house for a moment, then emerged with their laptop and a tool bag. He got to work, pulling a large box out of the van and struggling through the instructions. Before long he had assembled what appeared to be a very small helicopter.

A drone. The younger brother felt himself smiling. It was good thinking.

The older brother had already moved his attention to a smaller box, which was emblazoned with words, the largest of which were THERMAL IMAGING CAMERA.

The older brother soon had the entire contraption in the

air, hovering smoothly several hundred feet up. He studied the laptop screen, then set it down and made a beeline for the younger brother. About twenty feet short, he slowed, then stopped at a partially fallen tree, one whose trunk was leaning at a roughly twenty-degree angle against another tree.

He studied the root ball, looking at a spot where it had pulled away from the ground to create a tiny burrow. The younger brother had walked by it at least thirty times. It had just never occurred to him something could fit under there.

The older brother pulled back his boot and let loose a savage kick, clearing away a clump of dirt. He bent low and reached under the tree.

"Gotcha!" he yelled triumphantly.

The reward for his effort was a terrified, high-pitched scream.

60

Alison pulled into a slot one row from the entrance. Without noticing the rented Chevy that had followed her into the parking lot, she climbed out of her car and made a straight line toward the building.

I parked one row behind her and watched her disappear through the front doors. After that moment's hesitation, I went after her. Whatever thought I had about lying back and watching how this developed was now gone.

We weren't going to be a family that kept secrets anymore.

As I plowed through the doors, I could see Alison at the reception desk. Her back was to me. She was writing her name on a clipboard.

Just like all the other cancer patients.

As the door swung shut behind me, she put down the clipboard. Her focus remained elsewhere until her peripheral vision registered that a very familiar figure was coming her way. She turned toward me and her eyes went wide.

"Scott?" she blurted.

Then her shoulders—those shoulders I loved so much—slumped.

"Hi," I said quietly.

We stood there facing each other, perhaps five feet apart, each calculating what the other was thinking, each seeing the other in a slightly different way than ever before. Her face strained to keep in emotion. My wife wasn't one for public scenes.

"Do you want to sit down?" I asked.

"Sure."

We walked into a large, sunlit waiting area. A woman in what appeared to be a wig sat idly thumbing through *People* magazine. A gaunt man checked his phone, wearing the haunted look of someone who had already gone twelve rounds against Floyd Mayweather and knew he was about to do it again.

I gawked at them more than I should have. Somewhere inside these people were clumps of rogue cells that were trying to crowd the life out of them. And modern medicine was going to do its best to banish those cells, using tools that future generations would surely consider barbaric— bombing them with radiation, injecting them with poison, carving them with scalpels.

This was the reality of cancer. It was not just a diagnosis. It was, in a twisted way, a lifestyle. You didn't just have cancer. Cancer had you.

And this was what my wife was now facing. In addition to everything else.

My wife had cancer. I couldn't fully parse the implications. Alison had obviously been living with this knowledge for some time now. It was still so new to me.

I thought back to all the things that had been right in front of me. The weight loss, the vomiting, how tired she looked—symptoms I had chalked up to the stress of

Emma's disappearance.

And then there were those unexplained absences, which my paranoid mind had turned into visits with our daughter, rendezvous with kidnappers, or trysts with her old boyfriend. Really, they had been doctor's appointments for the disease she had been keeping from me.

She had selected two chairs in the corner that were as far from the other patients as we could get. We sat with our knees not quite touching.

"So," I said.

"So," she replied.

"How long have you known?" I asked.

"I noticed a lump in the shower the day after Sam came back."

"Jesus."

"I know."

"Where?" I asked.

She pointed to her right breast. "It was hard and had a weird shape to it. All the things they tell you to be on the lookout for. I knew I couldn't ignore it. Especially with Dad's history. I reached out to the doctor that morning."

I thought back to the burst of industriousness she had shown that Friday morning while I slept—calling the kids' school, her workplace, the lab in Williamsburg. The call to our doctor's office had been wedged in there. I had even seen it on her phone when I checked her call log. I had just thought it was routine.

"I was hoping it was just a cyst or a clogged pore or, I don't know," she said. "The doctor was able to squeeze me in that afternoon and give me a mammogram in the office. So at that point I knew it was some kind of tumor."

"Oh, Alison," I said, as gently as I could. "Why didn't you tell me?"

"I was going to that night, but . . . I don't know. As I was driving home, I had this thought that it would actually be selfish of me. I wanted at least one of us to be totally focused on Emma, not sidetracked by . . . whatever this is. I hope you understand I desperately wanted to tell you. Desperately, desperately. Just to be able to cry into your arms. But I felt like I couldn't."

"Okay," I said simply.

It really was that easy for me. Not only did I understand, I probably would have done the same thing myself.

She smiled weakly. "Thank you."

"You told your family, yes?" I asked, although I already knew she had. They had covered for her the afternoon of the nap that wasn't and probably half a dozen other times.

"Yeah. There was no way not to. I couldn't exactly bring Sam to this place and have him asking all kinds of questions. My mom has been pretty much a basket case about everything, but Karen has been great, just taking charge like always. She's been helping me sort out all the insurance and everything. She's made sure I didn't have to take Sam to any of my appointments."

"So he doesn't—"

"Oh God no. That little boy has enough on his mind already without worrying about Momma being sick.

"Anyway, I met with the oncologist for the first time,

let's see . . . not this past Thursday, but the Thursday before. Laurie Lyckholm is her name. She's really lovely. She did an evaluation and took some blood; then she scheduled me for a needle biopsy. That was last Wednesday."

In other words, while I had been fretting over Denny Palgraff no-showing for a deposition, Alison had been having a massive needle jammed into her breast.

"So"—this was the question I had been wanting and not wanting to ask the whole time—"do we know the results yet?"

She nodded solemnly. "It's called infiltrating ductal carcinoma. You can Google it if you want to. Dr. Lyckholm said it's the most common form of breast cancer."

"That means it's . . . I mean, it's treatable, right?"

"Oh yeah. Sure. That's why I'm here today. Dr. Lyckholm wants a CT scan so we can get a clearer picture of what's going on. Then we discuss next steps."

"But are we talking surgery? Chemo? Radiation? All of the above? None of the above?"

"I don't know yet," Alison said. "Dr. Lyckholm said it helps that I'm relatively young and in otherwise good shape. I guess it expands the options, treatment-wise. But it seems like every other question I ask, Dr. Lyckholm says, 'Well, we'll have to see what the CT scan says.' "

"Okay. And whatever happens, you're . . . you're going to tell me everything now, right? I mean, no more secrets, right?"

She patted my hand.

"No more secrets," she confirmed.

"Not even about little things, like cigarettes?"

She looked down at her lap.

"For what it's worth, I really did quit while I was pregnant with the twins, and then for a few years after," she said. "But then it started to become this thing I'd do at work and . . . Well, I guess I'm paying the price now."

She exhaled noisily.

"I'm sorry," I said. "I'm not trying to blame you for—"

"Forget it. I'm just glad you're here. How did you know about it? Did my mom finally tell you? She's been threatening for a while."

"No," I said.

She wore a question mark on her face.

"Don't get mad," I said, still trying to summon the courage to admit to the big, ugly thing I suspected her of.

"Mad about what?"

"I followed you coming out of the house. I rented a car so you wouldn't see me. I followed you up to the organic farm, and then here."

"Why?"

There was no point in hiding it anymore. "I actually thought there was a possibility you had something to do with Emma."

"What?!" she said, sharply enough that the woman in the wig turned to look at us.

If we hadn't been in a hospital waiting room, I'm sure Alison's reaction would have been even louder. She immediately quieted herself, but her whisper was ferocious. "What do you mean, 'something to do with Emma'? Scott, how could you think that for even one second?"

"Well, first there was Miss Pam saying you were the one who picked up the—"

"That wasn't me; that was—"

"I know, I know. I'm just saying, that's where it started. And then there was the day you took Sam to the Living Museum. After you got him settled, you left—that was the day of your mammogram, I guess. You thought Sam was too distracted by the sharks to notice you were gone. But he did. And when I asked you about it later, you lied about it. Several times, actually."

She looked at her lap again and nodded. "So then you got suspicious," she said.

"Yeah, I . . . Look, I'm not proud of any of this, but I also wasn't exactly in my right mind, you know? So I went into your Facebook account, which I know I shouldn't have done. It was such a violation of your privacy. But at the same time, I felt like I was, I don't know, entitled. Because you had lied. And I found this message from Paul Dresser, saying he had some news and that you should call him."

Alison cocked her head. "He wanted to tell me our favorite English teacher had died . . . Wait, what would Paul possibly have to do with this?"

"He works for ApotheGen."

"Yeah? So?"

"Well, I thought he knew I had been assigned this case and had enticed you into going along with this kidnapping scheme."

"And, what, then we were going to run off together?"

402

She actually laughed. It was the first time I had heard that sound in what felt like a century.

"Oh, honey," she said. "Paul is basically Peter Pan. He's the boy who won't grow up. His whole life is self-gratification. He goes on these fabulous vacations, but . . . I mean, all those times I talked about running off with him, I was *kidding*."

"He does work for ApotheGen, though. For what it's worth."

"Yeah, as, like, a sales rep. He works with ob-gyns. He's basically there to charm female doctors into pushing ApotheGen products on their patients, which I'm sure he excels at. But . . . Oh, Scott. I'm so sorry."

She covered her mouth and smiled, like she was a little embarrassed for me.

"Yeah, well, then that Thursday when you first met with Dr. Lyckholm? I called your mom's house and I talked to Karen. She told me you were napping. You came home and said the same thing. But when I asked Sam about it later, he said you were out doing errands."

"Wow. I guess he's not quite as oblivious as I thought," she said.

"He's not. And then this morning when you said you were going to the organic farm, I thought it was another time you were going to sneak off and do whatever it was you had been doing. So I followed you."

"And here I am," she said, forcing a brave smile.

"Here you are," I repeated. "Sorry I—"

She was already shaking her head. "I shouldn't have tried

to hide it. It was stupid of me to think I could. I actually sort of kept hoping you'd find out. I'm . . . I'm glad you did."

"Me too," I said.

I felt both of her hands, so warm, so pliant, so alive. I wanted to stop everything right there, to freeze this moment when she was only sort of sick, when things were bad but not as bad as they might become. Those rogue cells were inside her, making their insidious divisions. Was it possible one of them had broken free and colonized another part of her body? What would we do then?

There were so many questions. But I didn't want to be one of those people who got so fixated on the workings of the medical-industrial complex—the doctors, the insurance forms, the treatment options—that I ignored the bigger picture: My wife was in for the fight of her life.

And she might not win.

"So, Ali, are you . . . What does this mean?" I choked out, desperate for her to give me reassurance that she couldn't really offer. "You're going to be okay . . . right?"

"I don't know," she said honestly.

I lingered on that, but only a little. This new uncertainty—on top of all the others—was almost too much to contemplate.

"I feel like I've missed so much already," I said. "What can I do to help now?"

"Just worry about Emma. After Friday, you worry about me."

"No," I said. "I can't not worry about you anymore. It's too late for that. I'll still . . . Look, I'm not going to take my eyes off the ball with Emma, I promise you that. But there has to be something I can do to, I don't know, make this easier for you somehow."

She forced out a deep breath. "Oh, Scott," she said.

"What?"

"After all these years, you still don't get it, do you?"

Now it was my turn to wear the question-mark face.

"Do you remember the day we met?"

"Of course."

"No, no. I'm not talking about that fairy tale you tell everyone about me walking along in front of the student center with the sun glowing and the angels singing. I'm talking about later that night. You had asked me what I was doing that night and I told you I was probably going to a party."

"And I told you I was already planning on going to the same party, which was a lie."

"Well, I know. I probably knew it then too. But I showed up, and there you were. A friend later told me you had been there for an hour and a half already."

I smiled at the memory.

"And the thing was, you didn't just show up for that thing," she continued. "You showed up for the next thing. And the next thing. Anything you promised, anything you said you'd do, you followed through on. I had never met a guy like that. Not Paul Dresser. Not anyone. Maybe that doesn't sound very romantic—I fell in love with you because you were reliable—but you have to remember with my dad, nothing in my life had been rooted. It always seemed like just as soon as I made one or two attachments to a person or a place, it was, oops, Dad got promoted, time to go somewhere else. There had never been anything I could depend on, and then along you came. And you were this rock.

"So now you want to know what you can do for me? Just be yourself. Be that rock. You being you has always been enough for me."

She squeezed my hand again. We just sat there, holding hands, until a nurse approached. They were ready for her.

"All right," Alison said, dropping my hands and standing. "I'll see you at home later?"

"No, no. I'm staying right here. I've missed enough of this. You know you've already cost me my chance at a perfect attendance award, right?"

She bent down and kissed me. "I'll be back," she said.

"I'll be here for you," I assured her. "Right here."

61

I woke the next morning with what could only be described as an emotional hangover. The world was putting out too much sensory input for my tender circuitry. Even the colors outside the window seemed off, having been subtly redefined overnight by the knowledge of my wife's illness.

There probably should have been some relief in knowing Alison was not, in fact, scheming behind my back; and that Paul Dresser wasn't waiting to take her away; and that however bad things were, at least we were in this together. But those consolations were nullified by the intense ache of what had replaced them.

The greatest health crisis we had ever faced before this was when I got shot. It was noisy, gory, and shocking, yes. But, really, it was just physics. And simple, straightforward Newtonian physics, at that: A bullet carrying a certain amount of momentum had struck me, transferring its energy into my flesh, creating all kinds of musculoskeletal havoc before making its hasty exit. By the time I even realized I'd been hit, the damage had already been done. The recovery was, likewise, mechanical. There was no great mystery about what was going on, and, as much as it might have hurt, there was a certain comfort in knowing the worst was over.

This was far scarier. Cancer is like a bullet that hits you

slowly, over months and years. And the moment of impact is really just the beginning. We had no idea how big the wound was going to become.

What's more, the answers to all the toughest questions were expressed in the baffling terms of quantum physics. There were no certainties. There were just varying probabilities of outcomes that ranged all the way from the barely tolerable to the utterly unthinkable. I defy anyone to find comfort in studying charts of five- and ten-year survival rates.

The only thing that stopped me from shutting down altogether that morning was a stern lecture from Alison, reminding me that I had promised to stay focused on Emma.

The hearing was now two days away. My staff was fully ensconced in preparations, such that when I arrived at my normal time, I was actually the last one to get there.

I went through the motions of joining them. When I got buzzed by Mrs. Smith midmorning, I thought it would be another question from the defendant's lawyers about the use of visual aids or another petty squabble about courtroom seating.

Instead, she said, "Judge, Congressman Neal Keesee is calling for you. Would you like to speak with him?"

Neal Keesee. Hearing the name brought an instant spike to my blood pressure. It had been two weeks since the Michael Jacobs press conference, and I had—in the way that desperation breeds naïveté—thought the issue had been laid to rest.

"Of course," I said. "Put him through."

During my years in Blake's office, I had never dealt with Keesee, but I knew him by reputation. He was one of the most wonkish of our nation's 435 legislators, an incisive and detail-oriented technocrat who quoted Congressional Budget Office reports from memory. A feature in *The Washington Post* I now recalled revealed him to be an unabashed nerd— he was obsessed with model trains and was such a *Star Trek* aficionado he spoke Klingon. But those who dismissed him as nebbishy or ineffectual did so at their own peril.

I became aware I was holding my breath as I waited for the call to come through. I let it out slowly. The next sound I heard was Keesee's clipped voice.

"Good morning, Judge Sampson."

"Good morning, Congressman Keesee. How can I help you?"

"I know you're busy and I am too, so I'll get right to it: I'm having some continued issues with your ruling in *US versus Skavron* and I wanted to get it dealt with before Friday. I know you're hearing a very important matter that day."

"That's right," I said.

"Given the time constraints, it seemed most expedient to reach out to you directly. I'm sure you understand."

"Of course," I said, as if sweat hadn't just popped on my brow.

"Excellent. As you are aware, my colleague Congressman Jacobs has been rather loudly questioning your ruling with regards to Mr. Skavron. I recognized that at least some of his enthusiasm was driven less by the underlying issues of justice and more by the amount of attention he could garner for himself on Fox News. So before I brought the Judiciary Committee into this, I reached out to your chief judge, Mr. Byers, to better understand why he decided not to pursue this matter. He told me a story about a young man named Keith Bloom."

He was waiting for me to say something. So I threw in an "I see."

"Judge Byers apparently found your story very compelling, but I was interested in learning some more specifics, which he, of course, could not provide. So I asked a member of my staff to find a little more information about the Bloom case. And do you know what he found out?"

"No," I said, feeling the trap starting to close around me.

"Nothing. There was no record of a Keith Bloom having ever appeared anywhere in the District of Columbia court system. There was no recording of a plea deal, no sentencing, not a single mention of any Keith Blooms during the time when you worked for Senator Franklin. We knew the case wasn't sealed because you told Judge Byers that Mr. Bloom was no longer a juvenile. So my staffer took the extra step of contacting the US Attorneys Office for the District of Columbia. They didn't have any record of a Keith Bloom either."

"Huh," I offered, as if this puzzled me. My palm had been resting on the top of my desk. When I brought it away, there was a sweat mark in the shape of my hand.

"So now I'm reaching out to you. Do you have a phone number or an e-mail address for Mr. Bloom?"

"Uh, no. We're . . . not really in touch anymore. I think I told Judge Byers that."

"I understand. But I'm sure you can provide some helpful information. Perhaps where he went to college? Or the name of the high school where he works and coaches? Or the name of a family member who might know where to find him? I assure you this is not for public consumption. I'm not interested in cable news face time. I'd just like to confirm Mr. Bloom's existence and the basic facts of his situation as you've related them to Judge Byers."

I sat there holding the phone, trying to come up with anything that wouldn't get me in more trouble than I was already in. And I couldn't. Any lie I might concoct could easily be uncovered. Keesee had his teeth sunk in deep. And, in any event, my mind was too blank to come up with the first thread of a fabrication.

"You can't say anything right now because Keith Bloom doesn't really exist, does he?" Keesee said.

I didn't reply. If I told him the truth, there was no chance I'd hang on to *Palgraff*. It would be reassigned before the day was done. That made this a choice between my job and my daughter, which wasn't really any kind of choice at all.

There was a silence that I was not going to fill. At this point, words could only further damage my position.

"Judge Sampson, as I see it I have two choices here," he said finally. "One, you can offer me your resignation, and perhaps this will all just quietly go away. Or, two, I can begin impeachment proceedings against you."

"I . . . Can I think about it for a few days? Give me through the weekend."

"I'm sorry, Judge, but I cannot allow you to hear the ApotheGen matter under these circumstances. I have the public faith in the federal judiciary to consider. If you'd like to resign, which is what I'd recommend, you'll have to do it before the ApotheGen hearing."

"I can't do that."

"Very well. You should know I will be contacting Judge Byers and relating this conversation to him. I will be asking him to convene the circuit's Judicial Council immediately. It will be up to him to decide whether to do so, of course. But I'm going to recommend he do everything in his power to have your cases removed from you immediately."

My plea came out low and fast. "Please don't do that."

"Excuse me?"

"I said please don't do that to me. Please don't have Judge Byers take away my cases."

"I'm not sure I understand."

"I'm not sure I can explain it to you. But I need to keep hearing cases, Congressman. It's a matter of . . . of great importance to me."

I heard my own voice trembling. I'm sure it sounded the same to Keesee's ears as it did to mine:

Pitiful.

But apparently not worthy of pity.

"I'm sorry, Judge," he said at last. "You've given me no choice."

I hung up on him. There was nothing more to discuss and I had clearly reached the point where anything else I said could and would be used against me.

It didn't take much imagination to picture what would happen next. Neal Keesee would tell Jeb Byers I had lied to him—that I had made a fool out of him, really. And Judge Byers, understandably furious, would act swiftly.

The Judicial Council for the Fourth Circuit was comprised of an equal number of judges from the district courts and the court of appeals. It would take at least a few hours to find a time when all of them could get on a conference call. But Byers could get it done by the end of Thursday without much trouble.

The fact was, the walls were closing in on me. If I stayed quiet, the case was going to be stripped from me, which would be a disaster. But if I told Byers or Keesee the truth, it would put Emma's fate in the hands of FBI agents who wouldn't have an inkling of where to start looking for her— and who would need a miracle to find her in time, before the kidnappers figured out I was off the case.

The situation was hopeless. Truly hopeless.

I wanted to quit. Quit being a judge who had to hear cases of consequence. Quit being the husband of a wife who had cancer. Quit being the father of a daughter who wasn't there.

And I would have. If I felt like I had any choice in the matter. The reality was, for whatever Keesee had just said, nobody was really giving me that option. Not in any meaningful way. When you become a parent, you forfeit the right to quit.

So I stared at the clock on the far wall of my office, watching the second hand make sweeps around the dial until I returned to my senses and realized every tick was putting my family that much closer to tragedy. And I had to do something about it.

Before I really knew what my plan was, or what I was going to say to him, my fingers were dialing a phone number for the one man who might have the power, contacts, and wherewithal to get me out of this mess.

Blake Franklin might not take my call—given that our last conversation had involved me accusing him of living in Barnaby Roberts' pocket—but I was out of options.

After four rings, just when I thought I was heading for voice mail, Blake answered.

"Hello," he said. He sounded out of breath.

"Hey, Blake. It's Scott."

"Yeah, I know. Hang on."

I hung on. He had muffled the phone against his chest. Still, I heard some strange sounds coming through the earpiece. It was this high-pitched whining that may or may not have been human.

Then it—whatever it was—went away.

"Sorry about that," Blake said. "I'm at a goddamn animal shelter right now. My campaign manager thinks this'll make good visuals. I told him if I end up getting fleas he's gonna be looking for a new job. Anyhow, what's up? You calling to ask if I'm necking with Barnaby Roberts in the backseat? Because I can assure you he's not my type."

"No, look, about that. I'm sorry I—"

"Forget about it. You were under stress with the case and with that Jacobs moron. I'm under stress with the election. You were making some valid points and instead of taking a deep breath and talking you off the ledge I got defensive. It looks like the plaintiff's attorney backed off anyway, so it's all much ado about nothing. I'm willing to forget about it if you are."

It was a classic Blake Franklin compromise, the kind of levelheaded concession making that is increasingly rare in our nation's capital. And I was all too happy to accept it.

"Absolutely," I said. "And thanks for—"

"Don't mention it. And we definitely need to catch up soon. But if you don't mind, there are some puppies back inside who are just dying to have their picture taken with a US senator."

"Actually, there's something else. And it's really important."

"Oh yeah? What's up?"

As succinctly as I could, I told him about my phone call from Neal Keesee, finishing by impressing on him the urgency of the situation.

"Damn, son," he said when I was through. "First you kick a bees' nest; then you poke the bear that was there to eat the honey."

"Yeah, that's about the size of it."

"But catch me up on something here. If you didn't let that

Skavron fellow go free because of that football player, why did you cut him loose?"

I took a measured breath. "Blake, I know this sounds strange, but I can't tell you."

"Can't or won't?"

"Can't. All I can say is that it's a very unusual, very dire situation."

"How dire?"

"Life-and-death dire."

All I heard on the other end was his breathing. So I added, "And when I say life-and-death, I'm not exaggerating. It's something involving my family. But I really can't say more. You're just going to have to trust me."

Even though we were talking on the phone, I could picture exactly what Blake looked like as he considered this. He was probably running his hand through that thick gray hair of his—something he did only when he was lost in thought—and looking far off into the distance.

"Okay," he said. "What are you thinking I can do, exactly?"

"Intercede with Neal Keesee," I said. "You know him, right?"

"A little. I think we first met during your confirmation proceeding, if that's not ironic enough for you."

"As I see it, he's the linchpin of all of this. All you need to do is stall him a little. Just get him off my tail until next week sometime. Then I'll be able to explain everything to you. And to him. And then I think this will . . . Well, I can't say it'll go away. But it'll at least make sense to everyone."

"I'll see what I can do," he said. And then, cryptically, he added, "I probably owe you that much."

62

Even with Blake on the job, working his backroom magic, my adrenal glands went into overdrive every time the phone rang throughout the remainder of the day on Wednesday and into Thursday.

It made for a lot of anxiety. My phone was ringing constantly. The rest of the world—heedless of my personal drama—was charging full speed ahead toward the Markman hearing. *The Wall Street Journal* wrote an advance about it in Thursday's newspaper, calling it "the hearing of the decade for the pharmaceutical industry and the hearing of the century for ApotheGen." It also spoke about the "complication" that the presiding judge was "embroiled in a controversy that has cast an eerie shadow over the proceeding."

Steve Politi posted a piece on HedgeofReason, touting his vaunted "source," who reiterated my bullishness on the merits of the plaintiff's claim. Which meant the source, while knowing enough to give Politi my cell phone number, was otherwise dishing out information from a fantasized realm.

The UPDATE! confirmed that ApotheGen stock had dropped another two dollars and seventy-four cents. It was now down more than thirty dollars from its fifty-two-week high, having sunk to a level not seen since the Crash of 2008.

Meanwhile, my staff and seemingly everyone else in the building were preparing the Walter E. Hoffman United States Courthouse for an onslaught. The clerks set up a second courtroom, where an anticipated overflow of spectators could watch on closed-circuit television. The court security officers had spent half an hour with us, reviewing crowd-control protocols.

There was talk of moving the hearing to one of the larger courtrooms downstairs, but I nixed that immediately. I wanted whatever was going to transpire to take place in the most familiar setting possible. I had insisted on that, and also on scheduling the hearing for one day—and one day only. Expedience was now more important to me than ever.

Hemans seemed amenable to that. The defense team, however, was clearly displeased. In addition to Clarence Worth, there were thirteen other attorneys from Leslie, Jennings & Rowley and three other firms who felt the need to justify all the hours they had been billing. They wanted more time to show off—in front of me and, just as important, in front of their client. It made for a fair amount of haggling with lawyers who were, I could tell, losing patience.

The person who normally dealt with those matters, Jeremy, wasn't saying a word. He had simply withdrawn into his office, to the great discomfort of the rest of the staff. But they were either too confused or too polite to make an issue out of it. They just kept shuffling all those details on over to me.

It made for two hectic, stressful days. I handled it with a sustained burst of energy that came from one place: the knowledge that if I could somehow keep this messy train moving forward—and Blake could stop it from being derailed—it would continue taking me closer to Emma.

*

I can mark the exact moment when the energy finally ran out. It was Thursday night. I was reading Sam his bedtime story, ostensibly as a precursor to tucking him in. But the person who ended up nodding off first was me.

Roughly two hours later, I startled awake when a peal of thunder shook the house. An early-fall thunderstorm had overtaken Virginia's Middle Peninsula with all its attendant turbulence.

When I came to, I was in Sam's bed, still with the light on. A drool slick had accumulated next to my mouth.

Sam, who apparently thought nothing of his father collapsing with him on his bed, was wedged on the far side, up against the wall. Gently, so as not to wake him, I eased myself up, then looked down on him.

Watching your children sleep really is one of the great joys of parenting. And if I took a moment to savor his serenity, it was only in an attempt to absorb some of it myself.

He was wearing his beloved Captain America pajamas, the ones he had gotten when he was two and a half and were now so small he was bursting out of them. His arms were splayed out to the side. His mouth was open. Something in his face reminded me of how he looked as an infant. Yes, he was older now, with features that were becoming sharper and more defined with each growth spurt. I could almost start to imagine the man he would become. But the baby was definitely still in there, somewhere.

Do they grow out of that, eventually? Or can all parents, no matter what age their offspring, still see the vestiges of the tiny little newborn their child once was?

I thought of how, when we first brought the twins home from the hospital, Alison and I used to creep into the nursery and watch them breathe. Mostly it was that new-parent paranoia: We wanted to make sure they were still doing it. But I think part of it was also to enjoy the unfathomable miracle we had conspired to create.

It was a marvel to think of what he had become, this little thing whose heart I had first heard—beating in stereo with his sister's—when he was in his eighth week of gestation. To think he was now capable of such complex operations, even something as banal as putting on too-small pj's, astounded me.

It also made me wonder what Emma was doing. Right at this moment. Was she sleeping and drooling too? What was she wearing? What position were her arms in? It made me miss her so powerfully I could feel it squeezing my chest. I wanted to see her little baby face too; to marvel over the infant she had been, the girl she was, and the woman she would, I prayed, have the chance to become.

A bolt of lightning cracked nearby, followed a second later by the rumble of thunder. Jolted out of reverie, I went over to the wall and flicked off the lights, so if Sam came to he wouldn't be greeted by the odd sight of his father standing over him, weeping. Then I recrossed the room and pulled the covers over him, giving him a light kiss on his forehead. He didn't stir as I left his room.

The rest of the house was dark, which told me Alison was probably asleep. Now that she was no longer pretending to be healthy, she had been turning in early each night. She needed the rest.

Outside, a tempest roared. Bands of rain lashed the side of the house. The trees danced to the unpredictable rhythm of wind gusts. Somewhere nearby, our pack of feral dogs was howling at the storm, for whatever good it would do them.

I padded softly to our bedroom, where I became aware there was an extra shape sitting in our wide windowsill, watching the light show.

"Hey," Alison said.

"Oh hey."

"How's Sam?"

"He's good."

"Did he ask you to sleep with him?"

"No. I just passed out while reading to him."

She chuckled softly.

"Mind if I join you?" I asked.

She scooted up, making room for me to slide in behind her. She squeezed herself between my legs, with her back to me, and I wrapped both arms around her.

"He's really held up pretty well, all things considered," she said. "I mean, he gets these bouts of . . . I don't know if you'd call it melancholy or what. I know that's when he's thinking about her, when he's missing her. The rest of the time, he's been a real trouper."

"You think it's resilience or youthful ignorance?" I asked.

"Maybe both," she said.

She was about to say something when another bolt of lightning split the night, briefly illuminating our yard, the beach, and the river beyond it.

Once the boom of accompanying thunder had dissipated, she said, "So, are you ready for tomorrow?"

"As ready as I'll ever be," I said.

"I'm not talking about the trial. I'm talking about—"

"How things will go with Emma. I know," I said.

This was not the first time she had brought up the topic of how the hostage exchange would work. We had agreed that, with Sam, there were reasons things had been relatively straightforward. They gave us our son back because they had our daughter and still needed something from me.

It was different now. Much different. The moment I made that ruling, I would cease to be of use to them. So would Emma. She would become a liability, a witness who could testify against them if they ever got caught. That meant I couldn't issue my ruling until Emma was safe in my arms. We had discussed that fact many times, and I thought she was going to rehash it.

Instead, she just said, "We've got one shot at this, you know."

"I know."

She had turned toward me and was looking at me in a way that I'm not sure words can accurately describe. It was as deadly serious as I had even seen her.

"These people, they're not going to just give us what we want. We're going to have to take it from them. We have to be willing to do whatever it takes to get her back."

I didn't respond. I just stared out the window and watched that early-fall thunderstorm work out its fury on the York River, whipping it into a white-capped frenzy.

"Whatever it takes," she said one last time.

*

I slept a few, halting hours that night. Around four A.M., my bladder woke me up. By the time I returned from the bathroom, my heart was already pounding so much it felt like the thunder was still reverberating in my chest.

After perhaps fifteen minutes of deluding myself that I was still getting some form of rest, I gave up and went downstairs to brew a pot of coffee.

As the sun started its inexorable creep toward our eastern horizon, I sat on our back deck, thinking about my conversation with Alison and the severe way she had looked at me. I knew the end goal as well as she did, of course. What remained unclear was how the mechanics of the exchange would work.

Maybe it's different in other jurisdictions, but in the Eastern District of Virginia, we still file rulings—at least the big ones like this—in much the same way Walter E. Hoffman himself did. A hard copy of the document, hand-signed by the judge, is walked down to the clerk's office and handed to the case manager.

From there the twenty-first century takes back over: The case manager scans the document and enters it into the electronic case filing system, the attorneys are e-mailed digital copies of the document, the press downloads the PDFs, and so on.

But that first step—the one that matters most—is still done analog. And it required my putting pen to paper. As far as the federal judiciary was concerned, that was my only real power. I couldn't give it up until the last possible moment.

That was the simple part. The rest was more complicated. I couldn't imagine the kidnappers would want to come anywhere near the courthouse, a secure federal building filled with US marshals. Emma's captors would insist on the exchange happening elsewhere, in a place they would consider to be more neutral turf.

And yet the document had to be filed at the courthouse, on what was clearly my turf.

It was a paradox, one that I had been mulling for weeks now. One more pot of coffee and one more sunrise did nothing to resolve it. Eventually I gave up, went inside to get ready for the day ahead. I checked my e-mail quickly, just to make sure there hadn't been an e-mail from Jeb Byers saying that the Judicial Council had convened and ordered me to cease and desist. But I was still in the clear.

After kissing Alison and Sam good-bye, I was soon in my Buick, rolling up our long driveway. It was when I reached the end of it that my eyes went to the sky and I was filled with foreboding.

Ordinarily, I don't put a lot of stock in signs or omens.

I don't believe a radio station has played a certain song because there's a message I'm meant to hear. I don't think a rainbow means anything other than that there are water droplets in the sky. I couldn't read tea leaves if I wanted to.

But the last thing I saw as I turned onto our road was a small flock of vultures—probably the very same ones that had feasted on Herb Thrift—circling overhead.

63

Ever since the little girl's escape, the younger brother had lost whatever authority he once possessed.

The older brother was calling all the shots now. And this latest task was no different. The older brother insisted it had not been done well enough the first time.

So, really, what choice did the younger brother have? Out he went, shovel in hand, right after breakfast.

He was wearing long pants, long sleeves, gloves, and a hat. They were going somewhere sandy and sun soaked after this, a place with cheap booze and cheaper women. Hell if he was going to spend his first week in that paradise scratching at poison ivy.

The air tasted clean, like the previous night's thunderstorm had hit the reset button on the world. He inhaled deeply. High above, the morning sky was clear, with only a few jet contrails crisscrossing it in wispy strips.

He found the pine tree that marked his entry point, then plunged into the forest, ignoring the wetness from the dripping undergrowth. He walked due east, directly toward the rising sun, and counted his steps.

At a hundred, he saw the logs he had crossed over one another. He was still on course.

At two hundred, he found his second marker, two saplings

he had uprooted and pointed in the proper direction.

At three hundred, he reached his destination. He was off by only a few feet, which wasn't bad, considering how deep he was in the forest.

Gripping the shovel in both hands, he climbed down into the hole he had made the day before and got to work. He had already dug until he hit the water table, which wasn't very far in this soggy part of the world. The older brother insisted he go deeper.

The younger attacked the job steadily, tossing out one shovelful of mucky soil after another. He was deep enough now that he didn't have much resistance from tree roots, which had bedeviled him the day before.

He dug until he was up to his knees in water. That had to be good enough. He climbed out of the hole and took one last look at his handiwork. Satisfied, he retraced his steps back toward the house, eager for a shower.

If the older brother wanted that little girl's grave dug any deeper, he could dig it himself.

64

There were two court security officers at the employees' entrance that morning.

One was a big chunk of a guy who I knew only a little because he was usually assigned to one of the magistrate's courtrooms. The other was Ben Gardner. I greeted the large man first, then nodded at Ben.

"Morning, Judge," he said.

I passed through the forever-non-beeping metal detector, collected my bag from the X-ray machine's conveyor belt, and thought I would continue on my way toward the elevator, like usual.

But Ben said, "Judge, I'm going to walk with you to your chambers, if that's okay."

"Uh, yeah, sure," I said, a little confused.

"There's already a bit of a crowd up on the fourth floor. We just want to make sure there are no problems."

He followed me into the elevator. As soon as the doors closed, he cleared his throat.

"I know it's going to be a busy day for you," he said. "But I think I might have an answer for you a little later on that fingerprint thing."

"Great."

"My guy said he was going to run it this morning. If

there's a match, I should probably have a name for you around lunchtime."

"I appreciate that. Really."

"No worries," he said.

The elevator slowed to a stop on the fourth floor. I had thought Ben's line about there being a crowd had just been an excuse to get me alone for a moment. But he hadn't been making it up. I heard the noise even before the doors parted.

Then they opened and it was like walking into a large surprise party that didn't yet know the celebrant had arrived. There had to be a hundred voices, talking all at once, bouncing off the terrazzo floors and up to the ceiling.

It was so odd. The fourth floor is usually as quiet as a mausoleum and half as lively. Yet here were women in silk blouses and men in custom suits, leaning against the walls or gathered in small clumps in the middle of the hallway. They weren't allowed to have their mobile devices with them, so they had no choice but to talk to one another.

A few of them were less expensively dressed but just as loud. Those had to be the reporters.

"I'll lead the way," Ben said over the din.

I followed him into the scrum, letting him pick our path through it. Most of the throng didn't pay me any attention. Even though I had a CSO acting as a lead blocking back, I was just another guy in a suit. But I could tell, by the way certain heads were snapping in my direction, that a least a few people recognized me as I passed.

Who were all these people? The reporters, I understood. But the rest looked like . . .

Investment bankers.

Of course.

Every development in the ApotheGen case had a corresponding effect on the stock price. These were analysts and hedge fund employees whose jobs involved making educated bets on the way a stock like ApoG would move next. If they thought it was going up, they'd buy low; if they thought it was going down, they'd short it.

They followed their hunches based on the information they could assemble. And my courtroom had suddenly become the best source for information on ApotheGen's immediate future. If I wrinkled my eyebrows in a disapproving way as the plaintiff spoke, ApotheGen would gain fifty cents. If I overruled an objection by the defense, ApotheGen would lose fifty cents. Or twelve cents. Or a buck forty. Or whatever.

Point was, there was money to be made in the courtroom of the Honorable Scott Sampson on this final Friday morning in September. It was like the fourth-floor hallway had become the lobby of a casino, and a high-stakes game of chance was about to begin.

And none of them knew the tables were rigged.

*

As nine o'clock neared, the horde continued to mass. There was still no word from Jeb Byers and the Judicial Council, though the rug could still be pulled out from under me at any moment.

With half an hour to go, I asked the clerks to open the

doors to my courtroom and the overflow room, to give people time to jostle for seats.

Ten minutes out, I started my pretrial ritual. I combed my hair. I donned my robe. I checked my phone for instructions—there were none—then tucked it in my pocket.

Despite the exhaustion that had become my persistent sidekick, I felt myself moving with alacrity. I might get to see this thing through after all.

Buoyed by that thought, I emerged from my office. Jeremy—who ordinarily would have been there to greet me, to give me one last once-over and a few words of encouragement—was nowhere to be found.

"Jean Ann says everyone is in place," Mrs. Smith informed me.

"Okay," I said. "Let's do this."

The court security officer led me down the hallway I had walked hundreds of times before.

Then he opened the door, and any sense of normalcy was shattered. My courtroom, so empty so much of the time, was stuffed with spectators. I both heard them, with their unquiet chatter, and felt them. Their collective breath hit me like a great, flatulent wall of air as soon as I crossed the threshold.

"All rise!" my law clerk yelled, and then had to repeat herself because she hadn't been loud enough the first time.

As the clerk began the traditional cry, I surveyed the room. The defense team had annexed the side to my left, mostly so its surfeit of advocates, who had occupied the jury box, all had places to sit. To my right, there was Roland

432

Hemans, standing next to bearded Denny Palgraff and two associates from Cranston & Hemans.

Beyond the divider, in the six rows of benches that comprised the gallery, there was a sea of faces. I identified Andy Whipple, hedge fund genius and my brother-in-law's employer, whom I recognized from television. He was in the back on the aisle.

I also saw the round, bald, Charlie Brown head of Steve Politi in the third row; and Barnaby Roberts, in the front row, with his British-schoolboy white hair peeking out from behind his legion of lawyers.

Then there was a man whose attendance I had not expected: Blake Franklin. His barrel-chested girth was taking up a spot in the back row. My eyes must have settled on him for a moment, because he smiled at me.

Then he winked.

I didn't know if it was a go-get-'em-Tiger kind of wink, or, more optimistically, a mission-accomplished kind of wink. But I was grateful for it. And for his presence.

With the law clerk having concluded her intonations, asking God to save my honorable court, I took my seat. The rest of the room did the same, making the wooden benches creak with their combined weight.

I began the proceeding by putting on the record the expected things. Because so much about how we're presented makes us seem like we're above petty human concerns—the robe, the big desk, the highest seat in the room—people tend to think judges don't get nervous.

But we most certainly can be. Especially with a crowd

like this and with the ticking time bomb that was the phone in my pocket. As I got going, I was self-conscious about my delivery. I had practiced it, but it still ended up sounding halting and uncertain.

Nevertheless, I somehow guided us through the necessary verbiage to opening statements, which I had suggested to the attorneys shouldn't be more than twenty minutes apiece.

Then I invited the plaintiff to begin. The sense of anticipation in my courtroom was palpable.

The hearing of the century was finally under way.

65

Roland Hemans rose to his full, towering height. In the first row, necks had to crane upward to keep him in view.

His face was unreadable as he made his way to the podium between the two main tables. He opened a leather folder on the podium, arranged a few pieces of paper, then looked up at me.

"Good morning, Your Honor," he said in that bottomless voice of his.

"Morning, Mr. Hemans."

Then, with his head in his notes, he began a recitation of the basic facts of the case. Denny Palgraff, working in the solitude of his home laboratory, had been studying a then little-known protein called PCSK9. Theorizing it might play a role in diabetes, and knowing the devastation caused by that disease, he synthesized a substance that would block the uptake of that protein.

He then did what any sensible scientist would under the circumstances, and filed a patent to protect his legal rights to his invention. Hemans listed the date on which the patent had been applied for, then recited the steps by which it had been approved. This part of the opening was so dry he could have been lifting it directly from the US Patent Office website.

Hemans next moved on to his argument, which he stated in simple fashion: Palgraff was the rightful owner of a patent for a PCSK9 inhibitor; ApotheGen was trying to bring a PCSK9 inhibitor to the marketplace; therefore, ApotheGen was violating Palgraff's patent.

I had thought, at that point, he would begin ramping up the presentation: remind me that the law protected loner iconoclasts as surely as it protected mainstream pharmaceutical giants, throw in some references to Thomas Edison or George Westinghouse, play to the audience in some way. This was just a hearing, yes, but he had billions of reasons to give it everything he had.

Instead, he said thank you and sat down. He used a little more than half his allotted time.

There was a stirring in the courtroom. Hemans' logic had been straightforward enough. It was the delivery itself that struck me—and apparently not just me—as a little flat. What should have been the opening of this lawyer's life was, instead, wooden and mechanical. Was he just so sure of his position he didn't feel he needed to embellish it? Perhaps. Sometimes, especially in a matter that is going to be heard by a jaded judge—and not an impressionable jury—starting in an understated way was sound strategy.

"Thank you, Mr. Hemans," I said. "Okay, Mr. Worth, it's your turn."

The defendant's lead counsel stood and walked to the podium that Hemans had just vacated. He moved with measured steps, in no particular hurry.

He placed his hands behind him. He had no notes.

436

"Your Honor," he began, "if I said I had a patent for a bicycle, and if the US Patent Office had filed it as a bicycle patent, but if the language of the patent went on to describe a bicycle as having four wheels, an engine, and a circular blade for cutting grass, would I really have a patent for a bicycle? No, Your Honor. I'd have a patent for a lawn mower.

"I am perhaps oversimplifying this case by making this comparison. The science, admittedly, is a lot more complex. It delves into things we can't see with the naked eye, things we don't necessarily understand intuitively, things like amino acid chains and peptide bonds. To laymen like you and I, this might seem unimportant. What's two more carbon atoms within a massive molecule? But to people who spend their lives looking at the world on an atomic level, that's like saying, 'What's two more wheels?'

"Now, like I said, some of this is going to get pretty technical. I hope Your Honor remembers some of his high school chemistry. I certainly needed a refresher. But what you have to keep in mind as we go through it all in great detail, hearing from some of the very brightest minds in this field, is that the concept really is quite simple. What we have here is a man who claims to have a patent for a bicycle when really he has a patent for a lawn mower."

It was around this time that I saw Andy Whipple turn and begin making gestures in the direction of the back door. These, I could guess, were trading instructions. He must have had someone out there to interpret the hand signals, run outside to a phone, and deliver his orders.

"I know you're probably wondering how this is possible," Worth continued. "Your Honor will hear the defendant tell you how smart he is. And I won't be able to dispute it. Denny Palgraff is as smart as they come. But even smart people make mistakes. Denny Palgraff thought he was working with the PCSK9 protein. If you hooked him up to a lie detector and asked him if he had invented a PCSK9 inhibitor, he would say yes, and he would pass with flying colors. But he wasn't. The protein in question, while very similar to PCSK9, was not PCSK9. It was almost like looking at identical twins who had slightly different haircuts. They might have many things in common. They might be almost indistinguishable from each other. But they're still not the same person."

As Worth delved into the details of how ApotheGen had been the rightful discoverer of the true PCSK9 inhibitor, I glanced over to the plaintiff's table, to get some sense of whether Worth's introduction—a thorough evisceration of the plaintiff's claim—had any basis in fact.

Denny Palgraff was staring straight ahead, blank-faced. It was his attorney's posture that proved to be much more telling.

Mammoth Roland Hemans was shrinking in his seat.

*

It was, of course, just an opening. I had certainly presided over proceedings where one-sided beginnings were not borne out during the remainder of a hearing. Worth still had to prove, by a preponderance of the evidence, that what he said was true. No judge decides a matter based on the eloquence of openings alone.

Yet as we began the testimony, and Hemans called Palgraff to the stand, it was clear to all the plaintiff was in need of rehabilitation.

Hemans began with a series of softballs, asking his client to talk about his background and credentials as a scientist. Palgraff was only too happy to discuss the early and ongoing manifestations of his unmistakable genius. Hemans then shifted his questioning toward this particular discovery, having his client crawl through the process by which he had come to it.

Palgraff was predictably pedantic at times, but otherwise smooth and convincing. By the time he was done, the great unseen needle that measures legal momentum had swung back closer to the middle.

Then Worth came to the podium for his cross-examination, bringing with him a pencil and piece of paper.

"Your Honor, may I approach the witness?" he asked.

"Of course."

Worth walked casually up to Palgraff and placed the paper and pencil in front of him.

"Mr. Palgraff, could you please draw the protein that your patent describes?"

Hemans leapt to his feet. "Objection, Your Honor. This is just showmanship. My client is a scientist, not an artist."

"Your Honor, we're not looking for artistry here," Worth countered. "If Mr. Palgraff can't draw a rough version of the protein he worked with, how can we be sure he even knows what he discovered? This goes to the very heart of why we're here. If Mr. Palgraff likes, I have a copy of the patent here. He is more than free to consult it in order to make his drawing."

I nodded. "Objection overruled. Mr. Hemans, I am well aware Mr. Palgraff is not here because of his drawing ability. And I realize he's doing this freehand. The court is going to give him a lot of leeway. I'm not going to tolerate you getting picky, Mr. Worth."

"Of course not, Your Honor," Worth said.

Hemans sat down, his disgust plain.

"Mr. Palgraff, do you need to look at the patent or any of your notes?" I asked.

"No," he huffed.

"Then please comply with Mr. Worth's request."

Palgraff shot me an annoyed look, then bent his sweat-dappled brow over the paper and set to work. Worth returned to the podium and nodded at one of his associates, a young woman in a tailored suit, who began unpacking and unfolding what turned out to be a large easel.

Minutes passed. The benches creaked as members of the gallery shifted their weight, crossed their legs, then uncrossed them. I had to fight the urge to peer down at what Palgraff was drawing.

When he was done, he held out the paper for Worth. But the defendant's lawyer didn't leave his spot.

"Actually, Mr. Palgraff, could you please let the judge inspect your work?"

Palgraff turned to me, the drawing extended. The court

security officer went into action, grabbing it and handing it to me.

I studied it, to what end I'm not sure. I might as well have been looking at a game of hangman. It was just a jumble of letters, with lines, either single or double, drawn to connect them. I nodded when I was through and gave it back to the CSO, who delivered it back to Palgraff.

"Excellent, thank you," Worth said, then nodded at his young associate. She flipped up a large diagram that had been labeled PCSK9 and mounted on a piece of foam board.

"Your Honor, you will hear testimony from our scientists that this is the PCSK9 protein as we understand it," Worth said. "You will also hear from independent experts that this is a proper diagramming of the PCSK9 protein. This was sent to your chambers last week, labeled as Defense Exhibit Fifty-eight."

"Yes, thank you," I said.

"Now, Mr. Palgraff, I'd like to direct your attention to this part of the diagram and, in particular, this grouping of elements," Worth said, expertly aiming a laser pointer at a spot on the upper left corner of the poster.

Palgraff grunted.

"Mr. Palgraff, can you tell me, does the drawing you made contain a carbon atom in this exact position?" Worth asked.

The laser pointer had settled on one harmless-looking little C. Palgraff squinted at the exhibit. The courtroom had gone so pin-drop silent, I could hear his breathing, which was more like a pant. The man shifted in his seat. The leather squeaked under him. There wasn't an eye in the courtroom that wasn't trained on Palgraff. The moment of truth had arrived.

"Mr. Palgraff, is there or is there not a carbon atom here in your drawing?" Worth prompted.

Palgraff's Adam's apple bobbed up and down. He licked his lips.

"No," he said in a hoarse voice.

As soon as the word slipped out of his mouth, Whipple started making frenzied hand gestures. A few men in suits, who had apparently not been thoughtful enough to arrange a runner, started climbing over the spectators next to them and scrambling toward the swinging door at the rear of the courtroom. That, in turn, put a charge in a few others.

It was like light bulbs were popping on everywhere. And there was one going on over my head too. Palgraff had a tragic flaw, and it was that he was so sure of his own genius—and so dismissive of everyone else—it made him insufferable to be around. And so he worked alone. There was no one around to point out his simple mistake to him.

He had simply bulled forward, like a mathematician determined to finish an elaborate proof, not realizing he had a multiplication error in his first step that rendered the rest of his work moot.

I suddenly understood why he had disappeared the previous week. While preparing for his deposition, he must have laid eyes on Defense Exhibit 58 for the first time. When he realized his error, he fled in shame rather than own up to it.

He had likely told Hemans to drop the case. But the lawyer lured his client back down here because, one, I had threatened to hold him in contempt, and, two, there was still a chance, however slim, that ApotheGen would toss them a few million dollars to go away. It wouldn't have been the first time a protracted settlement negotiation had finally been concluded on the courthouse steps.

That none of that had happened explained the tepidness of Hemans' opening. He knew, at that point, he was beaten. And, yes, it was still worth coming to the courthouse today to see the thing through—settlements had been tendered during lunch breaks too. And perhaps something favorable to Palgraff would happen during the testimony that would make Barnaby Roberts nervous enough to offer one. But even that hope was now slipping away.

Everyone else watching seemed to realize it too. The exodus from the back of my courtroom was now more like a stampede. There would be no rehabilitating this witness, or this case.

The financial community had heard enough to decide: Denny Palgraff was getting his ass kicked.

66

By the time it was done, Worth had put Palgraff through a cross-examination that was the legal equivalent of a trip to the abattoir.

It left me even more deeply confused than I had been before about who might have my daughter. Hemans and Palgraff clearly had a dog of a case, and therefore every reason to try to win it by other means. And yet the moment they had filed that motion to recuse, they were no longer in play.

Likewise, ApotheGen and its employees now appeared to have even less incentive for kidnapping. Why resort to something so reckless when they knew they were going to win anyway?

At 11:40, when Palgraff was finally allowed to flee the witness stand, I called for a lunch recess. To anyone watching the hearing, it looked like a small act of mercy.

But I had the ulterior motive that was Ben Gardner and the fingerprint results he promised. I scrambled back into my chambers, removed my robe, and exited my office just as Blake Franklin was coming in the main door of the chambers.

"Hey, there's the man I'm looking to see," he said, his drawling voice full of its usual cheer. "Do you have a minute?"

I didn't, of course. But Blake was more than likely the only reason I hadn't been banned from the courthouse by now, so I said, "Yeah. Of course. Come on in."

He eased himself through the door to my office. Once it closed behind us, I said, "I'm thinking I owe you a pretty big thank-you."

"Well, I don't know about that."

"Have a seat, anywhere you like."

"No, no, I really don't want to take up that much of your time. I know you got a full plate."

Blake just stood there, looking strangely ill at ease. From his breast pocket, his phone made a noise at him.

"Sorry, let me shut this thing up," he said. "I told the guys downstairs I needed to bring this in because of a matter of national security."

He fumbled with the device until he got it silenced, then returned it to his pocket.

"So what's up?" I asked. "What happened with Keesee? Talk to me."

"Well, look, I'm not sure where to start here ... 1 ... Frankly, I'm not sure I should tell you about any of this. But you'll probably figure it out and I didn't want you to be mad at me after the fact for what I did."

"Blake, what are you talking about?"

"I tried to do this the good-ol'-boy way. You know, find some dirt on Keesee, get some leverage. You'd think a grown man who spends his time playing with toy trains has a skeleton or two in his closet. Or a little Vietnamese boy. Or something. But he turns out to be as squeaky-clean as they

445

come. So I made him a deal he couldn't refuse."

"And what was that?"

"That he'd call off the dogs on you, in return for which I'd guarantee his party would pick up a Senate seat this November."

"But how can you . . . ," I began, and then it struck me with a jolt. I just still couldn't fully believe it. "Wait, Blake, *which* Senate seat? Yours?"

"On Monday, I'll announce that I have greatly enjoyed serving the people of Virginia but that I am no longer seeking reelection."

Under any other circumstances, words to that effect from Blake's mouth would have been said only in jest. His sense of gallows humor was such that he predicted the end of his career roughly three times a week.

He wasn't joking now.

"No, Blake, you can't—"

"I sure can. You said it was life-and-death and that it involved your family, didn't you, now?"

"Yeah, but I didn't—"

"Well, then that's the end of it," he said. "I've had a hell of a run, son. Serving three terms in two different parties is more than a career. It's a dang miracle. The fact is, guys like me, guys who like to just get stuff done and don't assume that if a Republican thinks the sky is blue a Democrat has to think it's green, we're dinosaurs anyhow. It's time for me to go extinct."

"No, no, Blake, stop. This is insanity. I didn't need you to get Keesee off me forever. I just needed you to delay him a little. Come Monday, call him back and tell him you changed your mind. By then I'll be able to fight my own battle. You can't . . . I mean, thank you, but I can't have you throwing yourself on the sword for me like this. You don't owe me this."

"Oh, but I do."

He reached out with one finger and lightly tapped the spot on my chest where I would always bear the scar of one deranged man's idea of lobbying his senator.

"Oh now, hold on, because of that? Blake, it wasn't like I dove in front of you and took that bullet. I was just trying to scramble out of the way like everyone else. It was nothing more than a random, stupid accident. You don't carry some debt because of that. And even if you did, you got me this job. We were square a long time ago."

He was shaking his head.

"Look, I know now's not a good time," he said. "But it never seems like it's a good time. And I've been . . . This is something I've been wanting to tell you for . . . Well, ever since it happened. And even now, I don't quite . . . I'm not sure how to say this."

It was so unusual to hear the ever-eloquent Senator Franklin stumble over his words or express uncertainty, I think I was too surprised to even try to interrupt him.

"That bullet," he said finally. "It wasn't an accident. It was actually meant for you."

"What are you talking about?"

"You remember how we had been passing around that gun bill you wrote, trying to get everyone behind it?"

"Right. Of course."

"Well, I knew it was dead before we ever announced it. It had been made very clear to me that with the people aligned against it, and with what they were willing to do to sink the thing, it had absolutely no chance of passing. But I . . . I was so stubborn, I went ahead and announced it anyway. I really thought that once the world saw how . . . how reasonable it was, how good a job you had done writing it . . . I thought there would be this groundswell of public support and everyone would have no choice but to line up behind it."

"Blake, that doesn't make you responsible for—"

"I got this phone call," he said, not acknowledging I had tried to speak. "It was the day before the press conference. It came from a pay phone. I don't know how the guy even got my number. But he was pretty clear. Everyone on the Hill knew you had written that bill, and this guy, he said that if I went ahead and announced it, he was gonna . . . he was gonna . . ."

Blake swallowed hard, then expelled a large breath. "He said he was going to shoot you. He was very specific. He said, 'You hold that press conference, and your boy Scott Sampson is going to take one in the heart.' I thought it was a bunch of malarkey and I didn't want to seem like I was scared or intimidated. You get known as a guy who can be pushed around and . . . It was just arrogance on my part. That's all it was. Plain, stupid arrogance. I really thought no one would make a move against big, bad Blake Franklin or anyone on his staff. I could have asked you to skip the press conference or wear a bulletproof vest. I could have told the cops to be on the lookout. I could have done a million things. But I didn't. I was just full speed ahead, damn the torpedoes, thinking only about myself and my idiotic reputation.

"And then when that whackadoodle actually went through with it, I was just . . . I was so ashamed of what I had done, of what I had let happen. I couldn't even bring myself to tell anyone about it. Not you. Not the FBI. I was so worried about what everyone would think of me."

"Blake, you still can't blame yourself for—"

"Now, let me finish, damn it," he said, flashing a quick smile. "I know you're the judge now and you've gotten used to telling people to stop talking, but I'm still in the Senate for a little longer, and we get to filibuster, okay?

"What I'm trying to say is you're like a son to me. You were then and you are now. And I didn't do a very simple thing to keep harm from coming to you way back when. So I'm going to do a not-as-simple thing to keep harm from coming to you now. And it's not because I think I owe you some debt. It's because it's the right thing to do, and I'm not going to hear another word about it. Now, come here."

He enveloped me in a hug.

What Blake said had, in some way I couldn't fully appreciate in the moment, altered the narrative of my life. It would take a while to figure out how I felt about it, to decide how it impacted my relationship with Blake.

For now, I just knew his willingness to relinquish his seat in the highest legislature in the land, with all its trappings, both awed and humbled me. It also gave my daughter a lease on life she would have otherwise lost. And someday I hoped I'd be able to tell her the story of just what an angel her godfather had been to her.

"Blake, I'm not sure I even know where to start," I began.

"Then don't. I didn't tell you about this because I wanted you to gush all over me. I just needed to clear the air. Now, if you don't mind, I'm standing in the way of a judge who doesn't need to listen to an old man ramble anymore. I'll let myself out."

He clapped me on the shoulder once. Before I could resume my efforts to talk sense into him, I was looking at his back as he left my office.

*

I stood there for a full minute, trying to consider a future world in which Blake Franklin was no longer my senator.

Then I snapped back to the present. I could contemplate Citizen Blake some other time. I had some fingerprint results to collect.

The hallway had mostly cleared. There was only a small cluster of people at the elevator, waiting for it to take them down. Not wanting to be gawked at by a bunch of strangers—and hoping to catch Ben Gardner without a crowd around him—I took the stairs instead.

As I walked the three flights down, I pulled my phone out of my pocket, just to make sure I hadn't missed anything. I felt like the kidnappers should have reached out by now. During the *Skavron* case, they had texted me how many times? The relative silence was unnerving. As much as I hated hearing from them, not hearing from them was worse.

At the bottom of the stairs, I opened the door to find Ben Gardner sitting in his usual chair. It was about five minutes of noon, just in time to beat the lunch rush. He was alone.

He stood when he saw me.

"Hey, Judge, got some things for you," he said.

He handed me the brass keychain, still in its plastic bag. Then he pulled a folded slip of paper from his pocket and held it in the air for a moment.

"You tell your missus this comes straight from NGI. That's the latest and greatest in FBI fingerprint identification. It stands for Next Generation something-or-other. It's ninety-nine point nine-nine-whatever percent accurate, and between the criminals and the civilians, they got more than a hundred million names in there. You were right about them not being able to identify one of the sets of prints on there. But they got a hit on the other one."

He handed me the slip.

"Thank you, Ben, I really appreciate this," I said, taking it in my palm.

"Not a problem. Tell your missus I said hello."

Wanting to maintain the appearance of indifference, I gave him an easy smile as I passed by. As soon as I was in the parking lot, I took out the piece of paper.

I glanced to my left and right, as if anyone else knew the significance of the thing I held in my hand. But there was just the usual prelunch nothing on the street. My only spectator was one lonely seagull.

The paper had been folded in half. With a nod, I unfolded

it and peered down at the name.

Then I felt everything swirl. I actually had to lean on a parked car for support.

There is treachery in this world that we have become jaded enough to almost expect. The kindly widow has poisoned her three dead husbands. Everyone's favorite neighbor is actually a pedophile. Pastor Jim embezzles from the weekly offering.

We hold these things out as being surprising—but somehow still possible—because they do not come from that deep inner circle of people in our lives; people we have been able to observe at close quarters for decades; whose benevolent nature we have confirmed through repeated acts of good faith; whose motives we never need bother to question because, on some atomic level, they are always in sync with us.

Then comes this. Evidence of a perfidy that literally left me staggered, momentarily unable to pry myself off the side of the Subaru that was keeping me upright.

And it was committed by someone who first held Sam and Emma on the day they were born, who had never missed one of their birthday parties, who was listed in our wills as being the children's legal guardian should Alison and I meet an untimely death.

I read that slip of paper again, still in something beyond disbelief.

The name written in neatly printed letters was Karen Lowe.

67

I stumbled to my car and sat heavily inside it.

Karen. Alison's sister. My sister-in-law. My children's aunt.

Was this some kind of misunderstanding or . . .

Or had Karen really attacked our family like this?

There were, possibly, innocent explanations for her fingerprint being on that keychain. Maybe she recently drove the car without my knowing it. Maybe she and Alison had been in the Honda together and Karen grabbed the keys. Or maybe Karen had needed to borrow the car for some reason I didn't know about.

As for the non-innocent explanations, I could already start making some guesses. She knew we kept the key to the Honda on that hook right by the front door of the cottage. She would also know the cottage was never locked. And a Wednesday afternoon would be an easy time to pilfer the car for a few quick hours: Alison and I would be at work; Justina would be at class. She could take it and return it without us ever knowing.

I flashed to the footage from the Montessori school and replayed it in my mind. There was a slender blond woman with a ponytail pulled through the back of a pink cap. When I first saw it, I certainly thought it could have been Alison.

But it also could have just as easily been Karen. They had the same coloring, the same dimensions. As teenagers, they were sometimes mistaken for twins. Even now, you had to be able to see their faces to tell them apart. From the side or behind, which was the angle at which Miss Pam and the children would have seen her as they spilled out of the front door to school, she would have been indistinguishable from Alison.

And once she got them rolling in a minivan with those cartoons on, would the kids have noticed? Apparently not. Sam hadn't, anyway.

There was still the question of why, of course. What motivation would Karen have to kidnap her niece and nephew? What could she possibly gain from it?

Or, again, was there some perfectly benign way to account for that fingerprint?

I didn't know. But Alison might. Still in my car, I dialed her number.

"Do you have her?" Alison answered.

"No. Not yet. Sorry. We're just breaking for lunch."

"Oh," she said, her voice falling. "How's everything going?"

"Fine. Listen, I've got a really important question to ask you. Is there any possibility that in the few days before the kids were taken, Karen drove the Honda?"

"Karen? Why would Karen drive the Honda?"

"Just answer the question. Did she borrow the car? Did you drive with her in it or let her drive it for some reason?"

"No. Why?"

454

"Because I got the fingerprint results back. Her print is—"

Alison inhaled so quickly it made a squeaking noise. Her exhale came out as: "Oh God. Oh God, no. No, no. It can't be."

I immediately ached for my beautiful wife, already cancer bitten and daughterless, now having to wrestle with the possibility that her own sister had done something this terrible. She was breathing so fast I worried she was going to hyperventilate.

"But Karen is . . . I mean, she couldn't," Alison continued. "She just couldn't. Why would she do this? There's just no . . . This is Karen we're talking about. *Karen.* You should have seen her when I told her about the lump. She sprang right into action. It's like she made my cancer her part-time job. Are you sure there's not some mistake? I mean, I know our prints are in that database because of Dad, but . . ."

"I'm sorry," I said.

"But is there a possibility—"

"Yes, there is a point-oh-oh-something percent chance of a false match. But that means the chance of it being right is well beyond ninety-nine percent. This is the very latest technology from the FBI."

"Oh God," she moaned again.

"Look, just . . . think with me here for a second. Is it possible there's some perfectly harmless reason her fingerprint was on that keychain?"

But Alison was already putting things together.

"That was *her* in the security footage at school, wasn't it?" Alison said. "That was the back of *her* head."

455

"It sure seems possible."

"I have to go."

"Where?"

"To Karen's. I have to ask her about this."

"I'm coming," I said.

"Okay. I'm at my mother's right now. I'm leaving Sam here. I'll be at Karen's in five minutes."

"Wait for me."

*

The Lowes' subdivision was about fifteen minutes from the courthouse. Alison was parked at the entrance of it when I arrived.

I hopped out of my car and jogged over to hers. She rolled down the window. Her face, which had become so gaunt in the past few weeks, was sunken even further.

"Are you all right?" I asked, which had to be the dumbest question I had asked in a while.

She closed her eyes, bent her head, and shook it slightly. "Let's just get this over with."

"Okay," I said. "So how are we doing this?"

"I think we just present her with the evidence and see if she'll tell us the truth."

"You think she's going to be honest about having kidnapped our children?"

"Let's just confront her," Alison said. "I mean, why would Karen do something like this? To her own niece and nephew? To us? It just doesn't make sense."

456

"I know," I said. Then I caught a glimpse of a cylindrical piece of metal poking out from underneath a sweatshirt on the seat next to her.

"You brought the gun?" I asked.

"It was an impulse when I left the house this morning. I just wanted to have it."

I understood how she felt. "Okay. Did you hear anything from the doctor, by the way?"

"I can't think about that right now. Come on. Let's go."

I patted the side of her car and walked away. Then I drove behind her for the final two-tenths of a mile to Karen's place. We pulled alongside the curb and marched up to the front porch.

Ordinarily we just waltzed into the house like we owned it. This time, Alison rang the doorbell. Karen answered dressed in workout clothes, mystified to see us.

"Hey, guys," she said. "What's going on?"

"We need to talk," Alison said stiffly, then made a straight line for the living room before Karen could respond.

"Is everything okay?" Karen said, trailing after her.

Alison took a seat. Karen and I followed her lead.

"I need to ask you about our minivan," Alison said. "The Honda. The one Justina used to pick the kids up from school."

"Uh, okay, what about it?" Karen said.

"Have you driven it recently?"

Karen didn't miss a beat. "No. Why would I?"

"Think hard. Are you sure you didn't maybe borrow it or run an errand in it?"

This time, Karen twisted her mouth to one side and thought it over. "Not that . . . not that I can remember. I don't think I've ever even been in that van."

And there was the lie. That she delivered it without the slightest hitch was an insight into a side of my sister-in-law's character I had never seen. I knew the surface Karen: tough, yes; bossy, for sure; but ultimately, I thought, a straight-shooting daughter of a colonel who would never be capable of something so pernicious. Obviously, there was a lot more to her than I had ever dreamed.

Alison's eyes flicked toward me.

"Scott, do you have the keychain with you?"

"I do."

"Could you show it to Karen, please?"

I pulled it out of my pocket, where its brass bulk had formed a lump. I placed it on the coffee table in front of me.

"That's the keychain for the Honda," Alison said. "Can you explain why we found your fingerprint on it?"

Karen's head went from Alison, to me, back to Alison.

Then she burst into tears.

*

At first, Karen's words were unintelligible. She was gulping air and crying and trying to talk all at the same time.

The first thing I was able to understand was, "They made me do it."

"Wait, stop," I said. "Who made you do it?"

"These men . . ."

"What men?"

"I don't know. I had never seen them before and I never want to see them again. There were two of them. They had beards and accents and they were very . . . I mean, my God, they were just terrifying. It was like they didn't even care that I was seeing their faces or anything. They came to the house one day and they said I had to"—she paused for a large breath—"I had to pick up Sam and Emma from school for them. They told me I had to take the van from your property and then drive it to school. It was like they had been watching you and they knew everything about you. They knew that most days Justina drove the van. They knew that Justina had class on Wednesdays. They knew how everything was supposed to go.

"So they laid it all out for me. They told me exactly what to do and exactly when to do it. And then I was supposed to meet them near the school and let them have the kids and they would take it from there. And I didn't have a choice. I—"

"Didn't have a choice?" Alison snarled. "What in God's name do you mean, you didn't have a choice?"

Her fists were balled. There was a kind of fury on her face I'm not sure I had ever seen before.

Karen had been pouring all this out at me. But now she turned to her sister and, wiping her cheeks, sniffled out, "They said if I didn't do it, they would kill my best friend."

"What are you talking about?" Alison asked.

"You, okay?" Karen shouted. "They said they would kill you. They said they would rape you and torture you

459

and then you would die a horrible, agonizing death. They showed me all these pictures of you—at work, at home, at the store. They knew where you were at every moment and they said they could grab you anytime and they started describing all the things they were going to do to you and I just . . . it was . . ."

"You should have let them kill me," Alison said.

"Are you crazy? Ali, this wasn't some hypothetical psychological experiment where you have to push one person off a bridge or five people in China die. This was . . . this was the real thing. They were going to kill you. And they said if I cooperated the kids wouldn't be harmed. So it wasn't even like the psychology experiment, because on the one side it was you dying and on the other side it was the kids being a little scared in the short term but eventually being okay. They said they would keep the kids for a little while and then return them once they got what they wanted."

"Did they say what that was?" I asked.

Karen shook her head. "I assumed it was some kind of blackmail. I told them you guys didn't have a lot of money and they were wasting their time. I didn't even think this related to one of your cases until later."

"These men," I said, "tell me more about them."

I expected a minor improvement on the same rough description she had already given, which wouldn't really help us much at all. Instead, Karen dropped this bomb:

"Do you want to see them?" she asked.

Alison jumped out of her seat toward her sister, but Karen continued. "I took a video of them with my phone. It's not very good. I didn't dare let them see I was doing it, so I sort of had to hide the phone. And the sound is really bad. I think I must have been covering the microphone with my finger. But I got something anyway. Let me get my phone."

Karen rose and left the room. Alison briefly made eye contact with me.

"She should have let them kill me," she said again.

I didn't have a response. Alison just stared at the coffee table.

Karen returned moments later. She knelt in front of where Alison and I were sitting.

"It's not very good," Karen said again.

Karen hit the play button. Alison and I leaned forward toward the tiny screen of an iPhone that was a few generations behind current.

The first thing we saw was the ceiling of our Honda Odyssey. Then there was Karen's chin, nostrils, and the bill of her cap—like some kind of odd-angled selfie. Then the phone was turned and it captured an extreme close-up of the cracked leather on the side of the van's well-worn seats. The audio was, as promised, essentially nonexistent—nothing but squelchy rubbing sounds.

Karen was obviously keeping the phone low at first, either on her lap or down at her side. But, slowly, she got more courageous with it. The view rose and shifted until we were getting the scene outside the passenger-side window. It was a thin strip of grass that descended into a stand of scraggly, adolescent pine trees.

"You're about to see one of them," Karen said.

Sure enough, there was a flash of a man. Dark, bushy hair. Dark, untrimmed beard. Caucasian.

"Pause it, pause it," I said.

"You'll get a better look later," Karen said.

Then we saw the top of a blond head passing the window. I felt a stab in the gut as I recognized my son.

"That's Sam," Karen said. "They had the kids go one at a time. Sam went first."

Alison asked, "Did they force them or . . ."

"They're kids, Ali. They just did what they were told."

"But did the kids ask you if it was okay?"

"The men told me I wasn't supposed to speak. Like, not a word, the whole time. They were banking on everyone thinking I was you, the kids included. Hang on, this is going to be your best view of one of them."

She hit the pause button at the right moment, just as one of the men appeared outside the window. Alison and I took turns looking at him up close. He was mostly in silhouette, but he was twisted slightly toward the car, so you could get some sense of what he looked like. If I had to guess his age, I would say mid-thirties, though it was hard to tell because the beard was so extensive. About the only features you could really make out were his nose, which was large and hooked, and his eyes, which looked like really strong coffee, so brown they were almost black. You could barely tell the irises from the pupils. They reminded me of a shark's eyes.

"I've called him Alexi, just to have something to call him," Karen said. "It's not like they ever used their names around me."

462

Once we had all gotten our fill of the still screen, she got the video going again.

"You never do see Emma, though it was around this time they took her out," Karen narrated. "And then the one I call Boris returned to close the door to the minivan. This is the best view you get of him."

Again, she hit the pause button. This time, she didn't like where she had stopped it, so she monkeyed around with it a little, going back and forth until it settled on a frame she liked. Then she passed us the phone again.

Boris looked a lot like Alexi. He was a little shorter, a little heavier. His nose was maybe slightly more aquiline, but he had the same black eyes. They looked like brothers.

She resumed the video. Once Boris departed, Karen had gotten a little bolder with her camerawork. She swung the phone up and, positioning it just above the dash, captured an image of the upper half of a white, windowless panel van—the vehicle Sam had described to us.

The audio was back at this point, though it was essentially worthless. It was just Karen, breathing hard, and the muffled sound of the van's engine starting up from the other side of her windshield. As it drove off, she lifted the phone higher, allowing us to see more of the white van, eventually all the way down to the tires. But by that point it was already small in the distance.

"I tried to slow it down and see if I could get the license plate, but it was too fuzzy," Karen said.

"I'm sure it's either a stolen van or stolen plates," Alison conjectured.

The video ended shortly thereafter. It wasn't more than two minutes of footage. We watched it again. It was a moment I had been imagining for the better part of a month now—my children being secreted off by bearded men. Seeing it in living color made it both more mundane, because it was just kids hopping out of a minivan, and more terrifying, because of those men's eyes.

"You said they had accents," I said. "Could you place them?"

"I thought . . . Well, I might be wrong about this, but I thought maybe they were Turkish. Their accents sounded exactly like Justina's."

Alison's glare went straight to me. Had her intuition been right, as always? Had Justina really been trying to seduce me? For that matter, when Jenny saw her at the mall that day with the leather jacket, had Justina actually been following Jenny somehow?

For the first time, it struck me as a mistake to make Justina move out. We should have kept her close, where we could watch her. Giving her a free pass out of our line of sight—essentially letting her get away without any of the questions that would have arisen if she simply disappeared—might have been exactly what she wanted.

Karen continued. "I've obviously had a lot of time to think about this, and my theory is that they were somehow connected to Justina. They seemed to know all the things Justina would know, like where the keys were and how the pickup at school was supposed to go."

"But why didn't you just tell us?" Alison said. "I mean,

there we were, at our house, two days after it happened, bawling our eyes out—"

"Because they said I couldn't. I didn't tell anyone. Not even Mark. The men said the children being returned unharmed relied entirely on me doing exactly as I was told. And they said I couldn't say anything. That was like the first thing they said to me and the last thing: 'Say nothing. Say nothing.'"

68

Once it became clear Karen didn't know anything else—and that Alison was going to make her rehash it three or four more times anyway—I stuffed the brass keychain in my pocket and announced my departure.

I had a hearing to resume. I had recessed us only until one o'clock. A judge returning fifteen minutes late was nothing unusual, but I didn't want to push it beyond that.

As I drove, I replayed the video in my mind and thought about what Karen had said. In some ways, her confession—or the connection to Justina being made after all this time—didn't change any of the circumstances in front of us. There were still bad men who had Emma. They were men with beards and foreign accents. We knew that already. What Karen told us and showed us just filled in some of the details, like that the accents were apparently Turkish.

It was also further confirmation that the kidnappers were well prepared and well organized, disciplined and efficient. Just being able to watch them walk was instructive. Their movements were precise and direct, with nothing wasted.

And then there were those black, black eyes. Men with eyes like that could certainly shoot Herb Thrift in the back and head, then mutilate his corpse, then send me a finger in the mail. Men with eyes like that were capable of anything I could imagine and things that were far worse.

I put myself in Karen's position, being approached at home by these shark-eyed villains and ordered to kidnap my niece and nephew, under threat of my sister's death. What would I have done?

Probably exactly what Karen did. Possibly, I would have said something to the parents. No, I definitely would have. Selfishly, I would have wanted to unburden myself of that secret just as soon as possible.

Otherwise, Karen just did what I—or any reasonable person—would do when faced with a choice between the unthinkable and something far worse. Defying their orders wasn't an option. Men like that, making threats like that, demanded total obedience.

But there was something else about the men in that video that struck me. They were completely unemotional about what they were doing. They could have been moving anything out of that minivan—a load of bricks, stolen computers, two little kids. It didn't matter to them. They were professionals. This was a job, nothing more.

Which begged the question that, three weeks into this ordeal, I still couldn't begin to answer: Whom were they working for?

I somehow doubted it was Justina. She was the conduit to us, yes. And maybe she had known those two brothers from back in Turkey. But there had to be someone else in charge. Her parents? I had never met them. Her father was supposedly a university professor. Or was that just a cover story? Were they really involved in organized crime somehow?

But then I thought back to the voice I had heard that first night, the one that told me he had my kids and I better follow his instructions. That voice, filtered and muddied though it may have been, was definitely not Turkish. It was American.

That was who called the shots for Alexi, Boris, Justina, and everyone else. And we still didn't really know anything about who that person was or what, exactly, he was looking to gain by commandeering this case.

It was 1:08 P.M. when I pulled back into my parking spot behind the courthouse. Ben Gardner was not manning the employee entrance, so I nodded at another court security officer as I dashed through the metal detector. Then I hustled toward the (empty) elevator and down the (empty) fourth-floor hallway. It was apparent that everyone who still cared about the outcome of this case had packed themselves back into the two courtrooms, where they were waiting for me.

I hurried through the front door to my chambers into the reception area, where Mrs. Smith looked up at me.

"Hello, Judge," she said.

"Hi, Mrs. Smith," I said, not breaking stride as I continued toward my office.

But she stopped me with, "Judge, I'm sorry to trouble you, but someone dropped something off for you and it looks important."

She stood up and handed me a manila envelope. I felt myself squinting at it for a moment, then made out that too-familiar block lettering on it:

JUDGE SCOTT SAMPSON
PERSONAL AND CONFIDENTIAL. OPEN
IMMEDIATELY.

"Thank you," I forced myself to say.

The envelope was closed but unsealed, its flap held down only by the brass clasp. I lifted the wings of the clasp and withdrew a thin sheaf of papers from inside.

There was a sticky note attached. It read:

DELIVER THIS TO THE CLERK'S OFFICE FIRST THING
MONDAY MORNING. THE MOMENT WE SEE IT HAS
BEEN FILED, YOUR DAUGHTER WILL BE RELEASED,
UNHARMED, TO A SAFE PLACE. WE WILL CONTACT
YOU WITH DETAILS.

I lifted the sticky note to look at the document underneath. It was the ruling, already written out for me. I skimmed it and found it well written, obviously done by someone with legal training and a familiarity with all the filings in the case. There were the appropriate findings of fact, followed by a ruling in favor of ApotheGen.

So there it was. All along, this had been about ApotheGen winning. Which still didn't make sense. If Barnaby Roberts or someone at ApotheGen was at the controls all along, why force me to grant the preliminary injunction? Why not have ApotheGen's attorneys file a motion to dismiss and then order me to grant it? They could have ended the whole nightmare in just a few days, saving their shareholders

469

billions of dollars in losses and their CEO from what had likely been a month-long angina.

I reached the last page of the document. The only thing missing was my signature.

"When did this arrive?" I asked.

"Someone slipped it under the door during lunchtime," Mrs. Smith said.

"Oh?" I said.

And then I smiled, just slightly. It was probably my first real smile in a month. This was an unbelievable break.

I felt like I had been chasing the same lead runner in a marathon for twenty-five miles, always a few steps behind. And then, just as we entered that final mile, the guy I had been trailing all that time had suddenly tripped on his shoelaces and fallen flat on his face.

The kidnappers had finally made their first mistake.

*

The two cameras that covered the entrance to my chambers were concealed in fake light fixtures that hung down from the ceiling a few yards on either side of the door. Up until that moment, I might have questioned how much camouflage those two plastic bubbles really offered.

But I could now say, with authority, that they did their job. Because whoever slipped that envelope under my door neither saw them nor gave a second thought to the possibility that they might hide cameras.

Everything captured by those lenses was sent to the

computer on my career clerk's desk. The footage stayed on the hard drive for some length of time before being wiped clean—a week, a month? Definitely longer than an hour.

All I had to do to see who had slipped me that envelope was get Jeremy to work the software for me. He was the only one on my staff who had been trained in its use. And I might have been able to work around that, but he was also the only one who had the password.

Which meant I needed him. And he had been anywhere from standoffish to hostile toward me for two weeks now. Not that I blamed him.

A court security officer had already come out to the reception area, thinking I was going to slip on my robe and let the show resume. But I said, "Hey, can you give me just five more minutes?"

"Of course, Judge," he said.

"I'll call Jean Ann and let her know," Mrs. Smith said.

I shoved the ruling back into the envelope. Then I walked eight steps to Jeremy's domain. My tap on his doorframe earned me an enigmatic stare.

There were two ways to handle this: ask for his help or order him to give it to me. But, frankly, I just couldn't deal with another confrontation. It was time to make peace. I wanted more than just Jeremy's grudging cooperation. I wanted him as an ally again.

"Hey," I said. "I really need your help with something and I know I have no right to ask for it, given how I've treated you. But I have to ask you all the same. Can I come in?"

"It's your chambers, Judge," he said tersely.

I entered, closed the door behind me, and sat down.

"First of all, I owe you an apology for those pictures I had taken of you," I said. "I had no right to invade your privacy that way. I also owe you an explanation for my strange behavior over the last three weeks. But I need to swear you to secrecy. You can't tell anyone what I'm about to say. Can you agree to that?"

"Sure, Judge," he said. "You have my word."

I gave him the quick version. He gasped a few times, nodded solemnly at others. I could see his ever-logical mind filling in what had previously been blank spaces in the narrative of the last month. Things that had seemed terribly out of place suddenly clicked back in.

"I'm glad you finally told me," he said when I finished. "I knew something was up, obviously. There were probably ten times I was close to handing in my resignation. But I just . . . I knew there must have been something really bad going on."

"Well, thank you for staying. Sam and Emma thank you too."

"You're welcome. But, look, we can get all mushy with each other later. For now, you said you needed help. What can I do?"

A few strokes of the keyboard later we were looking at a split screen of two views of the hallway outside my chambers. I had him start the footage at 11:40 A.M., when I had recessed us. We watched in fast-forward.

With my chambers being behind the courtroom— and around the corner from the hallway where everyone congregated—there wasn't much for the camera to see. It captured me on my way out to Karen's place; and then Mrs. Smith, Jean Ann, and the law clerks on their way out to lunch. There was one woman—a clerk in one of the other courtrooms—who passed by but did not stop.

Then, at 12:32, there came a solitary figure up the hallway. We were watching at 8× fast-forward, so it all happened too fast to see any detail the first time. But what had transpired was unequivocal: A man in a suit had walked up to my door, leaned over, slid a yellow-brown rectangle underneath, and then slithered away.

"There's the envelope!" Jeremy shouted. "That's the guy!"

"Go back," I said. "Go back."

"Okay, hang on."

He clicked the mouse until he got the split screens back to the moment before the man made his approach. Then he played it back.

The moment the man appeared at 1× speed, I knew. I just still couldn't believe it. The man who slipped the envelope under my door had flaming red hair.

"That son of a bitch," I said.

"What?" Jeremy asked.

"That's my brother-in-law Mark Lowe."

*

Without another word, I dashed out of Jeremy's office. The next thing those cameras outside my chambers recorded was me throwing open the door and steaming up the hallway. I don't know why I thought Mark might still be out there—why hang around the scene of the crime?—but I still felt compelled to check.

He wasn't there. I gazed through the small window into the back of my courtroom. He wasn't there either. It was just six rows of benches filled with people who were starting to get restless and some antsy lawyers seated in front of them.

It was now 1:19. I was stretching the extent to which I could keep stalling this hearing. For all I knew, Mark had dropped off that envelope, then fled. He could be in North Carolina by now.

And I still had a hearing to finish. Even if it was a masquerade, both sides had to rest before I could issue Mark's ruling.

Mark's ruling. *Mark's ruling?* The very phrase sounded strange in my head. Mark wasn't the guy who made the rulings. He was the guy who followed them. He was the quietest voice in the room, the one you seldom heard at all during our boisterous family gatherings. He was the one who didn't assert himself enough at work, or home, or anywhere else. He was the pale-skinned ginger, the Lowe Man.

Had Justina and the Turkish brothers really been following his orders? It was hard to process. And I didn't have time to even attempt to create a scenario where it made sense. But I did need to find him. I wheeled around and returned to my chambers.

"Give me one more minute," I hollered to Mrs. Smith, the CSO, and anyone else who cared.

Going into my office, I grabbed my robe and shrugged it on, not bothering with my mirror check. Instead, I pulled out my phone and sent a text to Alison:

> Don't know what exactly is going on, but Mark is
> involved. Must go back into hearing now. I will recess
> us in one hour. Meet me outside the courthouse.

Before hitting the send button, I paused to decide whether I should add three more words. I took a deep breath; then my fingers made the decision for me, tapping out:

> Bring the gun.

69

With the tardy and apologetic judge resettled on the bench, the plaintiff's case resumed its wheezing progress.

Roland Hemans was executing his duties. And Clarence Worth was pounding him for it, objecting the nanosecond Hemans slipped, drilling to the heart of every matter with his questioning, not letting a single opportunity to score points pass him by.

My mind kept wandering. Primarily, I was trying to figure out what evil had seeped into my brother-in-law's veins. It was one thing to endanger his niece and nephew, who weren't really blood kin to him—if that mattered in some kind of Darwinian calculation. But Mark had also imperiled his own wife, sending Alexi and Boris, two demi-humans lacking any conscience, into his own home.

What kind of man would do that? Put the mother of his four—four!—children squarely in the path of a pair of human hurricanes?

Meanwhile, my eye was wandering too. Andy Whipple was in the back row. It suddenly occurred to me that Mark had probably been the person Whipple had been gesturing to earlier this morning. Of course he was. That was going to be Mark's alibi if I bumped into him: He was just here, innocently serving as his boss's runner.

I kept sneaking glances at Whipple to see if he was making hand gestures, because it would mean Mark was back at his post outside. But the celebrity hedge fund manager did not stir.

Barnaby Roberts had also returned to the same seat, directly behind his lawyers. He just couldn't seem to stay in it. Every time Worth drilled Hemans—a regular occurrence that afternoon—Roberts shifted with the restlessness of an overstimulated schoolboy.

Blake Franklin was still in the room as well, offering his silent support.

But the most compelling figure, in the strangest way, was actually Steve Politi. HedgeofReason's faithful correspondent was sitting in a kind of stupor, his head lolled to one side. His notebook, into which he should have been furiously scribbling, was resting, unopened, on his thigh. If he had a pen, I didn't see it.

He looked, more than anything, beaten. He had been the confident prophet of ApotheGen's demise since the beginning. He had gone on national television to tout his stories. His hundreds of commenters and untold thousands of loyally clicking readers had undoubtedly done wonders for his website's advertising revenues.

And now? It was clear to anyone with an Internet connection he was Dewey-Defeats-Truman wrong. Poor Charlie Brown. Lucy had pulled the football away from him again.

His reputation was in tatters. His website was a laughingstock. His livelihood was also in jeopardy. Blog traffic is notoriously fickle. Once those millions of unique visitors decided HedgeofReason could not be trusted, his revenues would be gone.

All because his source—his great, unnamed source—had jerked him around. Was that source Mark? Certainly, Mark could have been the one who gave Politi my cell phone number. Had Mark been able to use his relationship with me to manipulate the coverage in HedgeofReason? Had Steve Politi been just one more person who underestimated the mendacity of Mark Lowe?

I had an idea of how I might find out.

"Thank you, Mr. Hemans," I announced, when Hemans said he was done presenting his case and Worth was finished shredding it. "We're going to take a break for fifteen minutes and then I'll start hearing from the defense."

And then I looked directly at Steve Politi: "Why doesn't everyone go outside, get some sunshine on their backs? It's a nice day. And I'm guessing everyone is eager to check their messages. The reporters especially."

Politi remained slack-faced for the amount of time it took him to realize I was really talking to him. I held my gaze on him until I watched it dawn on him. Then he straightened and nodded slightly.

I lifted myself from my seat as the law clerk called out, "All rise."

As soon as I was safely behind the closed door of my office, I pulled out my phone and texted Politi.

Please come to my chambers, ASAP. I've got a deal for
you.

*

Knowing I had much to accomplish in the next fifteen
minutes, I didn't even bother to take off my robe before
leaving my chambers. I ignored the curious looks as I picked
my way through the crowded hallway, then took the stairs
down to the first level.

Ben Gardner had returned to his post at the employee
entrance.

"How's it going up there?" he asked.

"Just taking a quick fifteen-minute break. I needed some
air."

"There's plenty of it just out that way," he said, and
pointed toward the door.

I fake smiled. As soon as I was outside, I called Alison.

"Where are you?" I asked as soon as she picked up. "I
just walked outside."

"I see you. Turn to your right."

My head scanned ninety degrees before I found her,
standing on the street corner outside the employee parking
lot. We met halfway, at the edge of the parking lot.

"What did you mean by your text? *Mark* is involved? Are
you sure?"

I told her about the surveillance footage and the envelope
he had slipped under my door.

"Oh my God, I just saw him," she said when I was through.

"You did? Where?"

"He was outside the main entrance, talking on his phone. I was going to approach him but I still didn't know what you meant by your text, so I held back."

"Is he still there?"

"No. His car was at one of those one-hour meters right in front of the courthouse. When he was done with the call, he fed the meters, tossed the phone in the car, then went back in."

"So he's inside the courthouse right now?"

"As far as I know," she said. "But if he really is involved, what are we going to do?"

"That's why I asked you to bring the gun. You do have it, right?"

"Yeah," she said, lifting her handbag to indicate it was inside. "But how's that going to do us any good? We're not going to be able to get it inside."

"Actually, I think we can. Can you disassemble it again? The metal detectors at the employee entrance are set pretty loosely. If I take half and you take half, I think we can sneak it in."

I could scarcely believe it was me saying the words— me, the ever-cautious judge, coolly planning the details of a felony. It was at least a year in prison if we got caught. Maybe more, given that I could scarcely claim ignorance of the law. But I was beyond fretting over consequences.

So was Alison.

"You still have that screwdriver set in your car?" she asked.

"Sure do."

"Grab it for me."

As she got settled in the front seat of my Buick, I retrieved the tools from the back. Working with a speed and competence her late father would have been proud of, she reduced the gun to its component parts. She slid the barrel in her pocket. She took the spring and the empty magazine and stashed them in her purse, under the rationale that neither would look suspicious when separated from other gun parts and viewed in the X-ray machine.

I took the pistol grip—much of which was plastic—and the bullets. Both would certainly look suspicious under X-ray, which was why I stuffed them in my pants, under my robe.

"Okay," I said. "Here goes nothing."

We walked toward the employee entrance arm in arm, just a respected federal judge and his lovely wife out for a stroll. I opened the door for her and plastered an eighteen-tooth grin on my face.

"Hey, Ben," I said. "You remember Alison."

"Mrs. Sampson, a pleasure to see you again," he said.

Without my having suggested it, Alison played her part perfectly. She planted a kiss on his cheek. "Mr. Gardner, I just wanted to thank you for the favor you did for us. I really do appreciate it."

Ben murmured a few aw-shucks as Alison placed her bag on the conveyer belt for the X-ray machine. She walked through the metal detector without a sound. I don't think Ben so much as glanced at the ghostly image of her bag that appeared on the screen in front of him. He was too busy beaming at Alison.

Then it was my turn. I was thankful metal detectors couldn't discern when someone was holding his breath, because that's what I was doing as I approached. I tried to make like this was just another routine time breezing through security. I was a judge with lots on his mind.

The machine didn't buy it.

It beeped loudly.

Ben's head snapped toward it. His face pinched. This was probably the first time in three years he had heard that noise.

It was a good thing Ben was no longer paying attention to Alison, because she was aghast. This was about to fall apart.

Ben had already grabbed a yellow wand, the handheld metal detector marshals could use to pass up and down someone's body. All it would take was one pass over my pocket and a *Can you empty that, please?* for this to end in disaster. I couldn't exactly issue a ruling on ApotheGen from a holding cell at the Western Tidewater Regional Jail.

Just on the other side of the machine, I stopped and made a show of my bewilderment. This had to be the acting performance of my life.

I made a big, obvious eye roll. I lifted one side of my robe—the non-gun side—and pulled the brass keychain, still in its plastic bag, out of my pocket.

"Oops," I said. "Forgot about this."

I held the bag by the zippered end and let that chunk of metal dangle before Ben's eyes. I grinned sheepishly behind it.

Ben regripped the wand in his hand and raised it to pocket height.

Then he used it to make a shooing motion. He smiled and said, "Just go."

*

When I returned to my chambers, Steve Politi was waiting for me in the reception area.

"Hi, Judge," he said as I entered.

He extended his right hand. I grabbed it firmly and gave it a shake.

"Nice to meet you, Mr. Politi," I said.

He looked almost as tired as I felt.

"He said you wanted to see him?" Mrs. Smith said, sounding like she didn't believe it for a second.

"Yes, thank you, Mrs. Smith. Mr. Politi, why don't you have a seat in my office? I'll be right in."

He accepted that suggestion without a word. I shunted Alison toward Jeremy Freeland's office, tapping on his door.

"Hey, Jeremy," I said.

"Oh, hello, Alison," he said, as if he had somehow expected to see her.

"She needs to be alone in your office for a little while. Would you mind taking a walk?"

"I just remembered I have a few errands to run," he said.

"Thanks. And, look, I know I'm out of favors to ask you, but would you mind letting her borrow your cell phone? I might need to contact her quickly."

We could sneak a gun into the courthouse, but not her cell phone. Ludicrous.

"Sure," he said, pulling it out of his pocket and leaving it on his desk. Then he stood up. "Don't let Thurgood beg any food out of you while I'm gone, no matter how much he whines. He's getting chubby around the gills."

"Got it," Alison said.

As Jeremy cleared out of the room, Alison was already hoisting her bag up on his desk. I closed the door, removed the grip and bullets from my pocket, and deposited them in front of her.

"Thanks," she said.

I planted a short kiss on her cheek, then left her to her work and returned to my office. Politi was seated at one of the chairs in front of my desk.

"Thanks for coming," I said.

"I thought it might improve my day. It pretty much couldn't get any worse."

"Is that so?" I said, playing along as if I didn't know.

"Have you *seen* my blog?"

My response was to pull up HedgeofReason.com on my screen.

To his credit, Politi was reporting the proceedings accurately and without bias. His post after the morning session reflected the terribly one-sided nature of what he and everyone else had witnessed. But he also cautioned readers to remember the case wasn't over yet and that judges had been known to make unexpected rulings based on arcane points of law.

Wall Street was already betting otherwise. That stampede of analysts pouring out of my courtroom earlier that morning

484

had a lot more sway on the market than one lonely blogger, no matter what his readership was. The UPDATE! reported that ApotheGen stock had already surged nine dollars and seventy-four cents on heavy trading. Apparently, brokers just couldn't get their hands on the stuff fast enough.

There were 1,270 comments after the update.

The first: "Politi you douchebag!!!!! I'm losing my shirt!!!"

The second: "You better not come into work becuz im beyond the hedge of reason rite now and im gonna beat your face in."

And on it went. Hiding behind the safety of their keyboards, HedgeofReason's readers were pouring vitriol onto the blogger who had so recently been the subject of their paeans.

"Ouch," I said.

"The only reason I haven't been fired is because I own the website," he said. "But I'm thinking about firing myself anyway."

"Yeah, that's a bad day."

"Thank you. Now, you said you had a deal for me? Please start talking, because otherwise you're just standing between me and a long date with the hotel bar."

I leaned back and crossed my legs under my robe. "So this source of yours. He . . . she . . . really played you, huh?"

"Did you just bring me in here to taunt me? There's enough of that waiting for me online, thank you very much," he said, lifting his body from his seat.

"Wait, wait," I said. "Just slow down. Hear me out. The

485

point I was trying to make was: Your source screwed you, so why not screw him back?"

He sat. "How?"

"Tell me who it is."

He leaned over, put his elbow on the arm of the chair, then rested his chin in his hand. I could tell he was thinking about it, and that he was tempted.

I sweetened the offer. "I'll give you an exclusive on the ruling. I'll let you have it before I send it down to the clerk's office."

Having the ruling early was gold for Politi, and we both knew it. In one post, he could begin to restore his standing with his readership. His head seemed to be bobbing. Then he stopped.

"So, wait, you give me the ruling before it goes out, but I assume you want the name of my source right now?"

"Yeah."

"No good. I've been jerked around too much already. I'm not telling you squat until I know what the ruling is."

Now it was my turn to take a little time sitting in silent contemplation. If he put the ruling out on his website too early, before we had Emma back, Alexi and Boris might spook. Or, worse, they might think the ruling had already been filed and decide it was time to dispose of their living, breathing bargaining chip.

"I can let you see it right now. But you can't post anything until I'm ready," I said. "It would be disastrous for me in ways I can't even describe if you posted something before I was ready."

There was no danger in giving him a glimpse. Right now his credibility was so tarnished, no one would believe what he was posting unless it came with a scanned version of the document anyway.

"You already have it written? So the secret was true: You really did know what your ruling was going to be ahead of time."

"No, I didn't. It . . . I can't really explain it."

He looked at me quizzically.

"It's complicated," I said. "I'll tell you everything once it's filed. In the meantime, please understand if you post anything early, you'll be doing harm you can't understand. And, at that point, I'll file a ruling that is the exact opposite, just to spite you. It'll ruin you for good."

"Mutually assured destruction," he mused. "I like it."

"So we have a deal?"

"Okay. But you've got to give me at least an hour's worth of an exclusive after you send it to me, and it has to be when the markets are open. Otherwise it's no good to me."

"You got it," I said.

I reached out across the table and we shook hands.

Then I went inside my desk and pulled out the document Mark had slipped under my door. I handed it to Politi and was immediately looking at the top of his bald head as he bent down and started skimming words and flipping pages.

"You're going for ApotheGen?" he said. "Well, now I'm officially confused."

"Why?"

"Well, I guess I should start by telling you who my source

is. It's Mark Lowe. He claims to be your brother-in-law. He showed me family photos and everything. But now I'm even doubting that."

"No, he is."

"Then explain this to me," Politi said. "He said this whole thing was a scheme on your part to sell short on a bunch of shares of ApotheGen stock. He said you made him do it in his name so the SEC didn't get wise to it. He even showed me a short sale contract for a hundred thousand shares that he signed when the stock was still at ninety-whatever bucks.

"But then if that's true, why would you rule for ApotheGen? Wouldn't you want to see the price go even lower? I mean, unless you . . . Oh, you clever devil, you already executed the short sale, haven't you? So none of this even matters anymore."

"I'm sorry," I said. "I have no idea what you're talking about."

"Well, you know with a short sale, when the price goes down, the person holding the contract actually makes money. For every ten bucks ApotheGen stock lost in value, that hundred-thousand short sale contract is worth a million bucks. So you pulling the trigger, say, yesterday, before the markets closed, netted you a little more than three mil, am I right?"

"I understand the mechanics of how short sales work," I assured him. "When I say, 'I have no idea what you're talking about,' it's because I'm not involved in any kind of conspiracy with my brother-in-law. You have my word on that. Maybe he does have a short sale contract with my name on it. But I had nothing to do with it. Everything he's told you about me was a lie."

"Well, I guess I shouldn't be surprised at this point," Politi said. "It's pretty clear now the guy has been lying to me about everything else."

He shook his head at his own gullibility. "So we have a deal?" he said.

I nodded. "We do."

70

With my fifteen-minute recess having already stretched into more like twenty-five, I had to get back into the courtroom.

There wasn't really time to consider everything I had just learned. But I did find myself thinking back to the moments Mark and I had been together the past few weeks. He had sat on decks—his and mine—and coolly shot the breeze with me. Essentially, he had been patting me on the shoulder with one hand while the other was ripping my heart out. That took nerve I didn't know he possessed.

Still, the rudiments of it made sense. Mark Lowe—his wife ever complaining about their upside-down house, their lack of cash, and his shortage of assertiveness—had put together a scheme to make a few million dollars. And he cared about those millions more than he cared about my children. Then he went out and hired the muscle and the know-how—Justina and the Turks—to pull it off.

That meant finding him was now my top priority.

After waiting for Politi to clear away, I cracked open the door to my chambers and stole a quick glance down the hall. If Mark was still serving as Whipple's runner, he would be on one of the benches outside my courtroom.

He wasn't there. I might have assumed he was off somewhere, already counting his money, except Alison had seen him so recently. He was around. Somewhere. As quietly as I could, I crept down the hallway, to ascertain if perhaps he was just sitting in a different spot.

But no. The hallway was empty.

I returned to my chambers and approached Jeremy's office door, still closed. I knocked softly, said, "It's me," then entered. Alison was sitting behind the desk, the gun now mostly assembled in front of her.

"Almost done," she said, continuing her work as she spoke. "I wasn't liking the way it was dry firing so I had to go back and do it again."

"Mark's not out there anyway," I said.

"So what are you going to do?"

"Resume the hearing, I guess."

"Shouldn't we just go find him now? You're the judge. People will wait."

"Yeah, but he might be back outside the building. I don't want to go chasing after him out there. We'd have to sneak the gun back in if he wasn't there. Besides, outside, he might be armed himself. In here, I think we can be reasonably certain we're the only ones with a firearm."

"Good point. So what's your plan, again?"

"Well, he's going to come back inside eventually. His boss will be looking for him," I said. "You can use the gun to coerce him to join us in my chambers. He'll be trapped, unarmed, and without a cell phone to communicate with any of the men he's working with. It's as vulnerable a place as we'll ever get him in."

She snapped one last piece in place on the gun, turned

around, and aimed it at the window. She pulled the trigger twice. It made a snapping sound.

"Perfect," she said. "I'm good to go."

"Okay. Just sit tight. And keep Jeremy's cell phone with you."

As I left Jeremy's office, I felt Mrs. Smith's curious gaze on me. I couldn't begin to fathom what she was making of my actions or of the unusual guests. I made a display of looking down at my watch for a moment, not actually taking note of the time.

"You know what?" I said to her. "It's Friday afternoon. It's been a long week. I'll be busy for the rest of the day with the hearing, so I don't really need you here. Why don't you knock off early?"

"Thank you, Judge, but I have work to—"

"Joan," I said, which stopped her immediately. "Please just go. And tell the same to the rest of the staff. I'd really appreciate it."

She considered this for a moment, then said, "Sure thing, Scott."

*

As the courtroom was called back into order, I was relieved to see Steve Politi was still in the room, because it meant he hadn't scrambled out to post the big scoop he was sitting on. Blake Franklin was also hanging in. Perhaps he had already canceled all his campaign events for the rest of the day.

Clarence Worth, who had little to complain about the way

the case was going, was nevertheless looking exasperated. After an hour-and-a-half-long lunch recess, I had taken another half-hour break.

I apologized for the delay, mumbled something about another matter that required immediate attention, then invited him to begin his case.

His first witness was a neatly trimmed scientist. I had thought Worth might start slowly in his defense, like a symphony that begins with a single oboe player and then adds one or two instruments at a time until it builds to a thundering crescendo.

But no. I could tell almost immediately, Worth was going for the fortissimo straight out. This was his smoking-gun witness, the one who had first caught Denny Palgraff's big blunder. My tip-off was that Barnaby Roberts could barely contain himself as the scientist began walking through the explanation of just how flawed the plaintiff's claim was. Worth's laser pointer was back out. Defense Exhibit 58, the diagram of the true and proper PCSK9, stayed out the whole time. I was sure Worth was hoping I dreamed about it.

As the next hour wore on, Worth worked methodically, leading his scientist through an explanation that built one layer of understanding on top of another.

Then the witness hit what you might have called his highest note, revealing where, precisely, Palgraff had misstepped, and how it was possible an otherwise brilliant scientist could get the protein wrong and not know it. For those who had been following along closely, it was a riveting climax—the moment when all became clear.

Then the moment I had been waiting for coincided with it. Right when the scientist got to the payoff, Andy Whipple twisted around and held his hands in a curious position.

I had to restrain myself from jumping out of my seat. If Whipple was making hand signals, my assumption was that Mark was there to receive them.

Barely bothering to disguise what I was doing, I buried my attention in my lap, where I had my cell phone, and hammered out a text to Jeremy's phone:

Mark is out there.

Then I lifted my head up and went back to pretending to concentrate on the proceeding. I had to maintain a certain amount of blind faith that Alison was receiving my text, that she was acting on it, and that it was working out the way we hoped.

Worth had finished with the witness. As Hemans began his cross-examination, I wondered if I was going to hear a shout, a gunshot, some disturbance. Or was Alison handling this quietly?

Certainly, she had a considerable strategic advantage, one that came with nine-millimeter bullets. And Mark would know any of the Powell girls were not to be fooled with when it came to firearms.

But I had already made the mistake of misjudging Mark too many times. Did he have other surprises for us?

I took a glance down at my phone. Four minutes had passed since I sent my text. No word from Alison.

The witness was reiterating the point that had exposed Denny Palgraff in the first place, doing it in even greater detail than the last time. Hemans was a good enough attorney to know he was actually making things worse, the longer he kept the guy on the stand. Every word was like another shovelful of dirt on his own coffin.

Another peek down. Seven minutes. Still nothing.

Soon, Hemans was done with his cross. The witness had been too sure-footed to give Hemans any chance to shove him off-balance.

Worth was already calling his next witness. Another scientist. She came to the stand looking every bit as competent as the last witness. The annihilation of Denny Palgraff was turning to its next chapter. She was swearing to tell the truth and nothing but.

Then I felt a buzz on my thigh and looked down.

Got him. In your office.

The witness had just passed "so help me God," and Worth was asking her to state her name and occupation for the record when I interrupted.

"You know what? Before we get into this witness, I think I need another quick break."

Worth's face briefly flashed with you-gotta-be-kidding-me aggravation before he got it back under control.

"Of course, Your Honor," he said.

"Fifteen minutes," I said.

Worth may have greeted this pronouncement with more

disapproval. I couldn't say for sure. Whatever dirty look he gave me would have been bouncing off the back of my robe.

71

The scene that met me in my office belonged in a mob movie, not my life.

There was a man sitting in the middle of the room, in one of the chairs that ordinarily fronted my desk. He was a man I obviously knew, having shared Thanksgiving dinner and Christmas Eve with him for the last twenty years. Yet I had never seen him looking anything like this.

Mark Lowe's wrists were tied to that chair by what appeared to be his shoelaces. His legs were bound by strips of a white dress shirt—also his own, judging by the fact that he was now wearing only a T-shirt. He had a gash by his left eye. Rivulets of crimson flowed down the side of his pale face. He was also bleeding from the mouth.

There was a woman standing directly in front of him, glowering hatefully. I could say it was Alison, but really it was some translation of her. The new language in which she was being expressed was fierce and primitive, a dictionary filled with fire.

Her arms jutted out of her sleeveless blouse, looking lean and sinewy. It was striking me again just how much weight she had lost. Stripped of a layer of fat, the muscle in her right forearm rippled from holding the gun. Her face was also red, although not from any wounds. Her flush came from exertion. And anger—a deep, boiling kind of hatred.

Jeremy Freeland was in the room too. He was standing behind Mark, his face a grave mask.

My best guess was that Alison had forced Mark in here at gunpoint. And Jeremy, the only staff member left in chambers, had helped tie Mark to a chair while Alison covered him with the Smith & Wesson. And then this new rendition of Alison, the woman who I had seen nurse two infants simultaneously, had brutally pistol-whipped him.

And just to be clear: I didn't feel a shred of sympathy for him. I only wished I could have gotten in a few swings myself.

"What have I missed?" I asked.

"He claims he doesn't know where Emma is," Alison said.

"I don't, I swear, I don't," Mark said.

He was hunched over, flinching like the proverbial dog that had been beaten too much. This was the Mark I knew. Meek. Submissive. The Lowe Man. I still couldn't fully square it with the guy who had turned our lives inside out.

The only difference was, I now recognized it was an act, and I didn't buy it anymore. If he was as innocent as he claimed, he would have screamed for help, knowing that there were legions of court security officers and US marshals who could rush to his aid. But he had remained quiet, because he understood law enforcement was no friend to men who kidnap children.

I walked up to him and grabbed him by the throat.

"We know everything already," I said. "I saw the video of you sliding that ruling under my door. I know about the

Turks you hired to threaten Karen and then snatch the kids. I know you were Steve Politi's secret source. I know about the hundred-thousand-share short sale contract on ApotheGen stock. It's all over. You tell us where Emma is or I swear, you won't live out the hour."

As I squeezed, I watched his blood seep into the dark fabric of my robe. He made a gargling sound and tried to pull away, but I held fast. When I felt my point had been made, I released my grip.

He coughed, trying to clear his windpipe.

"I'm telling you, I don't know," he said, his voice now ragged.

My hand went back to his throat. But this time, I used the other too, grasping both sides of his neck and choking him as hard as I could. He bucked and thrashed but couldn't really get much leverage while tied to a chair.

When I let go, he took a huge gasp of air, then said, "Stop. It's not me."

Alison, who was next to me, drew back the gun and was going to let it fly at his head again.

And then Mark blurted, "It's Andy."

That stopped her.

"Andy?" she said. "Andy Whipple?"

"It was all Andy. Andy and Karen, okay? He learned you were going to be the judge on this case. I think someone at ApotheGen actually tipped him off about the whole thing. Andy gets insider tips like that from all over. How do you think he always manages to beat the markets?

"Andy heard about the case and knew I was related to

you. He approached me and said that if I didn't go along with his idea, he'd not only fire me; he'd blackball me and make sure no one in the investing world would ever hire me. Then he laid it out for me, how he would load up with a ton of short sale contracts. That hundred thousand was just the tip of the iceberg. That was just the payoff to Karen and I for cooperating. Andy is in way bigger than us. As far as I know, he ended up selling short on something like ten million shares. The whole idea was to manipulate the price down, execute all those contracts at the bottom, and then buy ten million shares and ride the wave back up."

That meant Whipple was making money both ways. If he had ten million shares he sold short, the thirty-dollar drop in ApotheGen shares had netted him roughly three hundred million. But then, as ApotheGen's price shot back into the nineties—or beyond—that was another three hundred million. Or more. It would put the Whipple Alliance well on its way to another banner year of returning huge profits for its clients and huge commissions for the celebrity fund manager.

"That's a great story," I said. "Can you prove any of it?"

"I already have, if you just think about it for a second," Mark said. "That short sale contract was in my name. Where would a guy like me get the leverage to enter into a contract of that size with anyone? You think I could stroll into a bank and say, 'Hey, look at me, I've got five grand in my checking account and a four-hundred-thousand-dollar house that's upside down, but you got my back for a contract that, if it goes the wrong way, could end up costing me millions, right?' My collateral for that contract was Andy."

I felt my fists balling. "So if I have this right, Andy learns I'm the judge on the ApotheGen case and says, 'Hey, help me kidnap your brother-in-law's kids and I'll make you rich?' "

"Yes and no. Andy thought he would be able to bribe you by offering you a piece of the action, because that's Andy's world. He thinks money can buy anything and anyone. I told him you weren't programmed that way and told him he could go ahead and fire me but I wasn't going to cooperate. It was Karen who said, 'No, no, no, if you lose your job we'll lose everything. Think about the kids.' She really thought with Andy blackballing me I'd never be able to get another job, or at least not another job that would pay even half as well. She was already doing the math that we'd lose the house and probably go bankrupt. But she also knew you weren't going to take a bribe. So she came up with this kidnapping scheme."

"You're lying," Alison spat. "Karen would never do that."

"You don't know your own sister very well." Mark turned toward Alison, looking her in the eyes even as the blood continued to ooze from the cut near his own. "Don't you realize how much she resents you? I mean, we all laugh when she'll bring up the band trip to England. But look deeper than that. You were always the one people made a fuss over. Jenny had the friends, but you had everything else—the looks, the grades, the résumé. Do you know what it was like being your older sister but living in your shadow? The funny thing is, I think she had actually gotten over it for a while. But then you guys had to move down here, and you were this constant reminder of all the things she wanted but didn't have."

"That's absurd," Alison said.

"Oh, come on. We live on a quarter acre. You live on this huge piece of waterfront property. She's married to an IT geek. You're married to a federal judge. She's unemployed. You've got this fulfilling job. It's like you're everything she'd thought she'd be but isn't. You know I'm right. And she was finally figuring out that there weren't any six-figure jobs in benefits administration waiting for her down here. She knew she was staring at this future where we were going to be just like everyone else, struggling to make ends meet, praying the cars didn't break down because we couldn't afford to buy new ones, and she . . . I mean, do you know how much it humiliated her to accept that quote-unquote 'loan' from you guys when the heat pump broke?"

He spat a bloody glob of phlegm and saliva on my carpet. "So at first it was, 'We have to do this. We have no choice.' But then she got to like the idea of having six million bucks squirreled away. It was like this was what she had been entitled to all along, and now she was going to get it. She started talking about how we were going to tell everyone that I had gotten a nice raise and that I was finally being recognized for all my good work, and then we were going to buy new cars, new furniture. I couldn't talk her out of it. It got to the point where Andy was going directly to Karen with the details. I told them both they were nuts. But Karen was gung ho, and with Andy's money behind her, she thought we'd get away with it easily. I don't know what you're talking about with Turks. The guys Andy hired are Macedonian."

I thought about Karen's actions throughout. During that first family meeting, she had insisted we "do something." That way, she would be the first to learn if we actually *were* doing something proactive. When she discovered I was out chasing a hunch that first Saturday morning, which she would have learned when she called Alison to apologize for her boorish behavior at the Living Museum, she immediately had the kidnappers text me and bring me back home. Probably because she didn't want me investigating anything on my own.

Next, she had established the night watch over our house, which was a nice way for her to keep tabs on us—one out of every three nights, anyway—while putting herself even more in control of our investigation, or lack thereof. It also might give her some plausible deniability if things did unravel because, look, she was the one protecting us.

There was also her insistence, after she saw the Emma torture video, that I go to the FBI—all the while knowing I wouldn't, because she already knew how dead set Alison and I were against police involvement. But, on the off chance I had the idea of going to the authorities behind Alison's back, at least Karen would be the first to know.

Then I flashed back to the video we had seen of her delivering Sam and Emma to the kidnappers. It was fiendishly brilliant in that it seemed to support the story she had told us. But there was nothing in it that contradicted Mark's version of the events, nothing that proved she was being forced to do what she did. All it really told us was that she was driving the van when the kids were taken, which she could have been doing voluntarily.

And, of course, there was no audio. For all we knew, Boris and Alexi were saying, *All right, thanks, Karen, see you later.*

I could easily imagine Karen, cagey Karen, betting the I'm-just-the-helpless-housewife routine, combined with the story about the scary men and the video to support it, would be enough to protect her from prosecution if things went bad. For our benefit, she had added the flourish that Alexi and Boris sounded Turkish, because she knew that would play into our preconceived idea that Justina was somehow involved.

Which she wasn't, of course. She never had been.

Alison wasn't saying anything. But I didn't need to hear her words to know she was believing him. Or at least seriously considering it. Her body language said it for her.

"Alison," I said. "I think we need to talk to Andy Whipple."

"I agree," she said. "But who is going to get him in here?"

All I said was, "Blake."

72

Blake Franklin had made a career out of being charming, eloquent, and persuasive. And if anyone could sweet-talk Whipple in here without Whipple even knowing he was being sweet-talked, it would be the senior senator from the Commonwealth of Virginia.

After all, Blake had been the one who taught me a simple truism that had since served me well, whether in the US Senate, the federal judiciary, or the local Food Lion. And it went like this:

If you want to get a man to do something for you, appeal to his ego.

Blake did it better than most. He could also approach Whipple without it looking strange. It would just seem like one powerful, important man gravitating toward another one. And I was thankful that, unlike the rest of the gallery, who couldn't make claims about national security, the senator still had his cell phone on him.

Two rings later, he picked up. I could hear from the background noise that he was in a crowded hallway.

"Hey there," he said. "Are you going to get things going again soon? I don't mean to complain, because it's not like I paid for this ticket, but we're getting bored with all the intermissions."

"I will. I need a favor first."

"Sure, what's up?"

"Do you know Andy Whipple?"

"Yeah, he was just chatting me up earlier. I think he's convinced if he keeps talking to me, he'll be able to completely undermine what little is left of Dodd-Frank."

"I need to see him in my chambers, right now. Could you please tell him I'm a big, big fan of his, that I've seen him on TV, and that I really just wanted to meet him?"

"Is any of that true?"

"Not remotely. But he'll believe it coming from you. It relates to that life-or-death family thing, so I'm going to need you to make it convincing."

Blake considered this for a moment. "All right. I'll give it my best."

"Thanks."

I ended the call and returned my phone to my pocket.

"Jeremy, would you mind manning the front door and escorting Whipple in here?" I asked.

"You got it," he confirmed, and disappeared into the reception area.

This left just Alison, Mark, and me. Mark had his head bowed. His breathing was still rough. Alison was staring bullets at him.

"You really don't know where Emma is?" she asked.

"I swear, I don't. Karen doesn't either. Andy hired these two Macedonian guys, a couple of scary-looking bastards. Supposedly they're wanted by Interpol and God knows who else. I have no idea what rock he found them under. I just know he's paying them five thousand dollars a day for their services, so they must be pretty good at . . . whatever it is you would say they do."

Alison pelted him with a stream of curses and insults that ended with, "How could you do that? How could you let Emma be held by men like that? She's your *niece*. She loves you. She trusts you. Doesn't that mean anything to you?"

Mark took a deep breath. "Look, I know this is no excuse for what we've done. But Emma really is safe, okay? The men were under strict orders not to harm the children. We gave them money to feed the kids. We set up these rules: no tying the children up, no striking them, no—"

"They sent us a video where they were torturing Emma!" I yelled, before remembering where I was and quieting myself. "It looked like they were administering a series of shocks. You call *that* not harming the children?"

Alison didn't wait to hear more. Her arm flashed in the air and she slammed the gun into Mark's face, taking a chunk out of his cheek.

Mark yelped. Alison pressed the barrel of the gun to his forehead. Her lips were drawn back to reveal her teeth. Her index finger, which she had previously kept parallel to the barrel as a precaution, was now resting on the trigger guard.

"That wasn't how it was supposed to go," Mark said quickly, looking more at the gun than at Alison. "That was a mistake. And we told them in no uncertain terms not to do that again. Look, the main thing is, she'll be fine in the long run. They were never going to cut off any body parts or . . . anything like that. The deal we worked out is that the moment they see the verdict has been posted, they release her near the Patrick Henry Mall and tell her to go find a cop or a security officer or whatever. It will all end well."

Alison leaned more of her body weight against the gun, grinding it farther into Mark's skull. He reflexively turned to the side, but that only meant the gun was now aimed behind his ear. There was venom in Alison's eyes, which had squeezed down to slits on either side of a nose that had wrinkled with rage. She moved her finger from outside the guard to inside, curling it around the trigger. One twitch, and half of Mark Lowe's brain was going to be on my carpet.

"You're a total moron, you know that?" she said. "You really think those Macedonian guys are going to leave her alive out of the goodness of their hearts? The moment they see that ruling is up, they'll kill her. As far as I'm concerned, you can die along wi—"

"Alison, no!" I said.

I leapt toward her, grabbed her wrist, and forced it down, so the gun was pointing at the floor.

"Let go of me," she said, struggling to free her arm from my grip.

"Stop, Alison, stop. This isn't helping. If Blake does his job, Whipple is going to be here any second. We can't have Mark sitting here with his head blown off. We can't have Mark sitting here, period. If Whipple sees him before he's in the room, he might make a run for it. He's the one who knows where Emma is. We can't go chasing him through the courthouse with a gun."

Alison stopped fighting me, but her body was still

spring-loaded. I kept my hand on her wrist.

"Come on," I said. "Quickly. I really need your help. We've got to get Mark out of sight. Please."

She breathed in and out, slowly recognizing that of the demons currently aligned against us, there were far greater ones than Mark. Finally, I felt some small amount of the tension ease out of her arms.

"Okay," she said.

"Get the bathroom door open for me. We can stash him in there."

I went around to the back of Mark's chair and began sliding it across the carpet to my private bathroom. Once I got him settled in there, I said, "You better not make a sound, you understand? Or I swear I'll let her shoot you."

And then, before I left him in there, in the dark, with the door closed, I couldn't help but add, "Say nothing."

73

It wasn't more than another minute or two before there was a soft tapping at my door. It was, unmistakably, a Jeremy Freeland knock.

"Judge," he said. "Mr. Whipple is here to see you."

This was the moment. We were walking on a razor's edge across the abyss now. There were a multitude of ways this could go horribly wrong, any of which would result in the end of Emma's life. And, effectively, ours.

Had I even paused to think about that—about how close we were to catastrophe—I'm sure I would have been crippled by fear, unable to make my body respond to any meaningful commands. But we were going on instinct, moving without allowing ourselves to consider the externalities.

Alison positioned herself to the left side of the door and pinned herself against the wall, in a place where Whipple would be unable to spot her when he entered.

She gave me a thumbs-up. I opened the door. Both of Andy Whipple's chins appeared before me.

"Hello, hello!" I said. "Come in, come in. Please."

I backed away to give him room. With Jeremy gently herding him inside, he took a few short steps into the room.

"When Senator Franklin told me you needed to talk to

me about a financial matter," he began, "I have to admit I was a little—"

Alison slammed the door behind him, leveled the gun at him, and said, "Shut up."

"What . . . what is this about?" he said, looking genuinely surprised and perhaps slightly indignant. No one pointed guns at masters of the financial universe.

"You know exactly what it's about," Alison said. "Where's my daughter?"

"Your daughter? I'm sorry, I'm not following—"

"Stop it," I said. "Mark Lowe told us everything."

"Mark Lowe," he said, as if my brother-in-law's name were an exotic dish on a menu and he wasn't sure he was saying it right. "Who is Mark Lowe?"

I walked over to the door of my bathroom and opened it. "This guy," I said.

Whipple peered into the darkness of my bathroom.

"You can stop now, Andy," Mark said in his now-hoarse voice. "They know about the stock manipulation, about the short sales. They know about the Macedonians. I told them everything."

Whipple's head tilted perhaps three degrees. Other than that, he was utterly impassive, to an extent that was actually chilling. In my courtroom, I have seen my share of sociopaths, people whose utter lack of feeling for others left me wondering if they were even part of the same species as the rest of us. They were like houses where all the wiring is done, except the electrician has forgotten to make that final connection to the thing that makes us human, leaving the entire dwelling dark and unfit for occupation.

But even those people show some emotion during the course of a trial. Even if it's just regret over being caught, or fear of the punishment I'm about to mete out, or dismay over the fact that no one seems to like them—which is difficult for many sociopaths to handle, since they're also deeply narcissistic—I get some sense of an inner torment.

Not here. Confronted with the knowledge that one of his coconspirators had turned on him, that we were all aware of the horrific thing he had orchestrated, that we were looking at him and his rotten core with pure loathing, Andy Whipple showed no reaction other than that slight twitch of his neck.

"Shoot me if you want," he said evenly. "But please know that whatever injury you cause to me, I'll have double done to your daughter. And if you kill me? You'll be killing her too. That is an ironclad promise. Those two Macedonian gentlemen won't hesitate to slit her throat if they stop hearing from me."

Alison's nostrils flared. Her finger was on the trigger, but I already knew that was just for show. Whipple wasn't bluffing. There was a reason he had amassed such a fortune. It was because he was ruthless, yes, but also because he was always thinking through various contingencies and planning accordingly.

"I suggest a fairly simple transaction here," Whipple said. "Really, it's the same deal I've been offering all along. Your daughter for a verdict. Are we agreed?"

Alison had tears pouring down her face. The gun was

starting to wobble. She unleashed an invective-laced tirade that finished with: ". . . you monster. Emma is not some commodity to be traded."

"Oh, but she is," Whipple said. "And it might help if you think about her that way for a short time. If you do, you'll see this is the best solution. You get your daughter back, your life back. That's a win for you. And I make some money. That's a win for me."

"*Steal* some money is more like it," Mark said from within the bathroom. "For every one of those short sale contracts, there's someone losing millions of dollars. You're a crook."

"And you're fired," Whipple countered. "But I suppose it won't hurt you too bad. Let me remind you, Mark, you're walking away from this with at least six million dollars. Three million from that short sale contract and at least another three million when ApotheGen stock jumps right back to where it started. See? I told you. Everyone wins.

"Oh," Whipple added, now looking at me. "And if you're thinking that when this is over you can just run to the police, you might want to think otherwise. I anticipated the possibility of a backfire like this, so I took out a little insurance policy. There's another hundred-thousand-share short sale contract that has been executed, and it's got your name on it, Judge Sampson. There's also a standing order to wire the money from your account with the Whipple Alliance to a bank in the Caribbean."

"I don't have an account with the Whipple Alliance," I said.

"Ah, but you do. It was set up just before this all began. If everything went perfectly, I was just going to fish the money out at my leisure. I have all the codes. But if push came to shove, I knew I could use that as a little enticement for you to go along with me. Or, if you didn't like that carrot, I could always go with the stick: I'll tell the authorities you were complicit in the scheme and you'll go down with me. If anything, you'll go down harder, the mandatory minimums for official misconduct being what they are."

"That would never hold up in court."

Whipple actually laughed. "But, you see, it would. You have no idea how guilty you look, Judge Sampson. Karen Lowe has a key to your house. She was able to get your passport, your social security number, everything we needed. And I assure you the signatures on all the paperwork are a match. I hired the best forger in New York and he did magnificent work.

"I know you think your 'But I'm a judge, I've been framed, I'm innocent' act would work with the prosecutor. But it would be your word against the documents, and I've got you nailed six ways to Sunday with the documents. It's all waiting for the US Attorneys Office with a neat little bow on it if I so choose."

There was a possibility he was inventing all this on the fly. But, somehow, I doubted it.

It went to the very nature of what a hedge fund was and how it had gotten its name in the first place. The whole idea of hedge funds was that they made money even in down markets—with short sales, derivatives, and a host of other financial instruments that were potentially profitable regardless of the direction of the markets. They were all ways of hedging your bets.

Which was exactly what Andy Whipple had done here.

"So," he said. "Do we have a deal or not? Just say yes and you'll be hugging your daughter within the hour."

"Yes," I said. "We have a deal."

I didn't see where I had any other choice.

74

The brothers had thought it would all be fairly simple: Get the call, kill the girl, toss her in the grave, and take off.

Their final destination was Venezuela. They could hole up for as long as they needed. It had plenty of beaches, plenty of rum, and didn't extradite fugitives to the United States.

It was all set. So when the Internet phone rang and the older brother answered, the younger was already going into the bag where he kept his hunting knife. He would wait until they were out at the grave before he slit the little girl's throat. Less cleanup that way.

"Yes," the older said.

"There's been a change of plans," Andy Whipple told them on speakerphone. "Bring the girl to the judge's house."

"Then what?"

"Then you let her go."

The older brother paused. "That wasn't what we agreed to."

"I know. I told you, there's been a change of plans."

"We haven't cleaned up yet. I don't want to leave behind evidence."

"I'll give you another hundred thousand," Whipple said.

The older brother glanced at the younger. He shrugged.

"Make it two hundred," the older said. "The little girl

has seen our faces many times. She would be able to identify us. That's a risk we weren't anticipating. We should be compensated for it."

"Fine," the man said, so easily, it made the older brother wish he had asked for five hundred. "But I need you to leave immediately."

"Very well."

The call ended.

"I did all that digging for nothing?" the younger said.

"Maybe not," the older said. "We'll see."

75

A child for a verdict.

It was what Andy Whipple had wanted all along. And while it galled me to give it to him, what mattered far more was that Emma was coming home. And Whipple was going to have a gun trained on his ear until she got there safely.

Whipple had his hedge. That Smith & Wesson was ours.

We decided the exchange would happen at the farm. Whipple made the call to the Macedonians before we left the courthouse to set it all up. What we agreed was that Whipple would stay in my Buick until the Macedonians got there with Emma. When Emma was let out, we would allow Whipple to go free as well.

And then, on Monday, once the attorneys rested in *Palgraff vs. ApotheGen,* I would file the ruling that had already been written out for me. Whipple was assured of my cooperation by the knowledge that he could release all those toxic documents if I failed to toe the line.

I think it helped—both with my conscience and with my willingness to go through with it—that it was the correct ruling.

We told Mark to stay behind, not wanting to attract attention by having a battered man hobbling with us through the courthouse. Jeremy volunteered to stick around and babysit him in my office. Jeremy was also going to have Jean Ann adjourn court for the day, explaining to everyone that the judge had become violently ill.

That left just three of us in my car. Alison went in the backseat with Whipple. I drove. I felt like I was chauffeuring the devil.

I stole occasional glances at him in the rearview mirror. He was sitting in total tranquility. I had never been in the presence of someone I hated more. I found it vile that this man—no, he wasn't a man; he was a subhuman *thing*—was even touching my car's upholstery. At one point, I heard him sigh. It revolted me I was breathing the same air. Only supreme love for my daughter stopped me from acting out my loathing for him in any number of violent ways, all of which I fantasized about as we got on the highway.

Unaware of my hatred—or, perhaps more accurately, indifferent to it—Whipple just stared out the window. It was well beyond my understanding how he could stand to look at himself while he shaved in the morning.

The only satisfaction I had was that, even as he thought he was winning, he was actually losing in the long run. All he had was money, the things it could buy, and the ever-increasing misery that way of life brought. He thought amassing more would make him happy. Yet this supposed financial genius was forgetting one of the simplest tenets of economics, the law of diminishing returns. It was working against him the whole time. Each dollar he earned or stole made him a little bit less happy than the previous one. It would continue that way, ever more, until eventually, he reached zero.

Which was exactly what he deserved.

If nothing else, this ordeal had confirmed for me what mattered. The simple pleasures of family life. The love of an amazing woman. The joy of children. Good health. Especially good health.

I never had taken those things for granted, even before this. I knew I never would now. Pancake Day and Swim With Dad never sounded so good.

The series of lights on Route 17 in Gloucester seemed interminable. If Whipple was going to dare make a break for it, one of those lights would be his best chance. But he seemed content to ride along, secure that he had everything under control.

Eventually, after a long and tense ride, I made the turn onto our sleepy little road. As I passed our property line, I noted the vultures were gone.

I slowed as my tires left the pavement and started rolling through the woods along the soft dirt, down that four-tenths-of-a-mile road that I once thought walled out the world. I would never again make that mistake. But I hoped, someday, we would at least be able to feel like we were not under constant attack.

That was, cruelly enough, the sweet thought going through my head as we made it to the clearing that preceded our farmhouse. And then I was jolted back to the bitter present.

There, waiting for us at the end of the driveway, were four vehicles: an unmarked Ford Taurus, a sedan bearing the seal of the state medical examiner, and two Gloucester County Sheriff's cars.

*

From the backseat, Whipple was suddenly alive.

"What the hell is going on? What is this? Are you—"

"Shut up," I hissed. "Just shut up. I have no idea. You think I want these guys here right now?"

"Well, then what are they doing here?"

"*I don't know.*"

Alison swore.

"Just stay put," I said. "Let me take care of this. This doesn't change anything. I'll get rid of them."

I drove about halfway between the clearing and where the cop cars were parked and pulled off to the side. It was as close as I dared get; otherwise, they'd see my wife holding Andy Whipple at gunpoint. I shut off the engine, got out, and jogged the final fifty yards.

What I had told Whipple was the truth. I really didn't know what the Gloucester County Sheriff's Office was doing here. The presence of the state medical examiner was even less explicable.

Maybe twenty-five yards in, I saw the shaved black head of Detective Sergeant Harold Curry Jr. emerging from the front door of my house and walking out onto the porch. He was followed by the beefy, baby-faced deputy who had been out to my house previously, along with one other deputy.

Curry descended the steps and met me on the front lawn.

"You better have a warrant," I said.

"We do."

"Let's see it," I said.

From his jacket pocket, he produced two sheets of paper that had been trifolded. He handed them to me. I started reading. It appeared to be perfectly proper, granting them the right to search my primary domicile and anything else they felt like searching, just like last time.

But this warrant had a few extra words the previous one did not.

"Instrumentality of murder? . . . The homicide of Herbert Thrift?" I said. "You guys think I killed Herb Thrift? Why would I possibly do that?"

"He was one of our own, you know," Curry said. "Retired, sure. But he still had a lot of friends in the department. They're all pretty upset right now."

"But I didn't have anything to do with that. You're making a terrible mistake."

"Oh?" Curry said. "Well, tell me, Judge Sampson, did you hire Herb Thrift?"

I knew I should have shut my mouth. The defendant's table in my courtroom was regularly occupied by people who were indicted and then convicted by the stupidity of their own words, which they uttered under the belief they could talk their way out of trouble. I knew that.

But right then, I just wanted these men to disappear. Which made me another idiot suspect who thought if he said the right thing, this would all go away.

"Yes, I hired him."

"To do some private detecting for you?"

"That's right."

Curry pulled a small notebook out of his breast pocket. "What was he doing for you?"

"That's why they call it private," I said. "Because it's none of your business."

"Okay. When is the last time you saw him alive?"

I scanned back in my memory. "It would have been . . . a Thursday. Thursday two weeks ago. Or, I guess I should say, two weeks and a day ago."

"Where did you see him?"

"In his office. I made an appointment. I'm sure he has a calendar; you could check it."

"Have you seen him since?"

"No." I was trying not to envision the images of his corpse my brain would never allow me to forget.

"Have you talked to him since?"

"Yes. Several times, on the phone. We talked about the work he was doing for me."

"When was the last time?"

"I . . . I couldn't . . . Monday, I guess it was. No, wait, Saturday. Yeah, it was the Saturday after I hired him. Again, roughly two weeks ago. I'm sure you could pull his phone records and check."

Curry was scribbling all this in his little pad. The baby-faced deputy was listening every bit as intently.

The detective lobbed out the next question casually. "Did you visit his office again sometime after that?"

A horrible sinking feeling came over me. The note. They had found the note I wedged in his door.

"Yes, I . . . I hadn't heard from him, so I went by his office and"—there was no point in trying to deny it—"I left him a note."

"Where did you leave this note?"

"On . . . on the back door. I kind of wedged it in there above the handle."

"The back door. You're talking about the entrance to his personal quarters?"

He emphasized the second-to-last word, and I could already hear Detective Sergeant Harold Curry Jr. testifying at my trial, *It seemed like it was personal.*

"Yes, that's right."

"What did the note say?

"I just . . . I asked him to call me."

"Were you angry with him?"

"No. No, I was . . . I was a little frustrated I hadn't heard from him."

"Frustrated."

"Yes."

"Not angry?"

"Angry . . . angry would be too strong a word."

"Did you knock on his door?"

"Well, yes, I'm sure I did."

"How many times?"

"I . . . Several, I guess. What does that matter?"

"Were you swearing a lot as you did it?"

Oh God. They must have spoken to the neighbor, the woman I snapped at.

Now I could hear her testifying too. *He was ranting and raving and cursing a blue streak. I was so scared I ran back in the house.*

"I'm not sure," I said.

"Had you paid Mr. Thrift for his services in cash?"

"Uhh . . . yes."

"And had he completed his work?"

"No. That's why I wanted to talk to him."

"Did that make you angry? Paying for something and not getting it?"

"No. Just frustrated, like I said."

"Did you have any other interactions with Mr. Thrift after that?"

"No."

"Did you call him again?"

"Probably. I'm sure I left messages. You can check that too."

"Actually, we already did. It seems like you stopped leaving messages for him last Saturday. You stopped calling him too. Why, if you were so eager to hear from him, did you suddenly stop calling and leaving messages?"

I felt my face flushing, even as I willed it not to. This was the kind of detail that juries just loved, the one that both showed the defendant to be a liar and tied him to the foul play in question. It was circumstantial, yes—as long as they didn't have a body, it was all circumstantial—but it was incredibly damning in its own way.

"I guess at that point I just gave up on him and decided he wasn't going to call me back," I said lamely.

"Did you go back to his home again?"

"You mean his place of business?"

"One and the same."

"Well, no," I said. "I didn't."

"Because you had given up hope of hearing from him."

"Yeah. I guess."

More scribbling. He was taking his time. I hated him for it. I needed him gone. While he was focused on his pad, I risked a glimpse toward the Buick. Whipple still appeared to be sitting in the same spot. So was Alison. I was sure she still had the gun on him, but she was keeping it low, out of sight.

And then Curry, having already allowed me to build my own gallows with my voluntary statement, invited me to also tie the noose.

"So," Curry said. "Can you explain how it was Herbert Thrift's body was found on your property?"

The words bored into my gut. Curry had just laid out his whole case: I had hired Herb Thrift, gotten angry with him over his failure to provide services, left messages for him, stormed to his house looking for him, left more messages for him until I stopped leaving messages for him—because by that point, I had killed him and buried him in my woods. Men had been sent to prison for murder on far less evidence.

I now understood why the state medical examiner was there. They were pulling clues from what was left of poor Herb Thrift.

"A pack of wild dogs dug him up," Curry said, shaking his head. "Some lady was driving along and suddenly there's some mutt dragging a human arm across the road."

Curry was no longer writing in his note pad. His eyes were trying to lock on mine. But mine were shifting around quite a bit, I'm sure.

I was so engrossed by this little drama I didn't really hear the engine coming down the driveway. But then a rapidly moving object drew my attention.

A white panel van, the vehicle Sam had described to us, the one we had seen on the video in Karen's phone, had burst into the clearing.

The Macedonians had arrived.

76

What transpired next didn't even take a minute, perhaps no more than thirty seconds.

That I remember it so well, and can recount it with such vivid detail, is only because I have replayed it thousands of times in my own head.

The Macedonians tore along unabated for perhaps another ten yards. That was how long it took for them to recognize they were heading toward what appeared to be a police ambush.

The driver slammed on the breaks, hard. The van skidded off our rutted dirt path and onto the combination of grass and pine straw that serves as our yard. Dust flew into the air as the van went from roughly fifty miles an hour to a dead stop.

For less than a second, it stayed there, perfectly still. Then it started going backward.

The Macedonians, a pair of wanted men with a kidnapped child in their cargo hold, wanted no part of explaining themselves to the Gloucester County Sheriff's Office.

It was around this time the door to the Buick opened. It was Alison. When I say she hit the ground running, I mean I had never seen my wife move so fast. She charged toward the van. The Smith & Wesson was a blur of metal in her hand.

She was closing in, quickly. First thirty yards out. Then twenty. The only problem was, the van had shifted into reverse and was accelerating. Soon, it was traveling backward faster than she could go forward.

There was no chance of her catching up. Those Macedonian men were going to drive off with Emma. It was difficult to imagine any scenario where we'd see her alive again. The Macedonians were on the run now. They would value their own freedom over whatever flimsy arrangement they had with Andy Whipple. They would dispose of Emma and climb back down into whatever dark hole they had first crawled out of.

Alison was obviously having the same thoughts. She leveled the gun and, still running, started firing.

She was aiming low, at the van's tires. I suspect it was because she didn't dare shoot at the body of a van that had Emma inside.

Three small puffs of dirt appeared in front of the van as her first rounds missed short. I had seen my wife in action on the range. Even being out of practice as she was, hitting a tire from less than a hundred feet should not have been a problem. Either her running was throwing her off, or she was being too cautious with her aim. I suspected it was the latter.

Then more gunshots started ringing out. They were coming from the passenger side of the van.

One of the Macedonians was returning fire.

The barrel of the weapon jutted out of the window. It was an AR-15, a deadly assault rifle with a long banana clip attached. It was semiautomatic, but he was pulling the trigger as fast as his finger could move, clearly unconcerned about running out of rounds. I could see the muzzle flashes sparking in rapid succession.

It wasn't a fair fight. The Macedonian had a superior weapon and more ammunition. He was also surrounded by several tons of glass and steel. Alison, meanwhile, didn't even have a blade of grass for cover.

My initial reaction was delayed by the shock of the gunshots, by the compulsion—one that was especially strong in me, given past events—to duck for cover when the lead started flying. But finally that impulse was overwhelmed by the urge to protect my wife. I started charging toward her.

"No!" I shouted. "No, Alison. No!"

I didn't get very far. Two cops weren't going to let a civilian—even one they suspected of murdering their former colleague—run toward a raging firefight. Harold Curry grabbed me by the back of my jacket, which slowed me just enough for the beefy, baby-faced deputy to grab me with both arms.

Seemingly oblivious to the danger she was facing, Alison actually stopped running. She assumed a classic shooting stance: legs braced, one slightly in front of the other; shoulders square to her target; hands thrust out in front of her. She fired twice. The van's front left tire exploded. She shifted her sights and squeezed off three more rounds, reducing the front right tire to a mass of shredded rubber.

I knew the magazine on the Smith & Wesson held fifteen rounds and that she had started off with it full. By my count, she was down to seven bullets.

The van was now essentially riding on its rims. The wrecked tires were no longer helping. If anything, they were now a hindrance. The vehicle was foundering badly, unable to get any traction.

By stopping, Alison had greatly improved her accuracy. She had also made herself an easy target.

I shouted again. Actually, I was probably shouting the whole time, though what I said neither mattered nor made sense. At some point, Harold Curry had grabbed the deputy's radio from his shoulder and was frantically telling the dispatch to send all available units to my address.

Help was coming. Alison just had to hang on.

She had shifted her efforts to the back passenger tire, which she blew apart on the second try. The van lurched to the right and was now almost completely disabled.

That was when the Macedonian who had been driving tried to make a break for it. It was a huge mistake. As soon as he was clear of the van—and was no longer unwittingly using my daughter as cover—Alison cut him down with two shots in the back. His arms flew out to either side and he fell facedown.

The other Macedonian, who was either not as foolish or a whole lot bolder because of his AR-15, kept shooting wildly. I was now praying for him to leave the van too. Or for him to run out of ammunition.

Then something almost as good happened. Alison was on the move.

She was running away, dashing toward the safety of the woods. And she was going to make it. I let out a ragged cheer. *She really was going to make it.* She knew the battle had been won and now she was going to let the rest of the Gloucester County Sheriff's Office win the war. Let the lone Macedonian just try to take on all those armed deputies. He would either surrender or die while trying to fight it out.

Alison was mere seconds away from the greatest escape of her life. The trees couldn't have been more than thirty feet away. They were her refuge, her sanctuary, their thick trunks offering all the protection she would need.

Then, to my horror, she tumbled.

The way she flopped to the ground, limbs akimbo, told me a bullet had hit her leg. She tried, just once, to get up. But her lower body wasn't up to the task.

She rolled just as the Macedonian unleashed a new volley. Mounds of pine straw exploded where she had been lying mere nanoseconds before.

Then she came up to a sitting position, her worthless leg in front of her, the gun raised. Incredibly, she had a perfect shot at him. She was also savagely exposed to his fire.

I couldn't tell you which in the following happened first. For all intents and purposes, they happened simultaneously.

With one of her three remaining rounds, Alison buried a shot in the Macedonian's forehead. His head jerked violently backward. A red mist splattered the inside of the van's windows.

Concurrently, the Macedonian's aim finally became true. Two bullets ripped into Alison's chest. Her arms splayed to either side.

She fell backward.

I'm not sure if I managed to break free from the cops or if they simply let me go. I sprinted toward Alison's wilted form, bellowing for help, my arms and legs pumping. Yelling and running. Yelling and running. I was moving at glacial speed. It was like one of those nightmares where the worst thing you can imagine is chasing you but your feet can't seem to gain any purchase and your thighs are too weak to move you and the harder you struggle the slower you go.

When I reached her, I skidded next to her body on my knees, ready to pound life into her heart or breathe oxygen into her lungs.

But there was no point.

The slugs had torn into her with lethal force, leaving two jagged, plum-size cavities in the center of her torso. The carnage was devastating.

Her chest was not moving. Her pupils were fixed and dilated. There was something about her stillness that was absolute. One moment there had been a fully functioning woman, in charge of all her motor functions, both large and small. And then someone pressed an off button.

She was already gone.

*

I have tried to tell myself this meant she died instantly, without much pain or suffering. Maybe it's because I like that version of things.

As long as I'm deluding myself, I tell myself she died with the full knowledge of what she had accomplished: that both

Macedonians were dead; that Andy Whipple, who had been cowering in the bottom of my Buick as soon as the bullets began flying, was going to allow himself to be arrested without resistance; and, most important, that Emma was safely in my arms not three minutes after the shooting ended.

Maybe she understood all that in her final, fleeting second of consciousness. Maybe she didn't.

All I can say is that I know the truth. She died so our daughter could live.

77

In the following minutes, hours, and days, so much happened that I'm not sure I can accurately recall the order of it.

Retrieving data from the dead men's phones, the authorities were able to track their hiding spot to a ranch house deep in the woods in Mathews, the next county over from Gloucester, a place so rural it does not have a single stoplight.

There, they found ample evidence of Emma's twenty-three days in captivity. They also discovered a piece of Tupperware in the refrigerator containing Herb Thrift's remaining fingers and all of his teeth, which effectively cleared me of that murder.

Andy Whipple, on the other hand, was just beginning his journey in the criminal justice system. He had made elaborate plans to mislead and frustrate the Securities and Exchange Commission, the FBI Securities Fraud Unit and the US Attorneys Office. He had not counted on the Gloucester County Sheriff's Office or the Virginia State Police, whose homicide charges took precedence over those financial crimes.

Murder for hire is a capital offense in Virginia. So is serial murder, which state statutes define as the taking of two lives in less than three years. So is murder in the commission of a criminal enterprise. The Macedonians in Andy Whipple's employ had killed both Herbert Thrift and Alison Sampson, all while engaged in a conspiracy to blackmail me by kidnapping my children. That put Whipple on the way to the needle in at least three different ways.

The prosecutor asked me if I thought he should pursue the death penalty. But I've never been all that interested in retribution. It wouldn't bring back my wife or restore Herb Thrift to his happy life. It wouldn't erase whatever emotional damage was done to Sam and Emma.

As it was, Whipple would never draw another breath as a free man. Karen's and Mark's testimonies were more than enough to put him away. The Lowes were also heading for what looked like many decades of incarceration, their cooperation in Whipple's prosecution notwithstanding. The only sadness I felt about that was related to their children. At least Aunt Jenny had agreed to take them in.

In the meantime, I was able to explain my *Skavron* ruling to Jeb Byers, who proved sympathetic. He saw to it the ruling was vacated, then issued a warrant for Skavron's arrest. The judge and I then agreed I should take some time off but that I could resume hearing cases when I was ready.

Neal Keesee was harder to appease. But he had the scalp he wanted: Blake Franklin followed through on his promise to pull out of the election. I felt more than a measure of guilt over it. But Blake, God bless him, assured me he was relieved to be done with the whole thing and that I was actually doing him a favor.

The matter of *Palgraff vs. ApotheGen* went away more

quietly. Roland Hemans, soundly beaten and not wanting to waste more of anyone's time, withdrew his complaint. The moment I heard about it, I alerted Steve Politi, then waited an hour until I notified the clerk of court. A promise was a promise.

In truth, all of that was happening on the periphery of my life. The center of it, more than ever before, was Sam and Emma, two children who needed me more than ever now that I was their only parent.

The three of us slept in the same bed at their grandmother's house that Friday night, and the two nights after that. They were just beginning to grieve for their mother, a process that would likely continue for the rest of their lives. And I was going to be their beacon of strength for all of it. Had I done differently, I have no doubt Alison would have found a way to come down from heaven and kick my ass.

I didn't return to the farm that weekend. I think I already suspected I never would. At some point on Sunday, Jenny and Gina bravely went back there and carried out a few precious items, the things that reminded us of Alison most. I planned to give the rest away and start fresh in a new house. Something near Gina, Jenny, and the cousins.

Just not on a cul-de-sac. I knew how Alison felt about those.

Mostly, I was still in shock, still trying to set in order what had happened, seeing Alison's final actions—heroic, selfless, and stupid as they were—in my mind a thousand times.

For the first few days, they still didn't really make sense to me. It was clear the Macedonians were going to get away if she didn't intercede. But why couldn't she have been more cautious? Why had she valued her own life so little?

Then, on Monday morning, at 8:43 A.M., Alison's phone rang. I had been keeping it with me, telling myself I was just being practical: People needed to know she had passed away. I'm sure any amateur psychologist could have diagnosed there was more going on.

Nevertheless, when it rang, coming from a number neither I nor the phone recognized, I answered with a simple, "Hello?"

"Uh, hello," said a female voice, one that was clearly expecting another female voice to answer. "This is Laurie Lyckholm. Is Alison there?"

"This is her husband, Scott," I said. "I'm afraid Alison passed away on Friday."

There was a silence on the line, followed by: "I'm very sorry to hear that. May I ask what happened?"

I told her as briefly as I could. Laurie Lyckholm listened without interrupting. I finished with: "I'm sorry, I know I should recognize your name, but there's been a lot going on and I can't place it."

"I was Alison's oncologist."

"Oh right," I said.

There was a pause on the line. Then the doctor said, "This is none of my business, so please don't answer if you don't want to. But I have to ask: Did she tell you about the conversation we had on Friday?"

"No."

There was another silence. Finally, she said, "I know

Alison wanted to keep her battle with cancer very private. But there's no point in withholding this from you now. Alison and I talked that morning. I told her that her blood work showed abnormally high liver enzyme levels and that her CAT scan had confirmed she had an enlarged liver. The cancer had spread from her breast to her liver."

"Oh," I said.

"We were going to finalize her treatment plan this morning. She said she needed the weekend to think about things. But I can tell you what I told her. Primary liver cancer, when a tumor starts in the liver, is very serious, of course, but it is curable. Secondary liver cancer, when it has come to the liver from somewhere else, is not curable."

"Not curable. As in terminal."

"That's right."

"And she knew that?"

"She most certainly did."

"How much time did she have left?"

"That's always difficult to predict. And of course it would have depended on what treatment she chose. But not very long. Three months? Four months? Six months? To be perfectly frank with you, the cancer was already fairly advanced. Whatever time she had left would have been increasingly difficult. And I had told her as much. So what happened to your wife, well, I would never call it a blessing. But in the strangest way, it was a more merciful, less painful end than what she would have faced otherwise."

"I understand," I said.

And this time I did.

We held the memorial service three days later, on a heartlessly perfect autumn afternoon, the kind I wished Alison had been around to enjoy. On the way to the church, I started having a conversation with her about how nice it was. I already sensed I would be doing that for a long time to come.

The church was full, naturally; overfull, actually, with people spilling out the back. Alison's colleagues, the children and families she had worked with at school, our friends and neighbors, people whose lives she had touched in ways large and small, they all came out to pay their respects.

I had asked for no flowers, requesting that people make a donation to a scholarship fund that had already been set up in Alison's name at her school. A bunch of folks had gone ahead and bought flowers anyway. The bouquets covered several feet on both sides of Alison, and their fragrance filled the sanctuary.

The casket was open. It wasn't, necessarily, my preference. Or, perhaps, Alison's. But Gina had insisted. She said she wanted to be able to see her daughter one last time. I didn't feel like I could deny a mother's last request.

Seeing Alison lying there was disorienting at first. She seemed so serene, so peaceful. None of her wounds had been to her face or head. I still was having a difficult time processing that she wasn't going to be at home with me that night, letting me hold her as we went to sleep.

The funeral home had used a light touch with the makeup. She was wearing the dress she had bought a few years earlier to celebrate our fifteenth wedding anniversary, a dress she loved. She looked beautiful.

We sang a few of Alison's favorite hymns. The pastor had asked me if I wanted to say something, but I assured him I wouldn't be able to make it through even half a sentence. Jenny delivered the eulogy instead, bravely forcing her way through it. Then the pastor gave a sermon. I think they were both nice, but I couldn't be sure. To be honest, I had a hard time concentrating on the words.

Part of me wasn't really there. I was back in our sophomore year, reliving the first time I saw her, that wow-who's-that? moment that started it all. I was seeing her hair, her shoulders, her very being radiating in the setting sun.

I asked myself: if I had known, at that very moment, how this would all play out . . . that we would have twenty-five years together . . . that we would make two amazing children . . . but that it would end with the worst agony imaginable. If I had full knowledge of all that, would I still have said hello to that incredible woman in front of the student center?

Of course I would have. My only regret was that I couldn't live every second of it all over again.

By the end of the service, I had managed to dial my attention back in. The pastor was giving instructions as to how the burial was going to proceed before we started singing the final hymn, which would then give way to the benediction.

But first, he said, there was one small addition to the service, something that wasn't listed in the program. This, he explained, came at the request of Alison's children.

I had no idea what he was talking about. Emma and Sam were on either side of me, tucked under my arms. I looked down at them, but they were already squirming out from under me. With a poise Alison would have loved, they walked toward the front of the church.

The pastor was leaning over. From somewhere inside the pulpit, he pulled out two small objects that I didn't even recognize at first, I think in part because my vision was so blurry from the tears. Then my eyes finally focused.

He was clutching two small stuffed animals. Emmabear and Sammybear.

The pastor walked out from behind the pulpit and met the children by the altar. Sam, naturally, got there first. The pastor handed him Emmabear. Emma, right behind him, accepted Sammybear.

The children approached their mother's casket. They climbed a stool that had been placed there for them, sharing space on the top of its platform. Sam reached out and patted his mother's shoulder. Emma grabbed her hand.

The church was dead silent, but for the sound of sniffling into handkerchiefs. Then Emma's clear, high, pure voice called out, "I'll miss you, Momma."

Sam followed with, "I love you, Momma."

If there were three hundred hearts present, I think every last one of them broke at that moment.

Then Emma and Sam took turns placing a stuffed friend on either side of their mother. Alison had been their momma bear, the one who kept them safe and loved, no matter what the cost.

And now, in their own, small, six-year-old way, they were doing the same for her.

The children climbed down. The congregation began singing the final hymn. As the pastor lowered the lid to the casket, I mouthed one last good-bye.

Acknowledgments

As a father who was in the delivery room for the arrival of both his kids, I ought to know better than to liken writing to childbirth.

But I swear the creation of this novel was probably as close as a guy can come. And I'd like to thank the series of literary doctors, nurses, and midwives who helped me bring this baby, squirming and bawling, into the world.

Alice Martell, my Jedi Ninja Pimp, became an indispensable voice during the end stages of this book's journey to publication. I can only imagine what a force she'd be if she actually knew how to buy a burner phone.

Jessica Renheim and Ben Sevier have been magnificent curators, cheerleaders, and champions for this work, and I feel fortunate to partner with them and the entire team at Dutton. That includes marketing gurus Carrie Swetonic and Christine Ball; publicity mavens Amanda Walker, Liza Cassity, and Becky Odell; copy editor Eileen Chetti; cover designer Christopher Lin; and a lot of other talented people at 375 Hudson Street. I'm so proud to call myself their author.

A number of eminent legal and medical professionals provided their expertise at various stages of the manuscript. That begins with two people, who I can't name, who were incredibly gracious with their time and insights into what it means to be a judge. I couldn't have written a credible Scott Sampson without them.

In addition, Shevon Scarafile and Greg Parks were my on-call attorneys. Arthur Hellman at the University of Pittsburgh Law School informed my understanding of judicial misconduct and its consequences. Drs. Laurie Lyckholm and Randy Ferrance served as my medical advisors.

Any slight discrepancies between how I did things in this book and the way the world actually works are because I decided to ignore their very fine advice.

My Hardee's family, including the regulars on the morning crew—like Anne, Monica, Kenny, Dina, Trudy, Angela, Virginia, Matthew, Ashley, and Justin—kept me in good cheer (and Coke Zero) during the writing and editing of this novel. I'm only sorry our matriarch, Miss Teresa, no longer joins our daily fun. I miss her sorely.

As for my actual family, all thanks and love to Joan and Allan Blakely for being such wonderful in-laws and grandparents; and to Marilyn and Bob Parks, who brought me into this world and continue to help me thrive in it.

Lastly, and most important, I need to thank my wife and children for their unflagging love, understanding, joy, inspiration, and support; and for being the best part of my life, every single day.

I am an incredibly blessed human being. They're why.